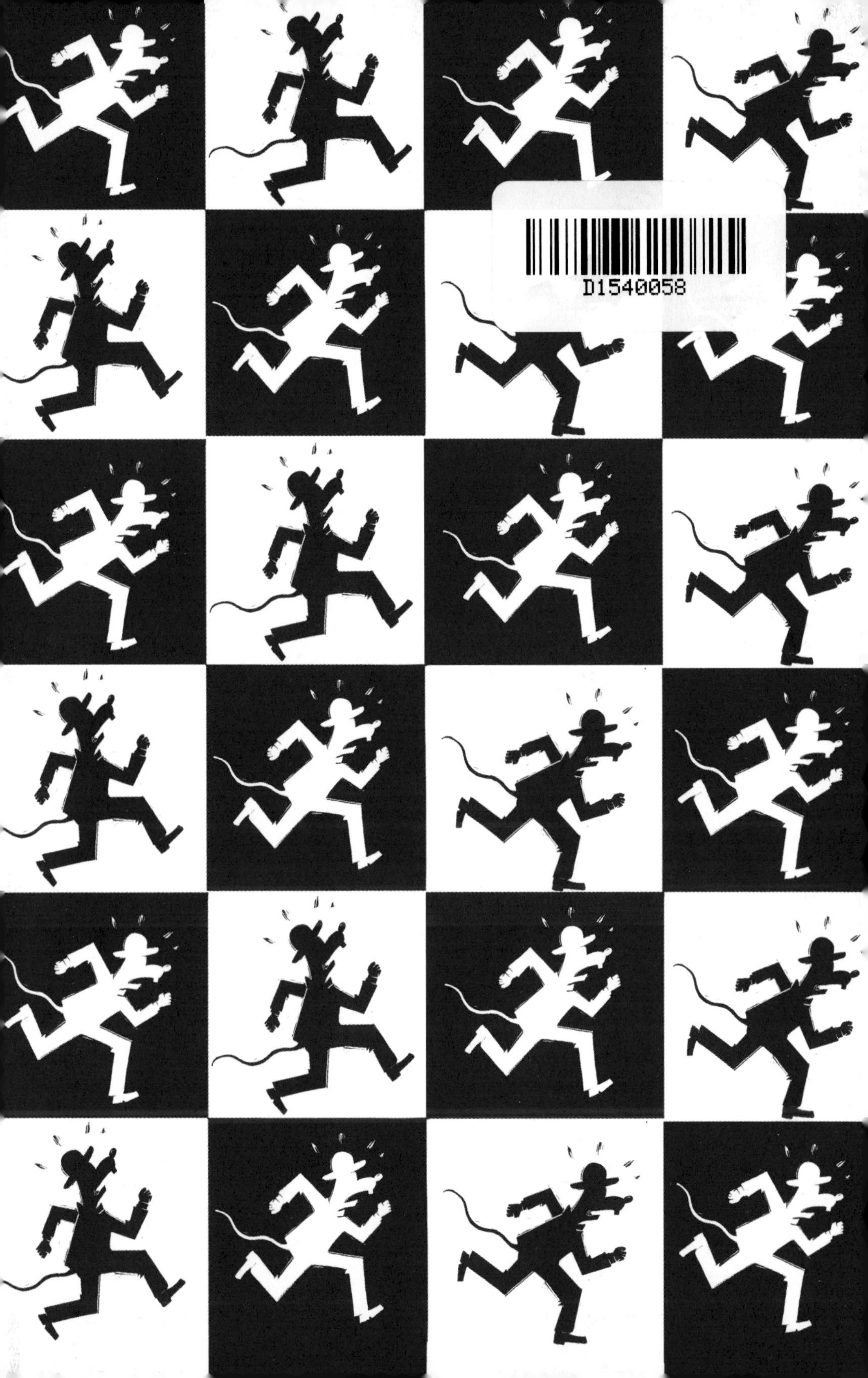

KAFKAESQUE

Also by Peter Kuper

Ruins
Drawn to New York
Diario de Oaxaca
Sticks and Stones
The Metamorphosis (by Franz Kafka)
The System
The Jungle (by Upton Sinclair)

KAFKAESQUE

Fourteen Stories

PETER KUPER

W. W. NORTON & COMPANY
Independent Publishers Since 1923
New York | London

Dedicated to Anthony Stonier,
who inspired this conversation with Kafka

Printed in the United States of America
First Edition

For information about permission to reproduce selections from this book, write to
Permissions, W. W. Norton & Company, Inc., 500 Fifth Avenue, New York, NY 10110

For information about special discounts for bulk purchases, please contact
W. W. Norton Special Sales at specialsales@wwnorton.com or 800-233-4830

Manufacturing by Versa Press
Production manager: Julia Druskin

Library of Congress Cataloging-in-Publication Data

Names: Kuper, Peter, 1958– author, artist.
Title: Kafkaesque : fourteen stories / Peter Kuper.
Description: First edition. | New York : W. W. Norton & Company, [2018]
Identifiers: LCCN 2018016252 | ISBN 9780393635621 (hardcover)
Subjects: LCSH: Kafka, Franz, 1883–1924—Adaptations. | Graphic novels.
Classification: LCC PN6727.K85 K34 2018 | DDC 741.5/973—dc23
LC record available at https://lccn.loc.gov/2018016252

W. W. Norton & Company, Inc., 500 Fifth Avenue, New York, N.Y. 10110
www.wwnorton.com

W. W. Norton & Company Ltd., 15 Carlisle Street, London W1D 3BS

1 2 3 4 5 6 7 8 9 0

CONTENTS

INTRODUCTION

KUPERESQUE

> "One must dare to dive and sink into the depths, in order to later rise again–laughing and fighting for breath–to the now doubly illuminated surface of things."
>
> –Franz Kafka

L IKE MANY STUDENTS, my first encounter with Franz Kafka's writing was *The Metamorphosis*, which I found . . . *disturbing*. Fortunately, a friend of mine liked to read Kafka aloud over beers. Hearing the absurd circumstances Kafka placed his characters into and their deadpan responses, I found myself guffawing. This wasn't just the alcohol talking; Kafka himself was known to laugh out loud when he read his stories to friends, his darkness interrupted by joy. So, back in 1988 when I first began translating Kafka into comics, it was the humor that drew me to his work. I continued adapting his stories over the years for their darker truths.

The moment I committed pen to paper, I discovered comics were ideally suited to illuminate what Kafka called his "scribbling." I found the stories inspired surprising interpretations that pushed my work in new directions. With Kafka's texts serving as an anchor, I could stretch and bend my panel and page designs without losing readability. In the comics' vernacular, surreal images flowed naturally and the contrary emotions of angst and humor coexisted happily.

For the artistic medium, I chose to draw on scratchboard, a chalk-covered paper that can be inked and scratched to approximate woodcuts. This evoked German expressionism and artists I loved, like Käthe Kollwitz, George Grosz and Otto Dix, who were creating concurrently with Kafka's time in Prague, Czechoslovakia. It also reflected my affinity for the work of artists like Frans Masereel and Lynd Ward, who created woodcut "picture stories," the forerunners of the graphic novel.

I've often wondered if any of the early newspaper comics crossed Kafka's desk. Kafka's stories were formed during the same time period and zeitgeist as many of the early comic strips, especially the work of geniuses like Winsor McCay, who under the

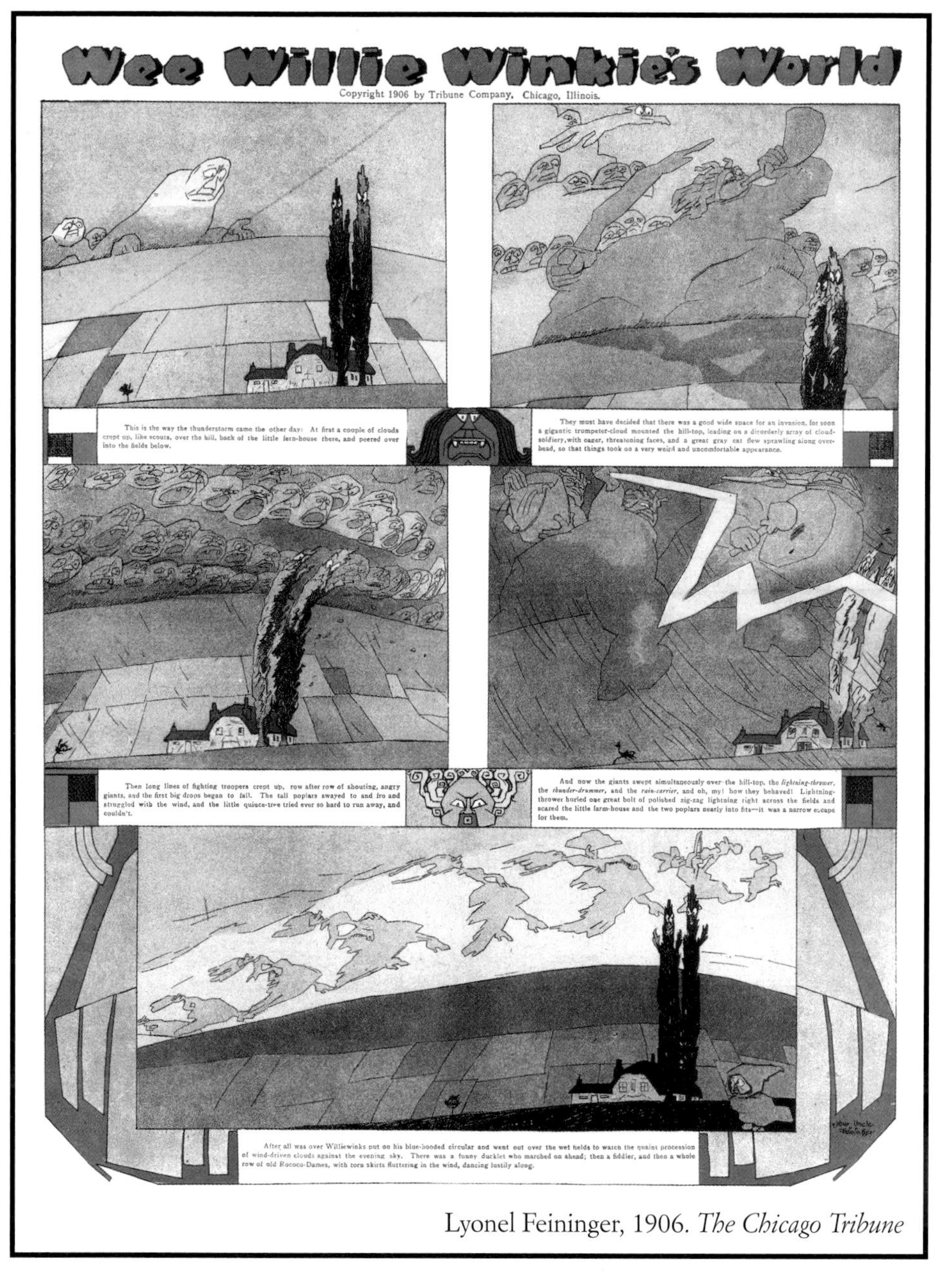
Wee Willie Winkie's World
Copyright 1906 by Tribune Company, Chicago, Illinois.
This is the way the thunderstorm came the other day: At first a couple of clouds crept up, like scouts, over the hill, back of the little fern-house there, and peered over into the fields below.
They must have decided that there was a good wide space for an invasion, for soon a gigantic trumpeter-cloud mounted the hill-top, leading on a disorderly array of cloud-soldiery, with eager, threatening faces, and a great gray cat flew sprawling along overhead, so that things took on a very weird and uncomfortable appearance.
Then long lines of fighting troopers crept up, row after row of shouting, angry giants, and the first big drops began to fall. The tall poplars swayed to and fro and struggled with the wind, and the little quince-tree tried ever so hard to run away, and couldn't.
And now the giants swept simultaneously over the hill-top, the lightning-thrower, the thunder-drummer, and the rain-carrier, and oh, my! how they behaved! Lightning-thrower hurled one great bolt of polished zig-zag lightning right across the fields and scared the little farm-house and the two poplars nearly into fits—it was a narrow escape for them.
After all was over Williewinks put on his blue-hooded circular and went out over the wet fields to watch the quaint procession of wind-driven clouds against the evening sky. There was a funny ducklet who marched on ahead; then a fiddler, and then a whole row of old Rococo-Dames, with torn skirts fluttering in the wind, dancing lustily along.

Lyonel Feininger, 1906. *The Chicago Tribune*

pen name "Silas" created *Dream of the Rarebit Fiend*, and Lyonel Feininger, who broke artistic ground with the short-lived *Wee Willie Winkie's World.* These strips could easily have been written by Kafka or inspired some of his own "disturbing dreams" like *The Metamorphosis.* They were certainly produced in the same stew of anxiety over bureaucracies, impending war, actual war and all the other joys of modern living.

The transformation of a text into another language is a, well, *metamorphosis.*

Without speaking German, I depended upon translators to not only convert Kafka to English but also to define his tone. I first read Kafka as he was translated by Willa and Edwin Muir and Tania and James Stern from the 1930s–1950s. Their translations represented the wonderfully stilted voice of Kafka for generations. I often found more recent translations, with modernized language, jarring. This wasn't the Franz Kafka I knew! For *Kafkaesque*, I recruited a German friend to do new translations that offered a stripped-down version of the text. Comparing old and new translations, it was fascinating to discover the different sentence structure and vocabulary each translator chose. This encouraged latitude in my own decisions. Kafka's stories inspire individual interpretation, giving each reader a unique personal context. For me, this process of interpretation and finding Kafka's voice through drawings and careful placement of type was the joy of adapting these stories. I chose different hand-lettering to create distinctions between characters, but I also used a standard typeface to remind readers that the text comes from source material.

The titles that, with few exceptions, had been chosen by Kafka's friend and executor, Max Brod, also varied from translator to translator. For example, the word "trip" in the title "Trip into the Mountains" could also be translated as "excursion" or "voyage," but I preferred the one-syllable "trip." I hope Kafka would have agreed, although ultimately everything done with Kafka's work contravenes his final request. He instructed Brod to burn all of his unpublished manuscripts, which includes most of the stories I adapted.

Thanks for ignoring him, Max.

Kafka died at the age of forty, nearly a hundred years ago, yet his stories resonate as though they were written yesterday. Or perhaps, as Kafka's disciple Gustav Janouch suggested, his writings are "a mirror of tomorrow." They belong here and now; his tales are road maps to our human condition. They warn us of the dangers

Lynd Ward, *Gods' Man*, 1929

DREAM OF THE RAREBIT FIEND
BY SILAS
OH! WHAT A HORRIBLE FEELING. WHY! THE BED IS ROCKING. OH! IT'S GOING TO TIP OVER. MERCY!
LAND SAKES ALIVE! WHAT AILS THIS BED? OH I'M GETTING SEASICK AND I'M GOING TO FALL OFF. OH. STOP IT!
WELL! IF THIS ISN'T PECULIAR. GOODNESS GRACIOUS! WHAT SHALL I DO? OH! OH! SOMEONE HELP ME! I MUST LET GO.
OH! MY HEAD. WHAT IS IT? OH WHAT IS THIS? I'M SO SICK OH! WHAT WILL BECOME OF ME?
I'M DYING. GOODBY! FAREWELL TO ALL. I DID NOT WANT TO GO THIS WAY. ADIEU! FAIR EARTH AND ALL
INTO EVERLASTING SPACE I'M PLUNGING. OH! HAVE MERCY ON ME! I PRAY FOR FORGIVENESS FROM ALL I—
OH! HELP ME OH! SAVE! WHAT WOULD MY INTENDED SAY IF HE SHOULD SEE. ME UP HERE? I'D RATHER DIE. MY HEAD IS BURSTING. HELP! HELP! OH! SAVE ME !!!!!!
W
N
S
E
PSHAW! HOW RIDICULOUS! WHO'D THINK MINCE PIE WOULD CAUSE SUCH A DREAM? WELL I'M GLAD IT WAS A DREAM. GRACIOUS!
SILAS

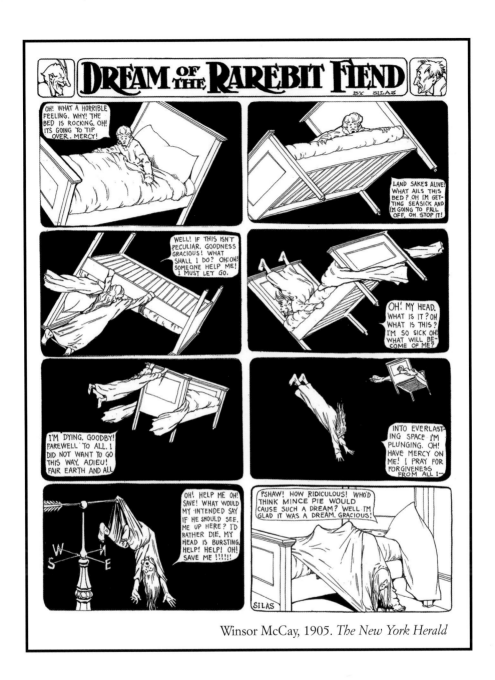

Winsor McCay, 1905. *The New York Herald*

of our institutions, remind us of our frailties and prod us to laugh at our absurdities. As our world increasingly reflects the adjective "Kafkaesque," we can find renewed meaning in all the messages Kafka whispers in our ears and between the panels.

–Peter Kuper
New York City
2018

TRIP INTO THE MOUNTAINS

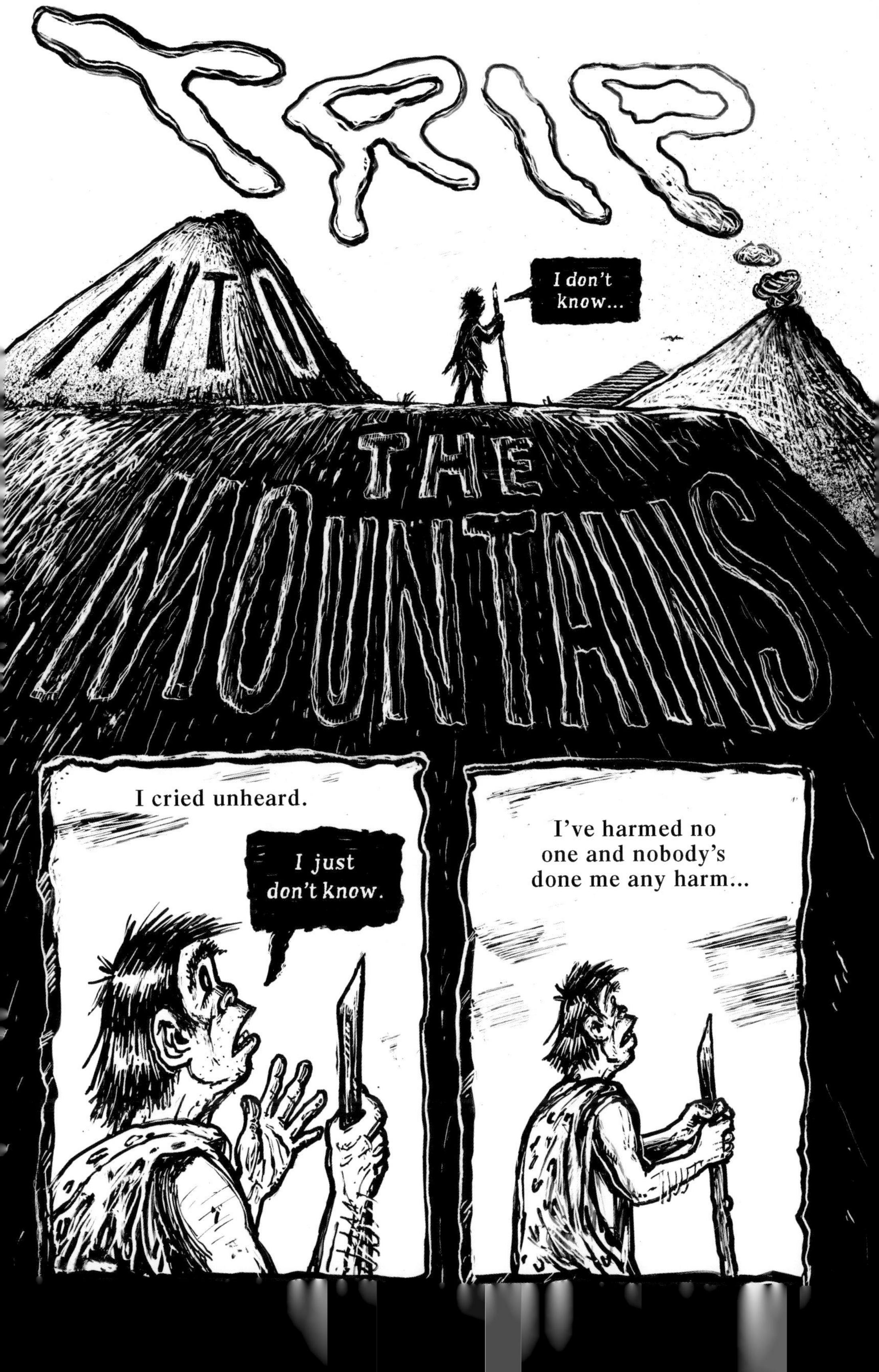
TRIP
INTO
THE
MOUNTAINS
I don't know...
I cried unheard.
I just don't know.
I've harmed no one and nobody's done me any harm...

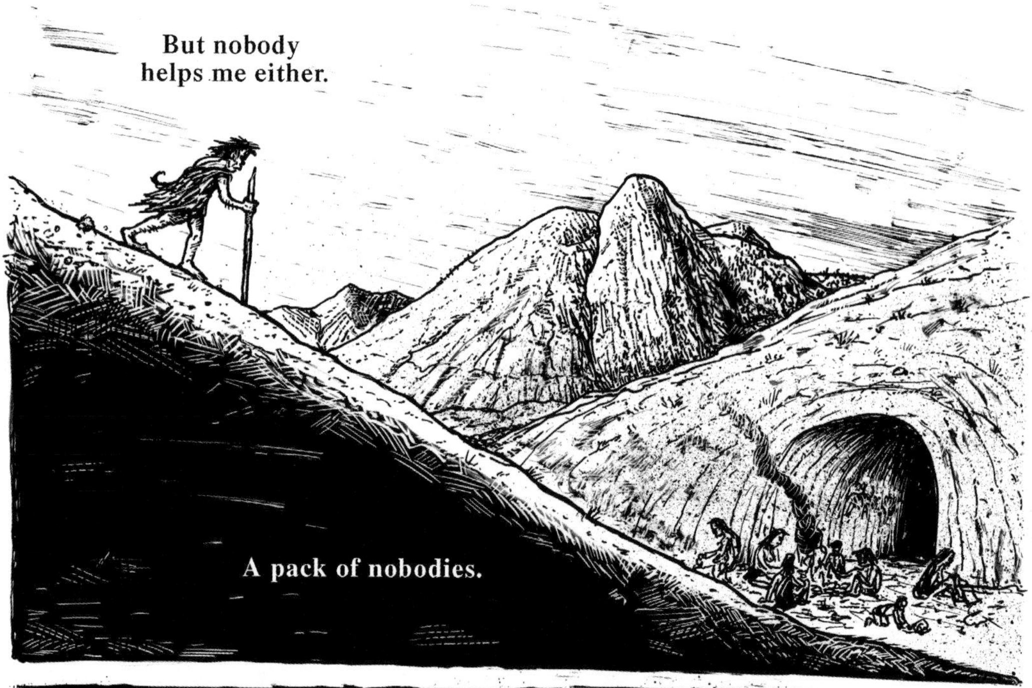
But nobody
helps me either.
A pack of nobodies.

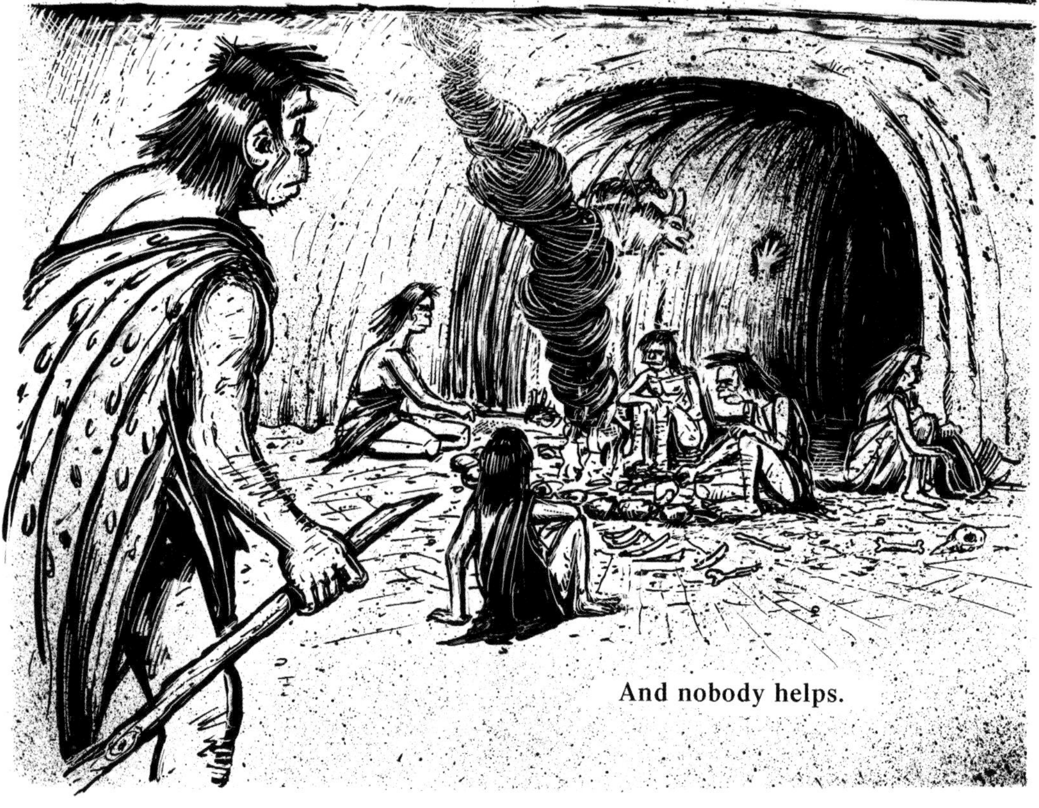
And nobody helps.

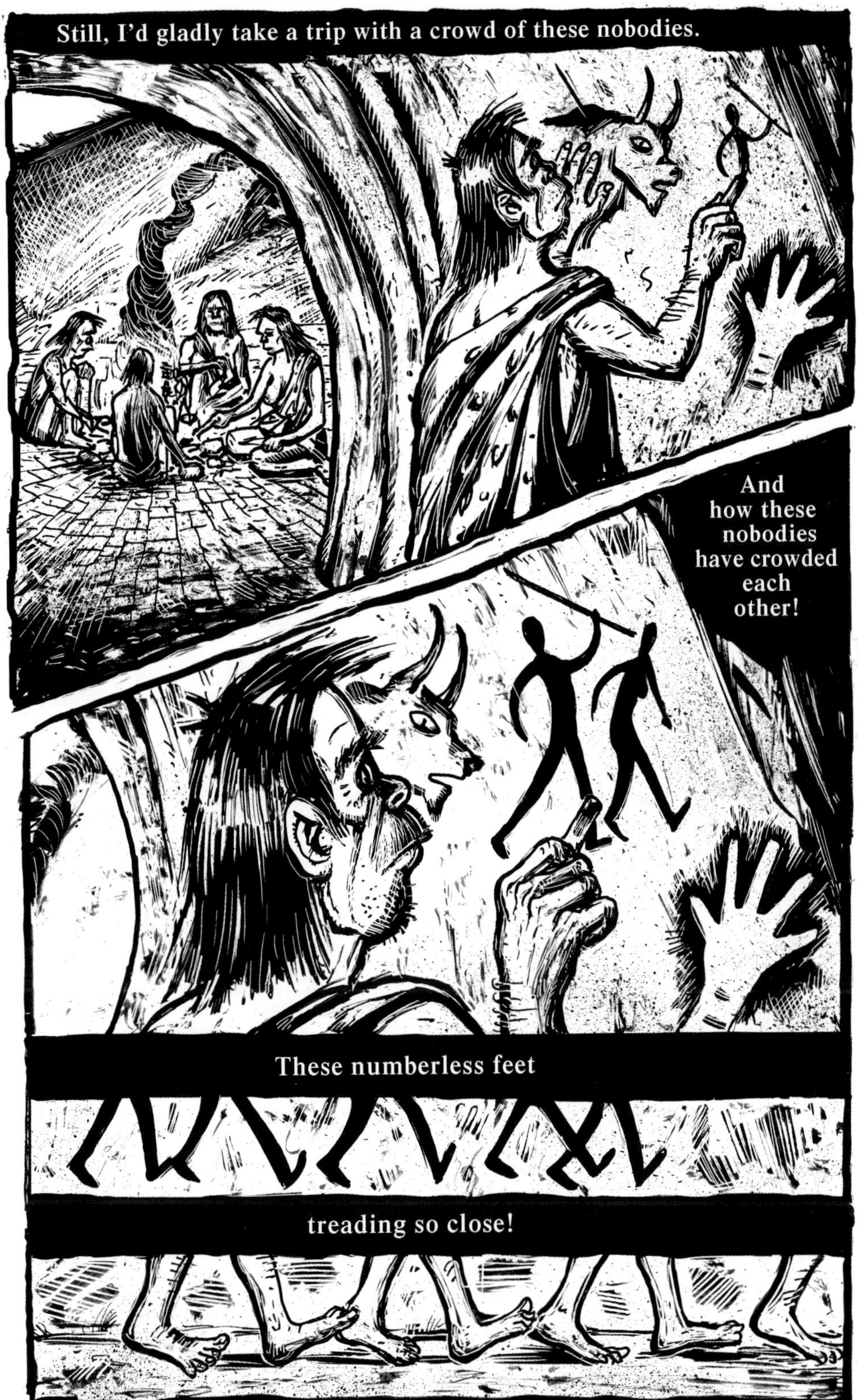
Still, I'd gladly take a trip with a crowd of these nobodies.
And how these nobodies have crowded each other!
These numberless feet
treading so close!

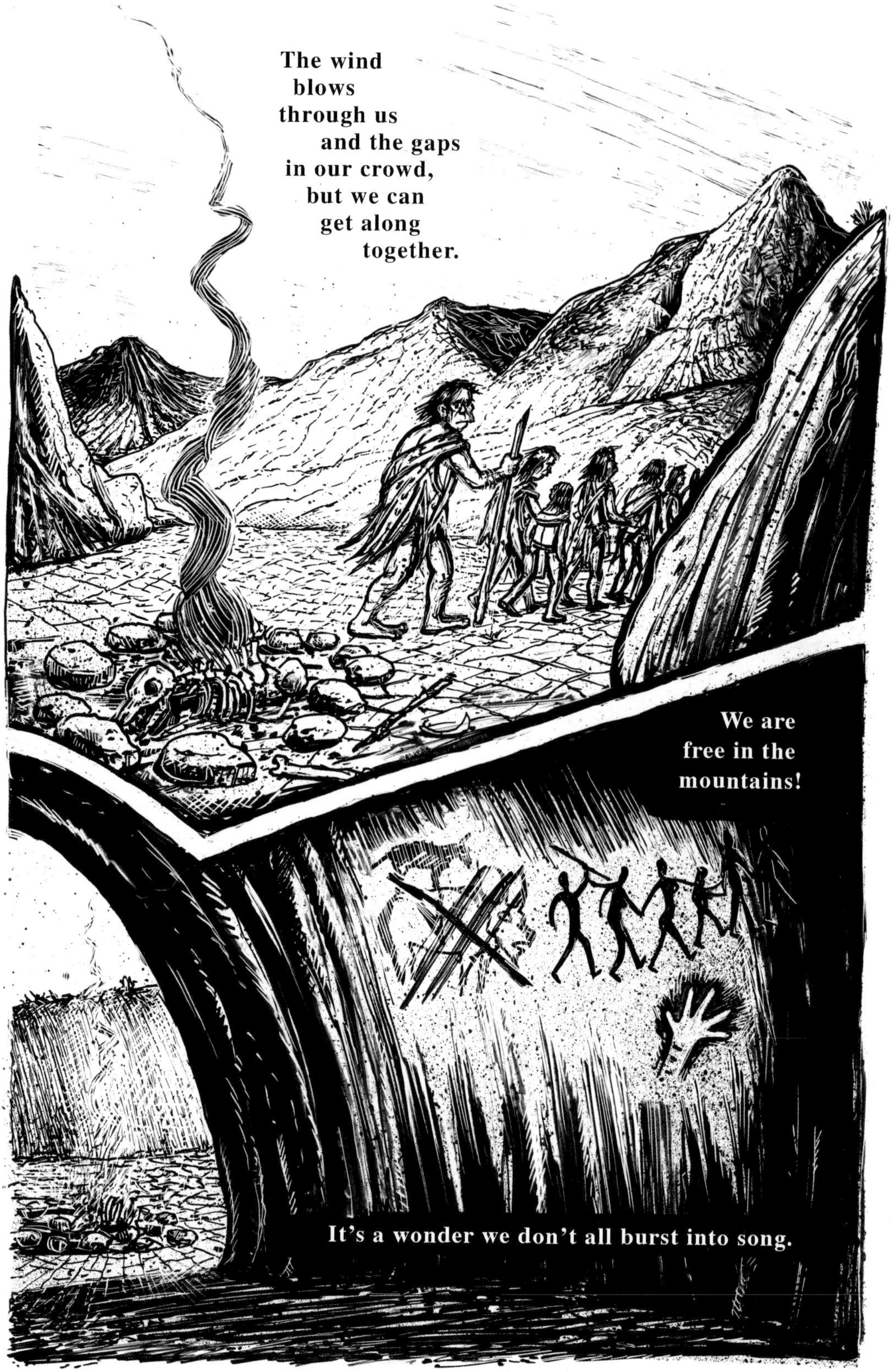
The wind blows through us and the gaps in our crowd, but we can get along together.
We are free in the mountains!
It's a wonder we don't all burst into song.

A LITTLE FABLE

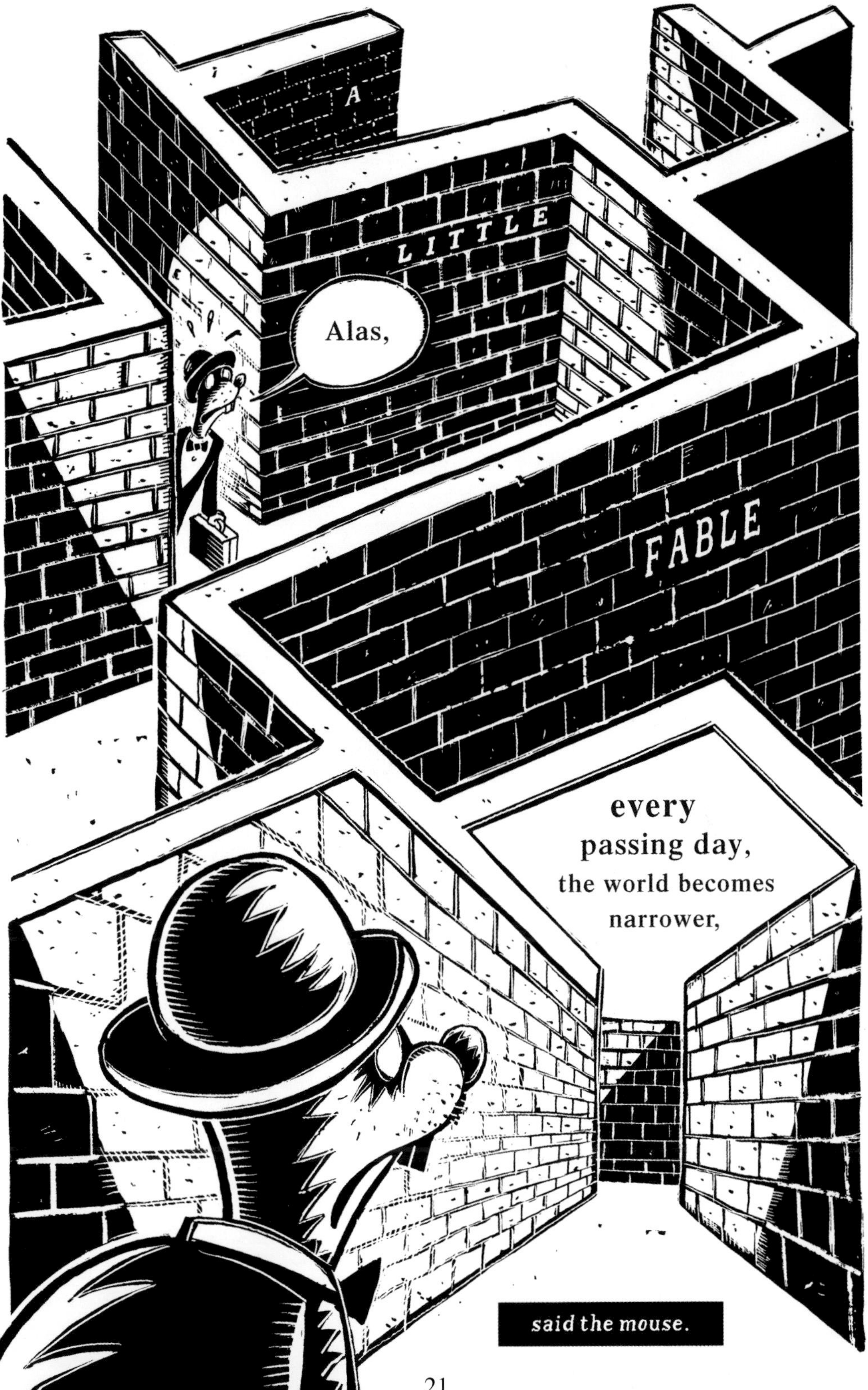
A
LITTLE
FABLE
Alas,
every passing day, the world becomes narrower,
said the mouse.

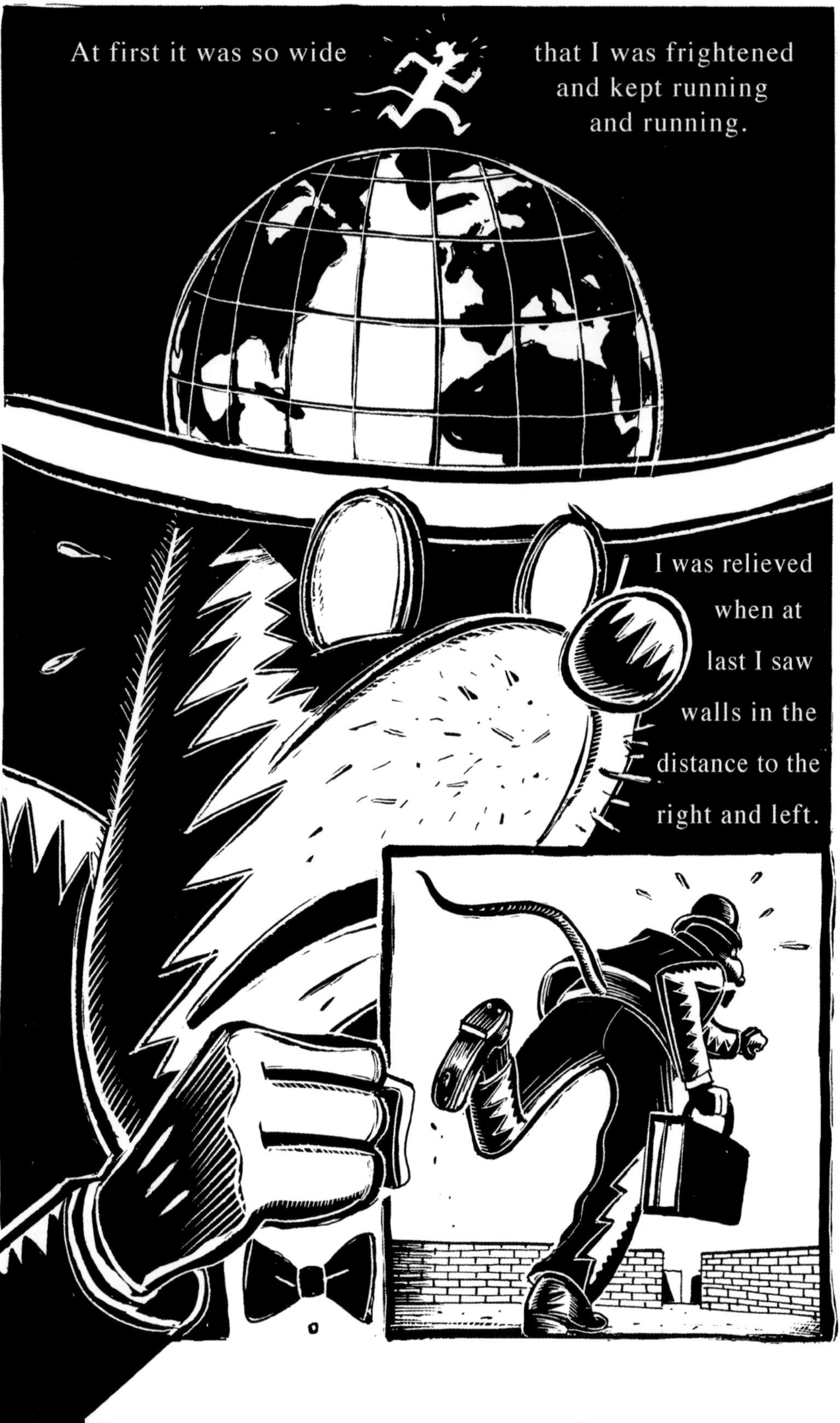
At first it was so wide
that I was frightened and kept running and running.
I was relieved when at last I saw walls in the distance to the right and left.

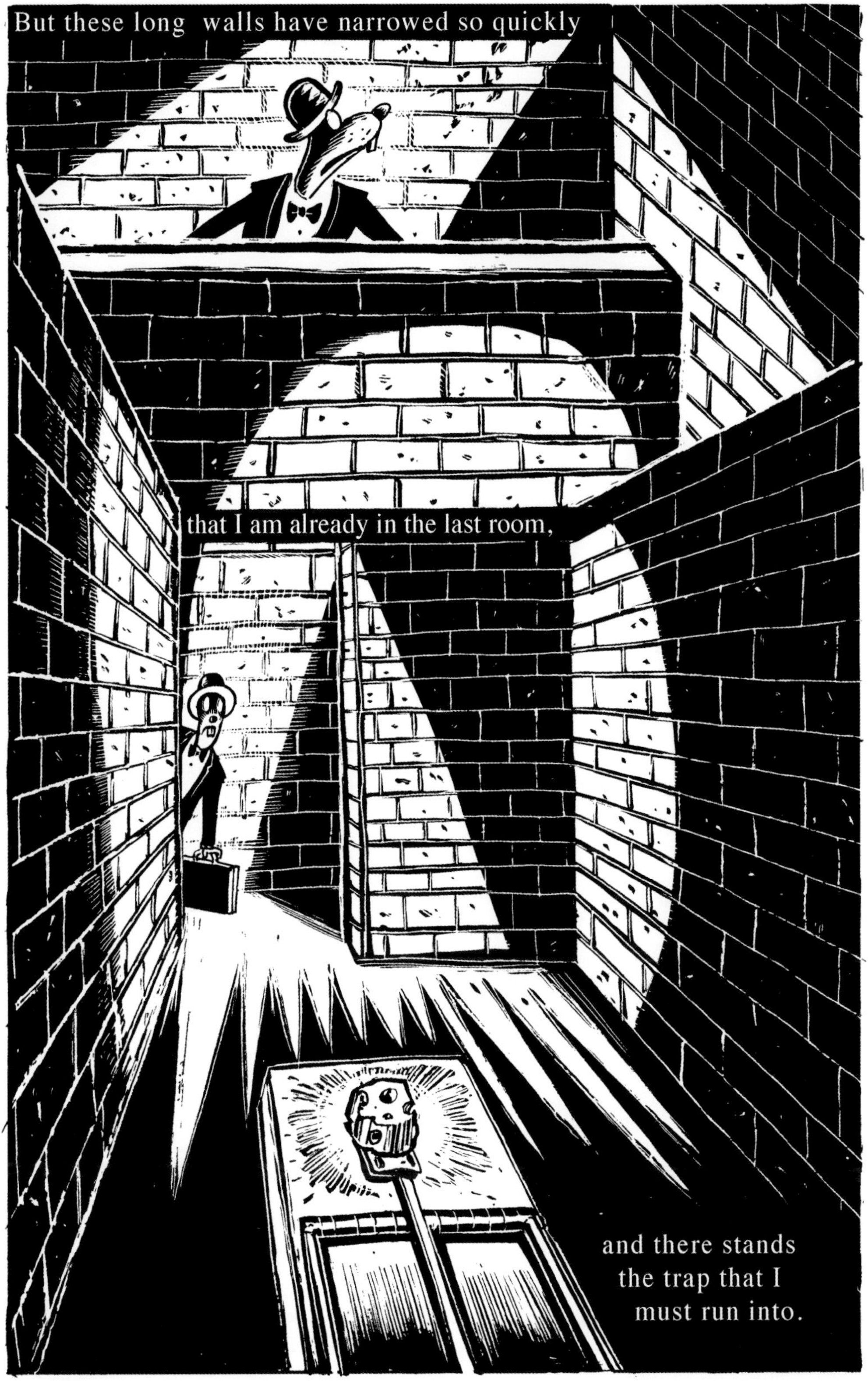
But these long walls have narrowed so quickly
that I am already in the last room,
and there stands the trap that I must run into.

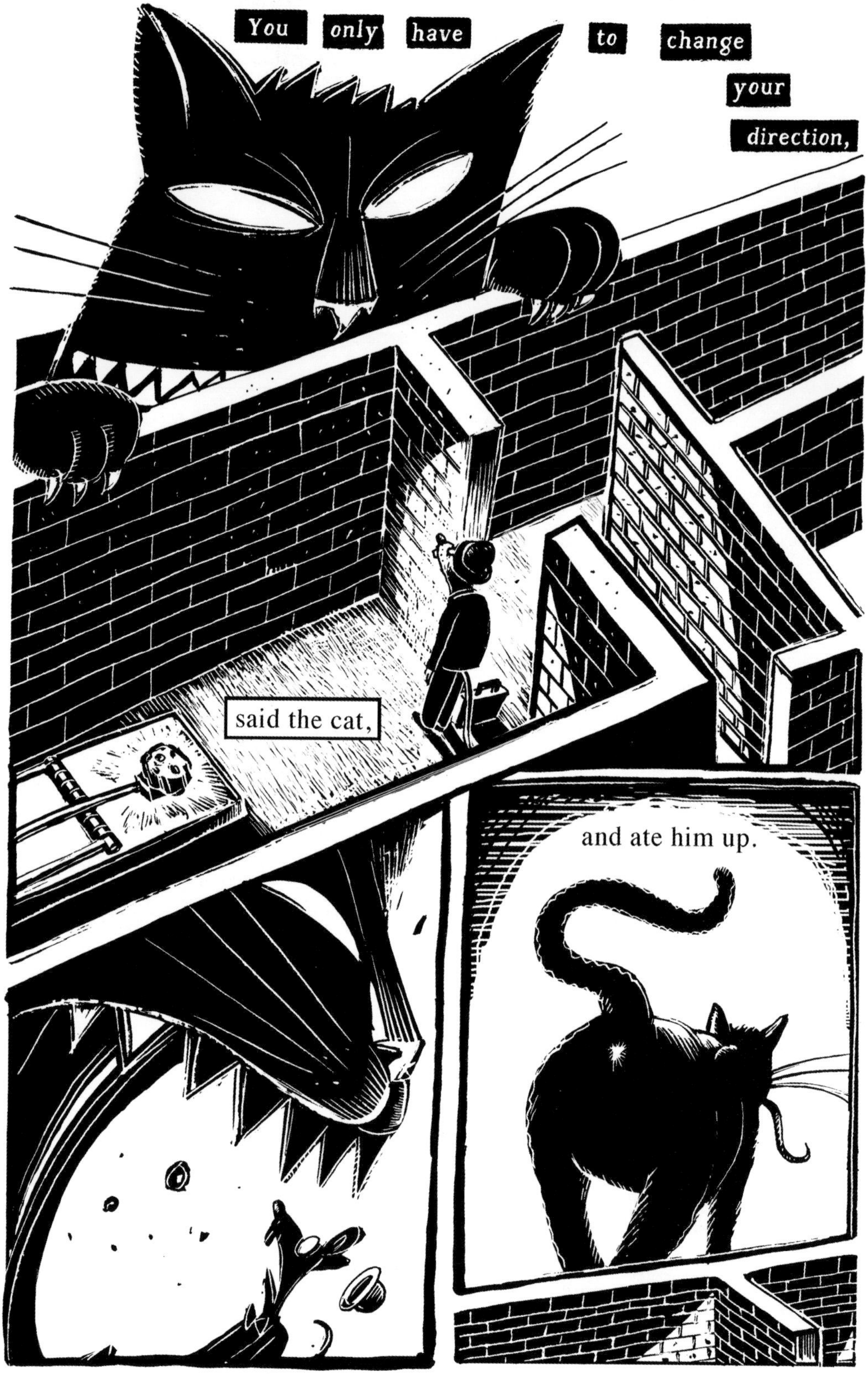

You only have to change your direction,
said the cat,
and ate him up.

THE HELMSMAN

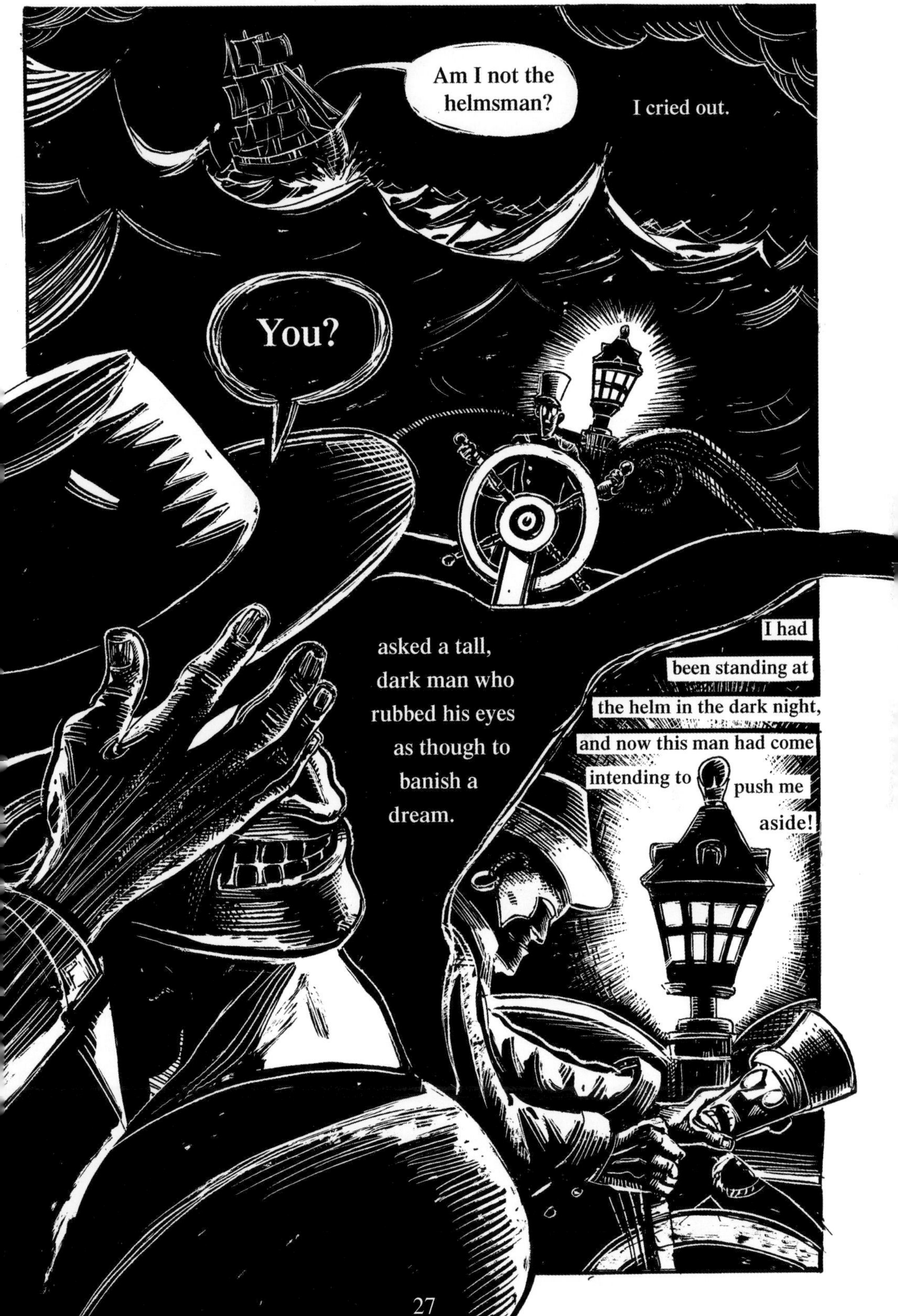
Am I not the helmsman?
I cried out.
You?
asked a tall, dark man who rubbed his eyes as though to banish a dream.
I had been standing at the helm in the dark night, and now this man had come intending to push me aside!

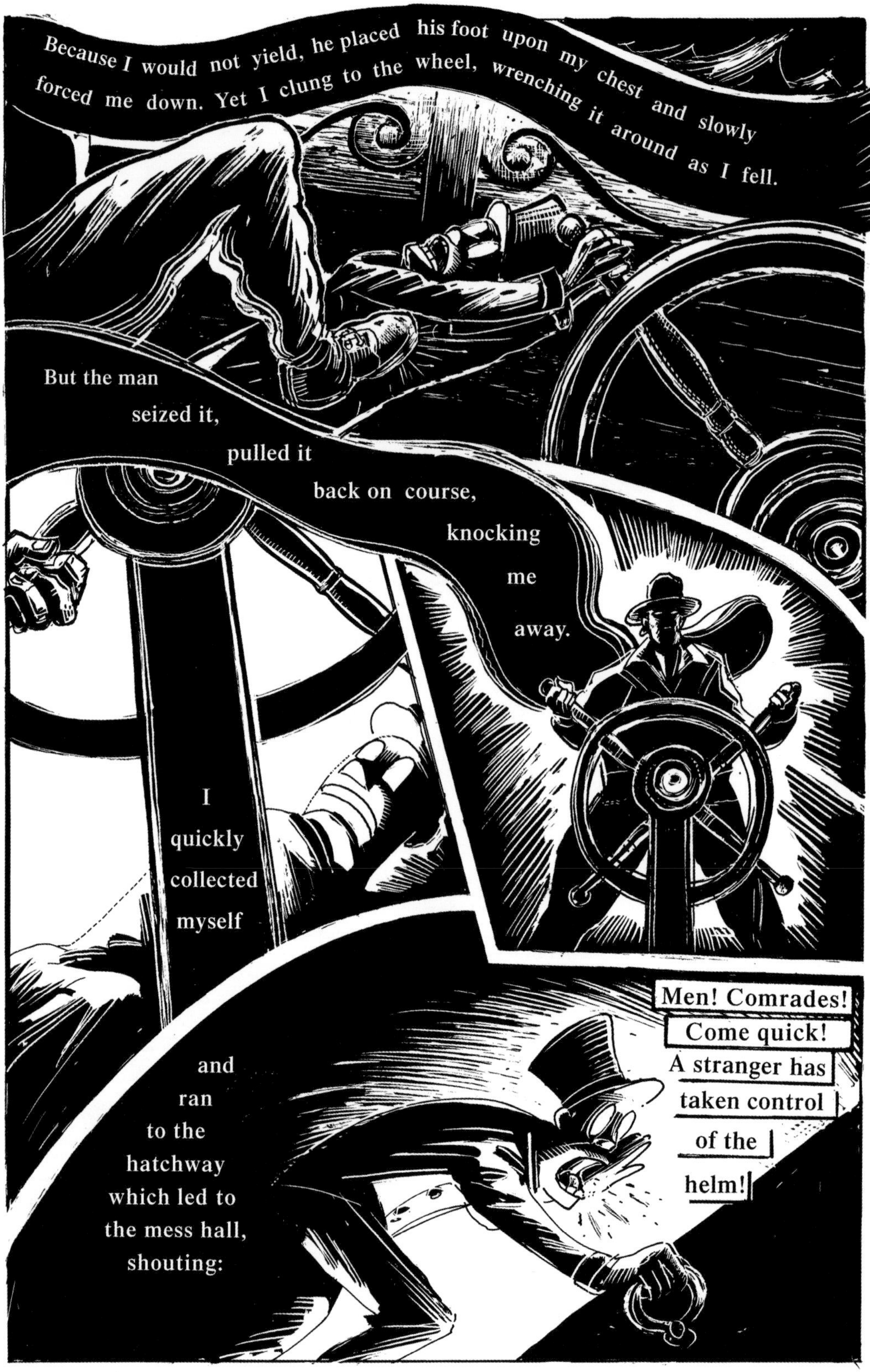
Because I would not yield, he placed his foot upon my chest and slowly forced me down. Yet I clung to the wheel, wrenching it around as I fell.
But the man seized it, pulled it back on course, knocking me away.
I quickly collected myself
and ran to the hatchway which led to the mess hall, shouting:
Men! Comrades! Come quick! A stranger has taken control of the helm!

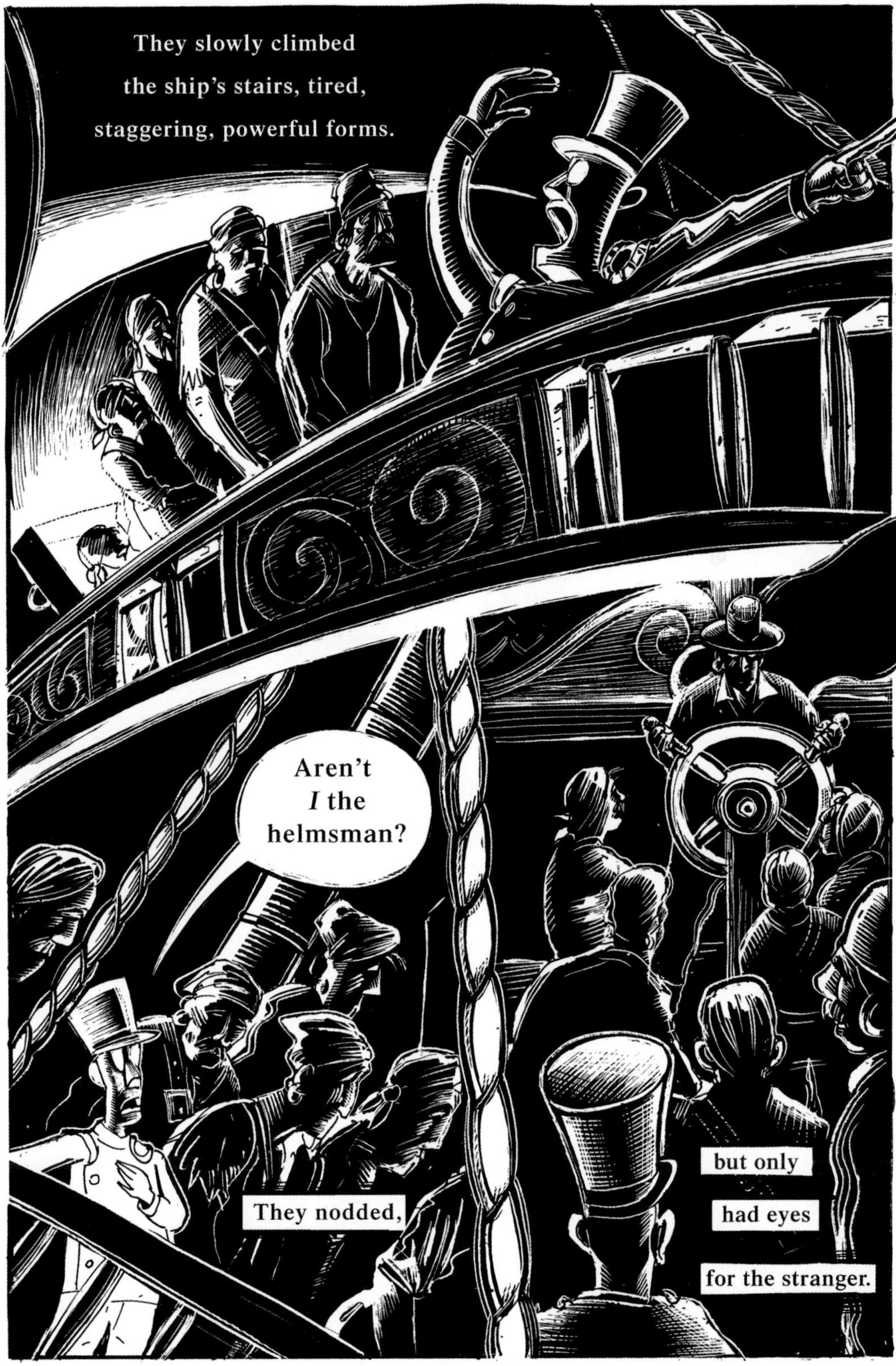
They slowly climbed
the ship's stairs, tired,
staggering, powerful forms.
Aren't *I* the helmsman?
They nodded,
but only
had eyes
for the stranger.

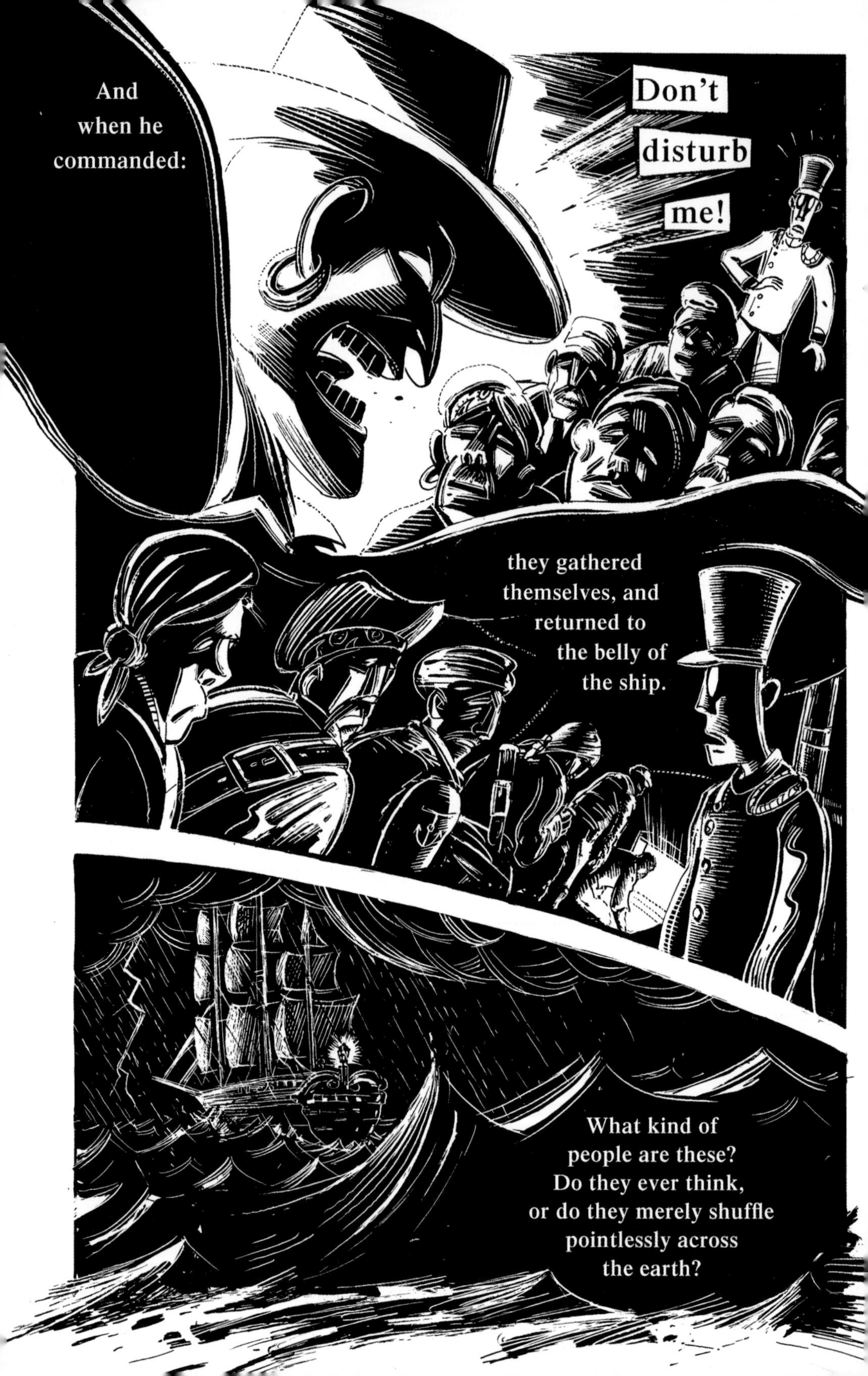
And when he commanded:
Don't disturb me!
they gathered themselves, and returned to the belly of the ship.
What kind of people are these? Do they ever think, or do they merely shuffle pointlessly across the earth?

THE SPINNING TOP

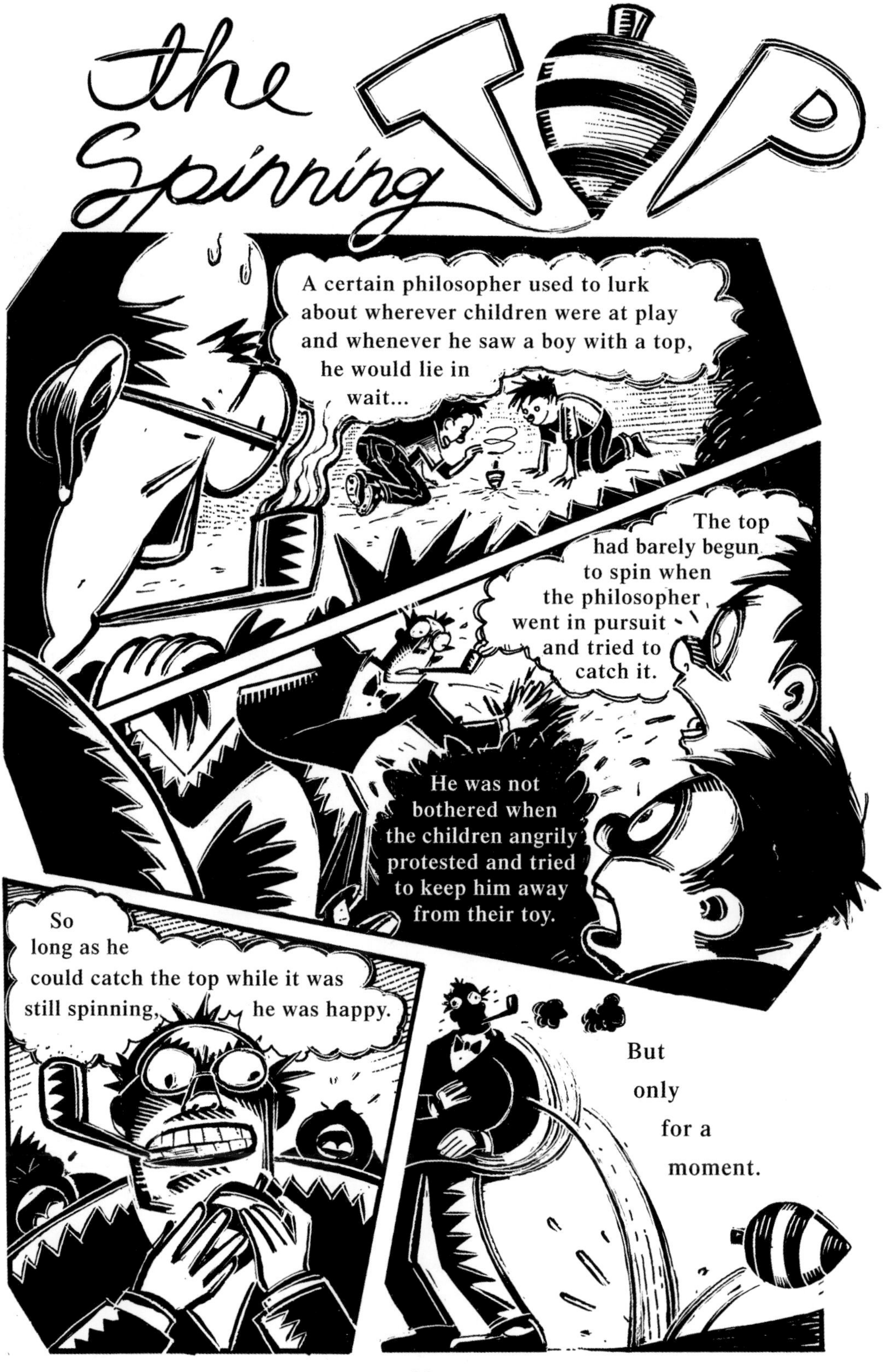
the Spinning TOP
A certain philosopher used to lurk about wherever children were at play and whenever he saw a boy with a top, he would lie in wait...
The top had barely begun to spin when the philosopher went in pursuit and tried to catch it.
He was not bothered when the children angrily protested and tried to keep him away from their toy.
So long as he could catch the top while it was still spinning, he was happy.
But only for a moment.

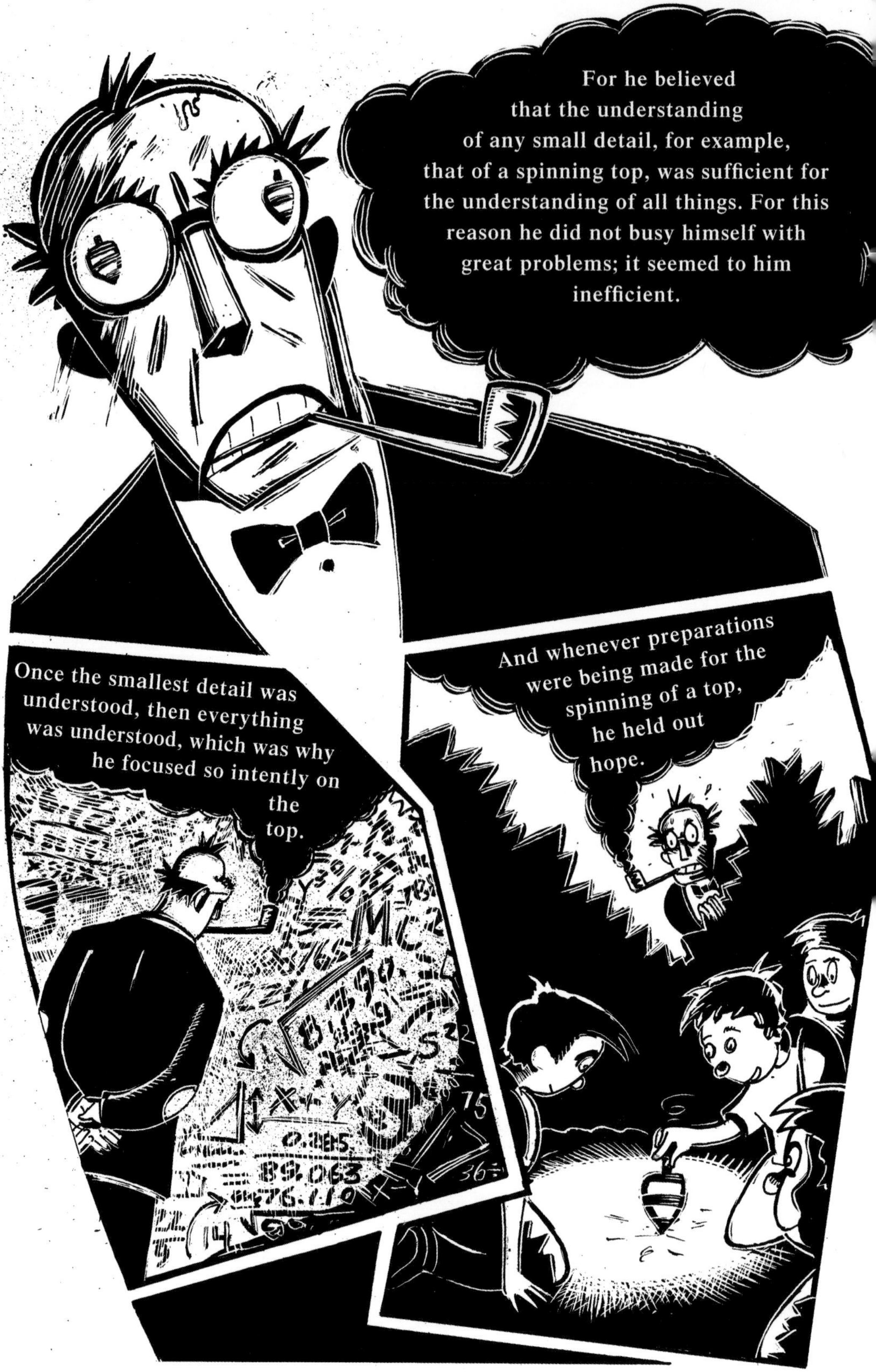
For he believed that the understanding of any small detail, for example, that of a spinning top, was sufficient for the understanding of all things. For this reason he did not busy himself with great problems; it seemed to him inefficient.
Once the smallest detail was understood, then everything was understood, which was why he focused so intently on the top.
And whenever preparations were being made for the spinning of a top, he held out hope.

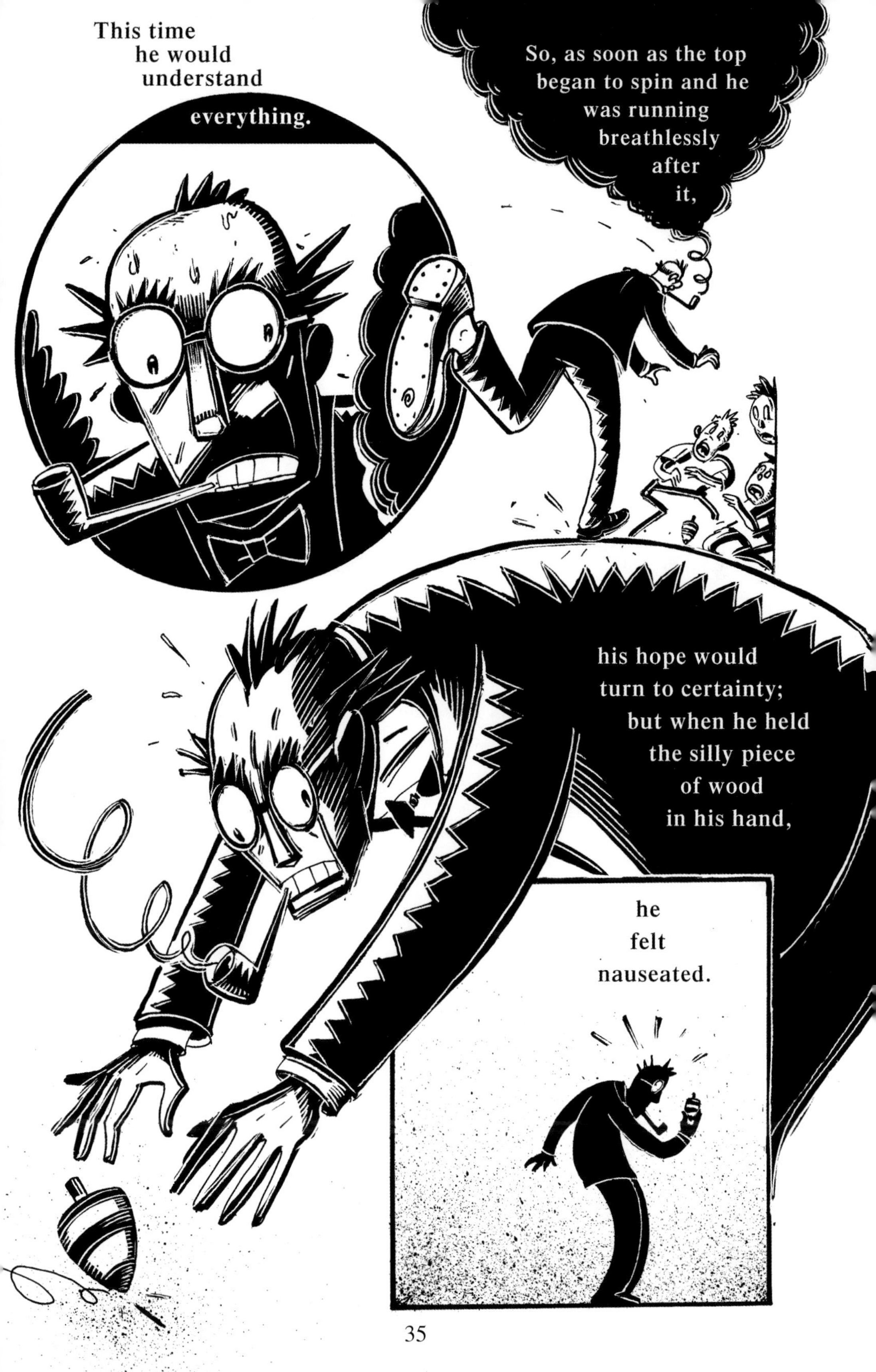
This time he would understand
everything.
So, as soon as the top began to spin and he was running breathlessly after it,
his hope would turn to certainty; but when he held the silly piece of wood in his hand,
he felt nauseated.

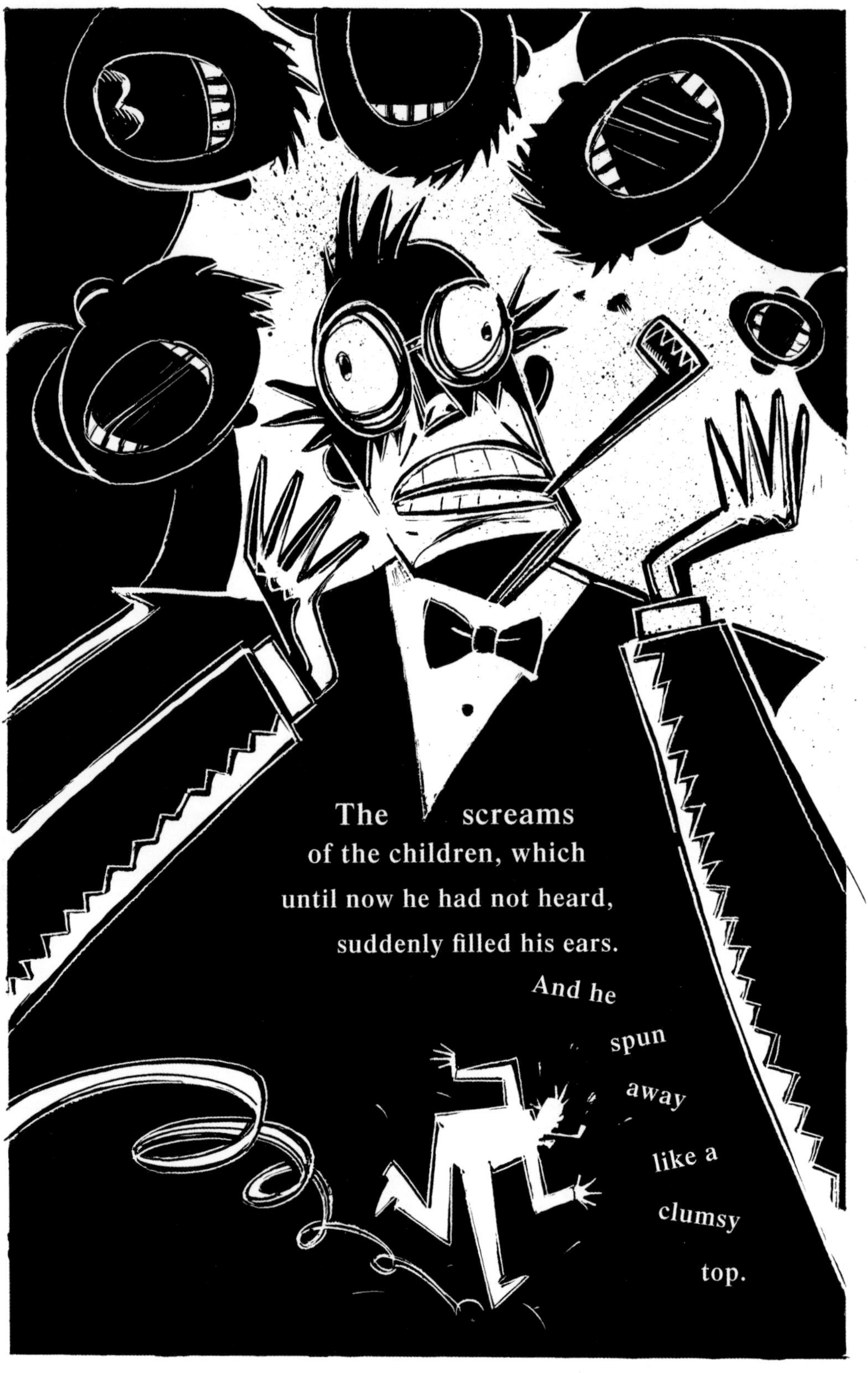
The screams
of the children, which
until now he had not heard,
suddenly filled his ears.
And he
spun
away
like a
clumsy
top.

THE BURROW

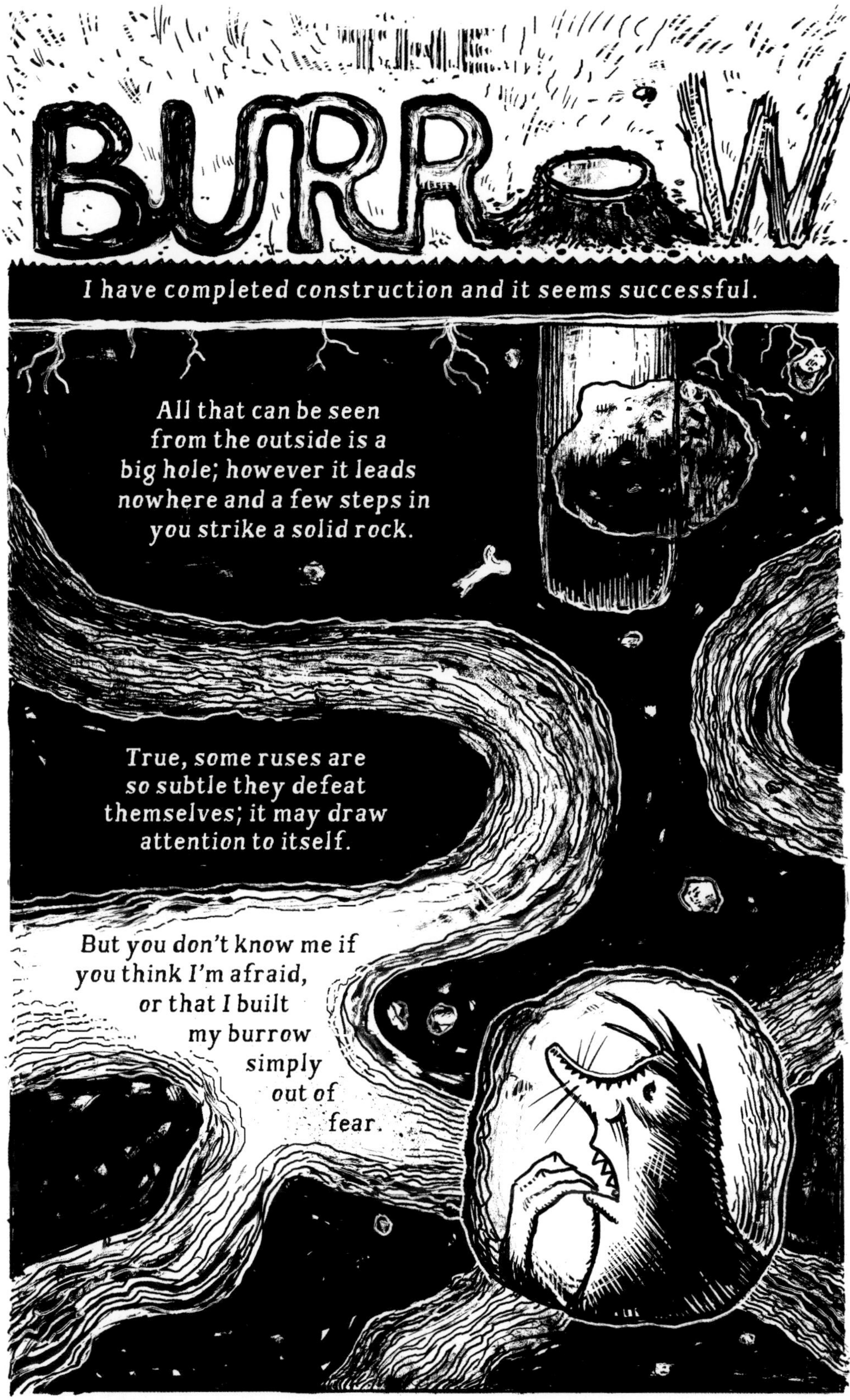
THE
BURROW
I have completed construction and it seems successful.
All that can be seen from the outside is a big hole; however it leads nowhere and a few steps in you strike a solid rock.
True, some ruses are so subtle they defeat themselves; it may draw attention to itself.
But you don't know me if you think I'm afraid, or that I built my burrow simply out of fear.

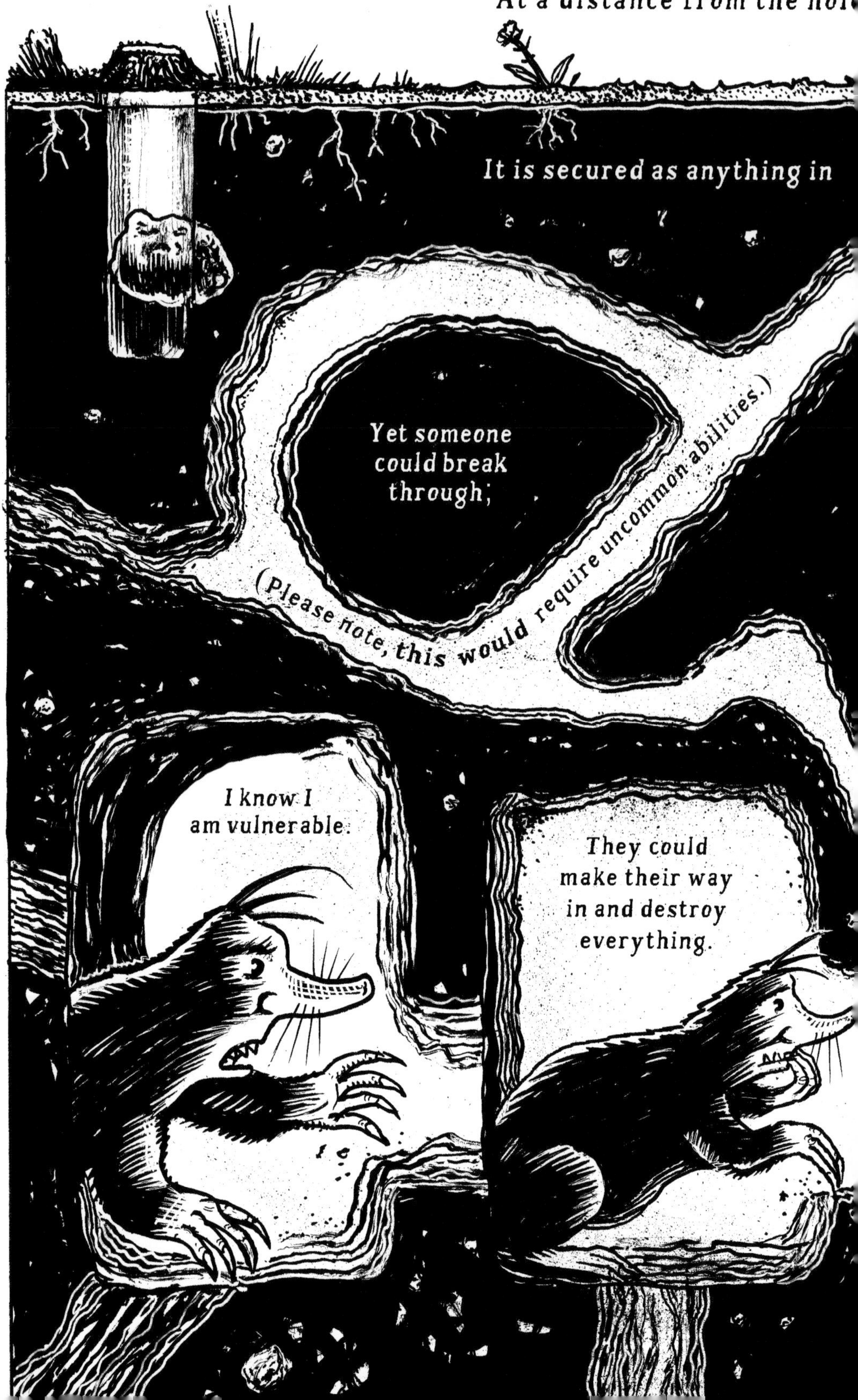
At a distance from the hol
It is secured as anything in
Yet someone could break through;
(Please note, this would require uncommon abilities.)
I know I am vulnerable.
They could make their way in and destroy everything.

ies the real entrance.

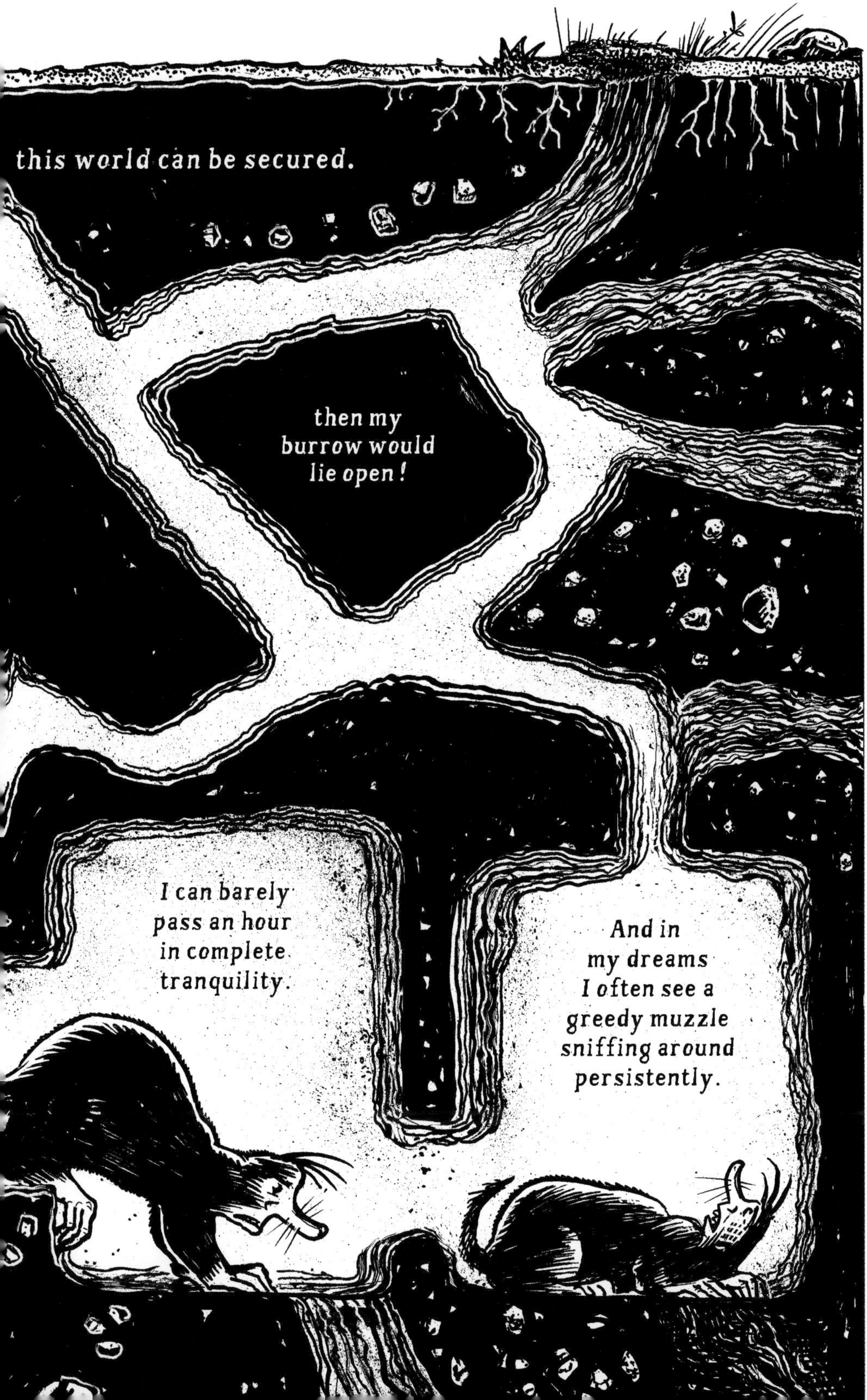
this world can be secured.
then my burrow would lie open!
I can barely pass an hour in complete tranquility.
And in my dreams I often see a greedy muzzle sniffing around persistently.

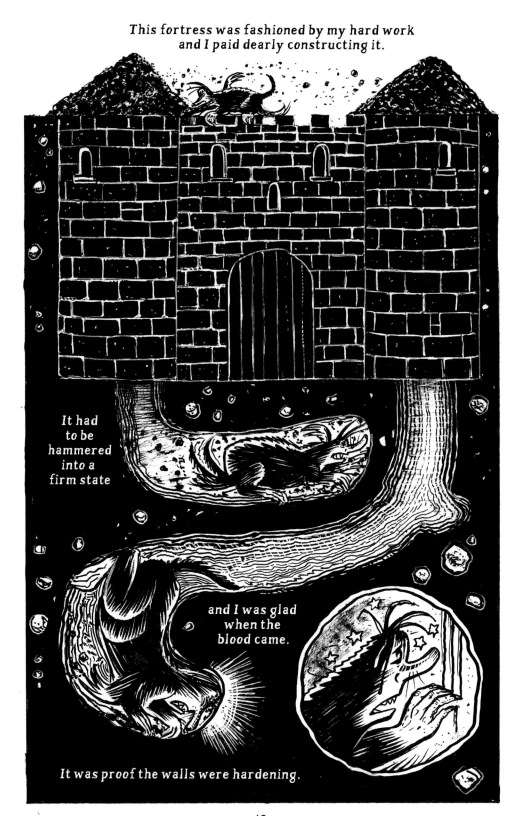

This fortress was fashioned by my hard work and I paid dearly constructing it.

It had to be hammered into a firm state

and I was glad when the blood came.

It was proof the walls were hardening.

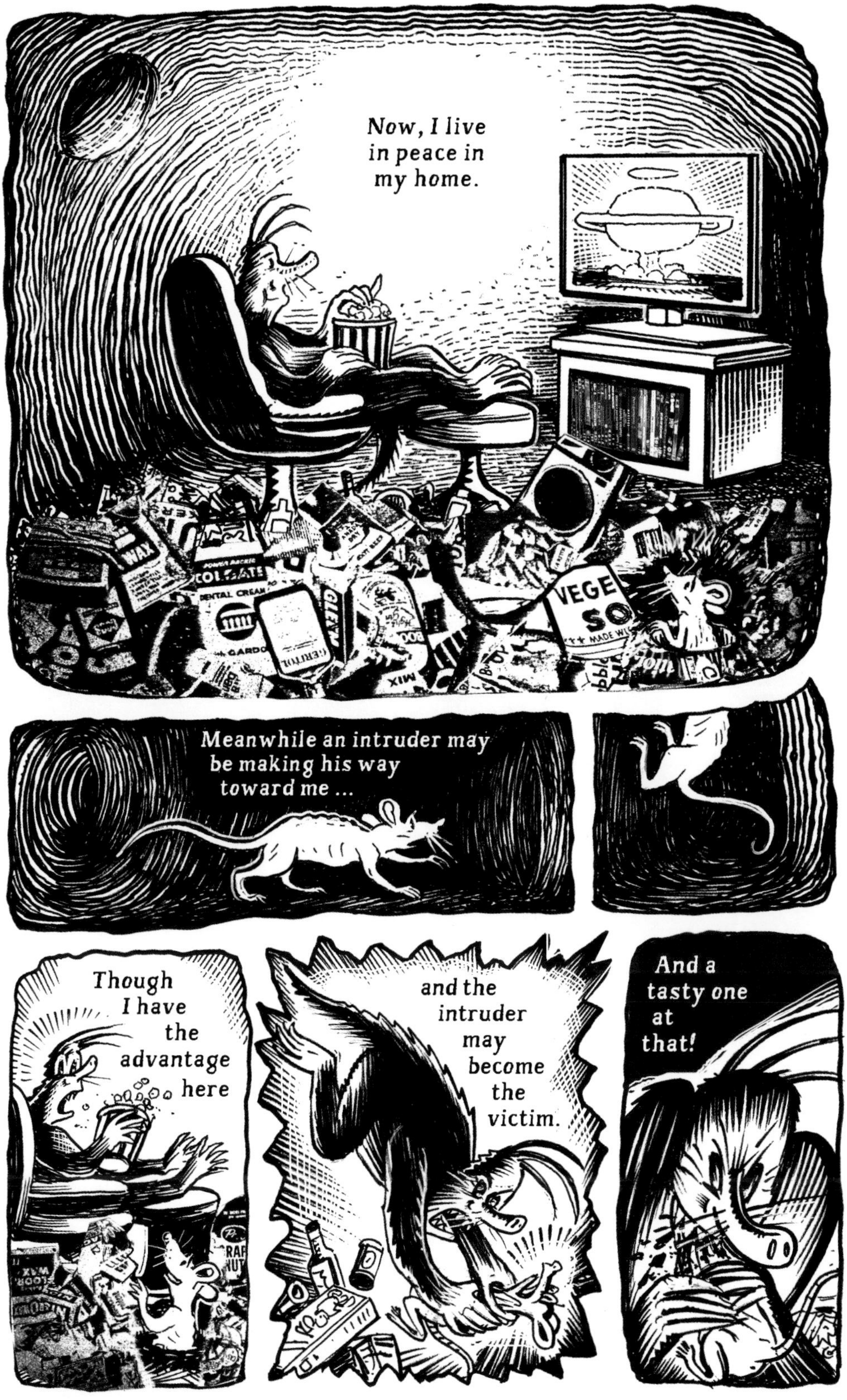
Now, I live in peace in my home.
Meanwhile an intruder may be making his way toward me ...
Though I have the advantage here
and the intruder may become the victim.
And a tasty one at that!

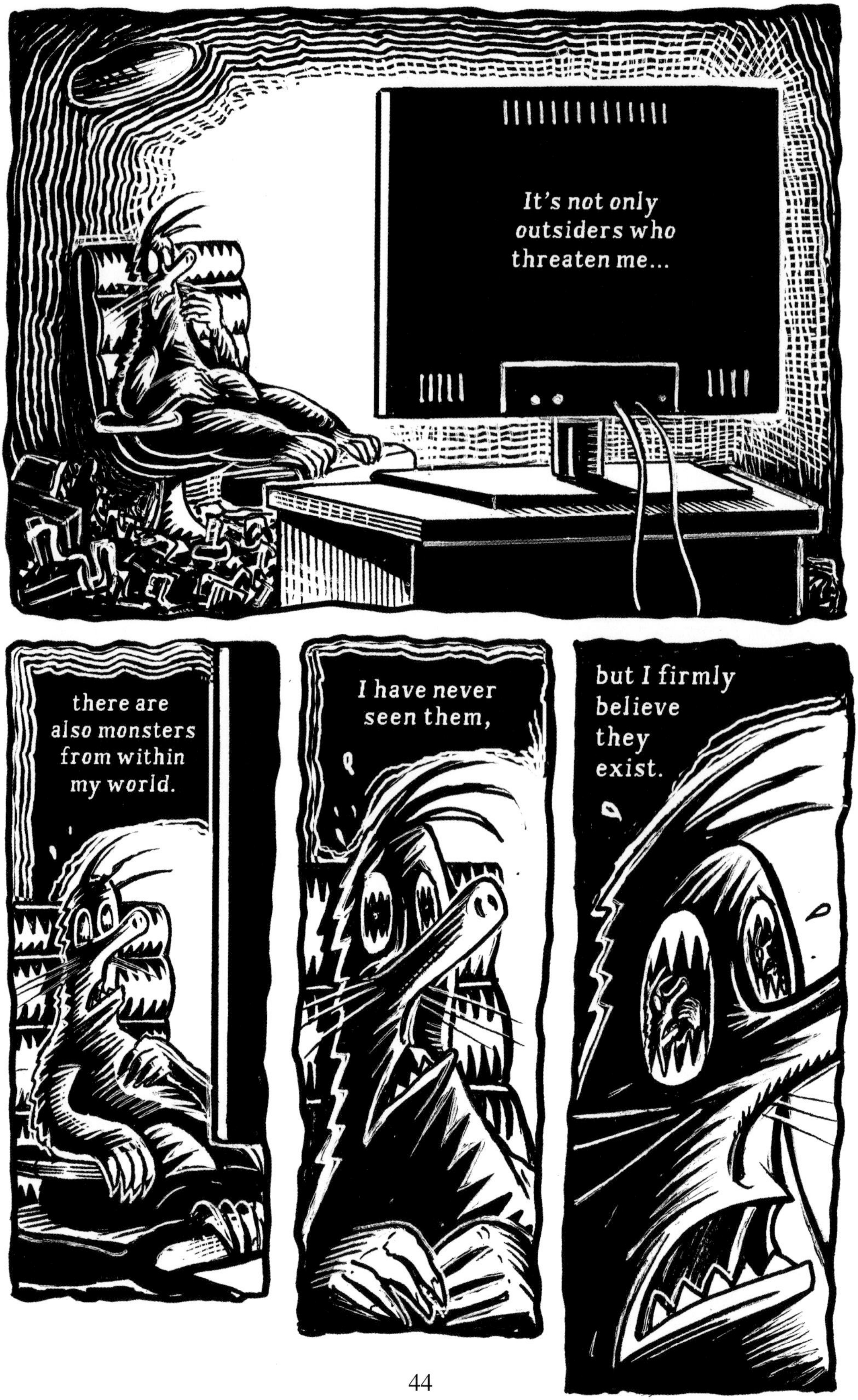
It's not only outsiders who threaten me...
there are also monsters from within my world.
I have never seen them,
but I firmly believe they exist.

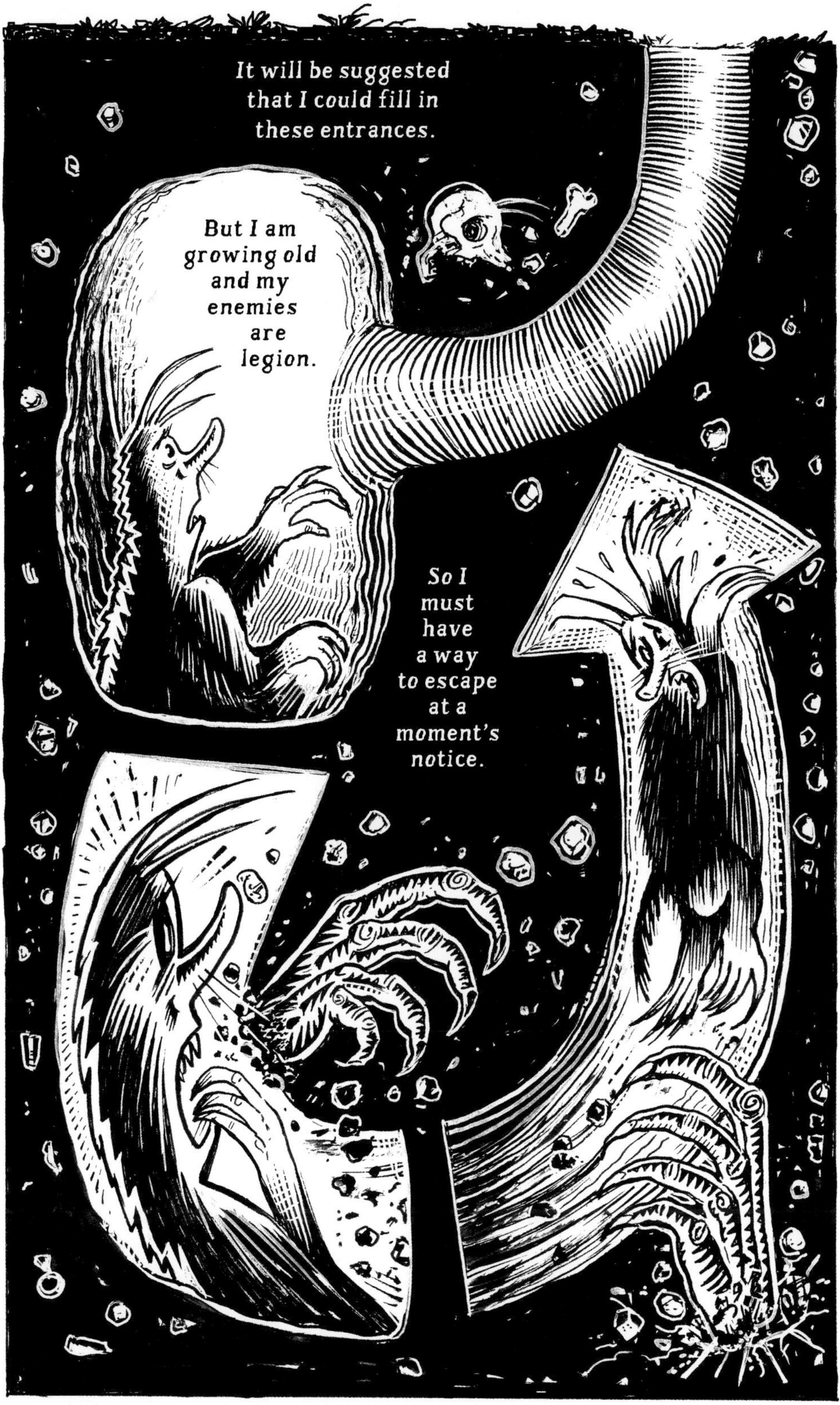
It will be suggested that I could fill in these entrances.
But I am growing old and my enemies are legion.
So I must have a way to escape at a moment's notice.

The most beautiful aspect of my burrow now, is its stillness.

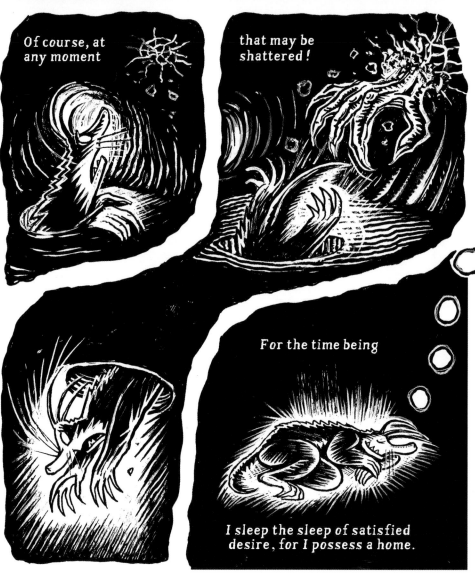

Of course, at any moment

that may be shattered!

For the time being

I sleep the sleep of satisfied desire, for I possess a home.

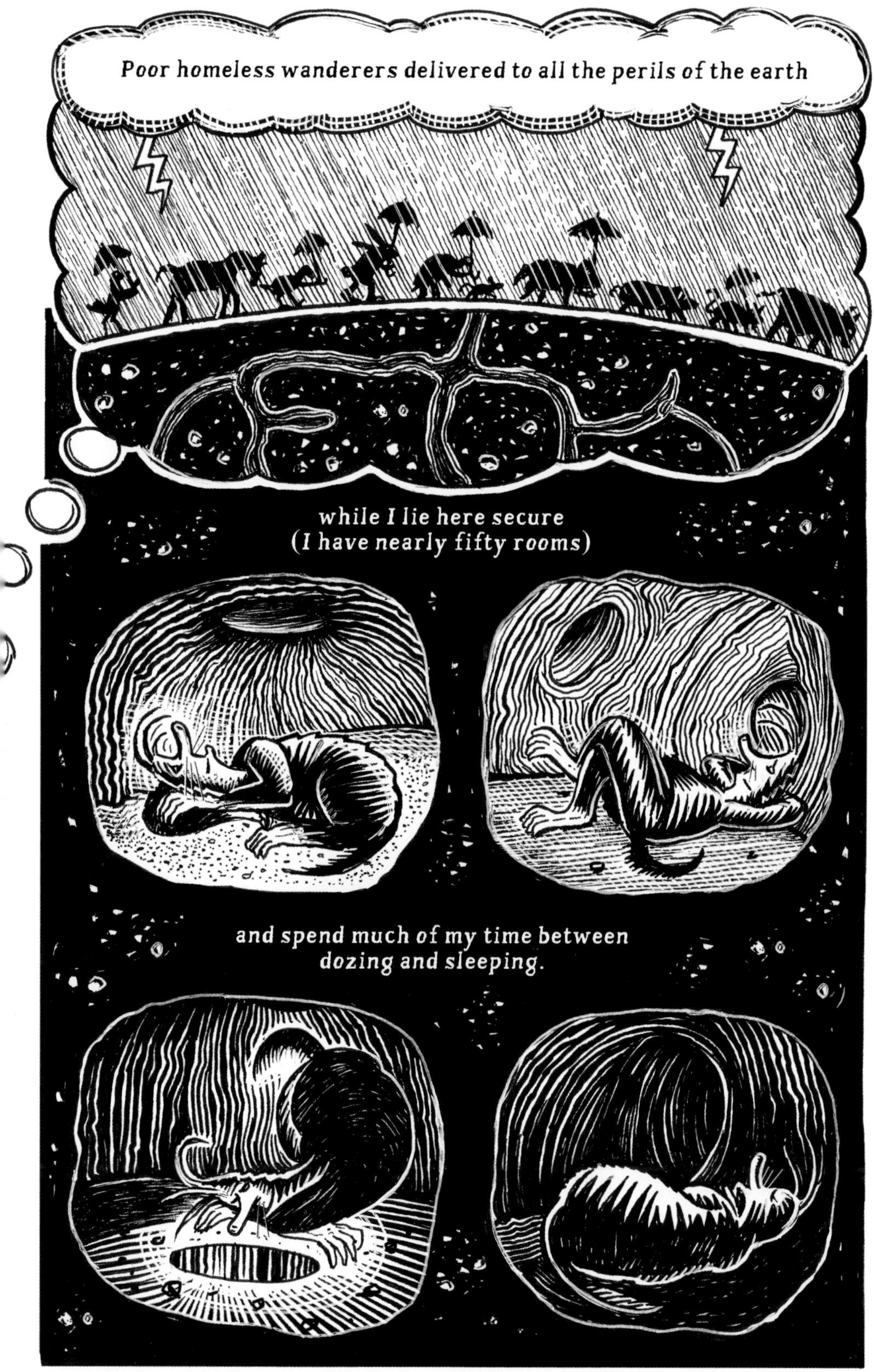
Poor homeless wanderers delivered to all the perils of the earth
while I lie here secure
(I have nearly fifty rooms)
and spend much of my time between
dozing and sleeping.

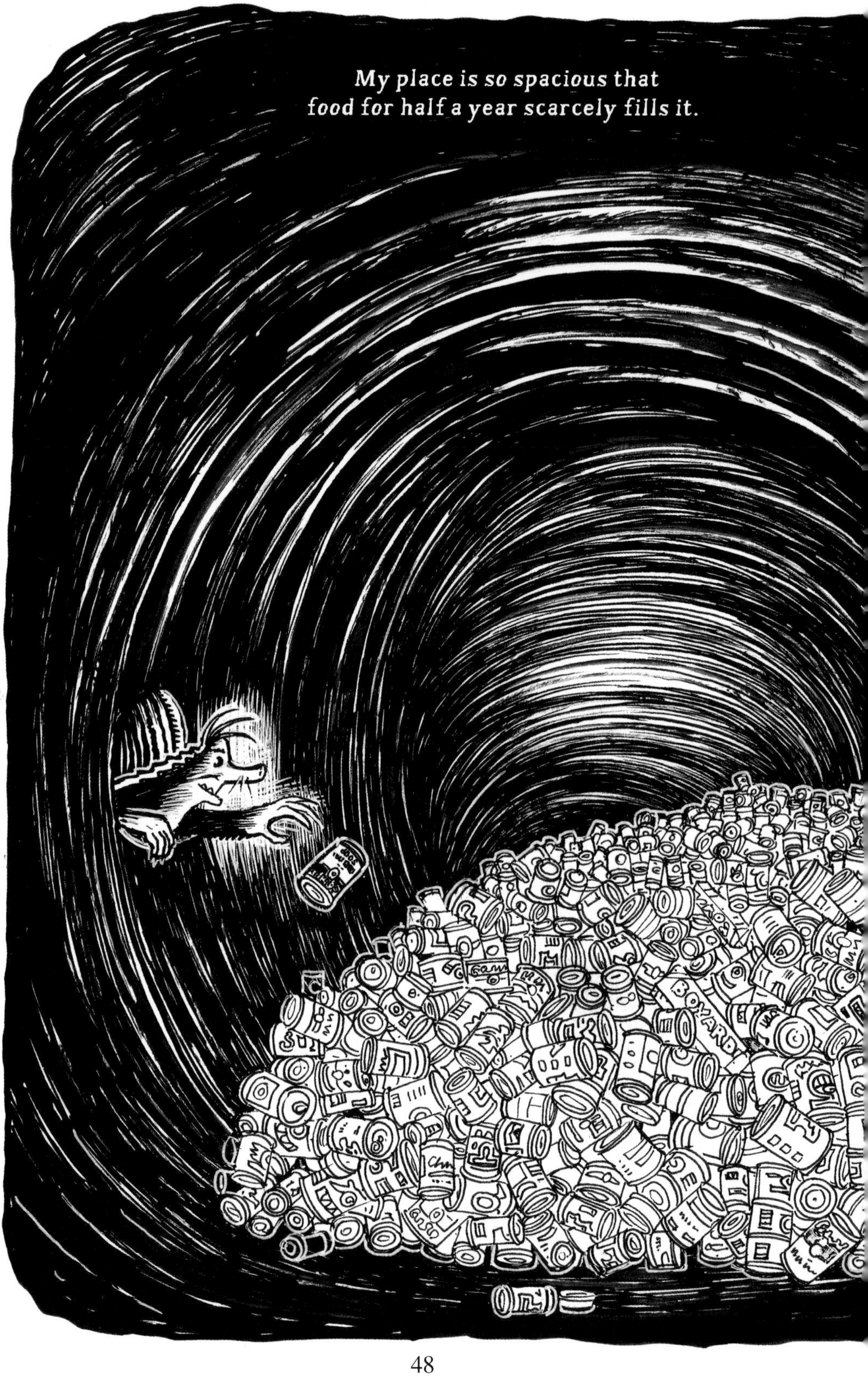
My place is so spacious that
food for half a year scarcely fills it.

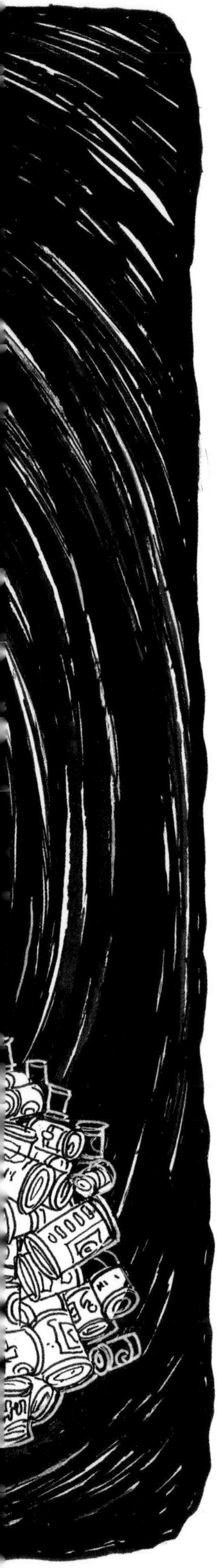

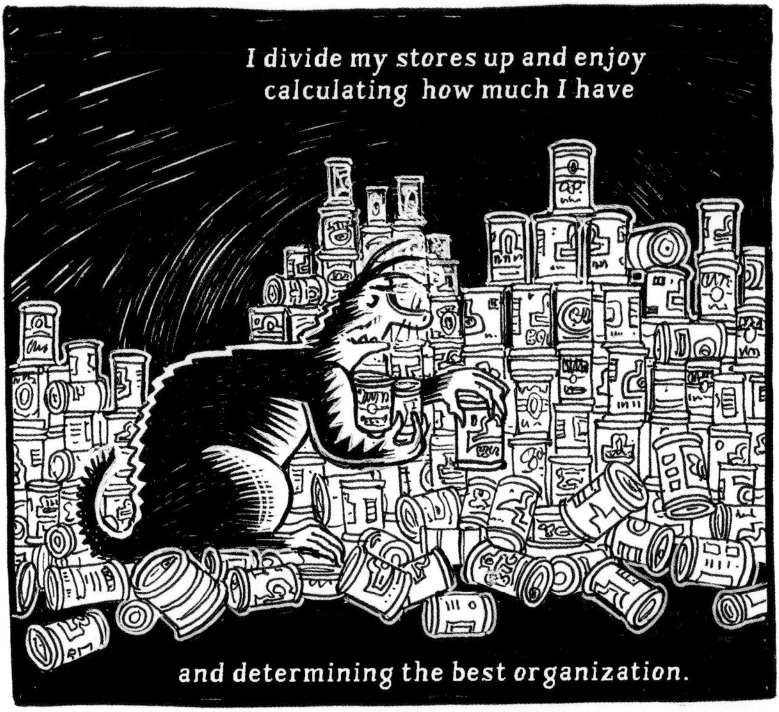
I divide my stores up and enjoy calculating how much I have
and determining the best organization.

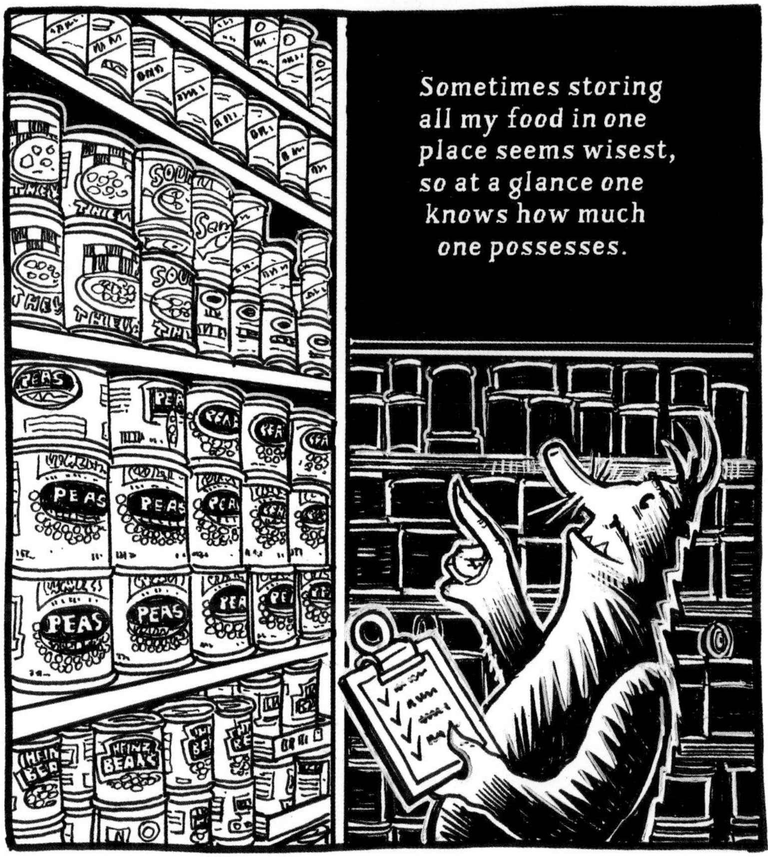
Sometimes storing all my food in one place seems wisest, so at a glance one knows how much one possesses.

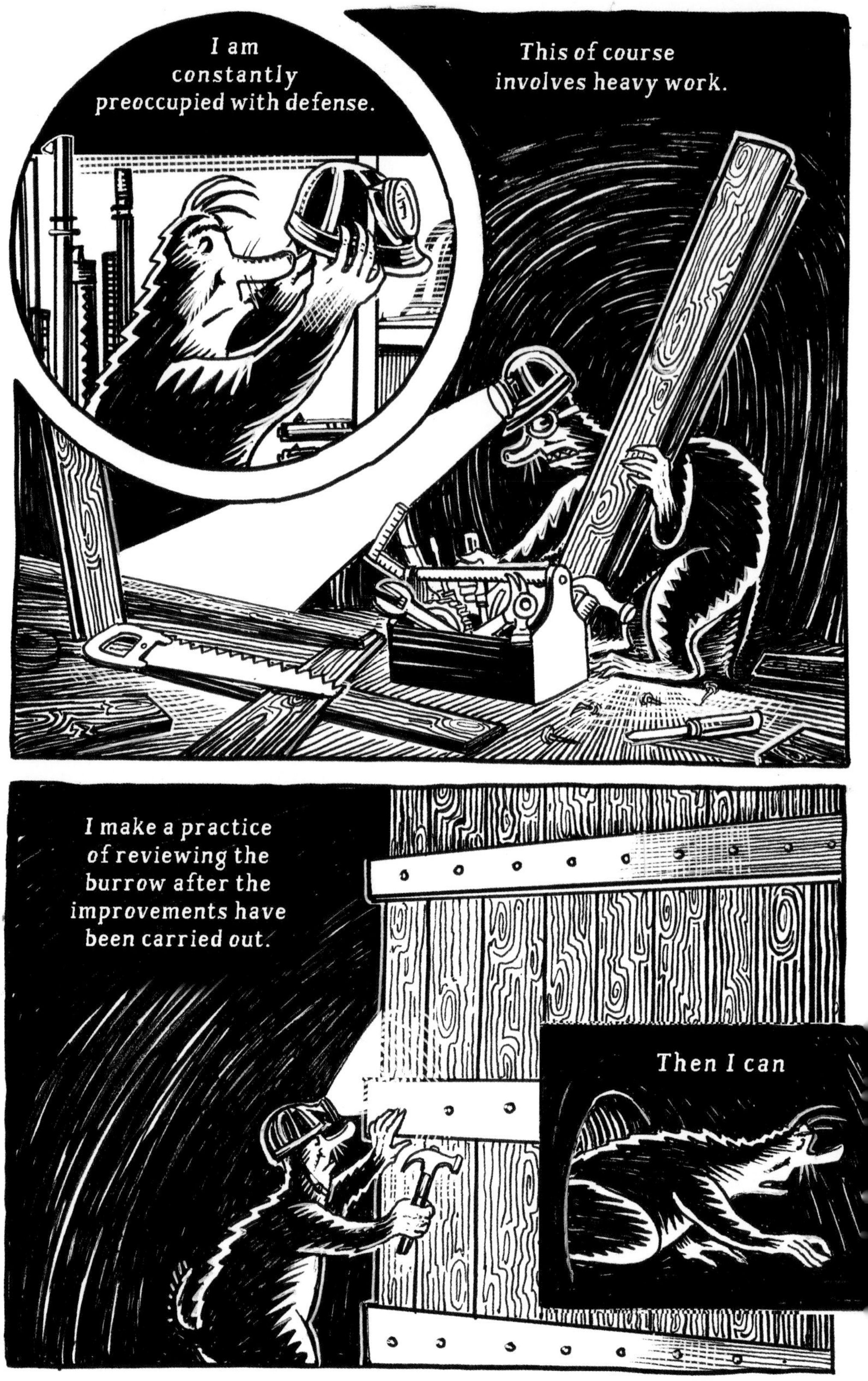
I am constantly preoccupied with defense.
This of course involves heavy work.
I make a practice of reviewing the burrow after the improvements have been carried out.
Then I can

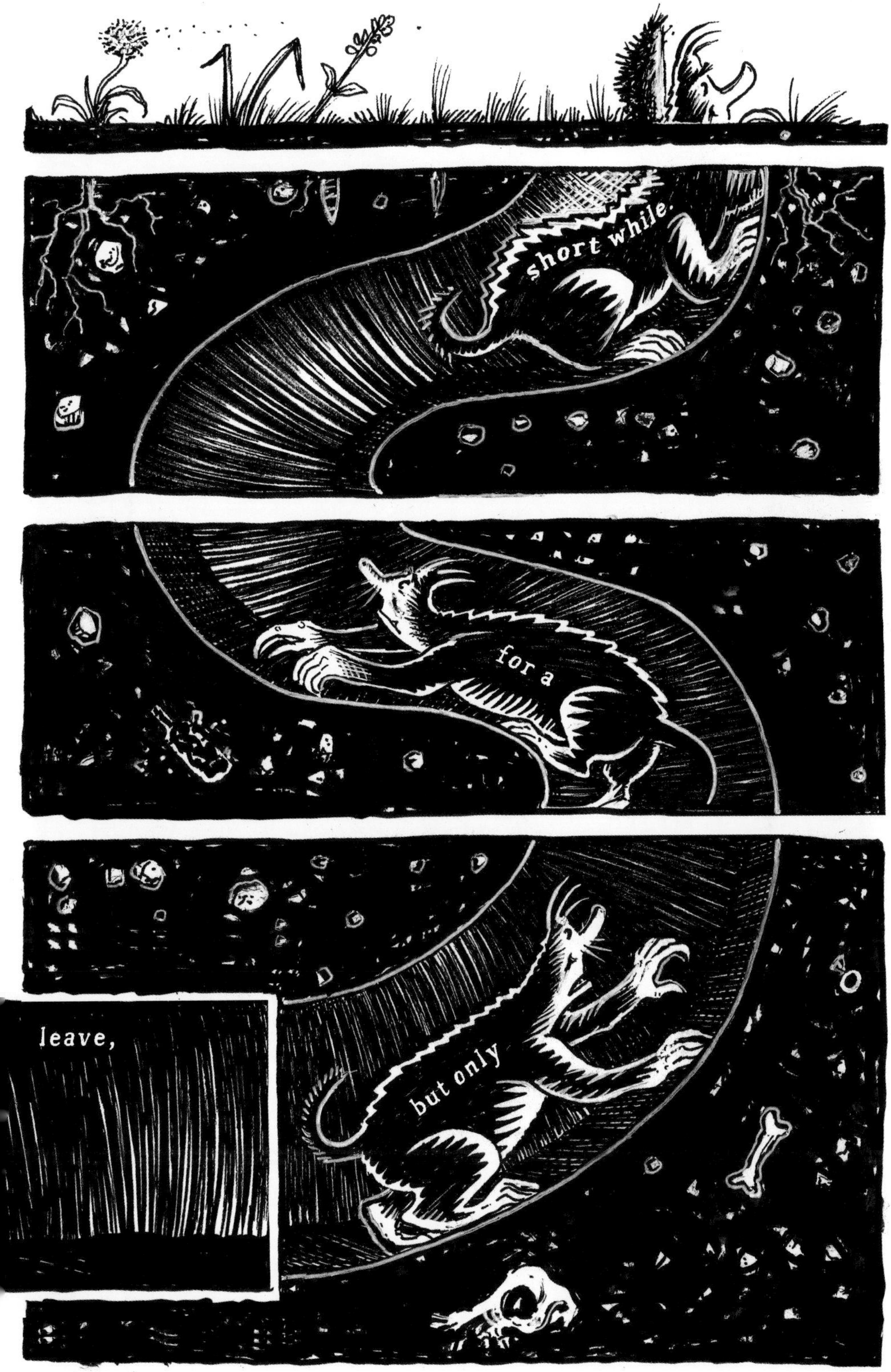
leave,
but only
for a
short while.

It is always with a certain amount of dread that I exit.

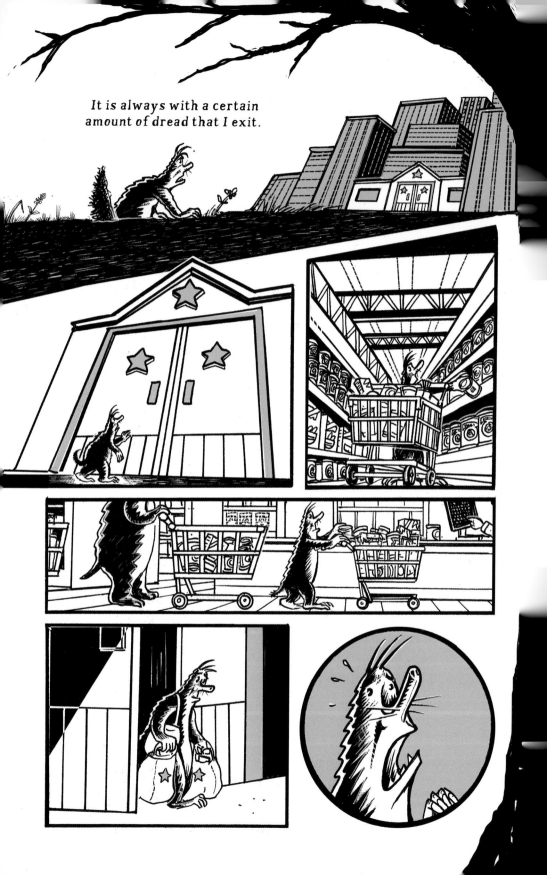

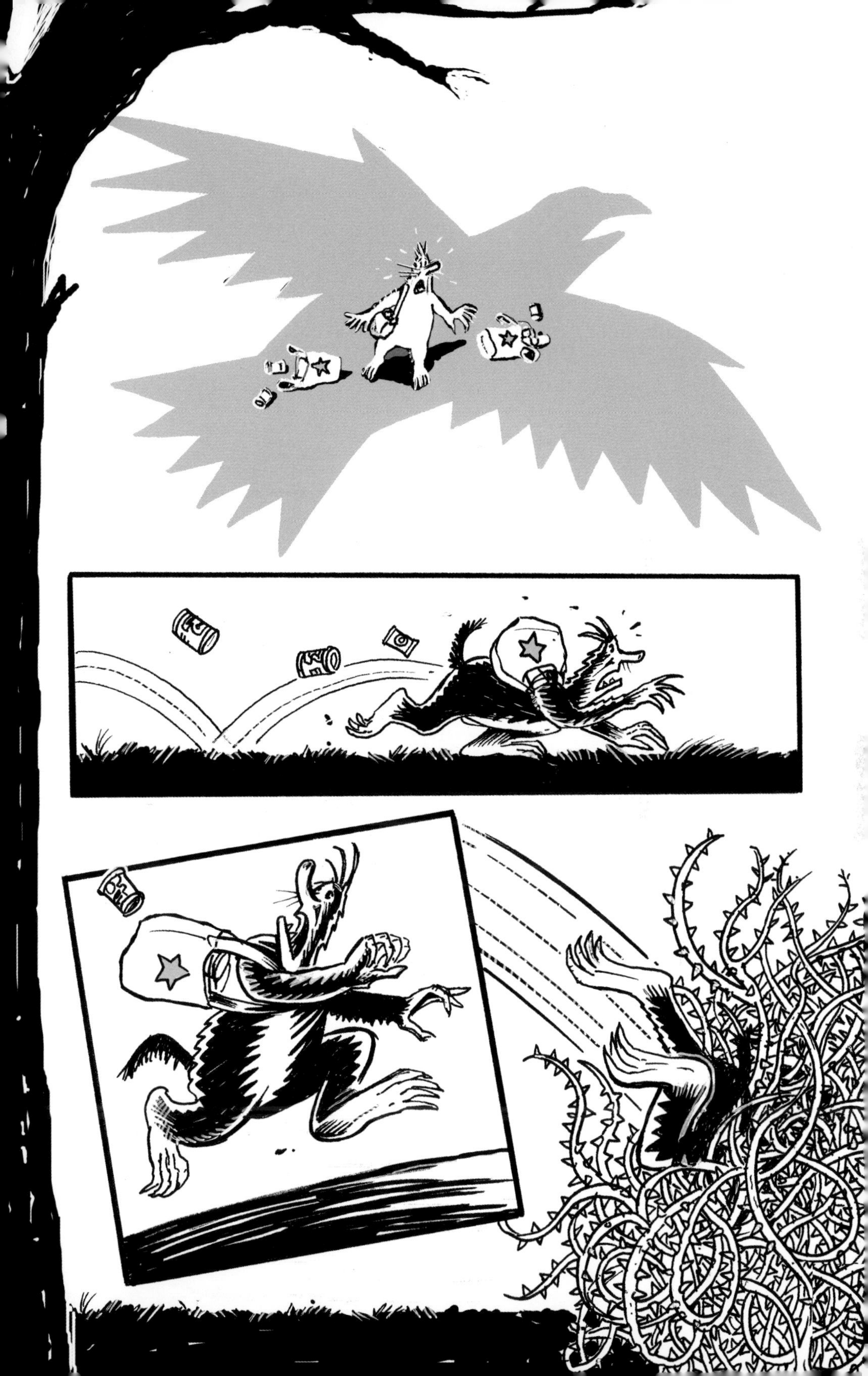

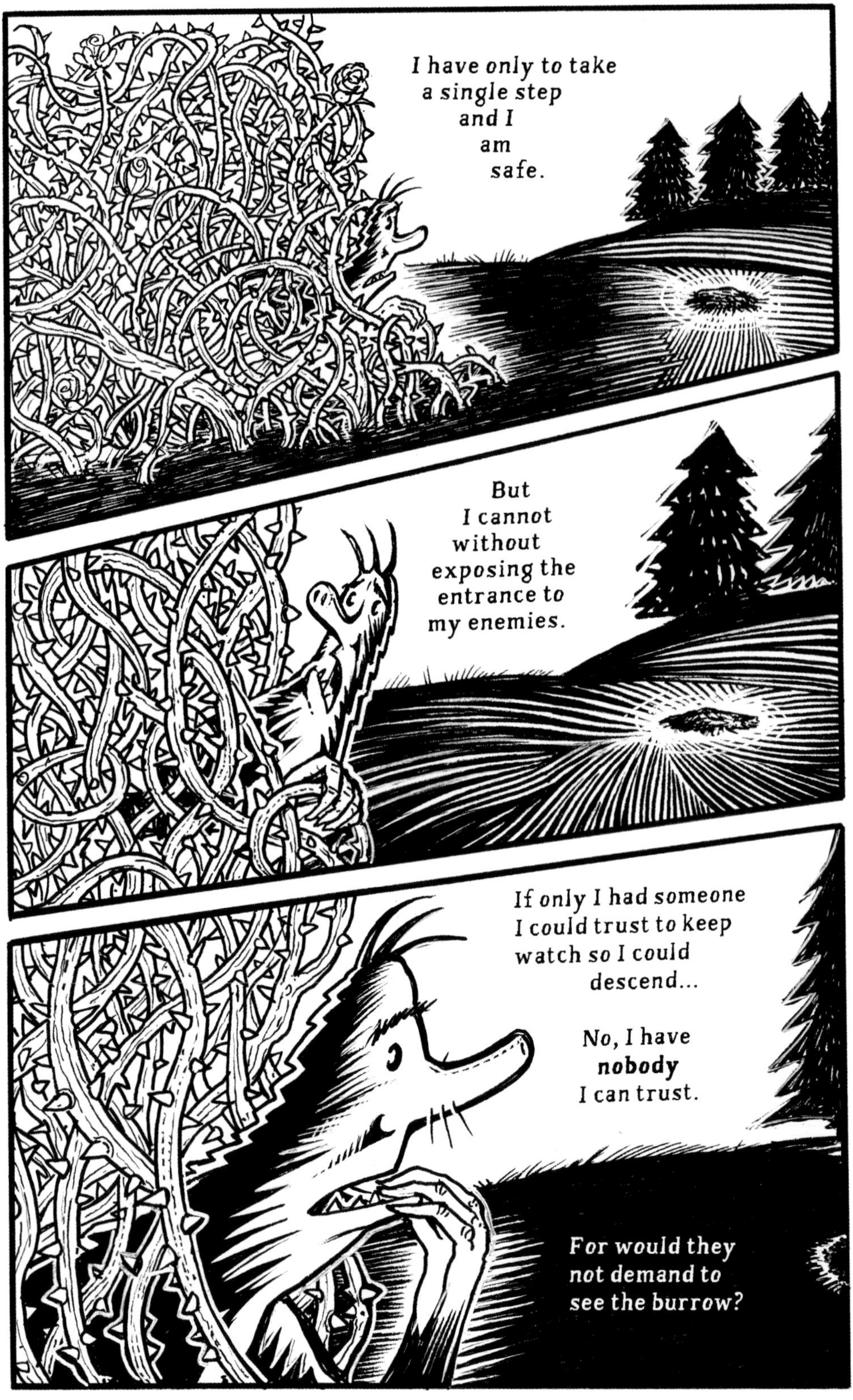
I have only to take a single step and I am safe.
But I cannot without exposing the entrance to my enemies.
If only I had someone I could trust to keep watch so I could descend...
No, I have **nobody** I can trust.
For would they not demand to see the burrow?

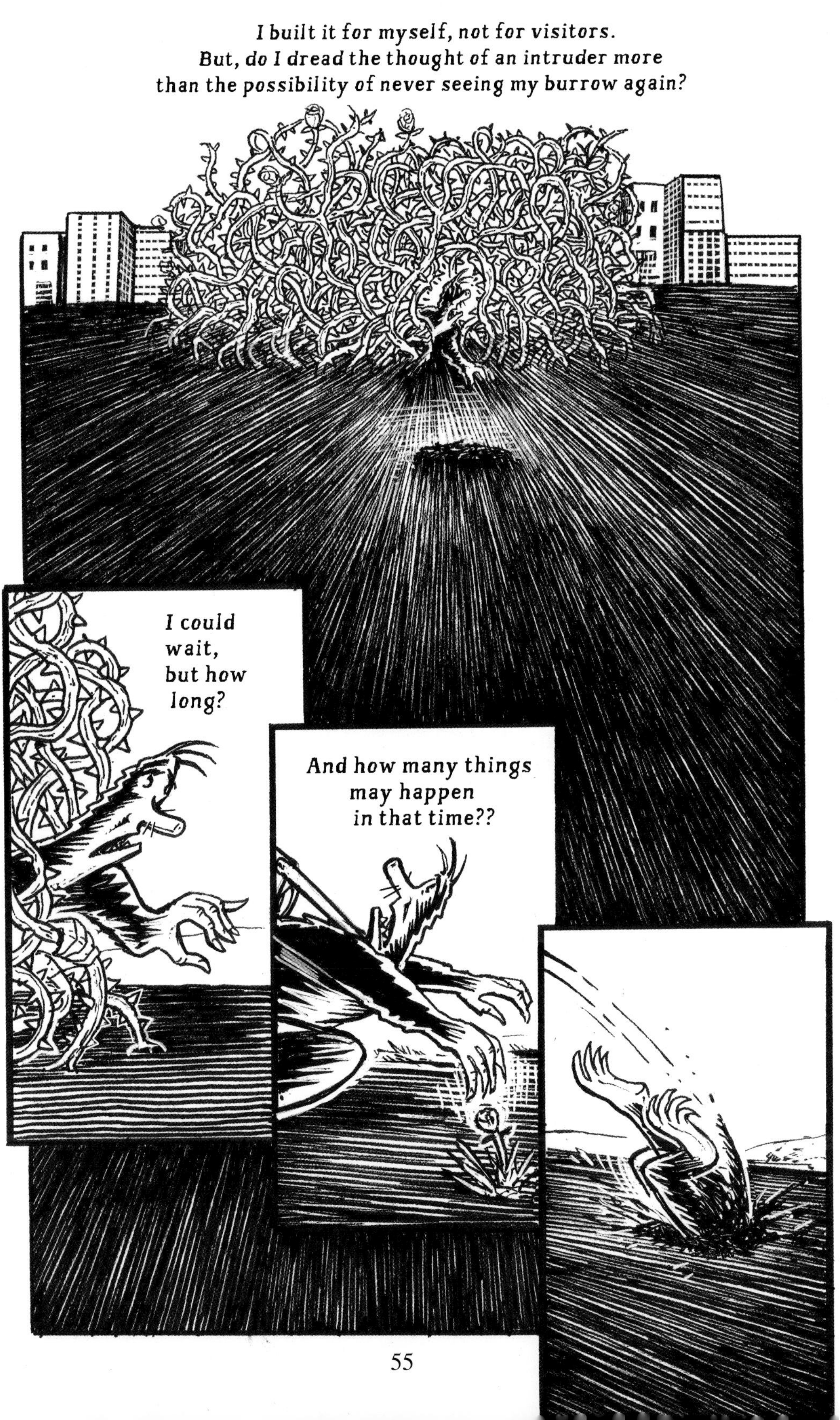
I built it for myself, not for visitors.
But, do I dread the thought of an intruder more than the possibility of never seeing my burrow again?
I could wait, but how long?
And how many things may happen in that time??

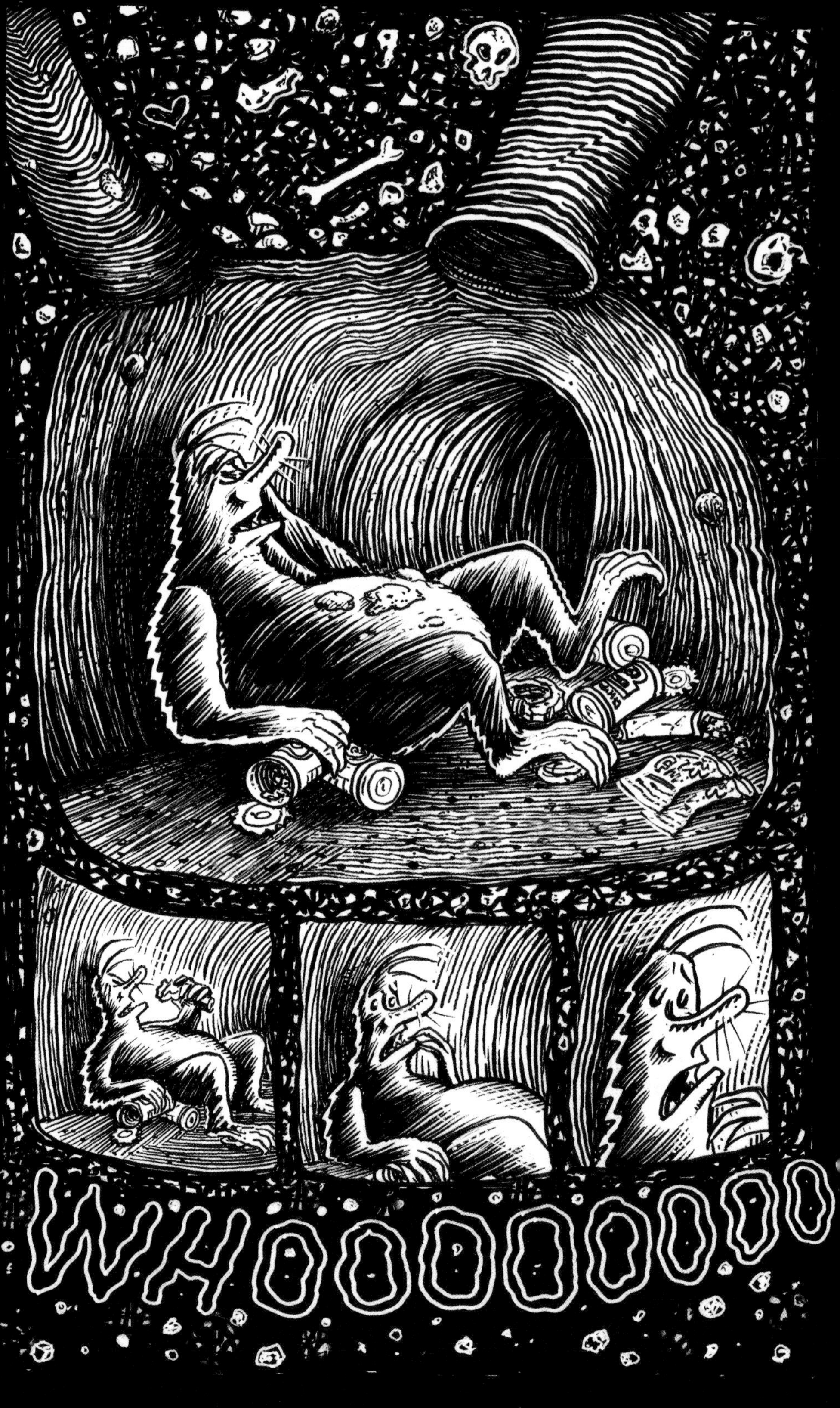
WHOOOOOOO

That whistling—some migrating creature? Has it
just grown fainter? No, no it has grown louder.
I keep very quiet. It simply cannot have heard me.
Perhaps it could have heard me, but if it had
I would have   some sign. The thing to do is
carefully   consider every way to defend
        the burrow. My mind is taken up
        with the whistling in my walls.
        It grows louder, it comes nearer.
        I must assume that the beast is
        encircling me. It has probably
        already made   several
        circles arou   my burrow.
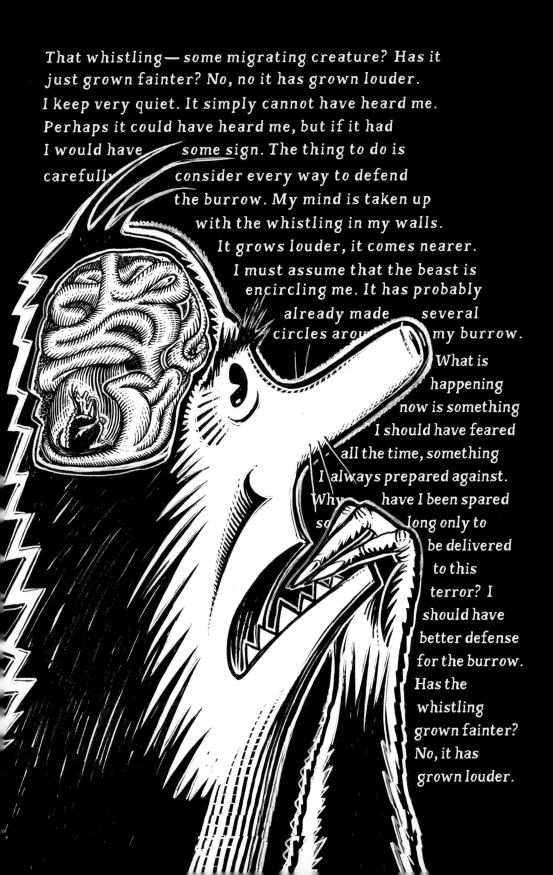
What is
happening
now is something
I should have feared
all the time, something
I always prepared against.
Why   have I been spared
so   long only to
        be delivered
        to this
        terror? I
        should have
        better defense
        for the burrow.
        Has the
        whistling
        grown fainter?
        No, it has
        grown louder.

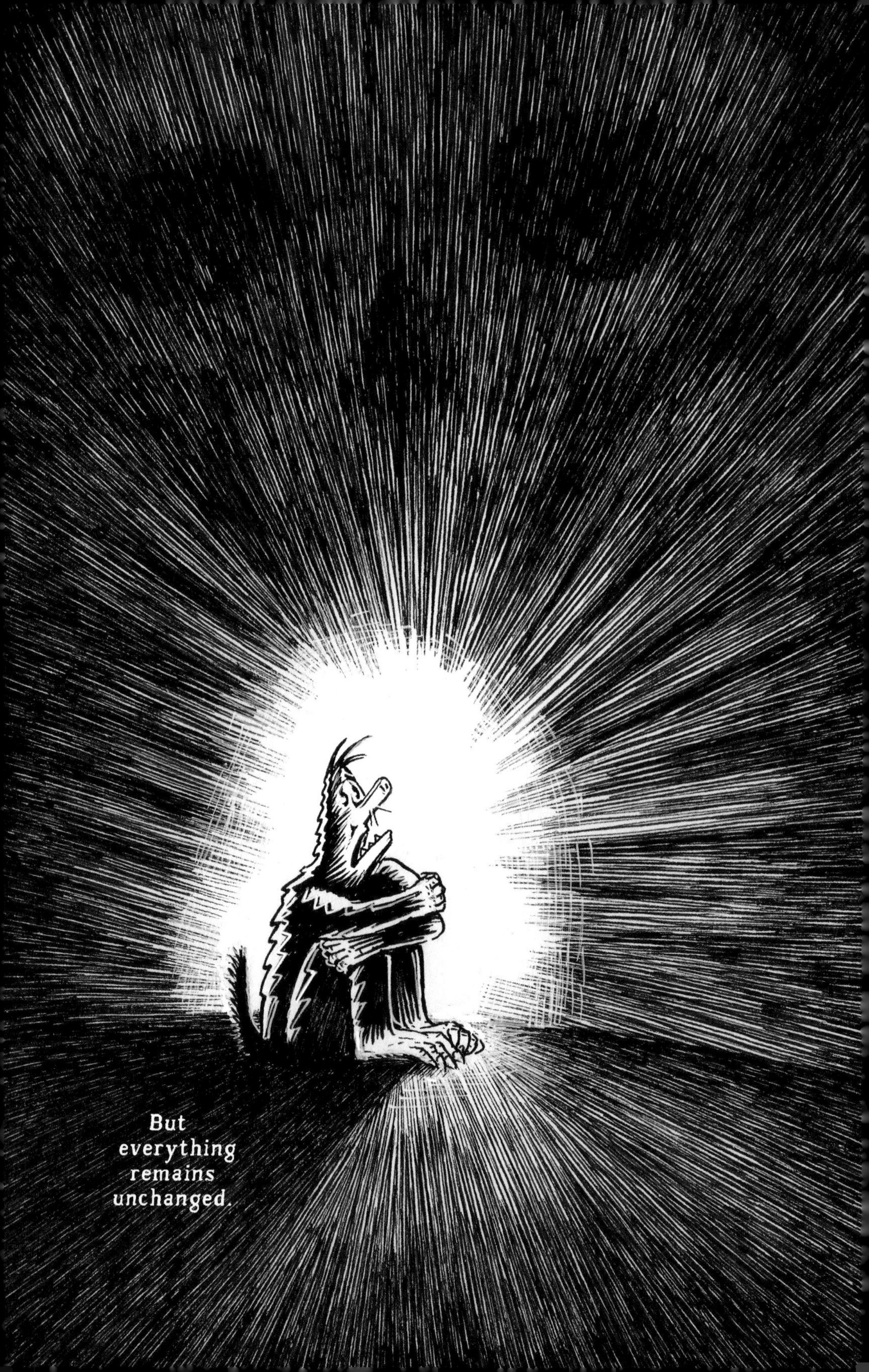
But
everything
remains
unchanged.

GIVE IT UP!

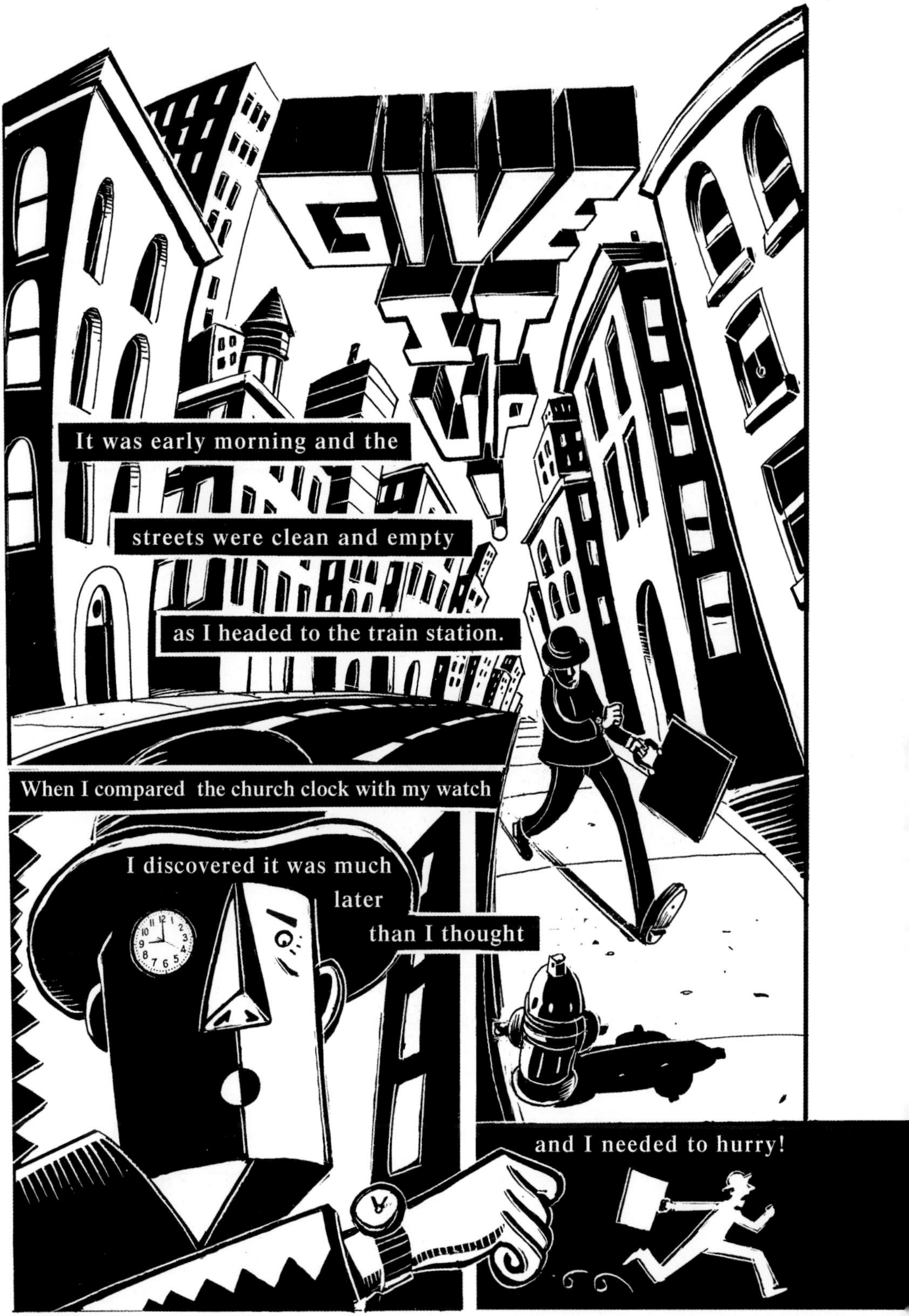
GIVE IT UP
It was early morning and the
streets were clean and empty
as I headed to the train station.
When I compared the church clock with my watch
I discovered it was much
later
than I thought
and I needed to hurry!

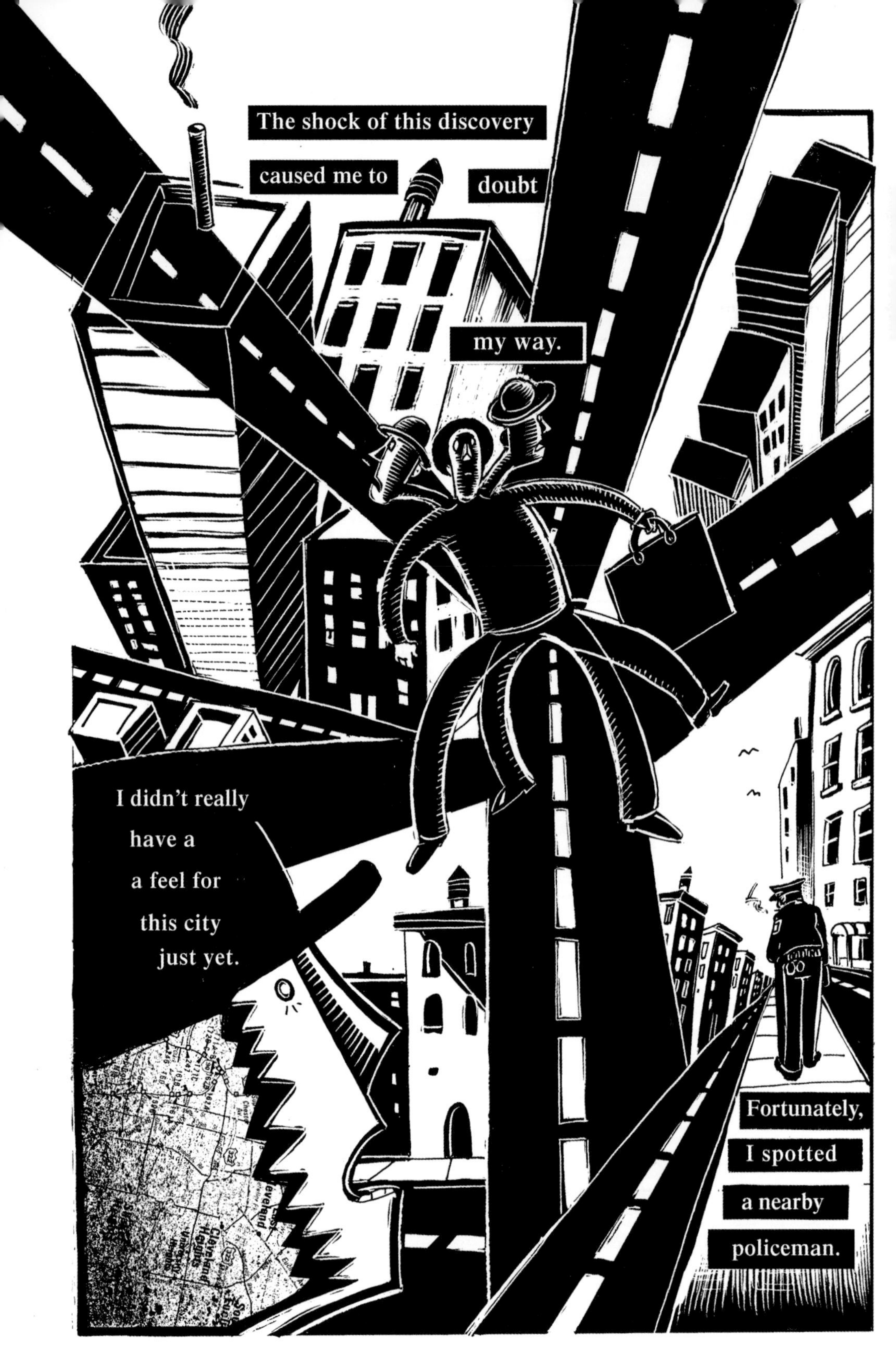
The shock of this discovery
caused me to
doubt
my way.
I didn't really
have a
a feel for
this city
just yet.
Fortunately,
I spotted
a nearby
policeman.

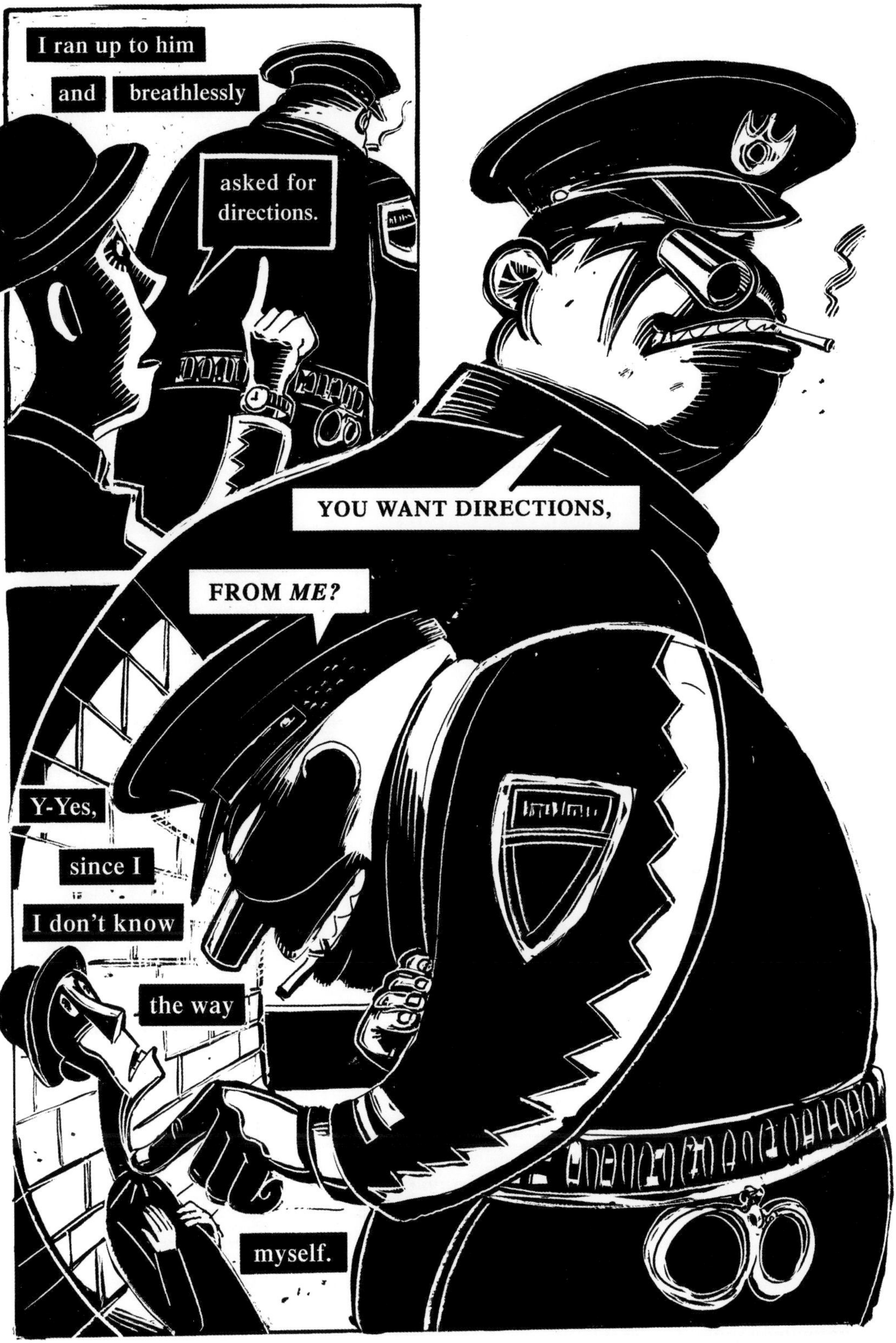
I ran up to him
and
breathlessly
asked for directions.
YOU WANT DIRECTIONS,
FROM *ME?*
Y-Yes,
since I
I don't know
the way
myself.

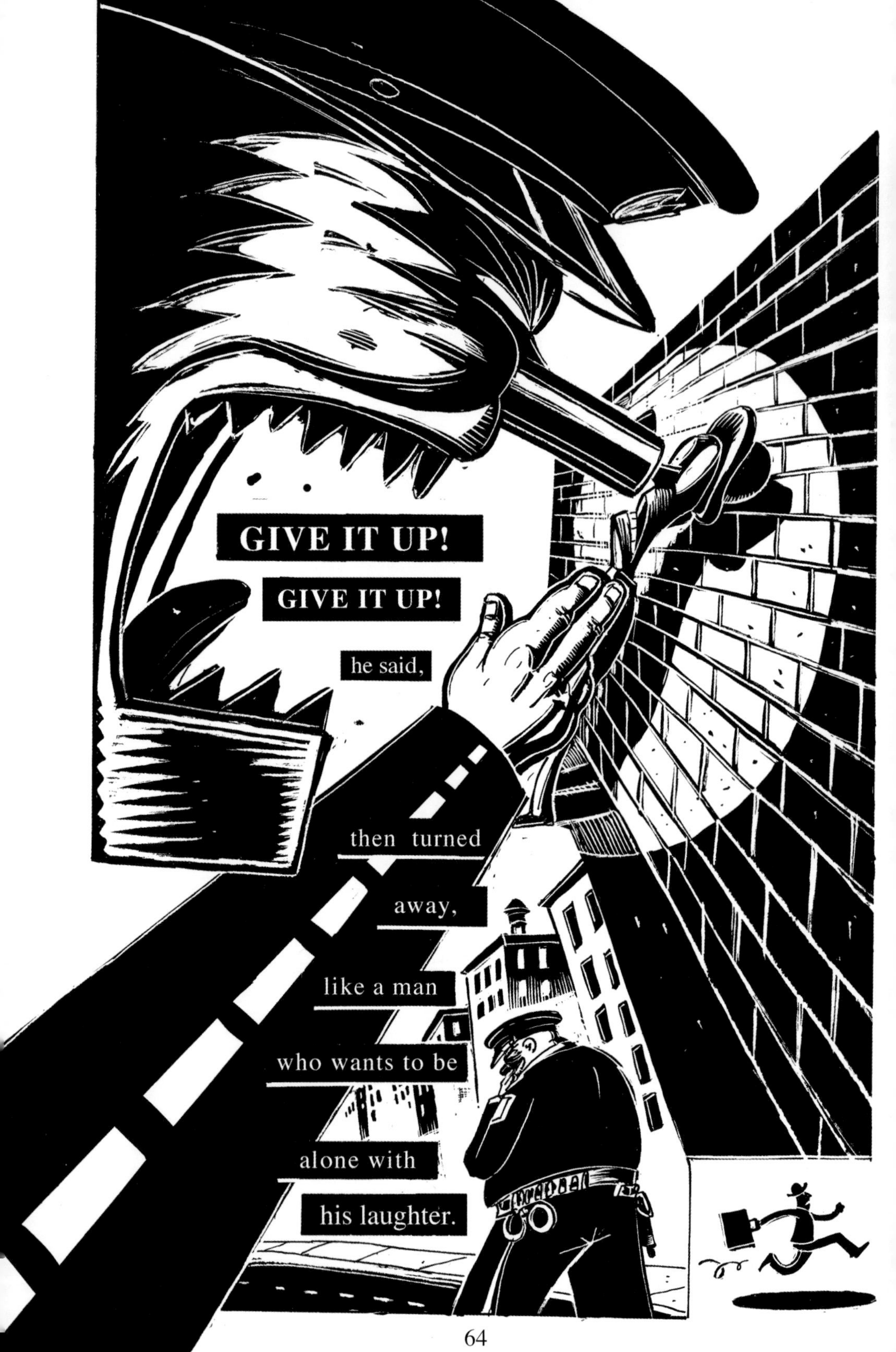
GIVE IT UP!
GIVE IT UP!
he said,
then turned
away,
like a man
who wants to be
alone with
his laughter.

COAL-BUCKET
RIDER

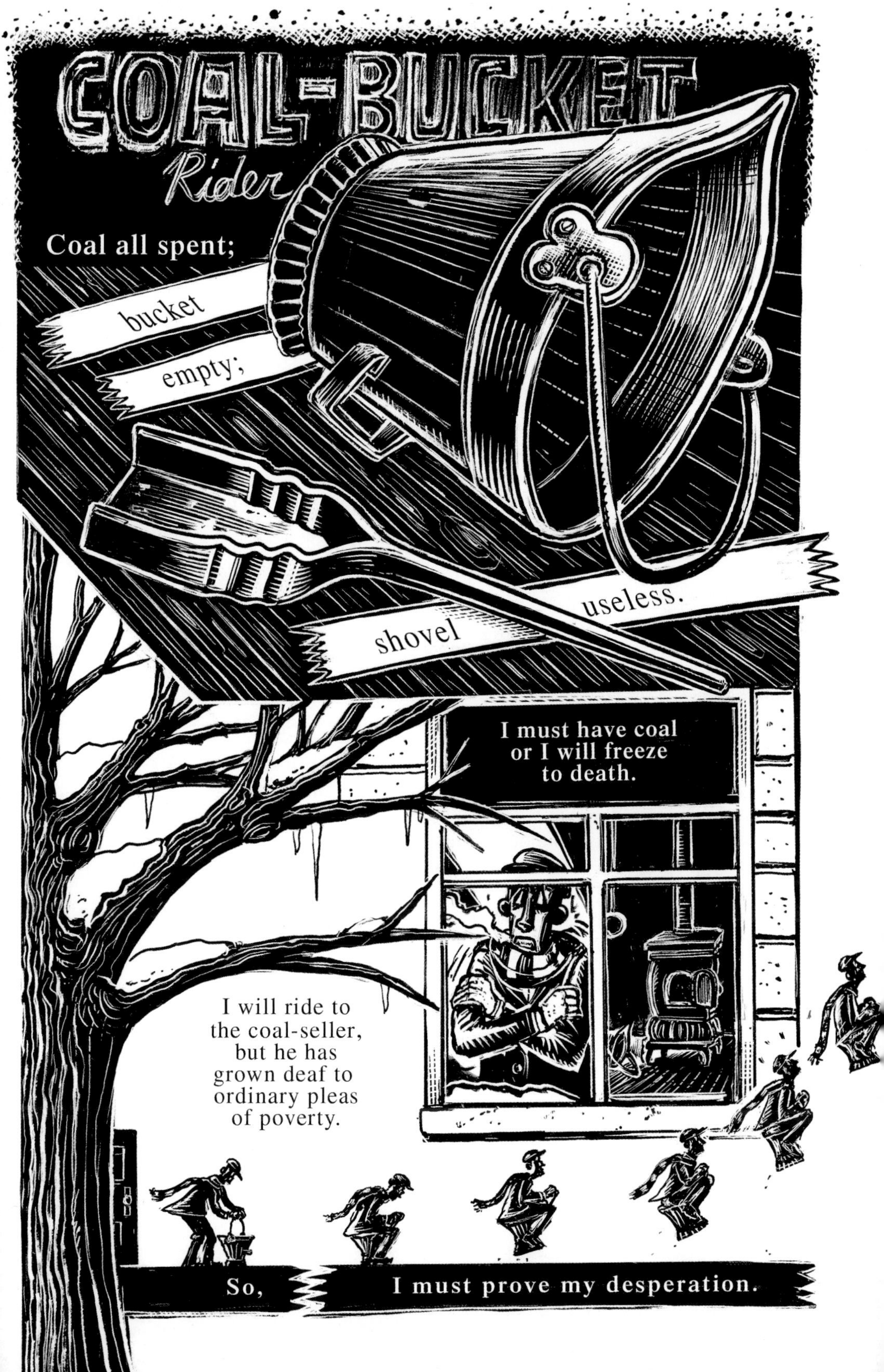
COAL-BUCKET
Rider
Coal all spent;
bucket
empty;
shovel
useless.
I must have coal or I will freeze to death.
I will ride to the coal-seller, but he has grown deaf to ordinary pleas of poverty.
So,
I must prove my desperation.

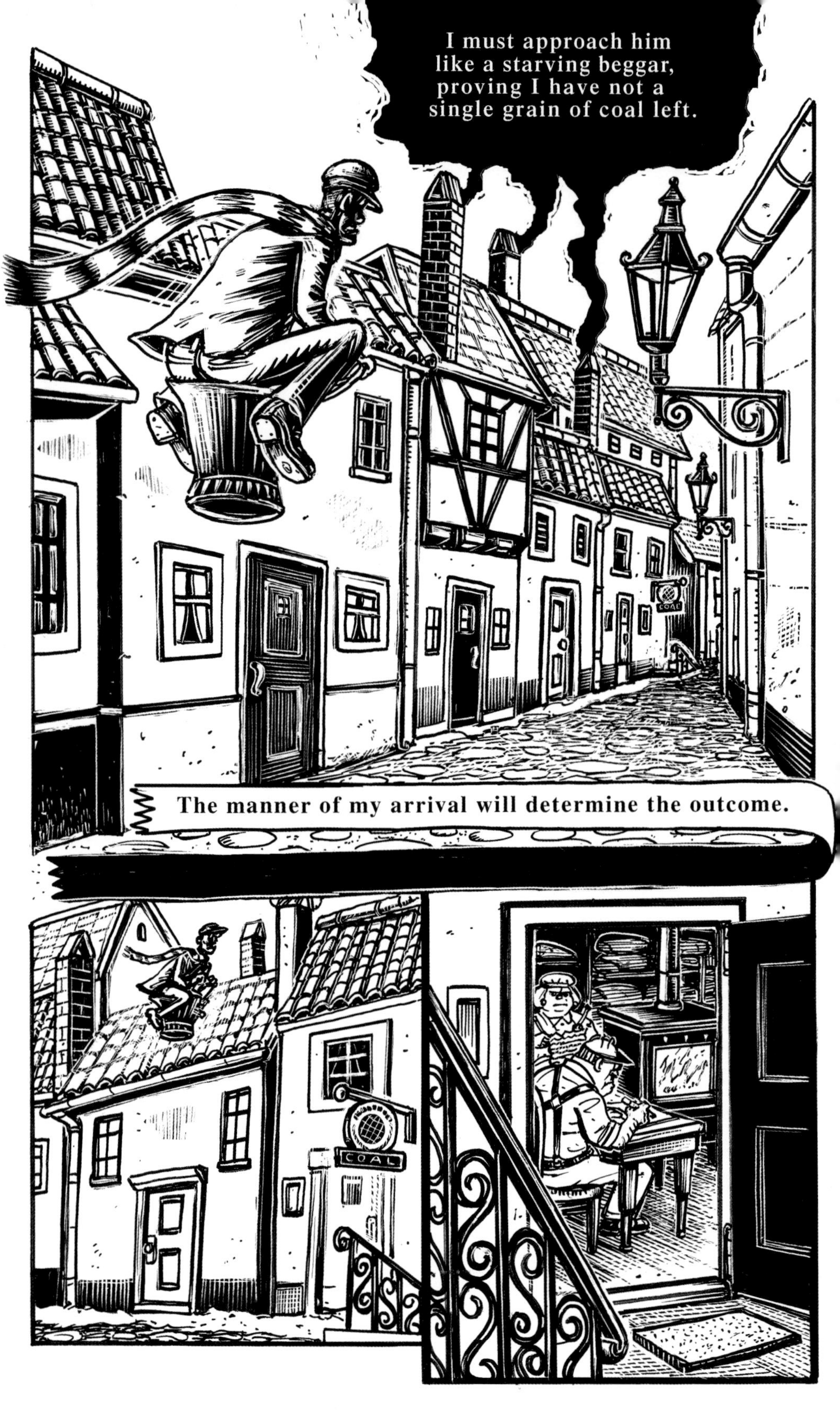
I must approach him like a starving beggar, proving I have not a single grain of coal left.
The manner of my arrival will determine the outcome.
COAL
COAL

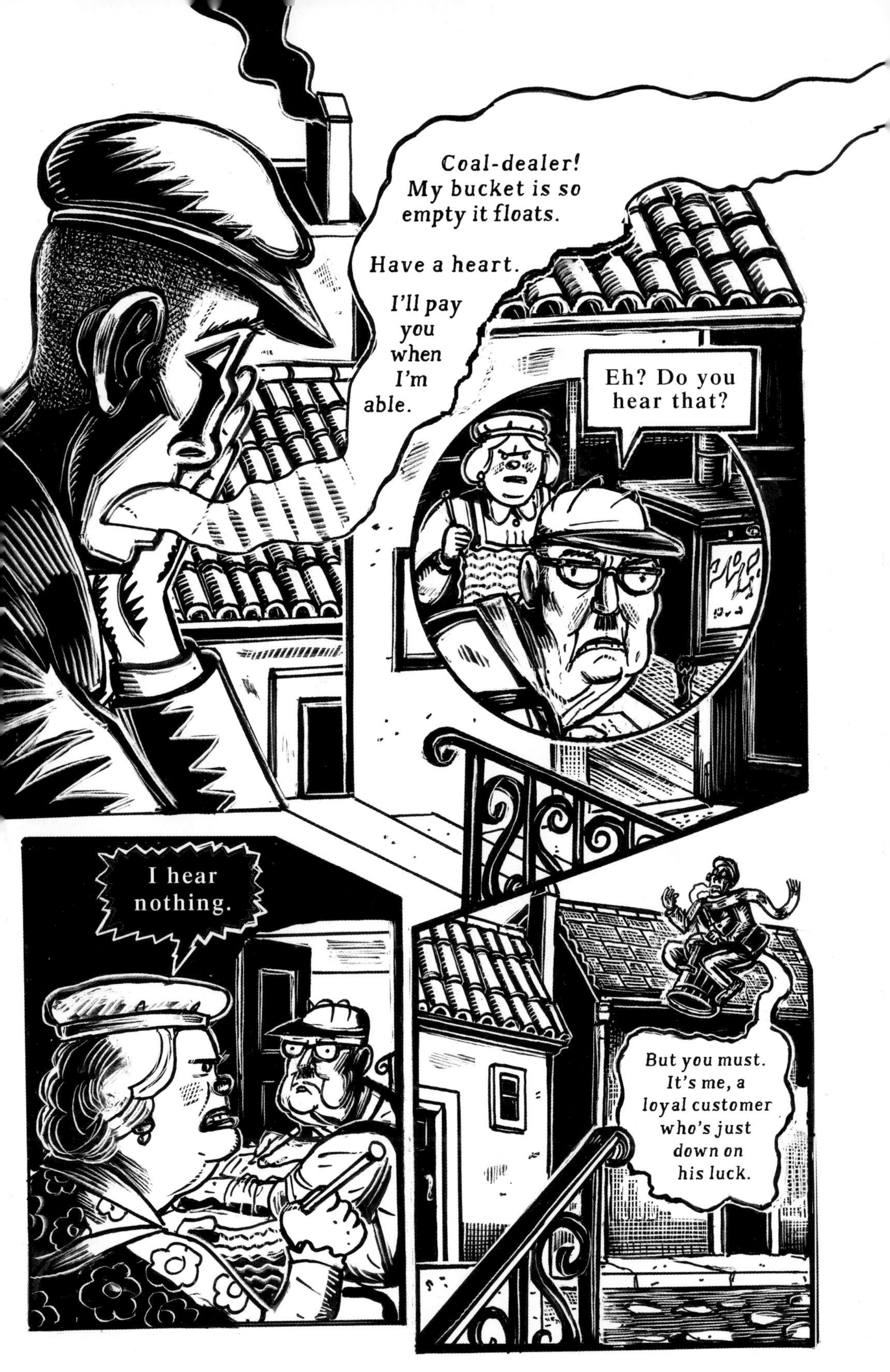
Coal-dealer! My bucket is so empty it floats.
Have a heart.
I'll pay you when I'm able.
Eh? Do you hear that?
I hear nothing.
But you must. It's me, a loyal customer who's just down on his luck.

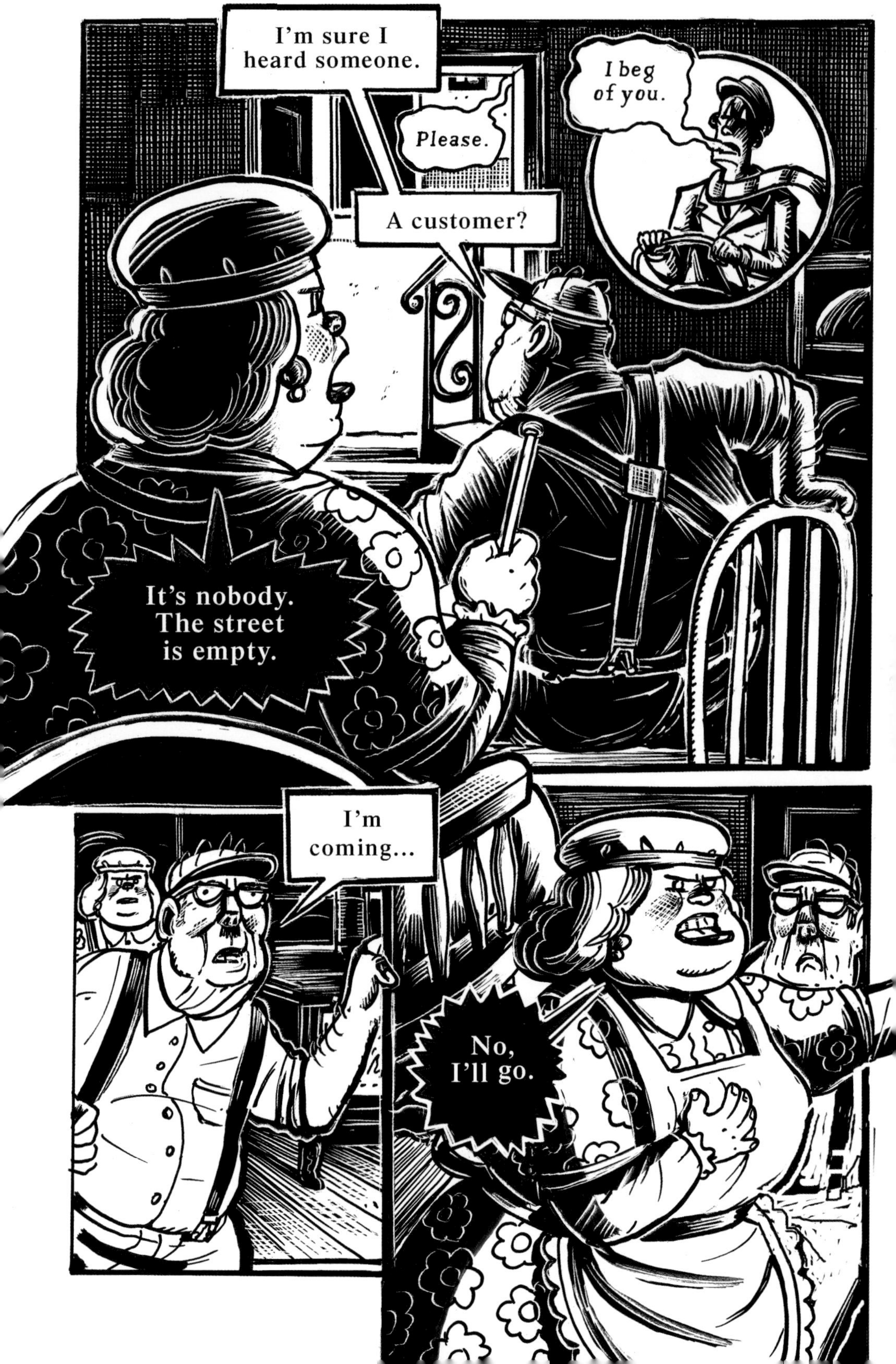
I'm sure I heard someone.
Please.
I beg of you.
A customer?
It's nobody. The street is empty.
I'm coming...
No, I'll go.

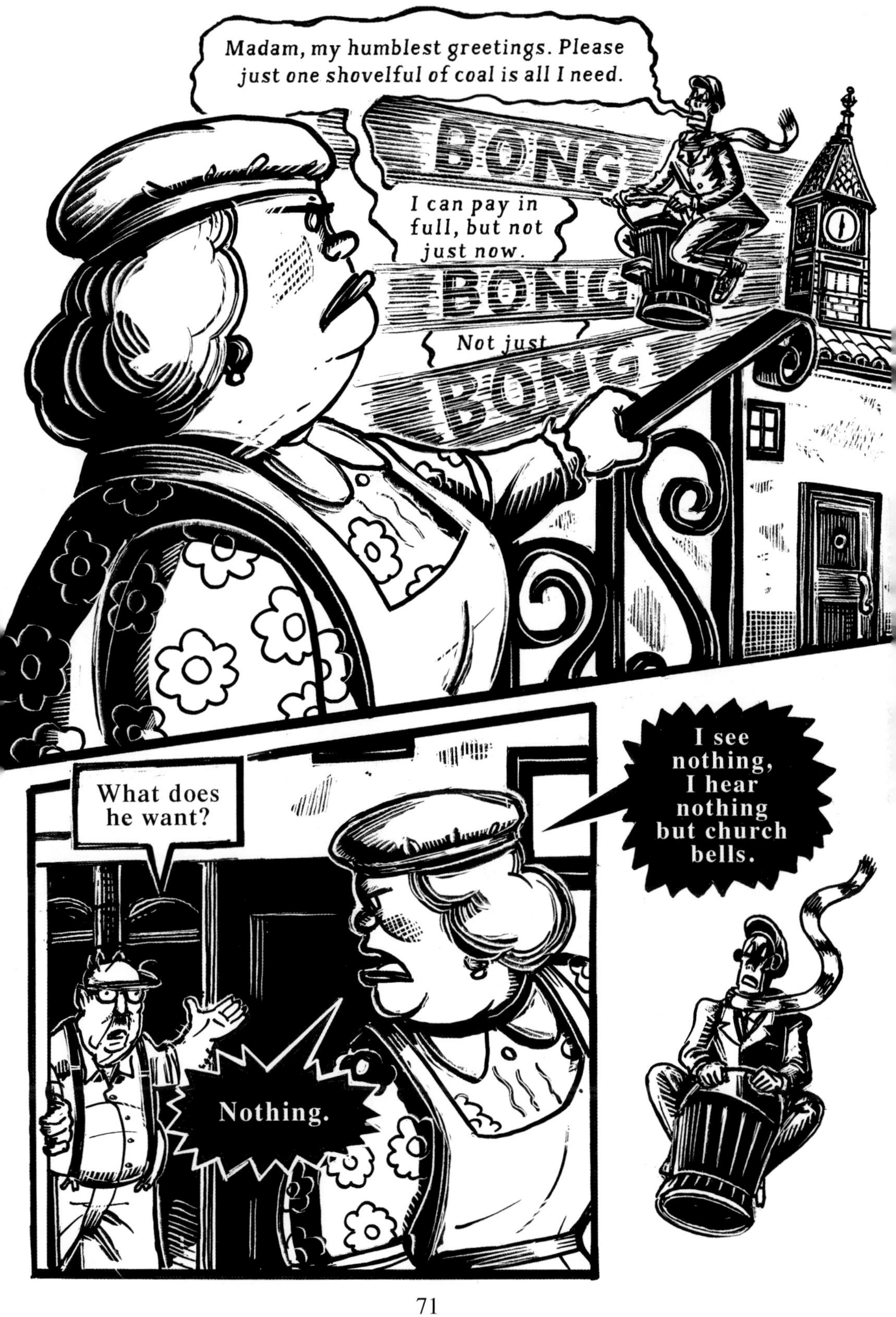
Madam, my humblest greetings. Please just one shovelful of coal is all I need.
BONG
I can pay in full, but not just now.
BONG
Not just
BONG
What does he want?
Nothing.
I see nothing, I hear nothing but church bells.

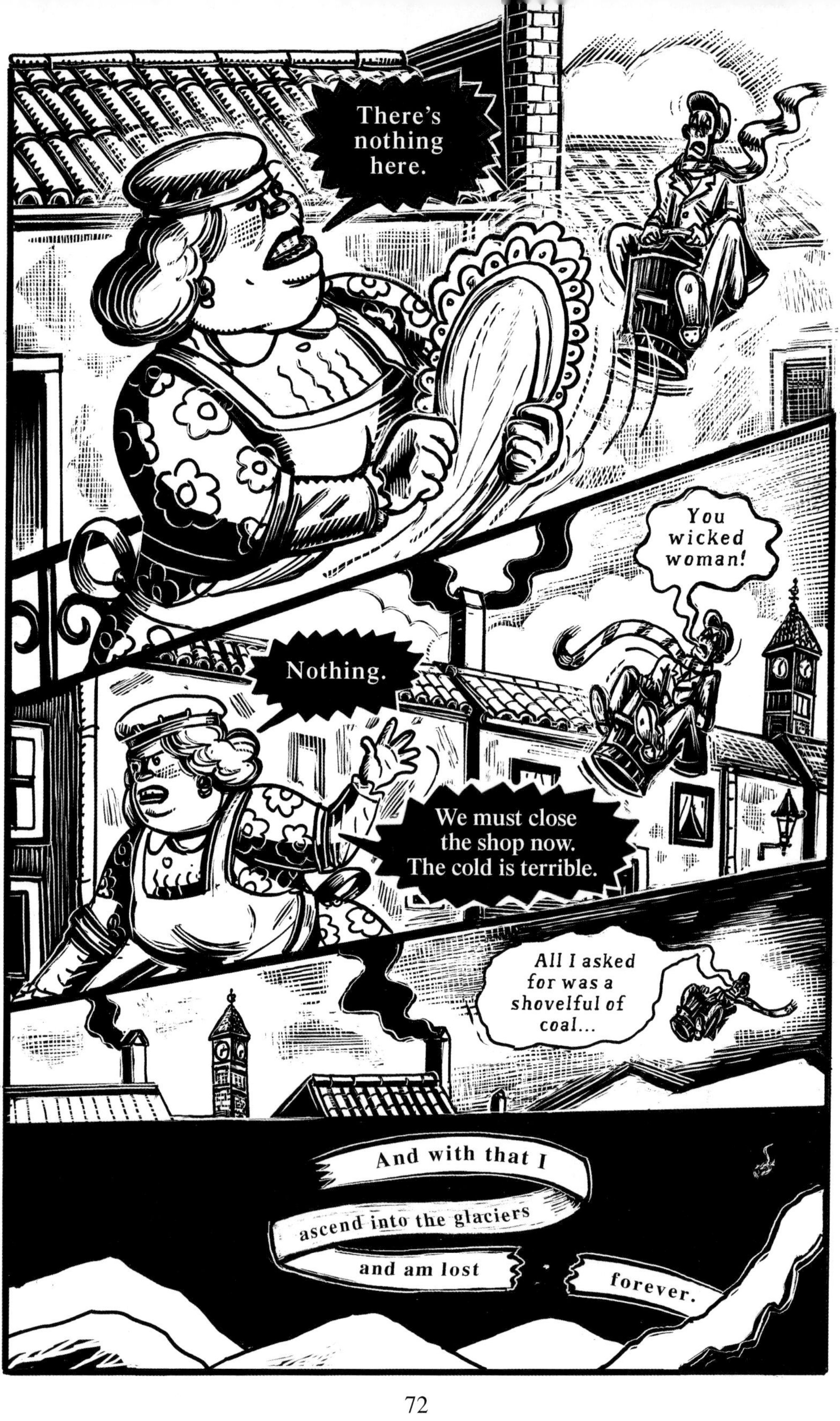
There's nothing here.
You wicked woman!
Nothing.
We must close the shop now. The cold is terrible.
All I asked for was a shovelful of coal...
And with that I
ascend into the glaciers
and am lost
forever.

A HUNGER ARTIST

Over the last few decades the interest in professional fasting has declined considerably. At one time the whole town took an active interest and the artist could make a fine living, but today that is impossible. Times have changed.

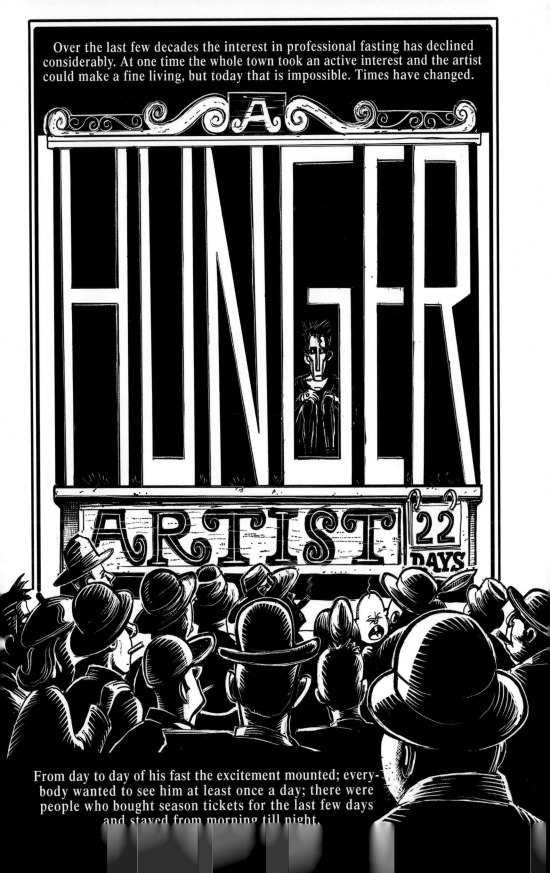

A HUNGER ARTIST

22 DAYS

From day to day of his fast the excitement mounted; every-body wanted to see him at least once a day; there were people who bought season tickets for the last few days and stayed from morning till night.

Besides casual onlookers there were also permanent watchers. This was merely a formality; the artist would never swallow the smallest morsel of food.

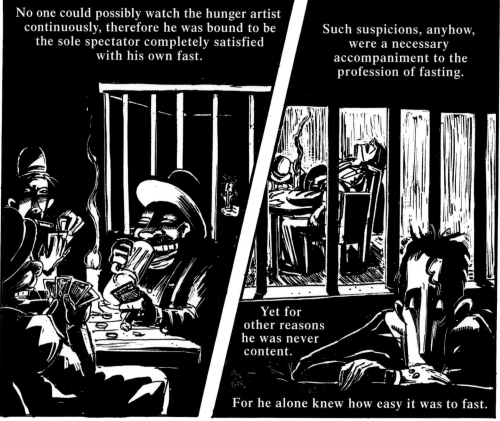

No one could possibly watch the hunger artist continuously, therefore he was bound to be the sole spectator completely satisfied with his own fast.

Such suspicions, anyhow, were a necessary accompaniment to the profession of fasting.

Yet for other reasons he was never content.

For he alone knew how easy it was to fast.

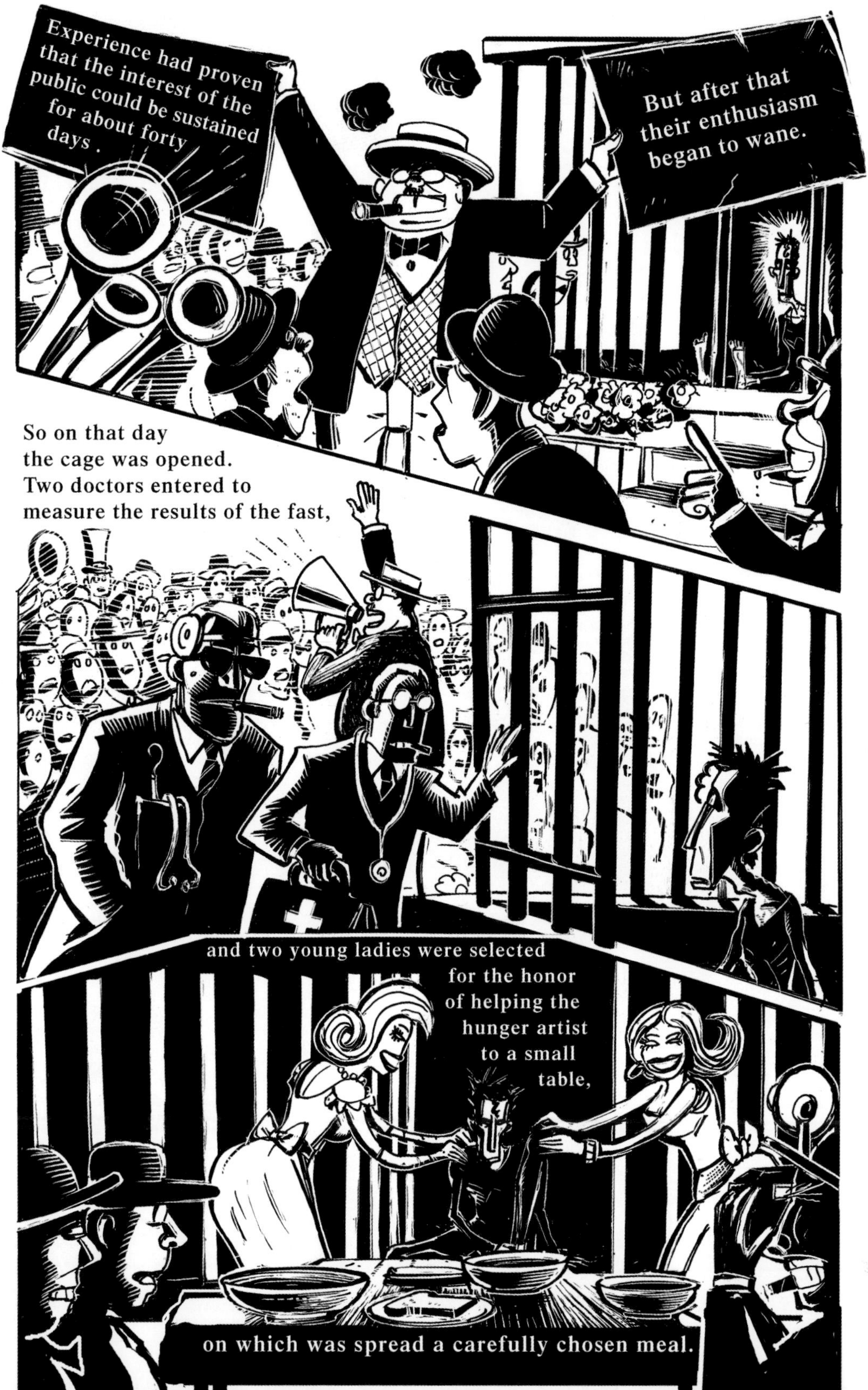
Experience had proven that the interest of the public could be sustained for about forty days .
But after that their enthusiasm began to wane.
So on that day the cage was opened. Two doctors entered to measure the results of the fast,
and two young ladies were selected for the honor of helping the hunger artist to a small table,
on which was spread a carefully chosen meal.

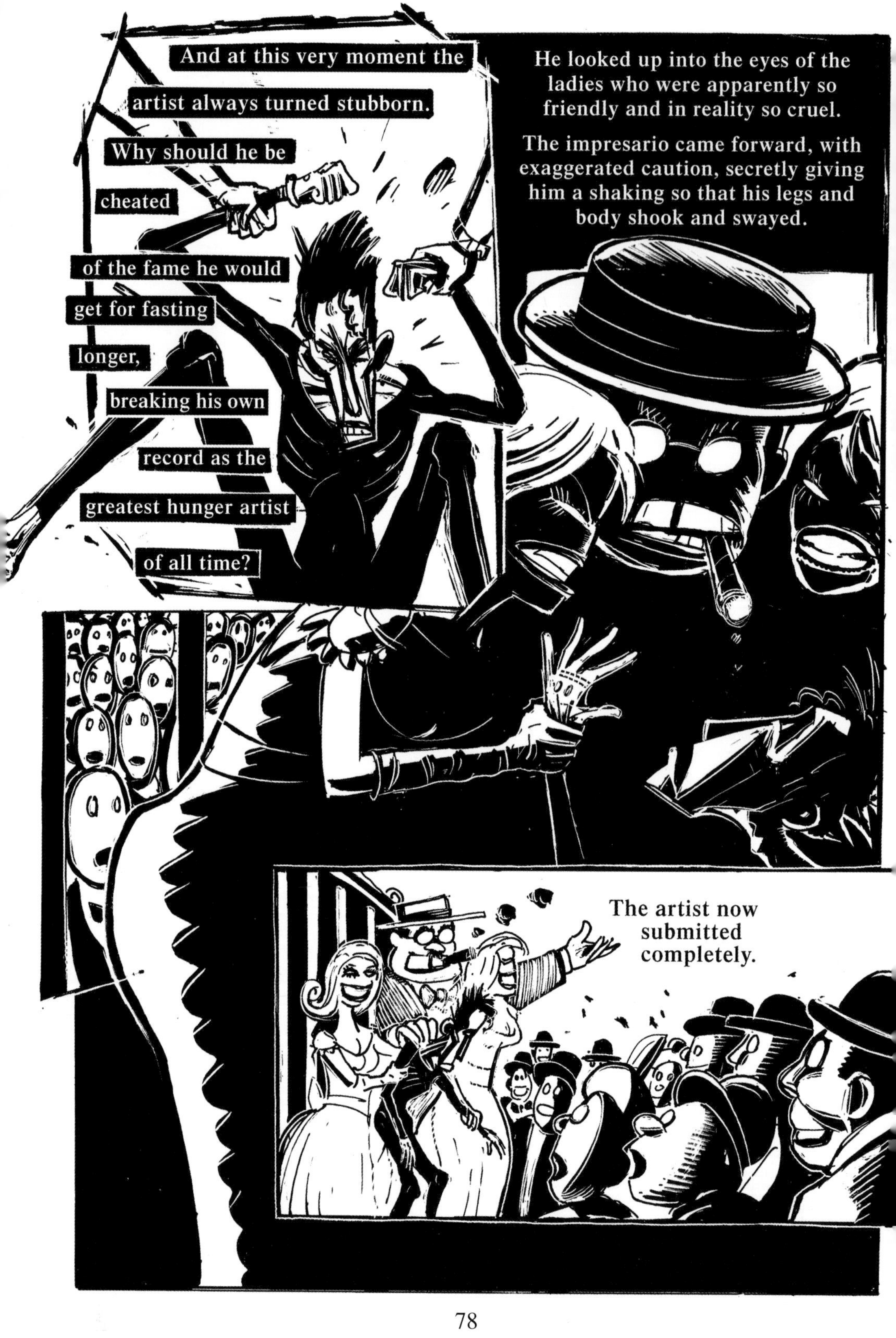
And at this very moment the
artist always turned stubborn.
Why should he be
cheated
of the fame he would
get for fasting
longer,
breaking his own
record as the
greatest hunger artist
of all time?
He looked up into the eyes of the ladies who were apparently so friendly and in reality so cruel.
The impresario came forward, with exaggerated caution, secretly giving him a shaking so that his legs and body shook and swayed.
The artist now submitted completely.

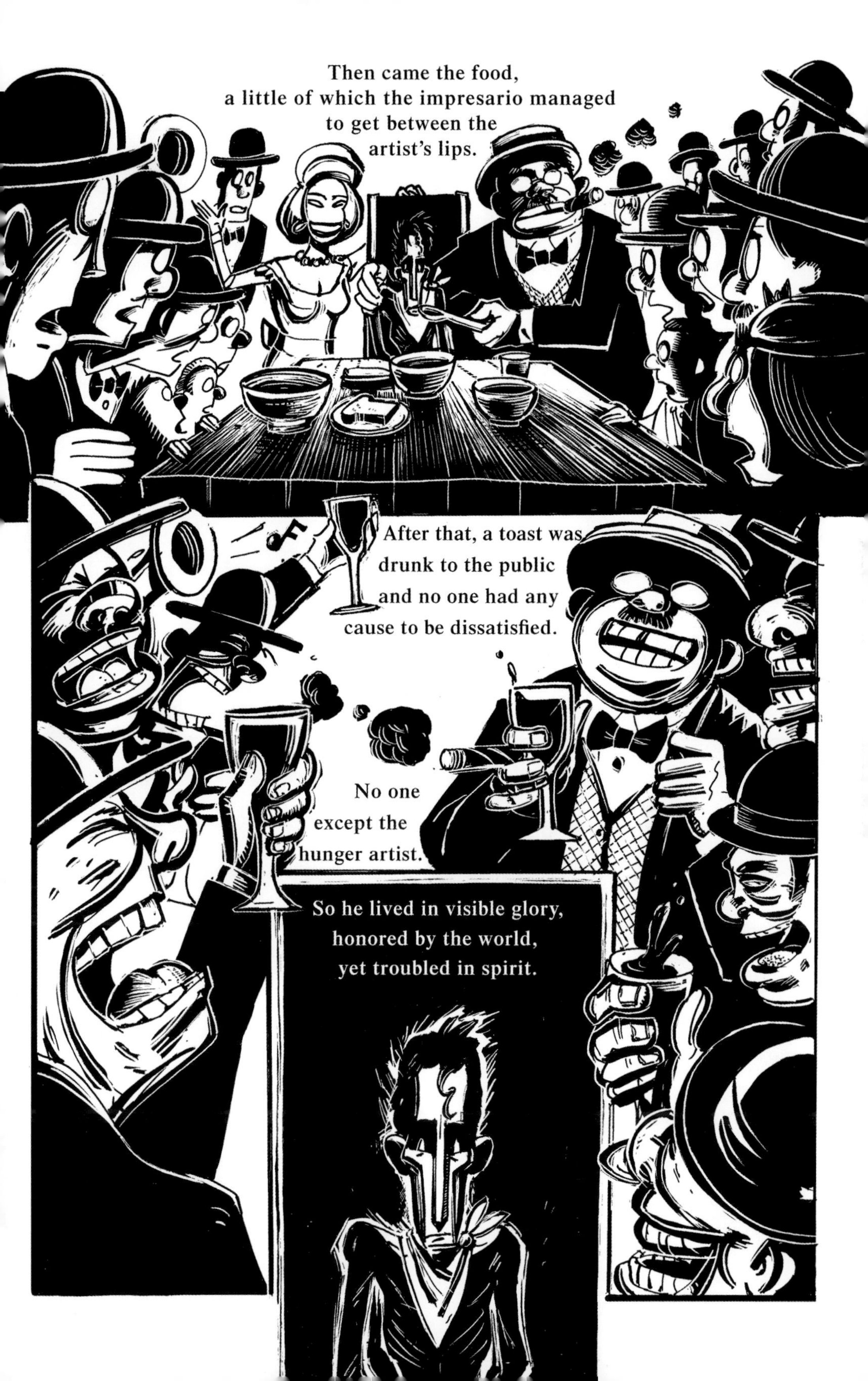
Then came the food, a little of which the impresario managed to get between the artist's lips.
After that, a toast was drunk to the public and no one had any cause to be dissatisfied.
No one except the hunger artist.
So he lived in visible glory, honored by the world, yet troubled in spirit.

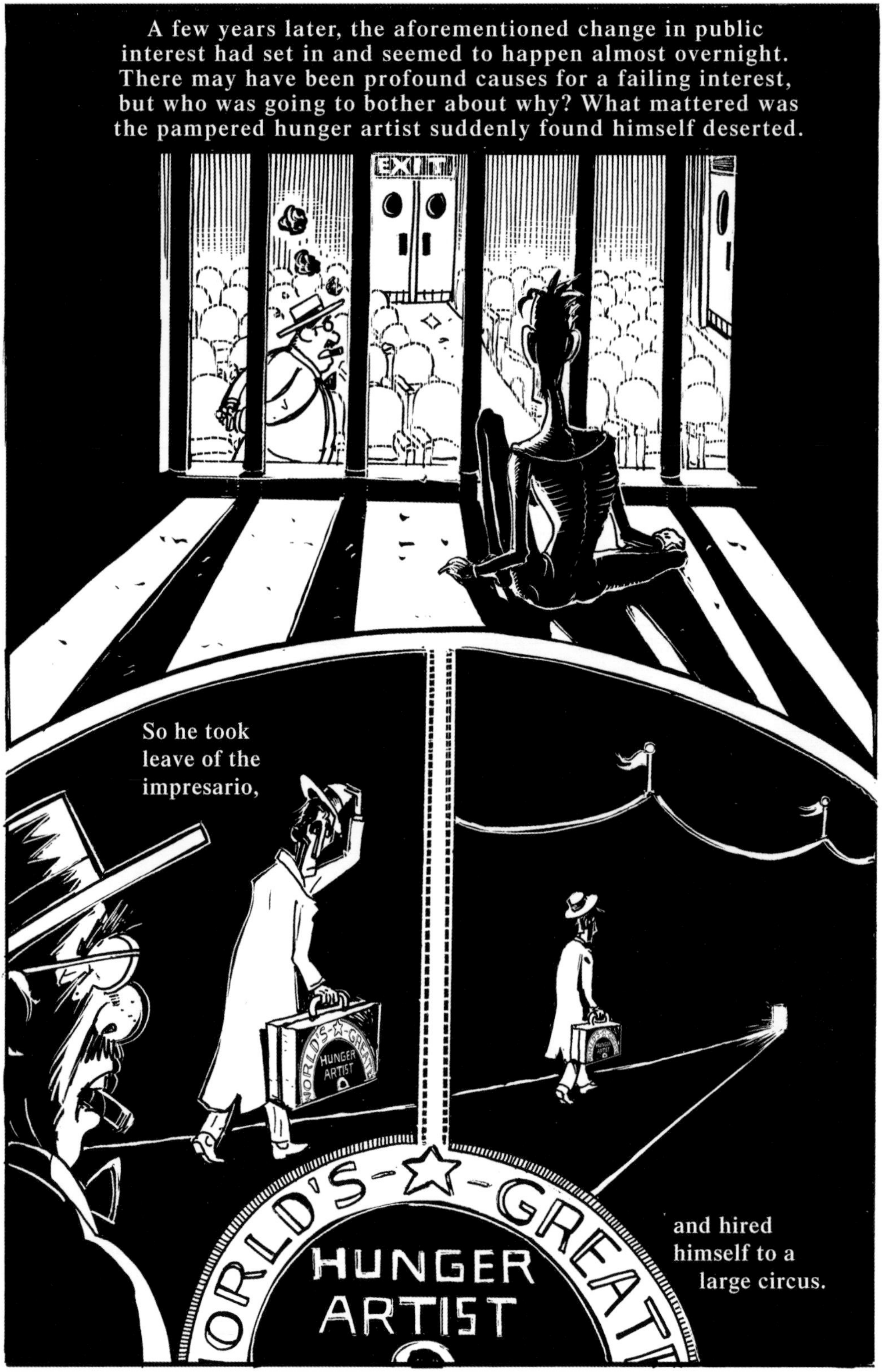
A few years later, the aforementioned change in public interest had set in and seemed to happen almost overnight. There may have been profound causes for a failing interest, but who was going to bother about why? What mattered was the pampered hunger artist suddenly found himself deserted.
EXIT
So he took leave of the impresario,
WORLD'S-☆-GREATEST HUNGER ARTIST
and hired himself to a large circus.
WORLD'S-☆-GREAT
HUNGER ARTIST

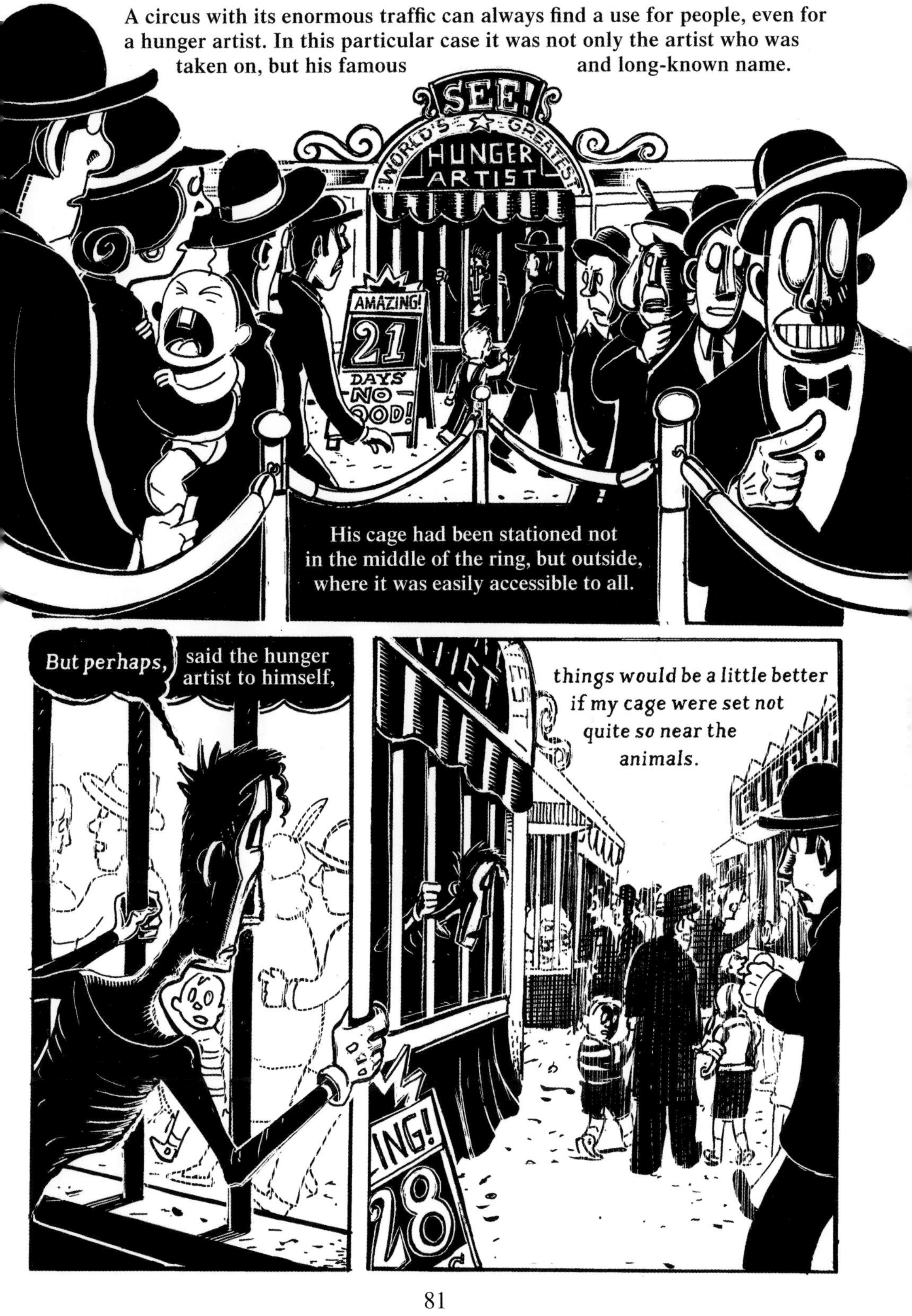
A circus with its enormous traffic can always find a use for people, even for a hunger artist. In this particular case it was not only the artist who was taken on, but his famous and long-known name.
SEE!
WORLD'S ★ GREATEST
HUNGER
ARTIST
AMAZING!
21
DAYS
NO
OOD!
His cage had been stationed not in the middle of the ring, but outside, where it was easily accessible to all.
But perhaps,
said the hunger artist to himself,
things would be a little better if my cage were set not quite so near the animals.
ING!
28

He might fast as much as he could, but nothing would save him now. The fine placards grew dirty and illegible, the notice board telling the number of fast days achieved had long stayed at the same figure; even this small task seemed pointless.

And so the artist simply fasted on and on, as he had once

dreamed of doing.

But no one counted the days, no one, not even the artist himself, knew what

records he was already breaking.

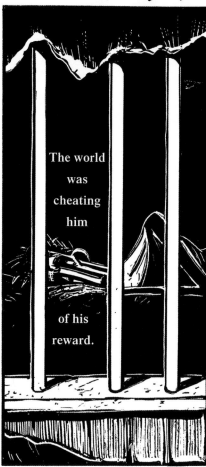

The world was cheating him

of his reward.

One day, the ringmaster's eye fell upon the cage and he asked:

Why?

this perfectly good spot should be left standing there unused.

Nobody knew, until one man remembered about the hunger artist.

Are you *still* fasting?

Forgive me, everybody.

I always wanted you to admire my fasting. But you shouldn't admire it.

Because I have to fast, I can't help it.

And why can't you help it?

Because I couldn't find the food I liked. If I had, I should have stuffed myself like

you or anyone else.

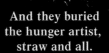

These were his last words, but in his dimming eyes remained the firm conviction that he was still continuing to fast.

And they buried the hunger artist, straw and all.

They put a young panther into the cage.

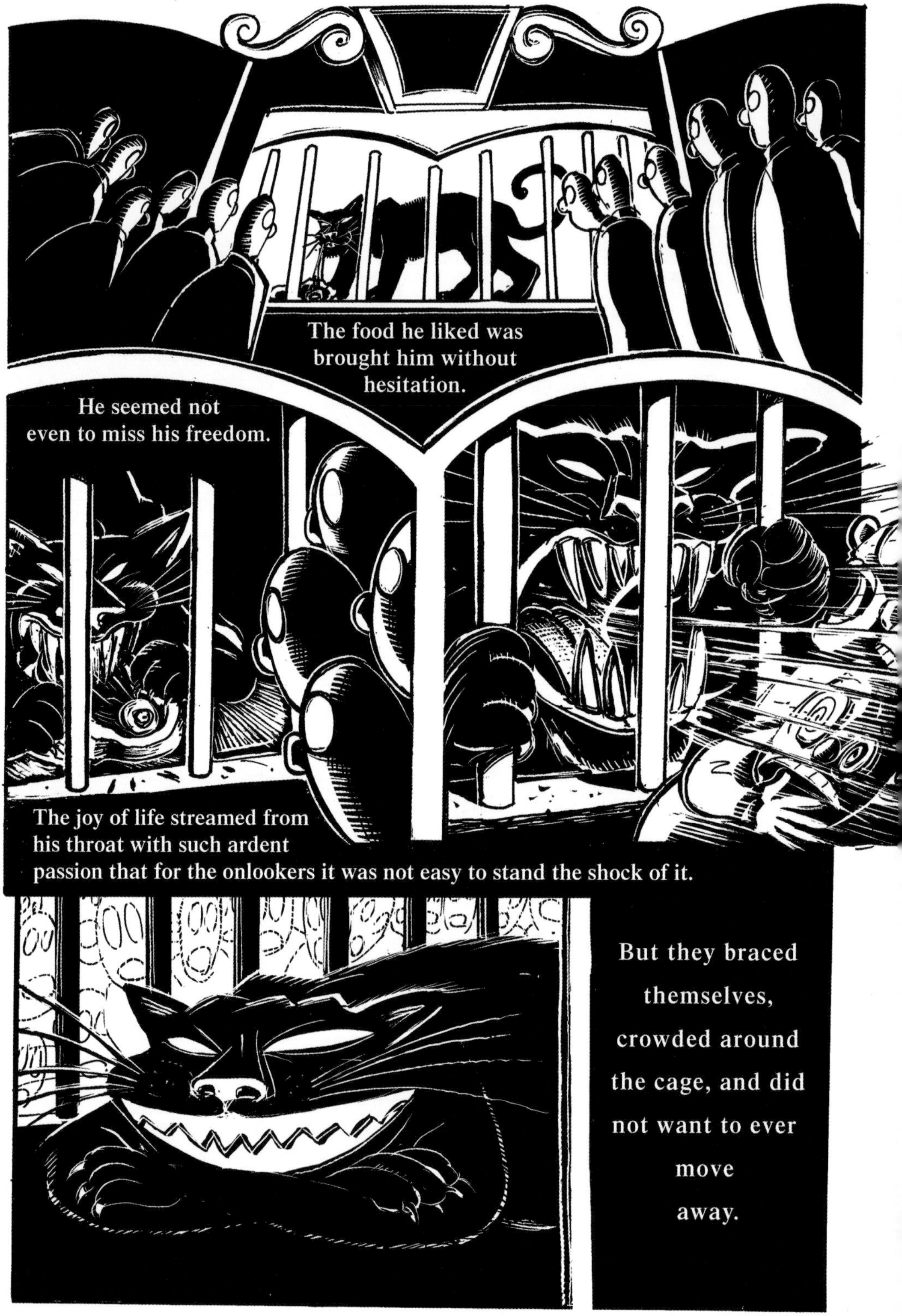
The food he liked was brought him without hesitation.
He seemed not even to miss his freedom.
The joy of life streamed from his throat with such ardent passion that for the onlookers it was not easy to stand the shock of it.
But they braced themselves, crowded around the cage, and did not want to ever move away.

A FRATRICIDE

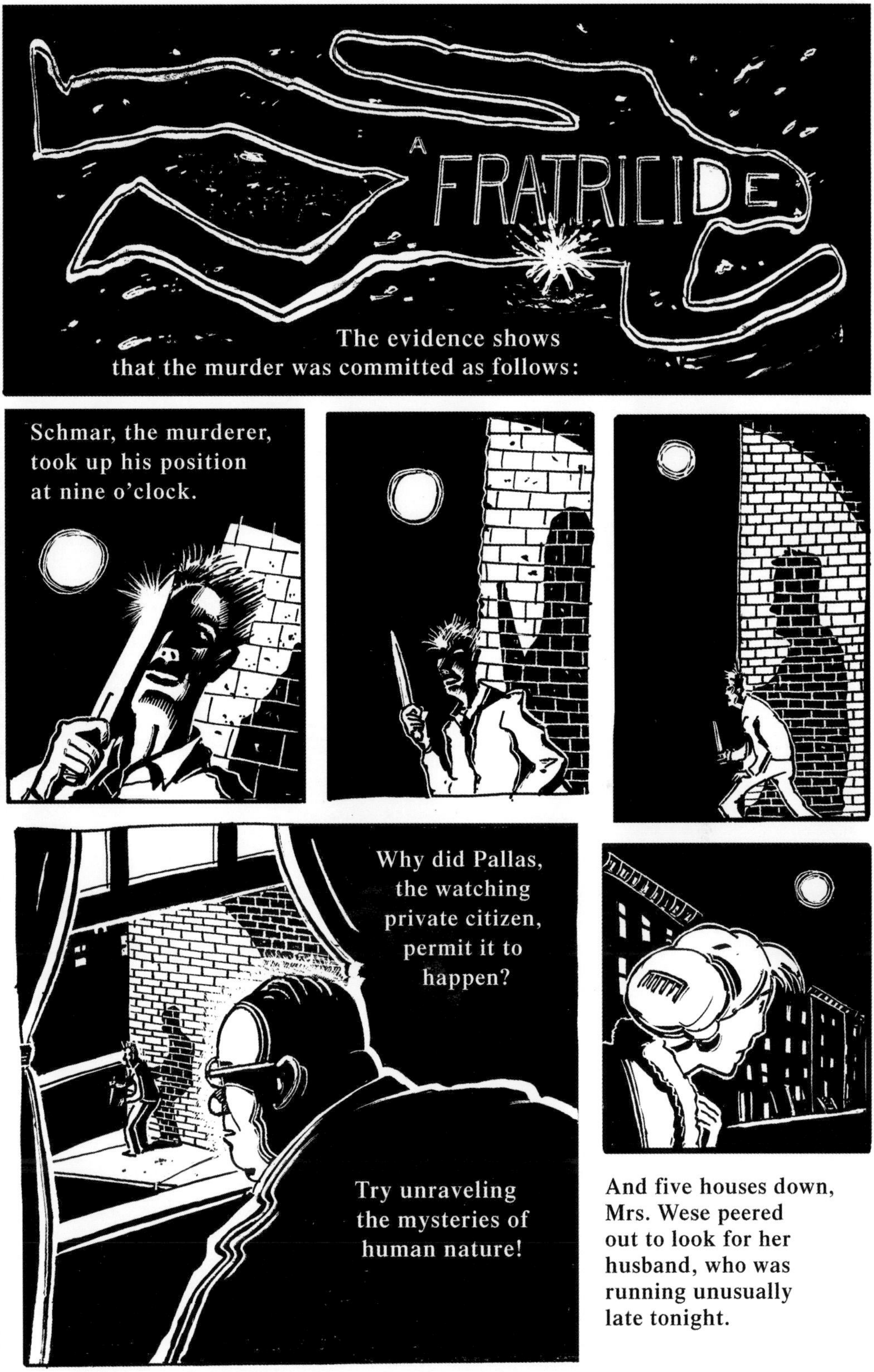
A
FRATRICIDE
The evidence shows that the murder was committed as follows:
Schmar, the murderer, took up his position at nine o'clock.
Why did Pallas, the watching private citizen, permit it to happen?
Try unraveling the mysteries of human nature!
And five houses down, Mrs. Wese peered out to look for her husband, who was running unusually late tonight.

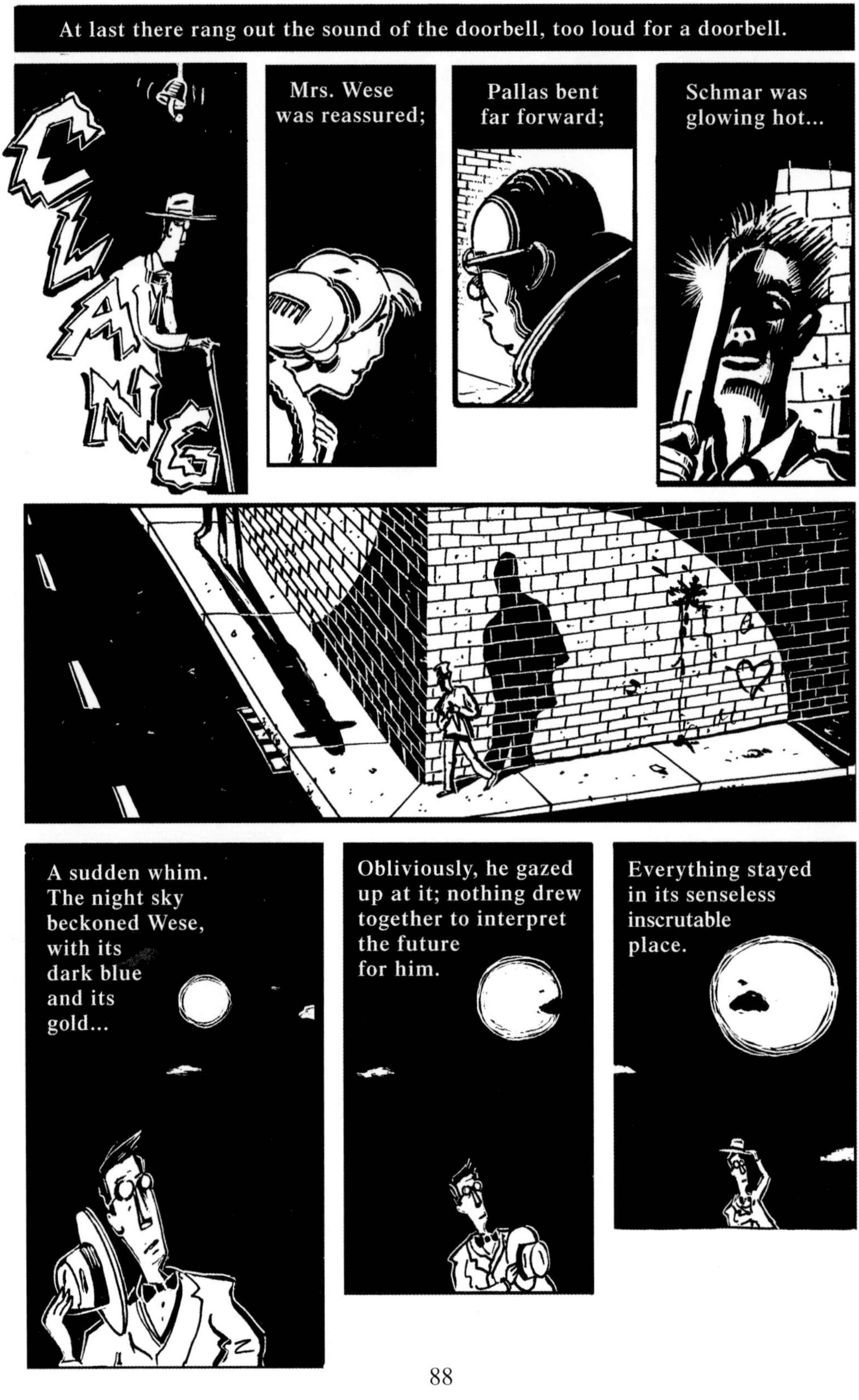
At last there rang out the sound of the doorbell, too loud for a doorbell.
CLANG
Mrs. Wese was reassured;
Pallas bent far forward;
Schmar was glowing hot...
A sudden whim. The night sky beckoned Wese, with its dark blue and its gold...
Obliviously, he gazed up at it; nothing drew together to interpret the future for him.
Everything stayed in its senseless inscrutable place.

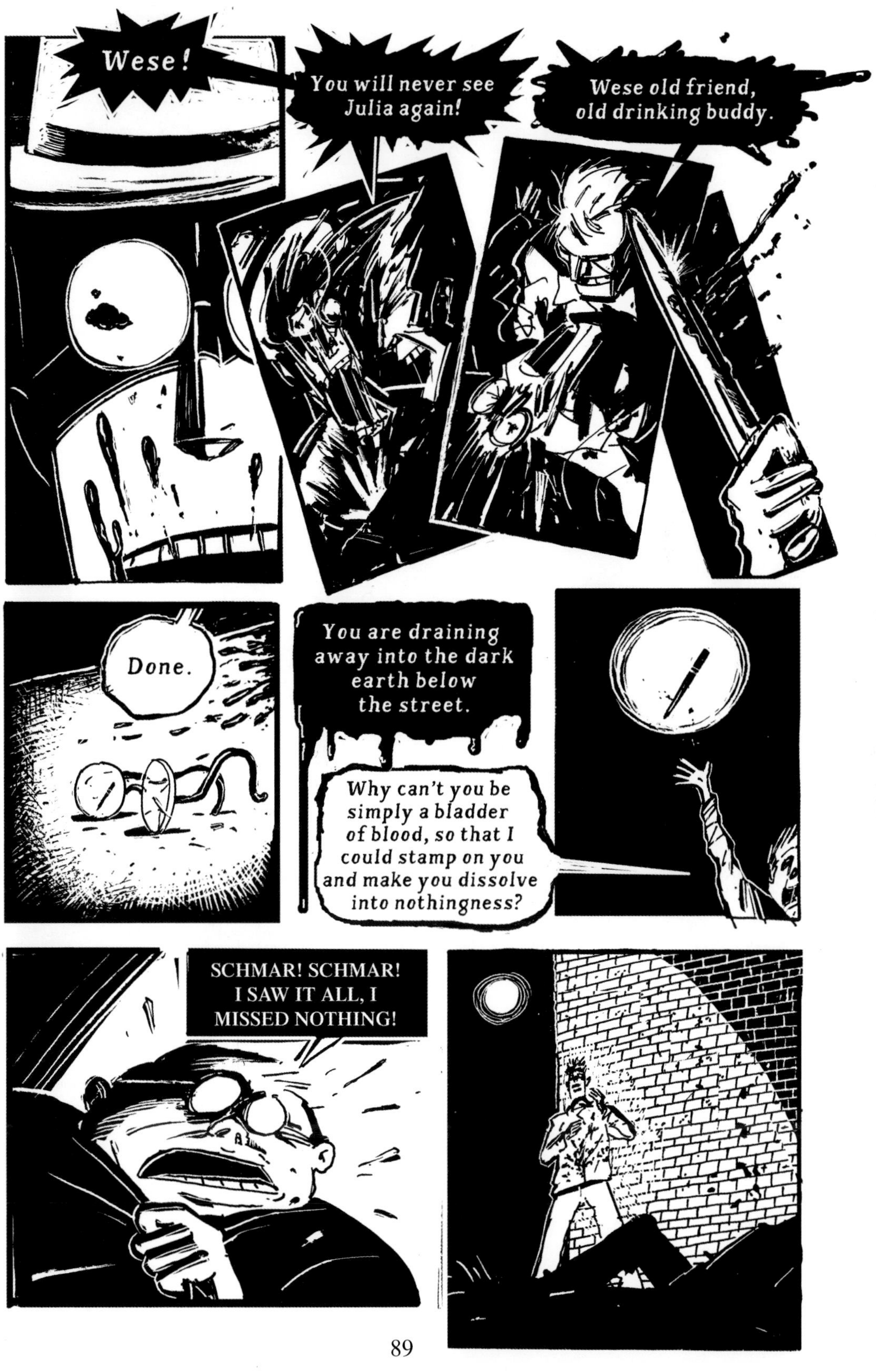

Wese!
You will never see Julia again!
Wese old friend, old drinking buddy.
Done.
You are draining away into the dark earth below the street.
Why can't you be simply a bladder of blood, so that I could stamp on you and make you dissolve into nothingness?
SCHMAR! SCHMAR! I SAW IT ALL, I MISSED NOTHING!

Pallas and Schmar scrutinized each other. The result of their scrutiny satisfied Pallas,

Schmar drew no conclusion.

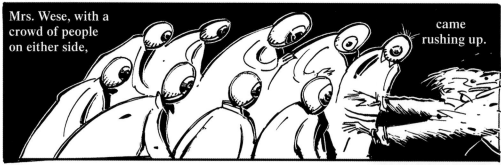

Mrs. Wese, with a crowd of people on either side,

came rushing up.

Schmar, fighting nausea, pressed his mouth against the shoulder of the policeman who, stepping lightly, led him away.

THE TREES

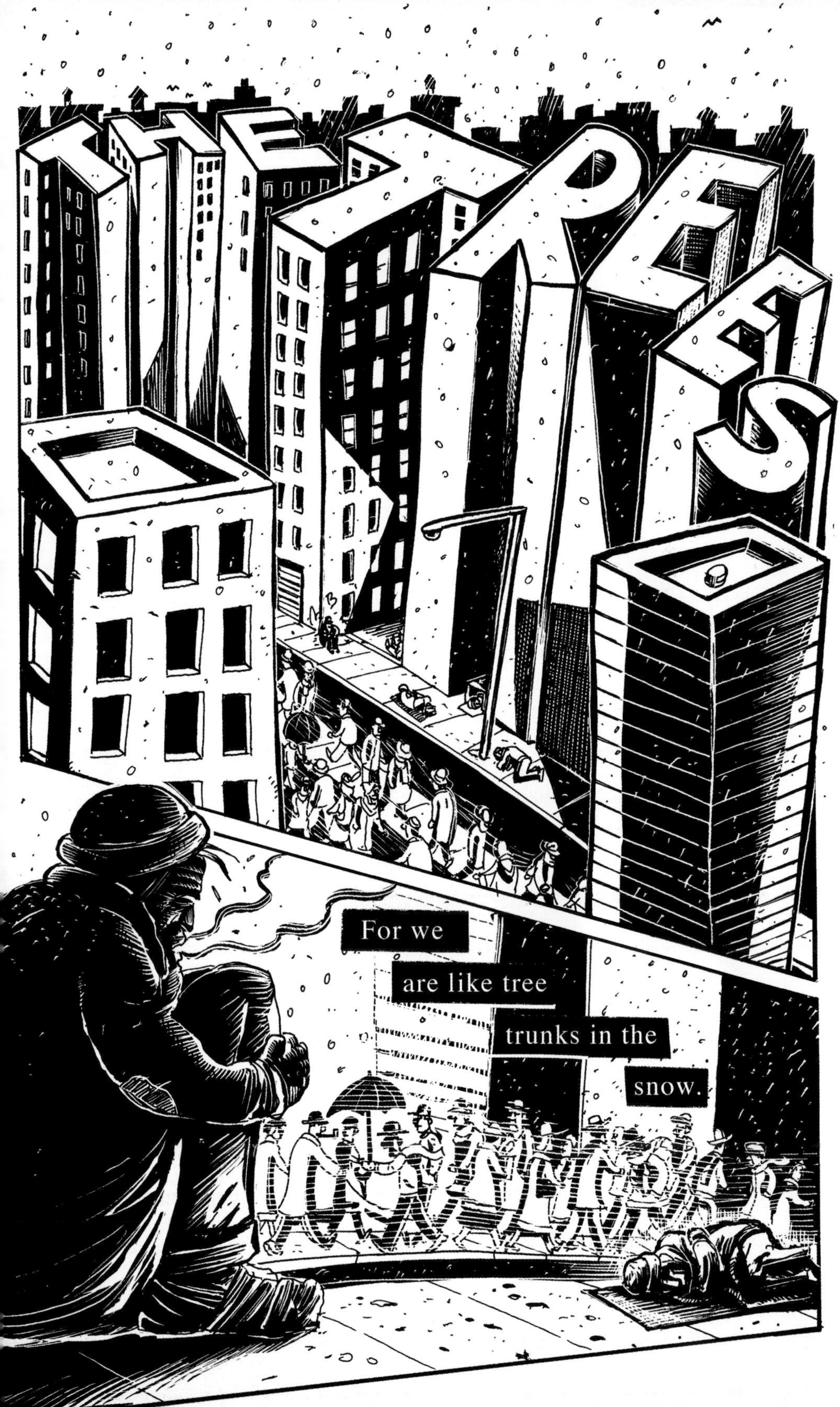
THE TREES
For we
are like tree
trunks in the
snow.

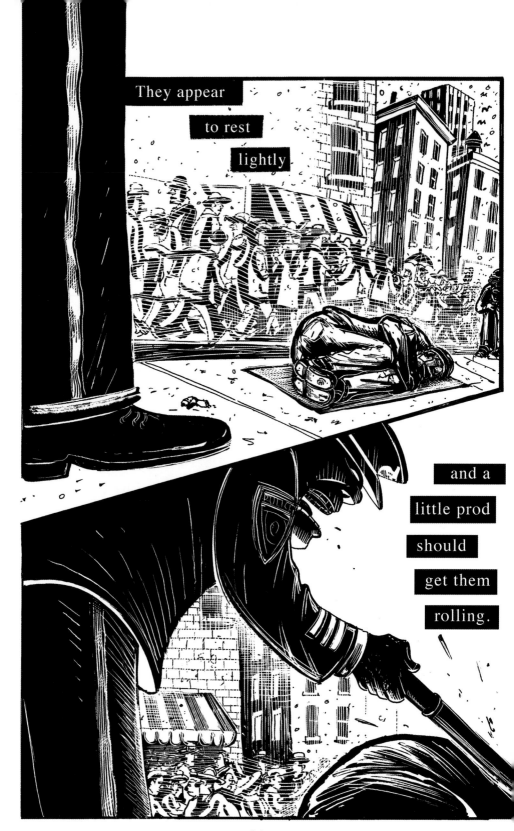

They appear

to rest

lightly

and a

little prod

should

get them

rolling.

94

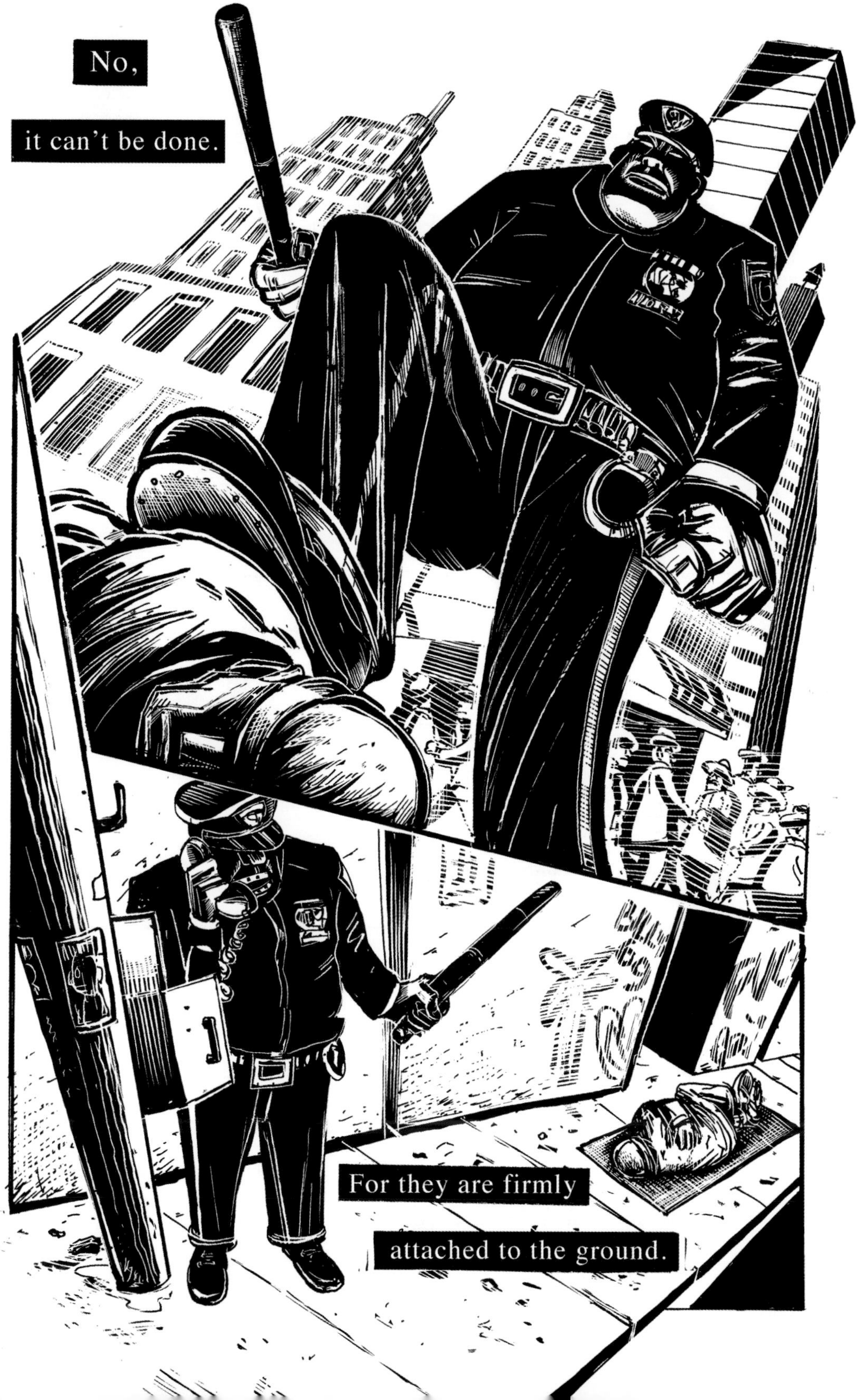
No,
it can't be done.
For they are firmly
attached to the ground.

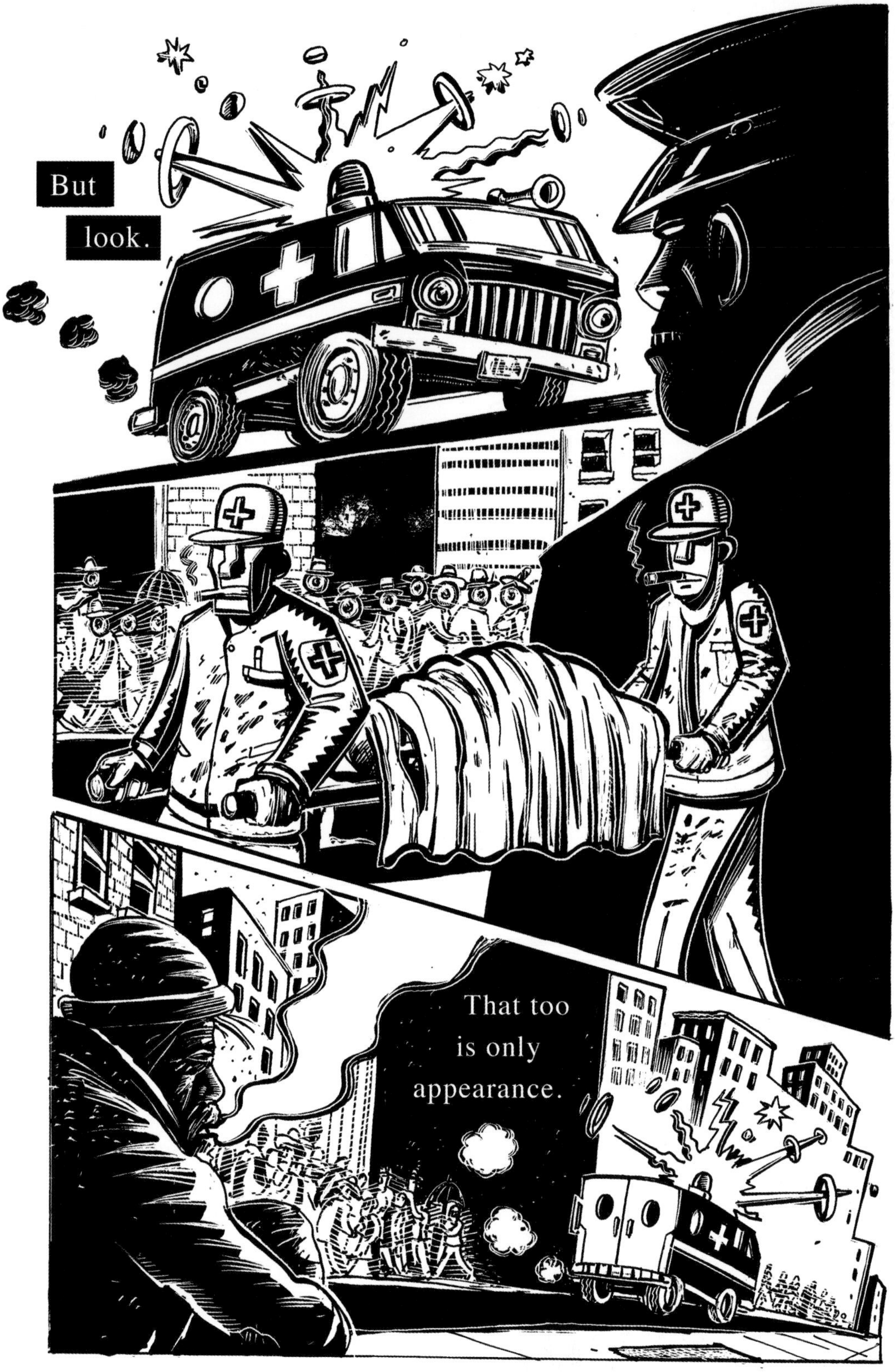
But
look.
That too
is only
appearance.

BEFORE THE LAW

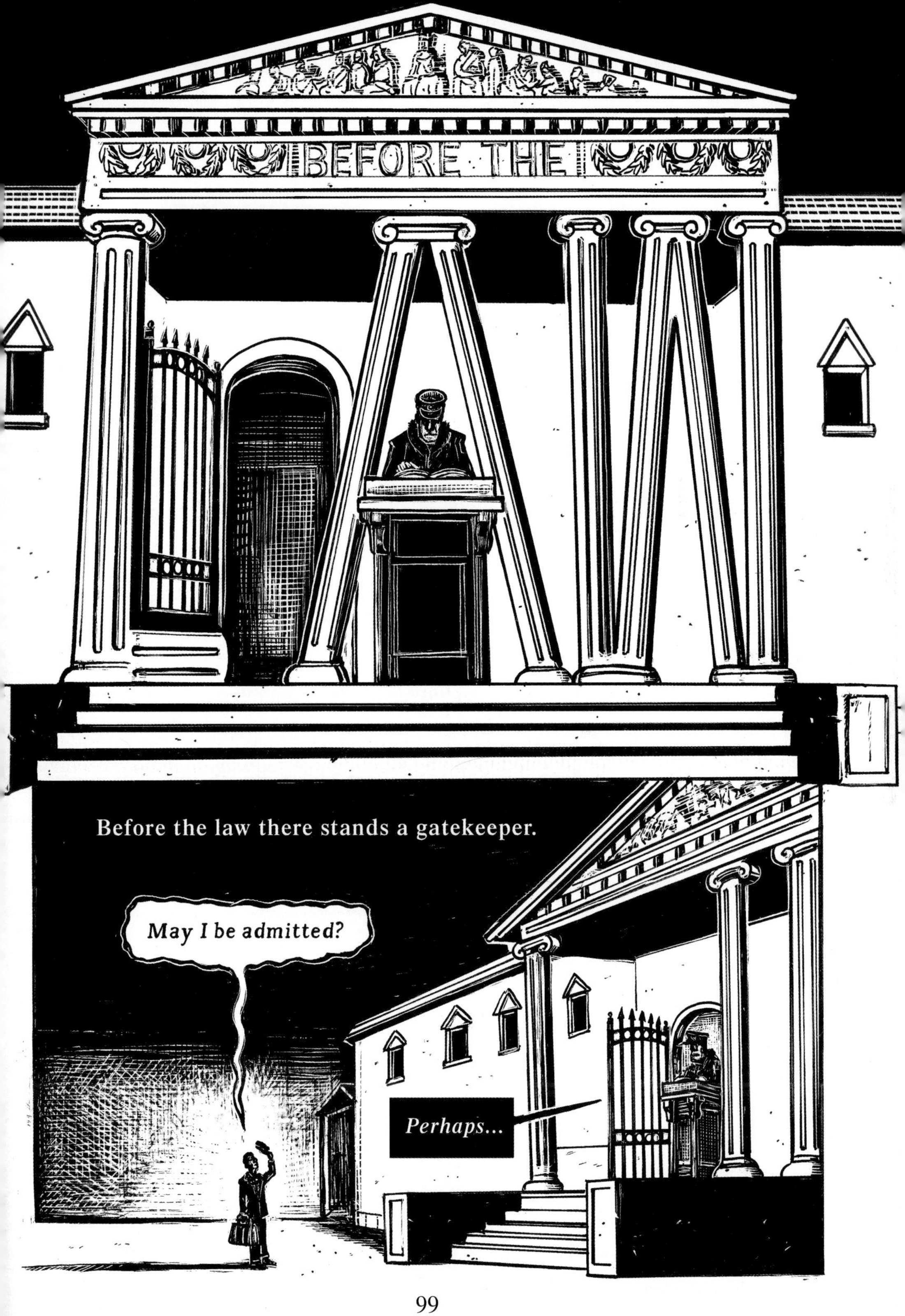
BEFORE THE LAW
Before the law there stands a gatekeeper.
May I be admitted?
Perhaps...

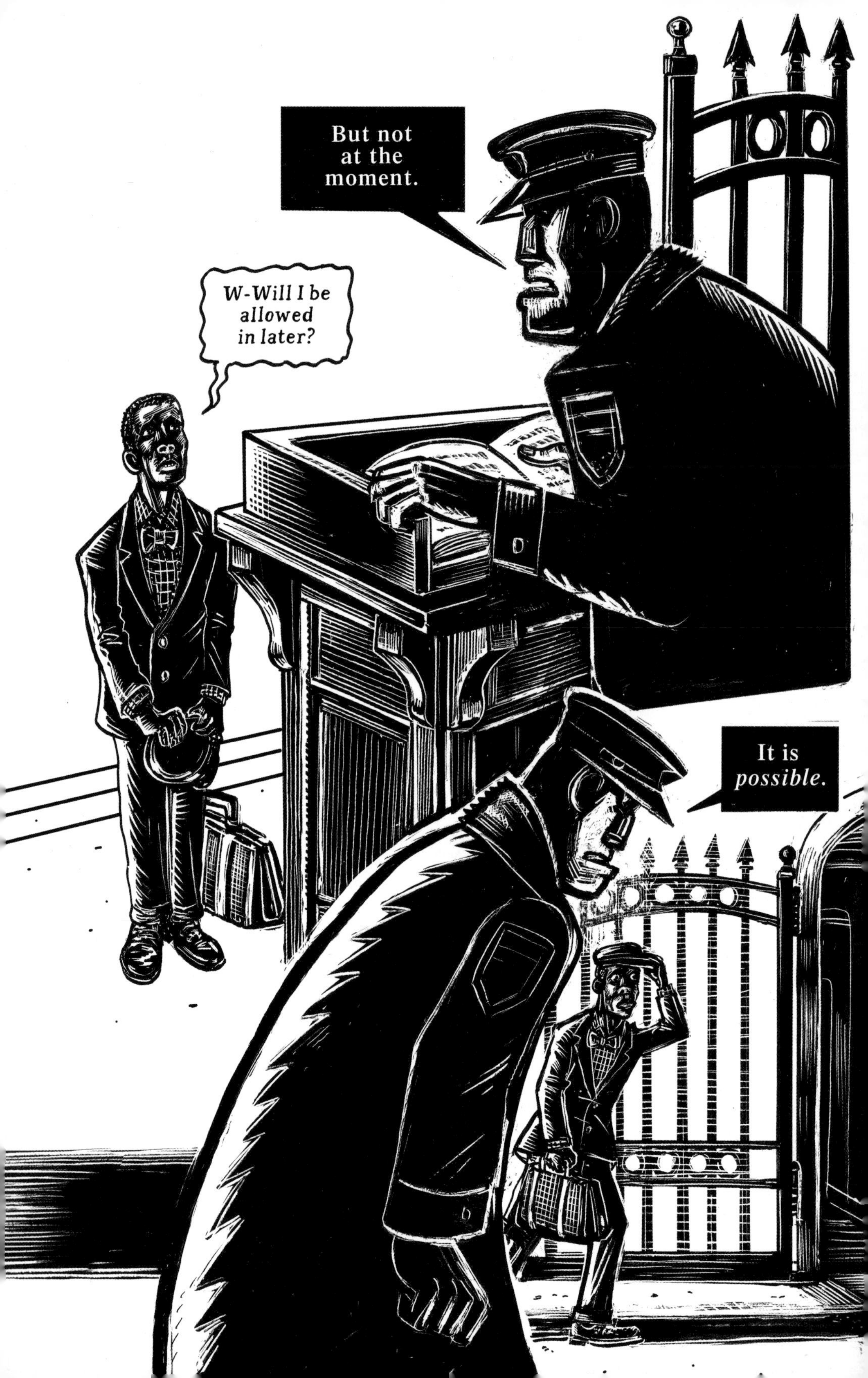
W-Will I be allowed in later?
But not at the moment.
It is *possible*.

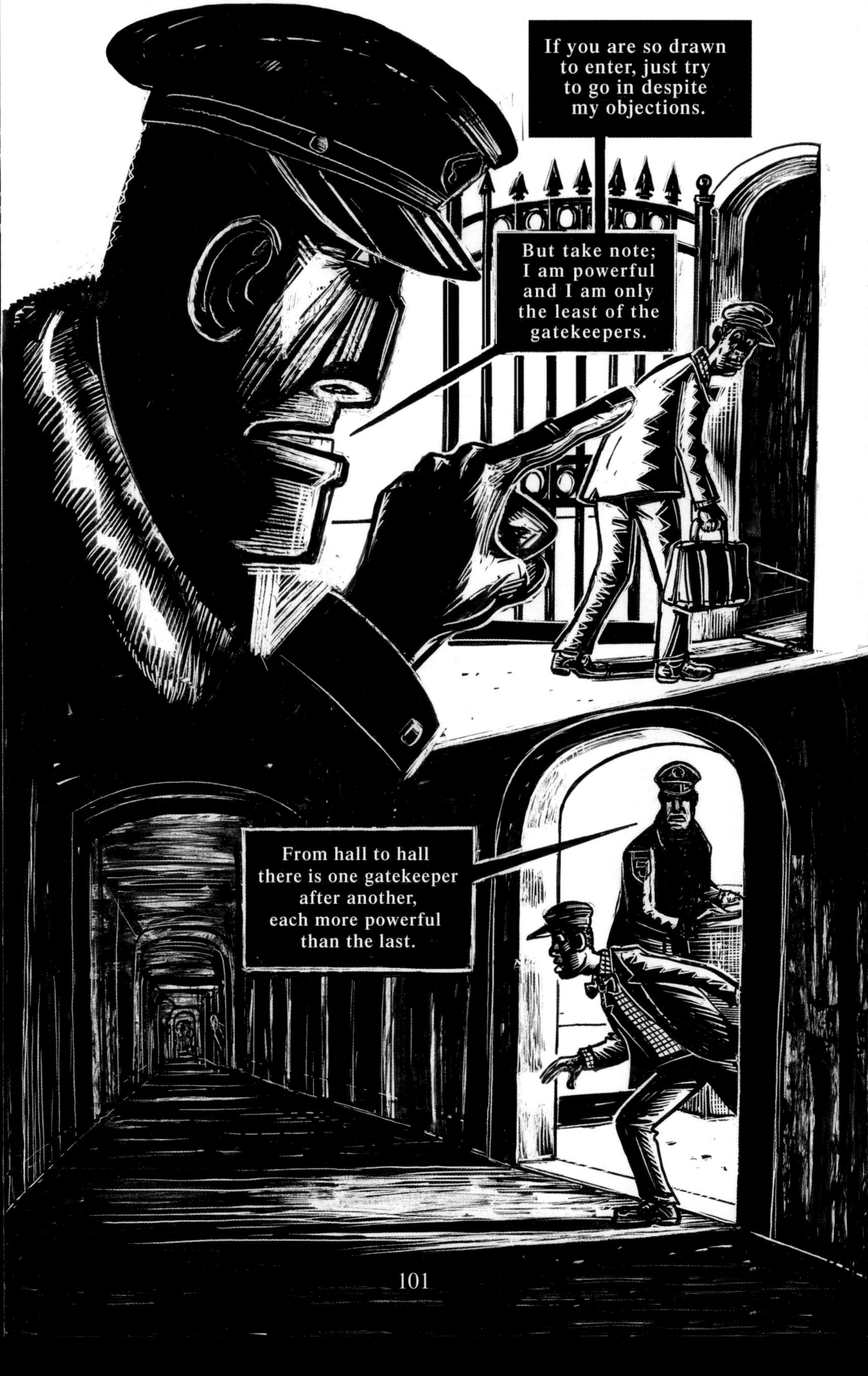

If you are so drawn to enter, just try to go in despite my objections.
But take note; I am powerful and I am only the least of the gatekeepers.
From hall to hall there is one gatekeeper after another, each more powerful than the last.

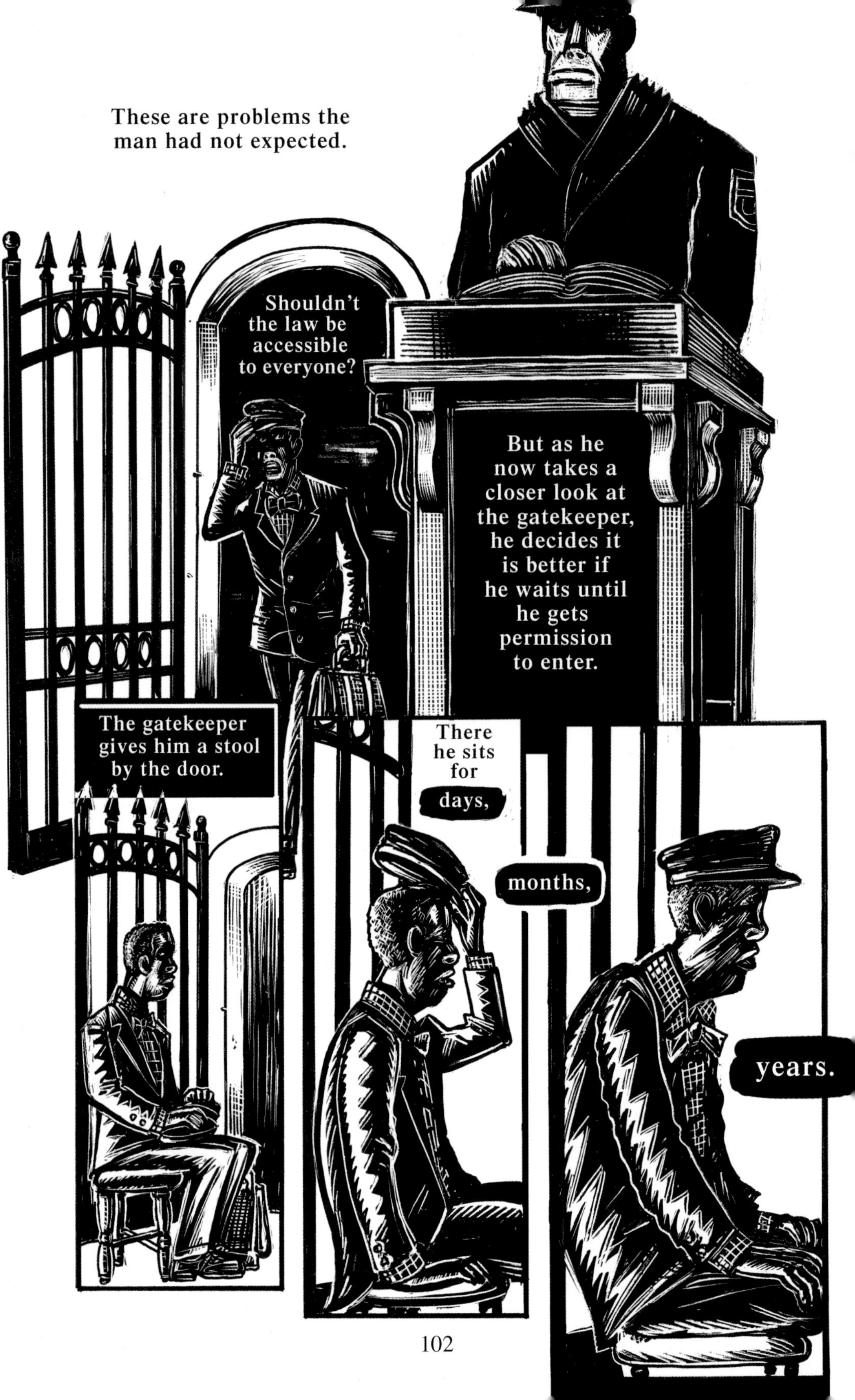
These are problems the man had not expected.
Shouldn't the law be accessible to everyone?
But as he now takes a closer look at the gatekeeper, he decides it is better if he waits until he gets permission to enter.
The gatekeeper gives him a stool by the door.
There he sits for
days,
months,
years.

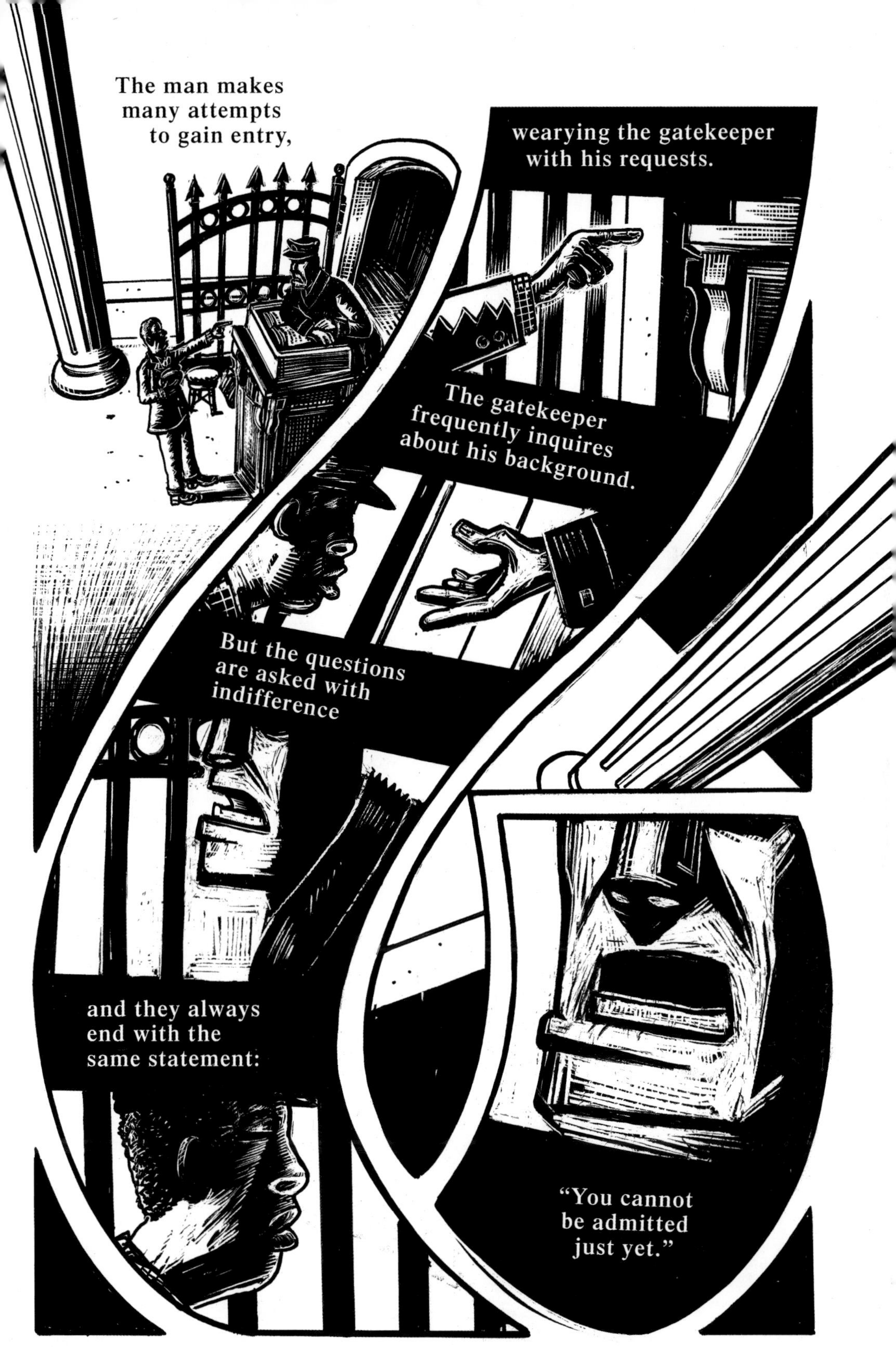
The man makes many attempts to gain entry,
wearying the gatekeeper with his requests.
The gatekeeper frequently inquires about his background.
But the questions are asked with indifference
and they always end with the same statement:
"You cannot be admitted just yet."

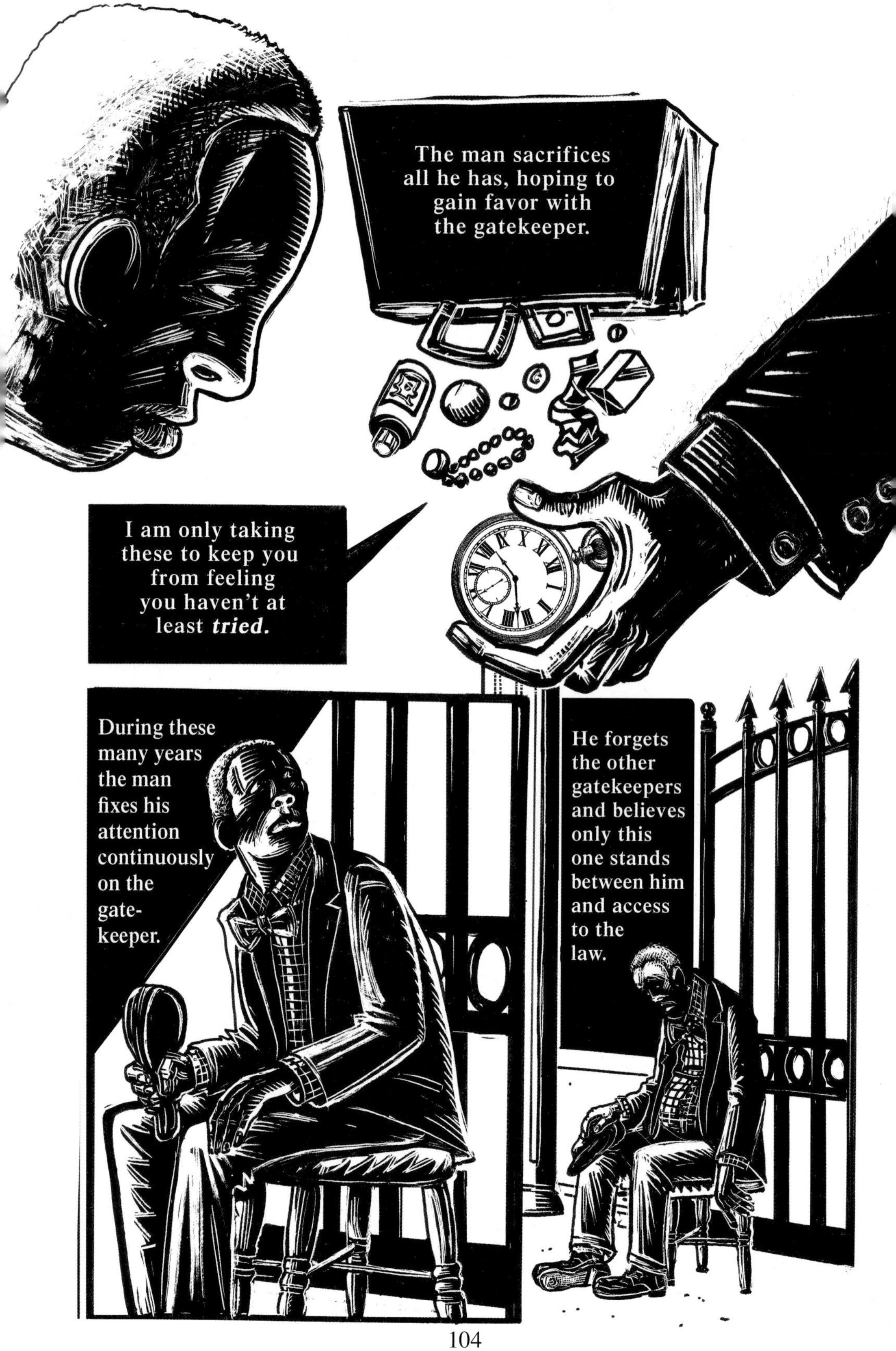
The man sacrifices all he has, hoping to gain favor with the gatekeeper.
I am only taking these to keep you from feeling you haven't at least *tried.*
During these many years the man fixes his attention continuously on the gate-keeper.
He forgets the other gatekeepers and believes only this one stands between him and access to the law.

In his youth he had boldly cursed his bad luck. Now as he grows old, he only grumbles to himself.

In his years of contemplating the gatekeeper, he came to know even the fleas in the man's collar...

and begged them

to change

the gatekeeper's mind.

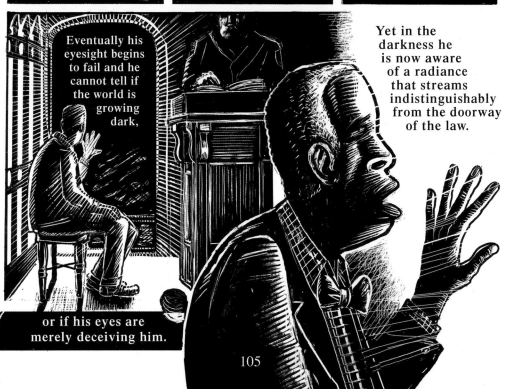

Eventually his eyesight begins to fail and he cannot tell if the world is growing dark,

Yet in the darkness he is now aware of a radiance that streams indistinguishably from the doorway of the law.

or if his eyes are merely deceiving him.

Now,
he hasn't
long to live.

Before
he dies,
all his
experiences

in these

long
years
gather
themselves

into

a
question

he has
not yet

asked.

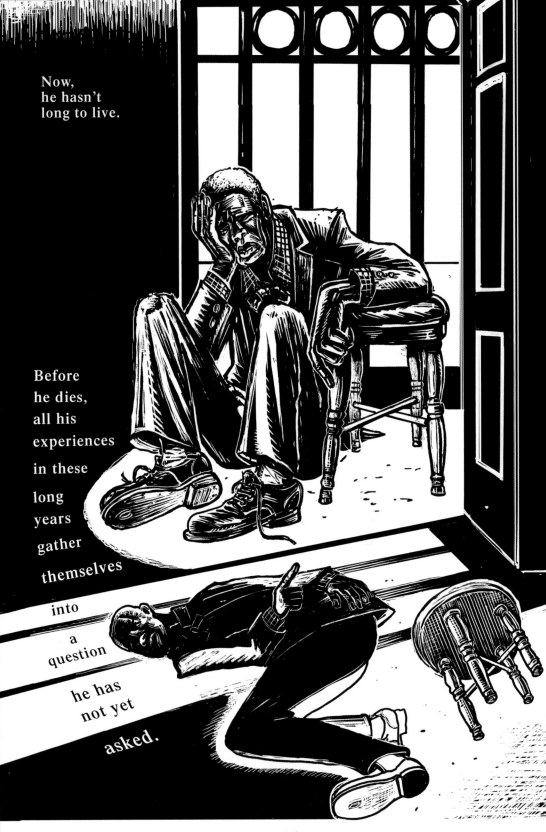

106

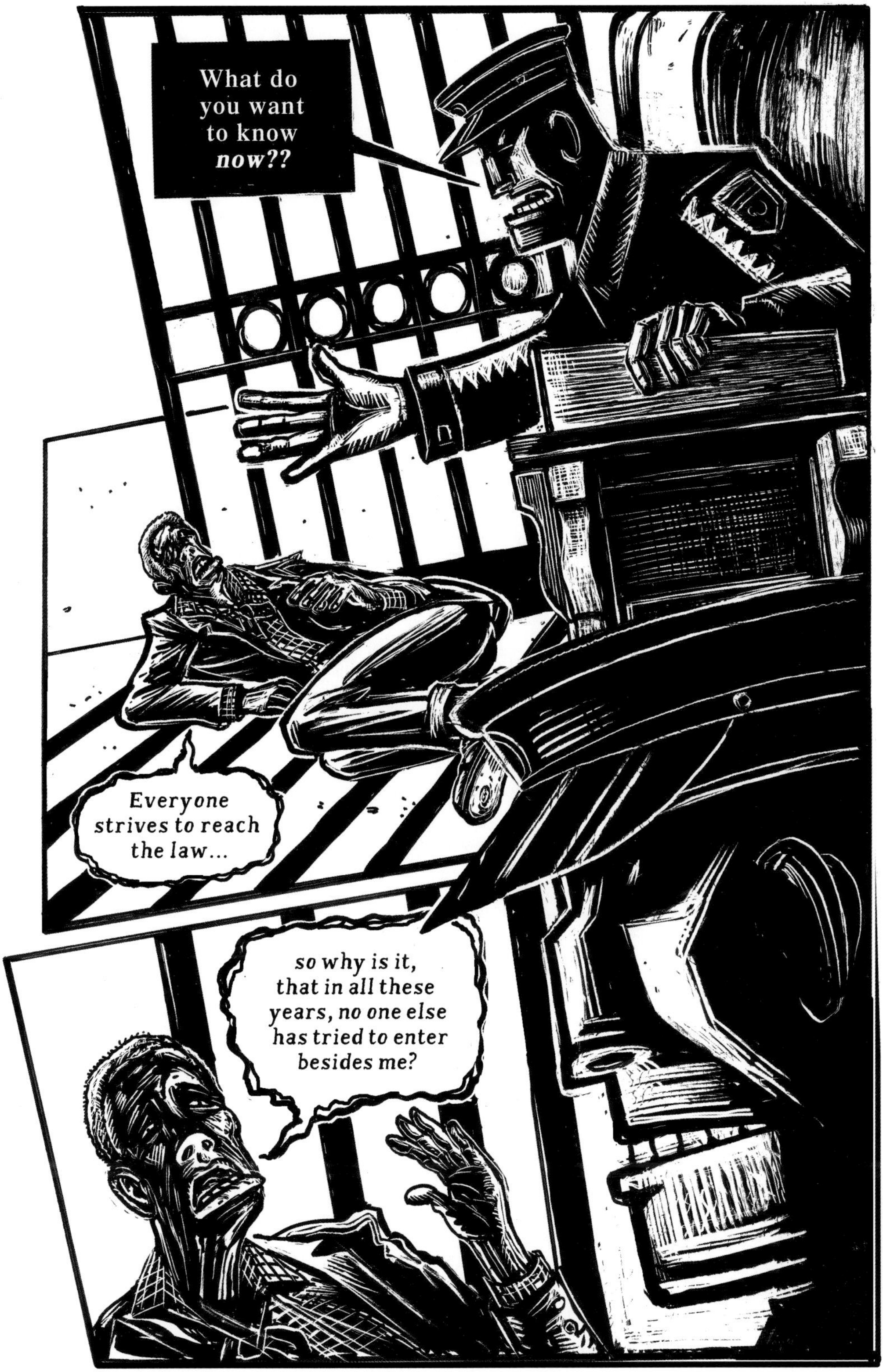
What do you want to know *now*??
Every*one* strives *to* reach the law...
so why is it, that in *all* these years, *no one* else has tried *to* enter besides me?

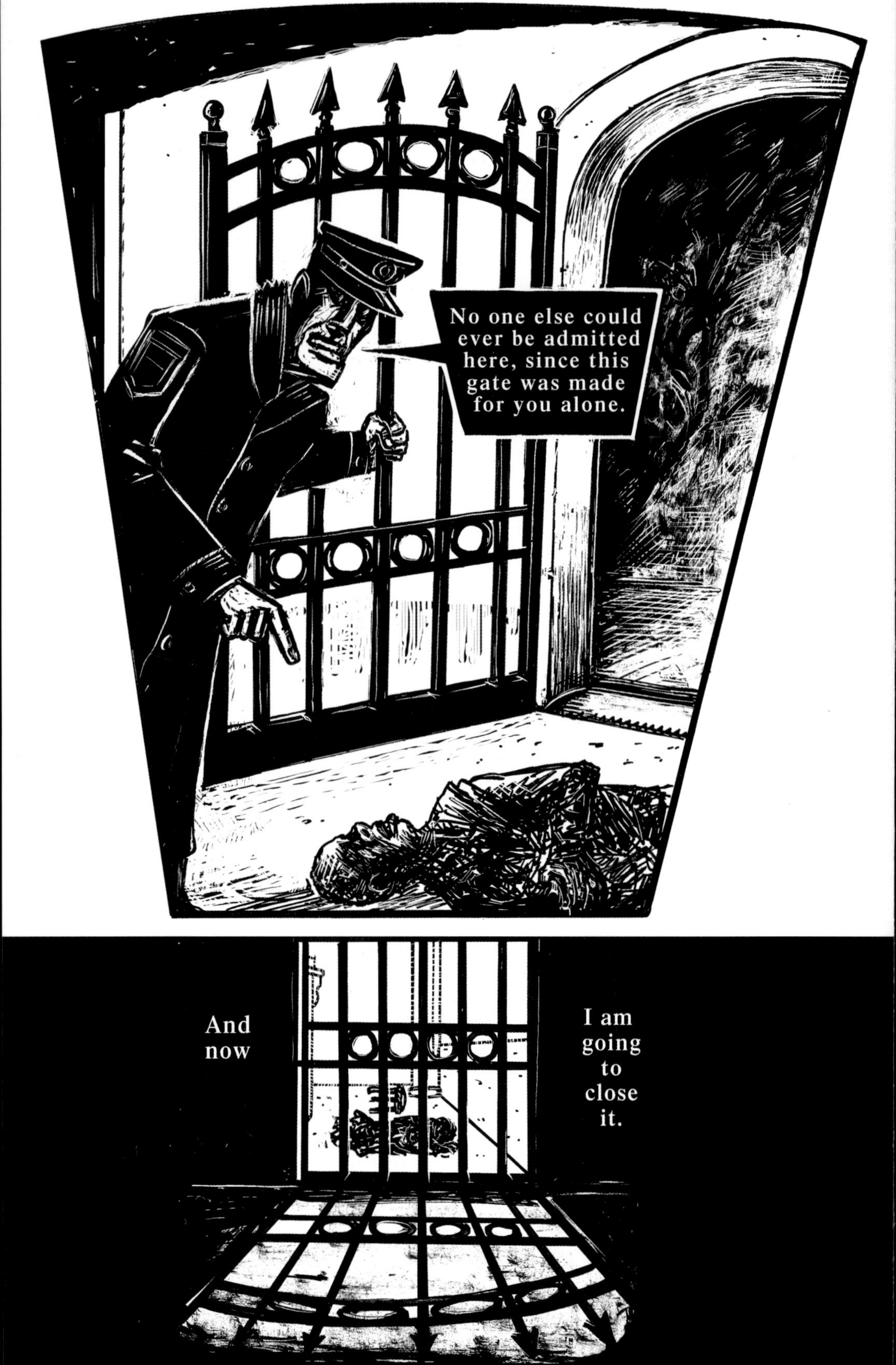
No one else could ever be admitted here, since this gate was made for you alone.
And now
I am going to close it.

THE BRIDGE

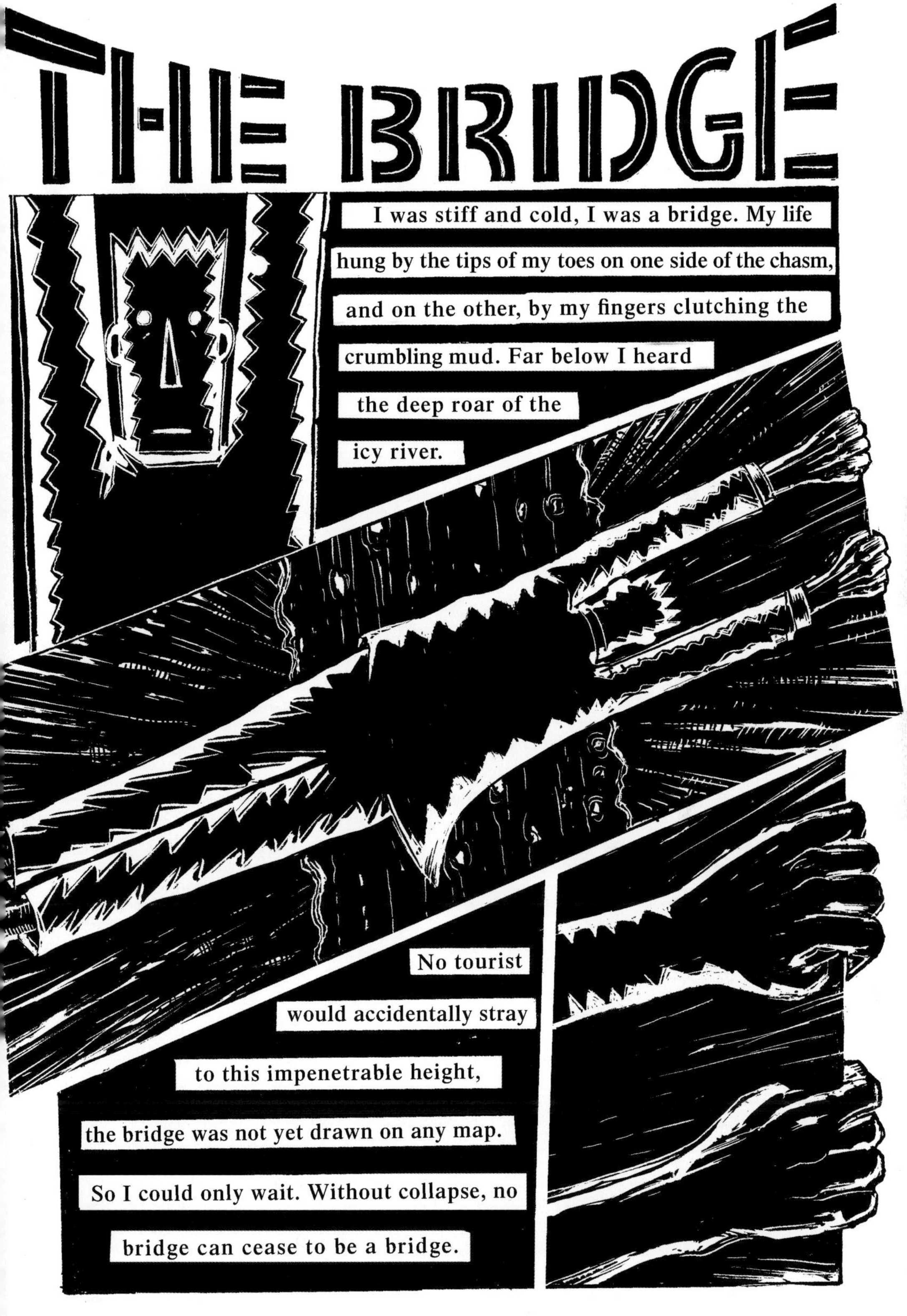
THE BRIDGE
I was stiff and cold, I was a bridge. My life hung by the tips of my toes on one side of the chasm, and on the other, by my fingers clutching the crumbling mud. Far below I heard the deep roar of the icy river.
No tourist would accidentally stray to this impenetrable height, the bridge was not yet drawn on any map.
So I could only wait. Without collapse, no bridge can cease to be a bridge.

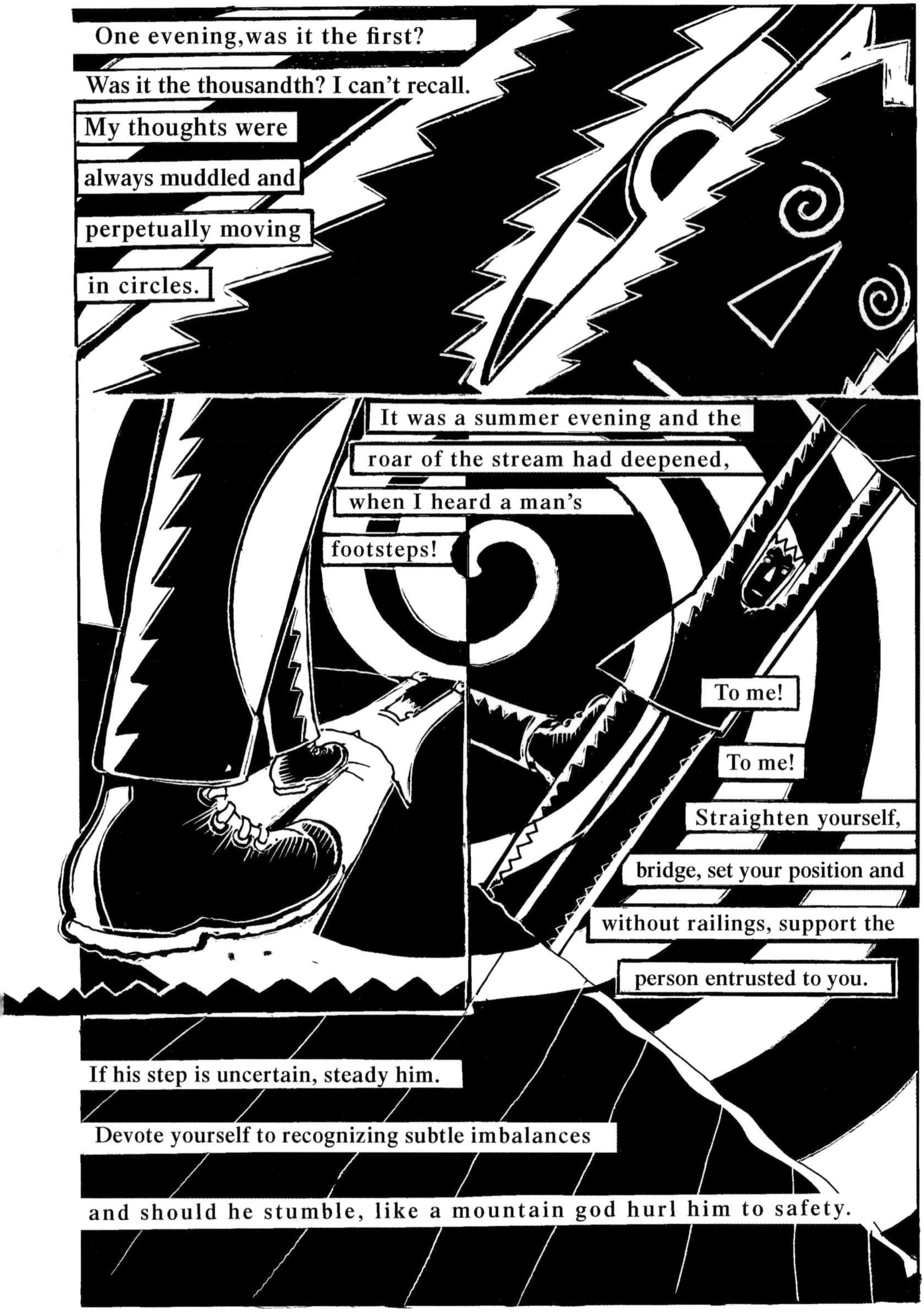
One evening,was it the first?
Was it the thousandth? I can't recall.
My thoughts were
always muddled and
perpetually moving
in circles.
It was a summer evening and the
roar of the stream had deepened,
when I heard a man's
footsteps!
To me!
To me!
Straighten yourself,
bridge, set your position and
without railings, support the
person entrusted to you.
If his step is uncertain, steady him.
Devote yourself to recognizing subtle imbalances
and should he stumble, like a mountain god hurl him to safety.

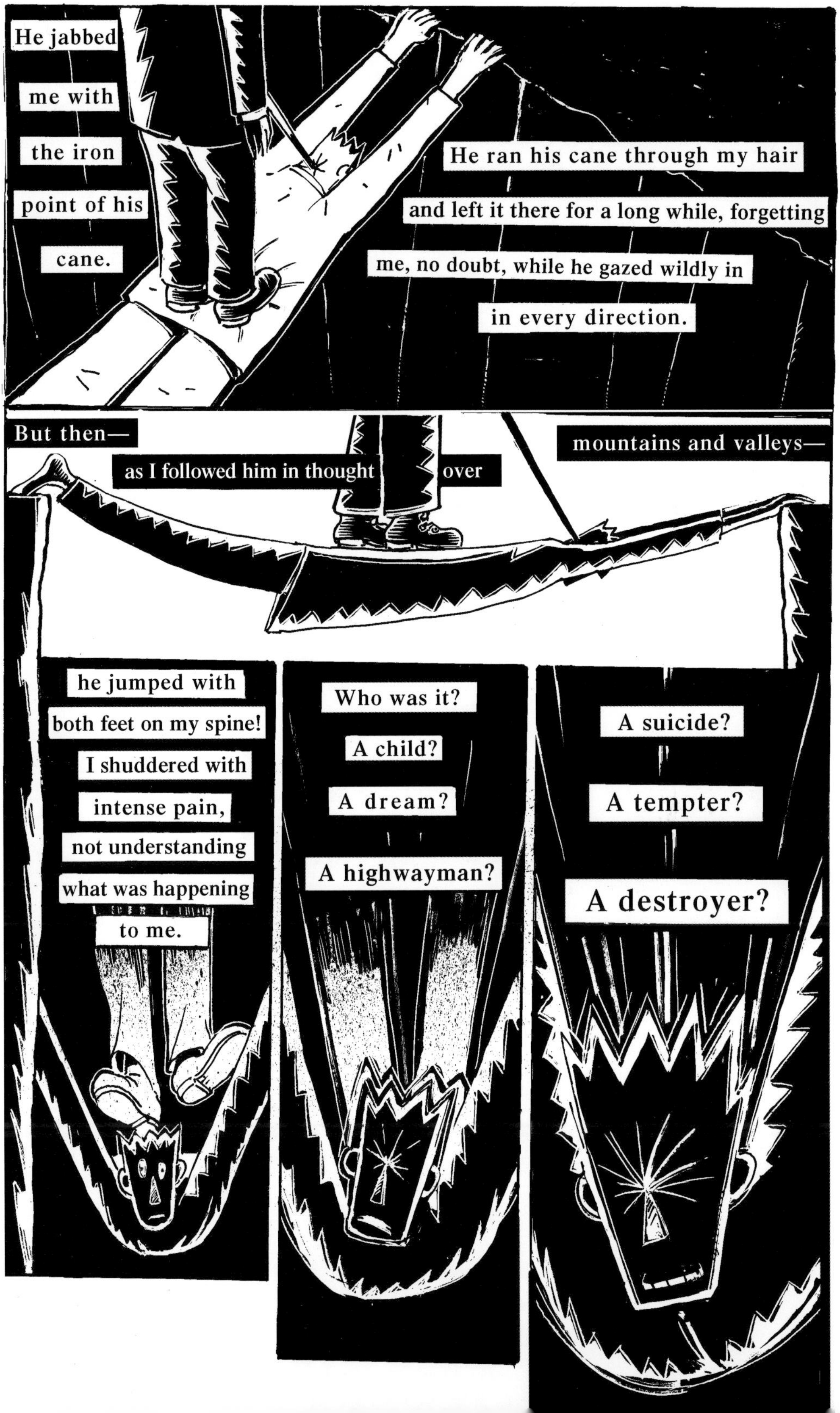
He jabbed
me with
the iron
point of his
cane.
He ran his cane through my hair
and left it there for a long while, forgetting
me, no doubt, while he gazed wildly in
in every direction.
But then—
as I followed him in thought
over
mountains and valleys—
he jumped with
both feet on my spine!
I shuddered with
intense pain,
not understanding
what was happening
to me.
Who was it?
A child?
A dream?
A highwayman?
A suicide?
A tempter?
A destroyer?

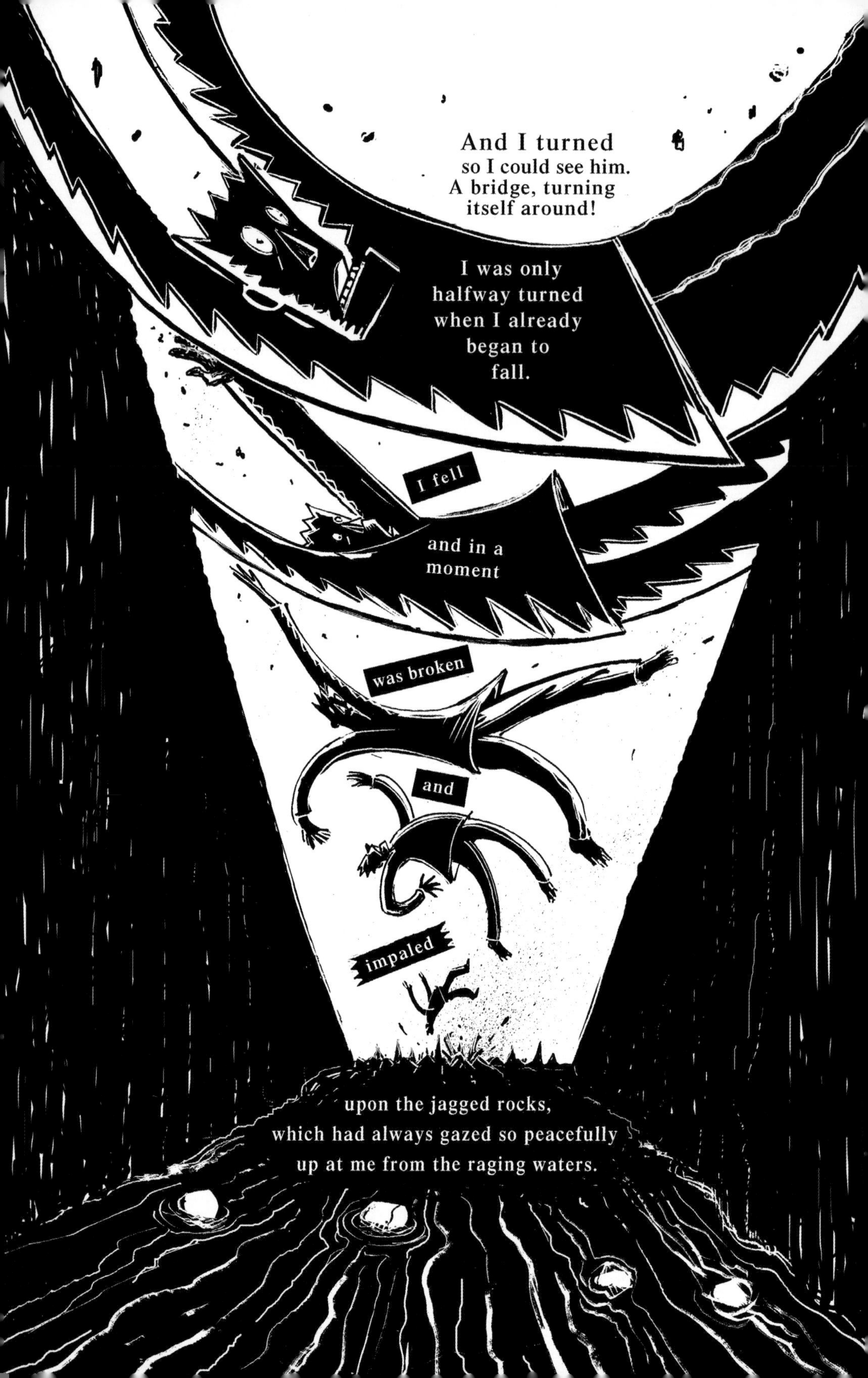
And I turned
so I could see him.
A bridge, turning
itself around!
I was only
halfway turned
when I already
began to
fall.
I fell
and in a
moment
was broken
and
impaled
upon the jagged rocks,
which had always gazed so peacefully
up at me from the raging waters.

IN THE
PENAL COLONY

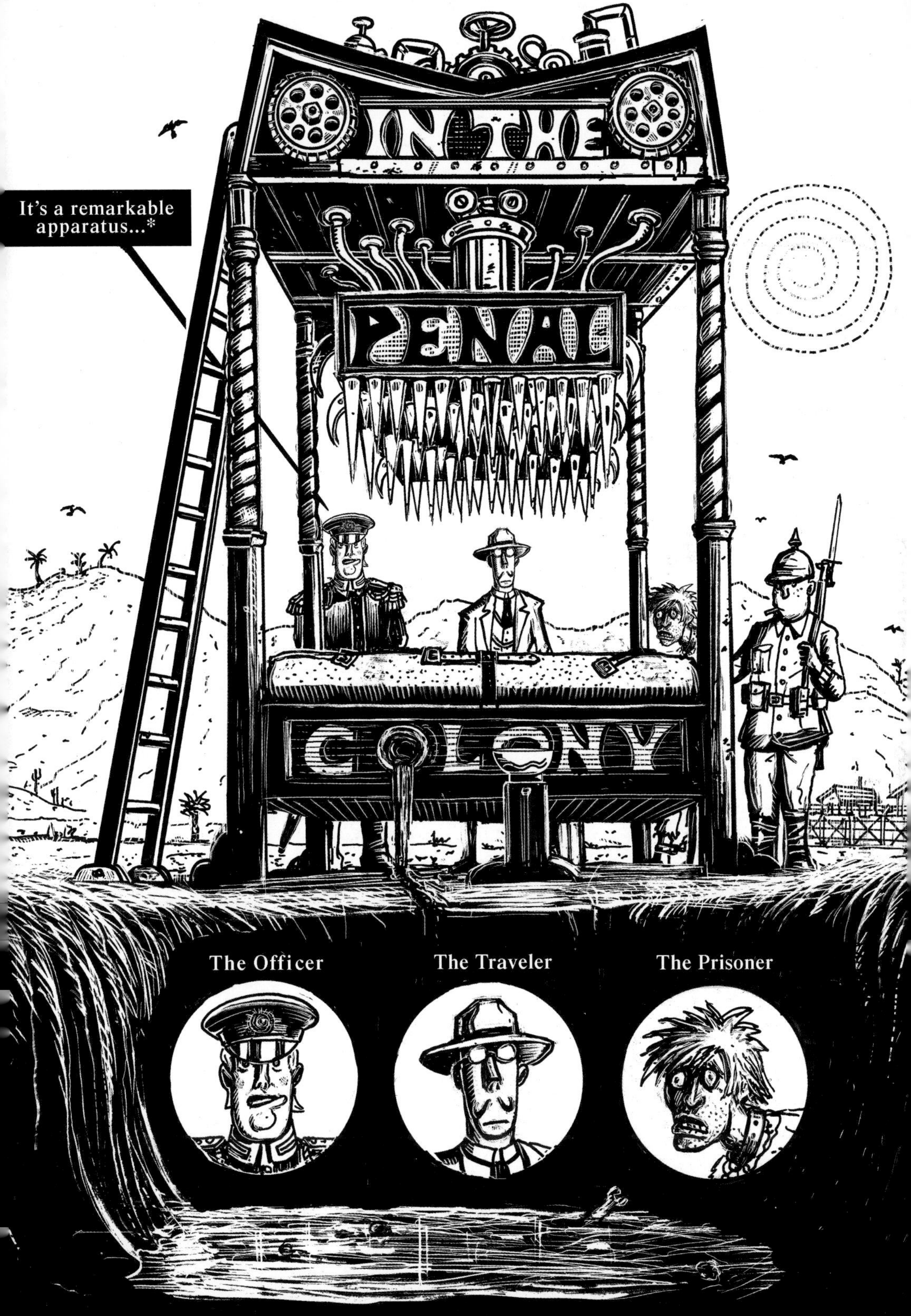
IN THE
PENAL
COLONY
It's a remarkable apparatus...*
The Officer
The Traveler
The Prisoner

* French (which the prisoner does not understand)

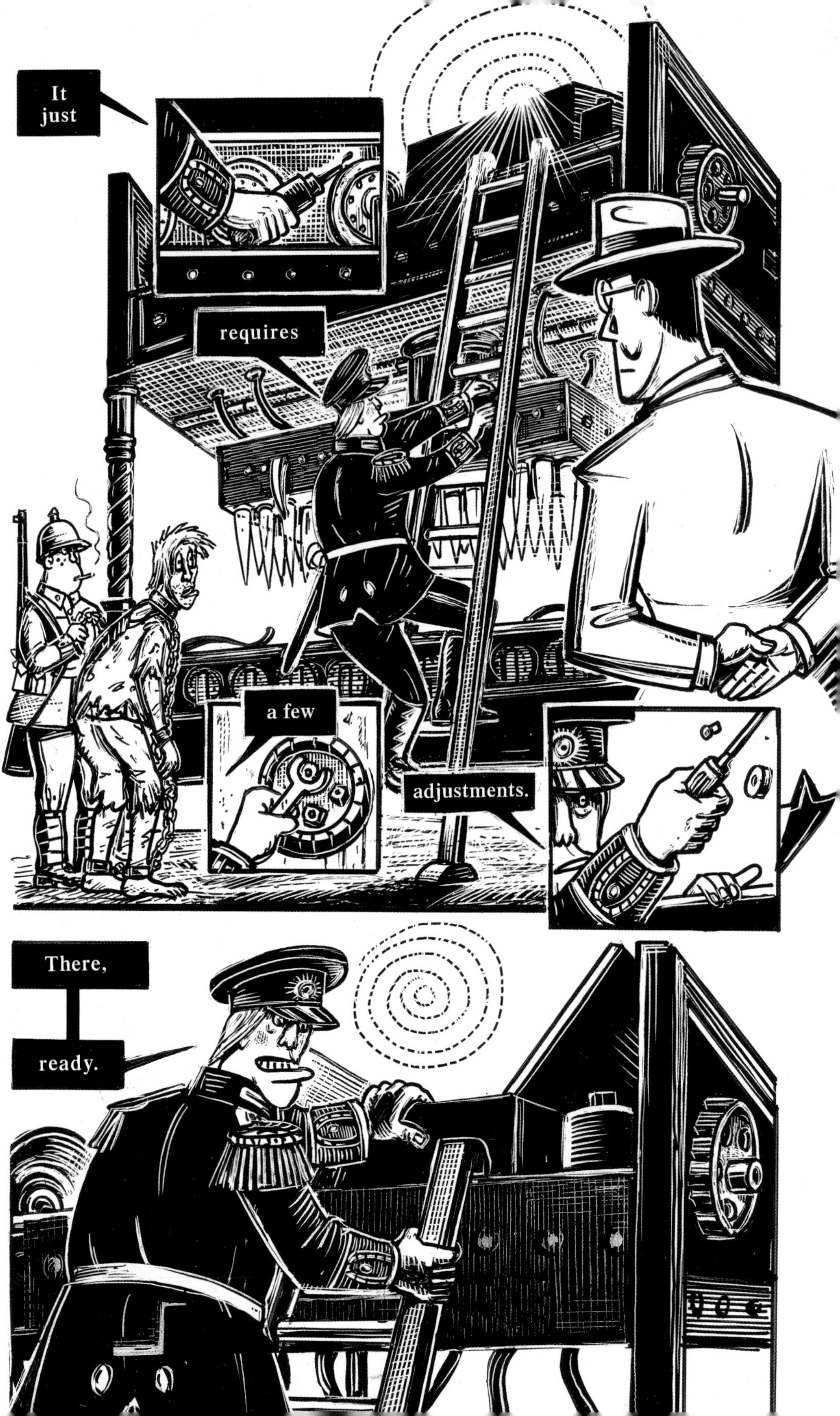
It just
requires
a few
adjustments.
There,
ready.

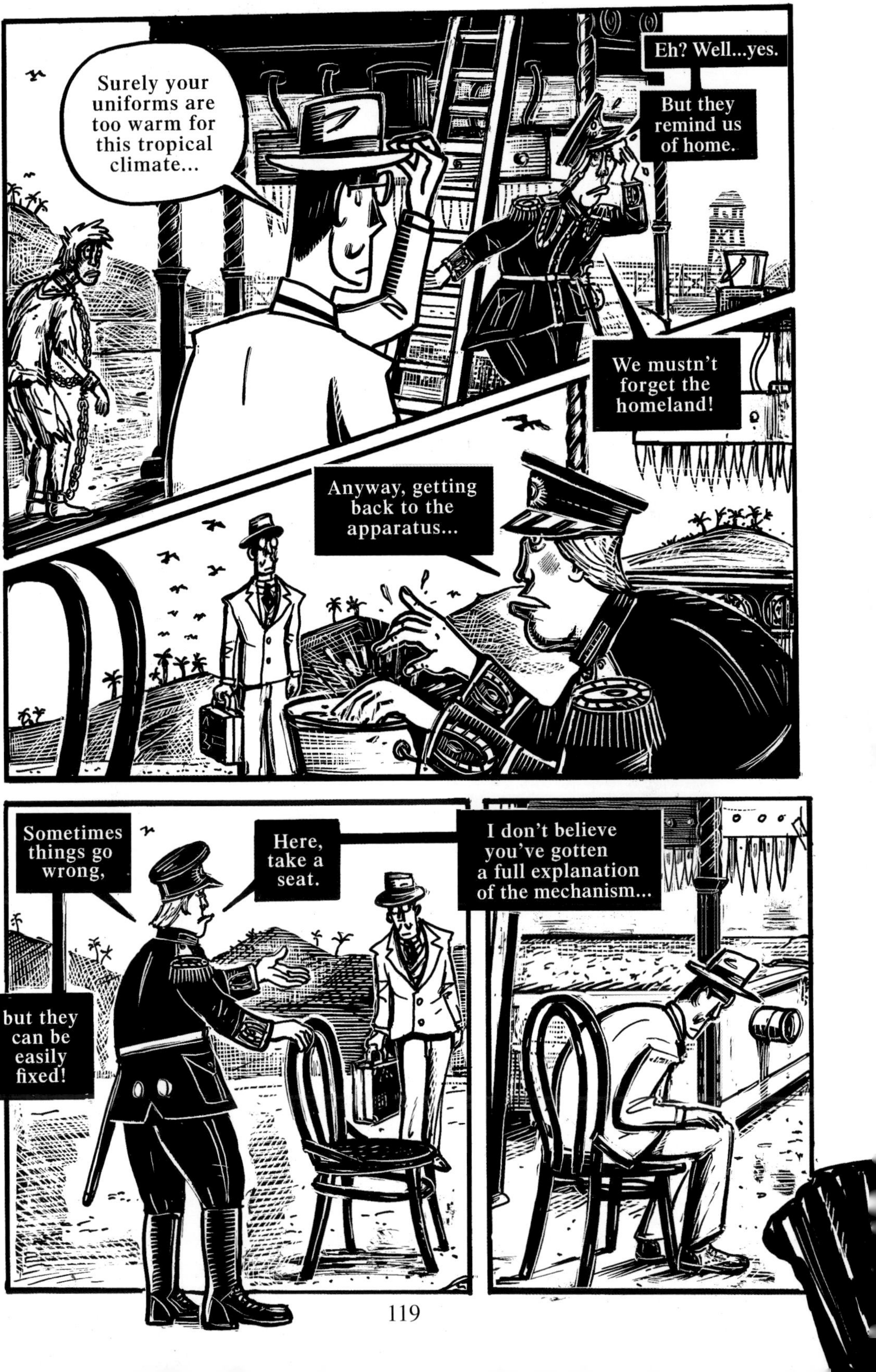
Surely your uniforms are too warm for this tropical climate...
Eh? Well...yes.
But they remind us of home.
We mustn't forget the homeland!
Anyway, getting back to the apparatus...
Sometimes things go wrong,
but they can be easily fixed!
Here, take a seat.
I don't believe you've gotten a full explanation of the mechanism...

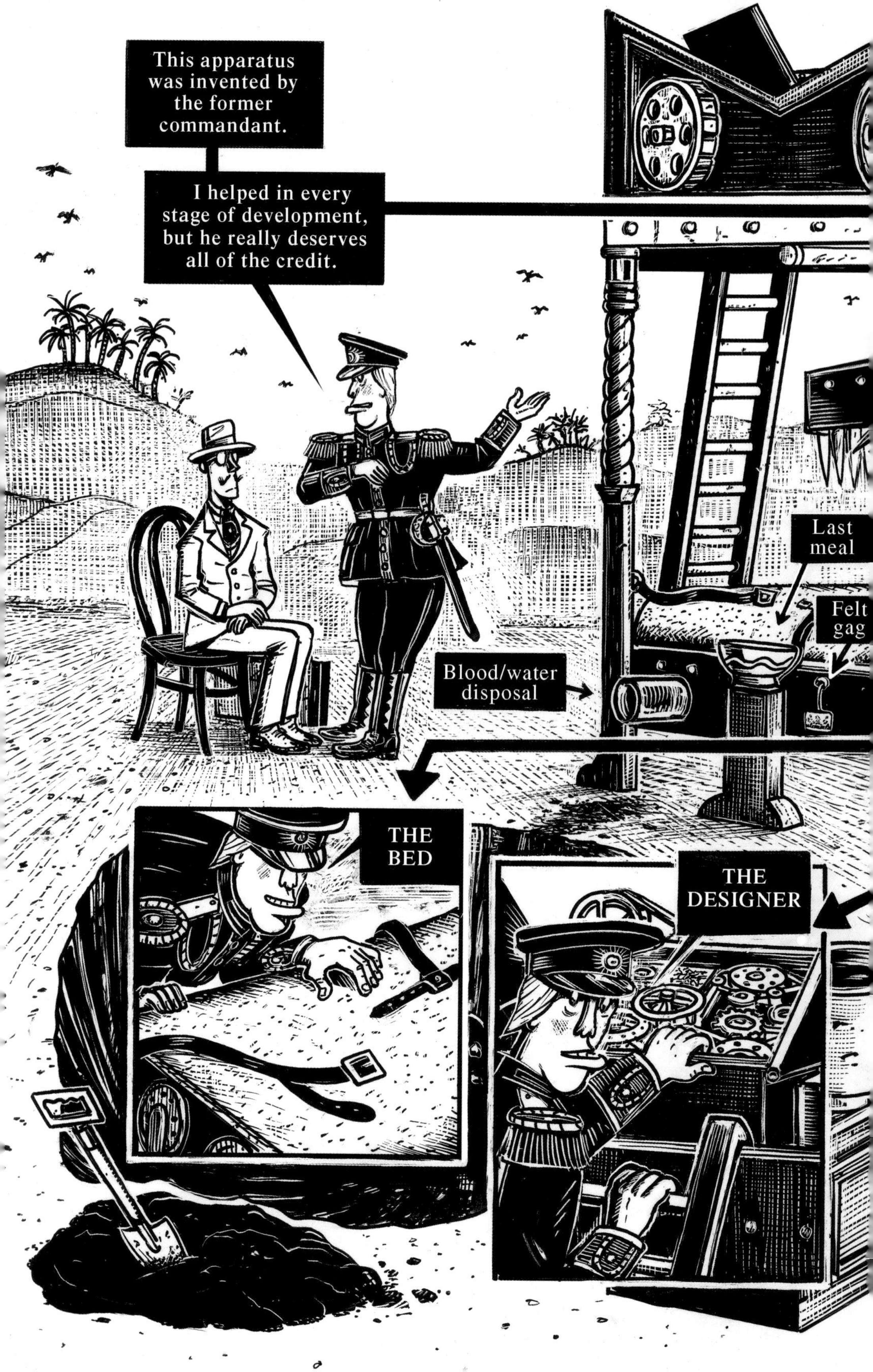
This apparatus was invented by the former commandant.
I helped in every stage of development, but he really deserves all of the credit.
Last meal
Felt gag
Blood/water disposal
THE BED
THE DESIGNER

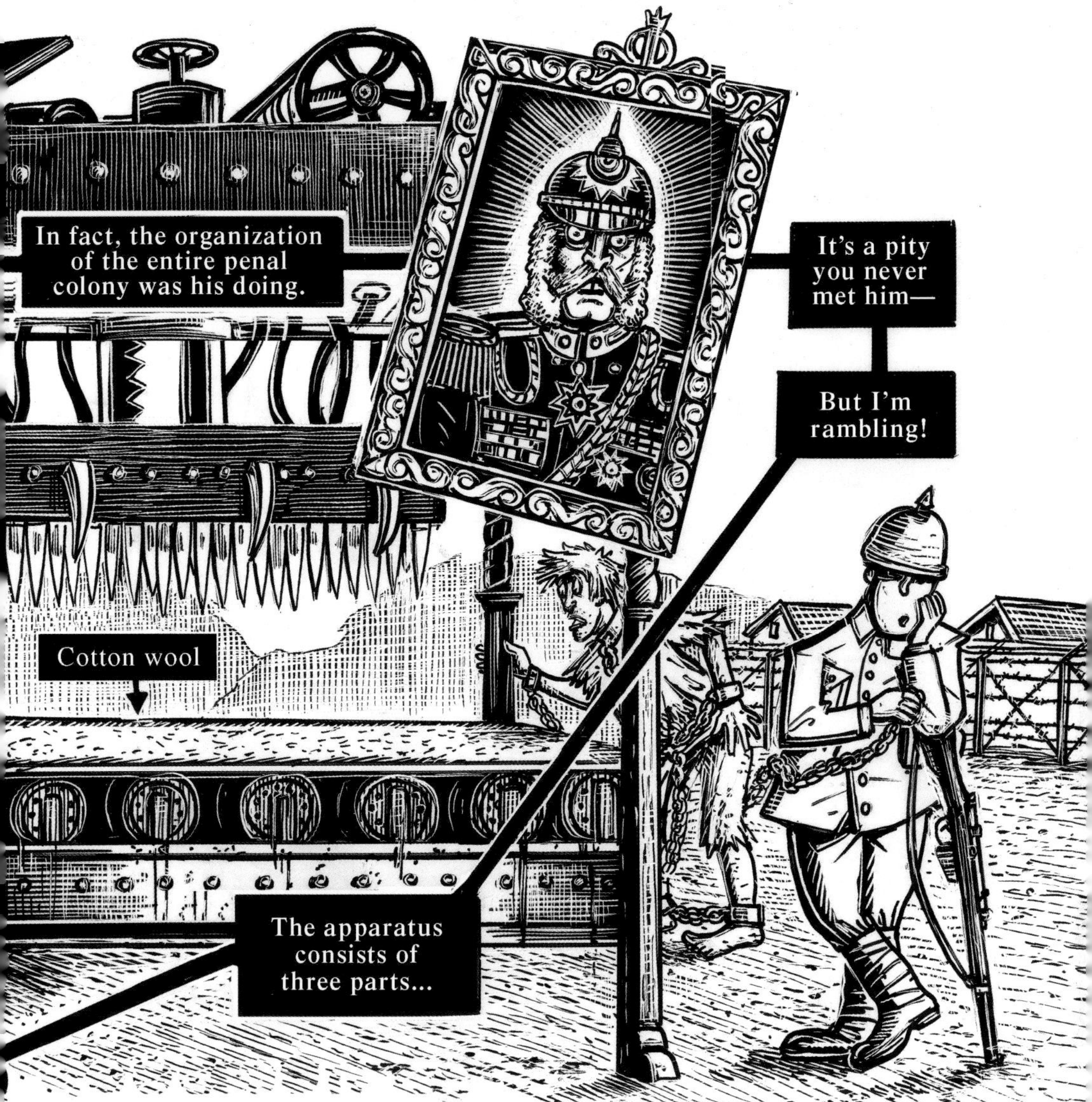
In fact, the organization of the entire penal colony was his doing.
It's a pity you never met him—
But I'm rambling!
Cotton wool
The apparatus consists of three parts...

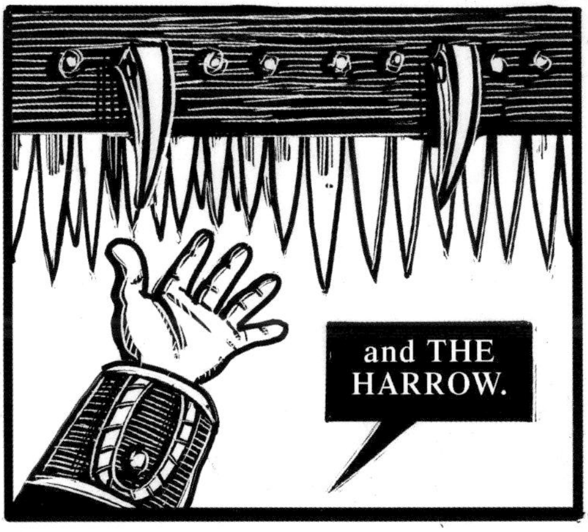
and THE HARROW.

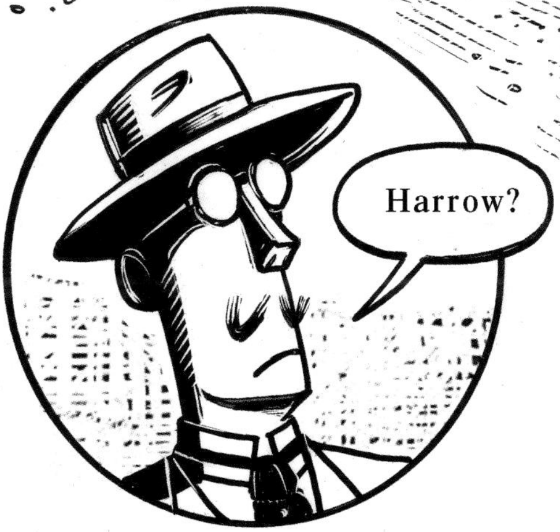
Harrow?

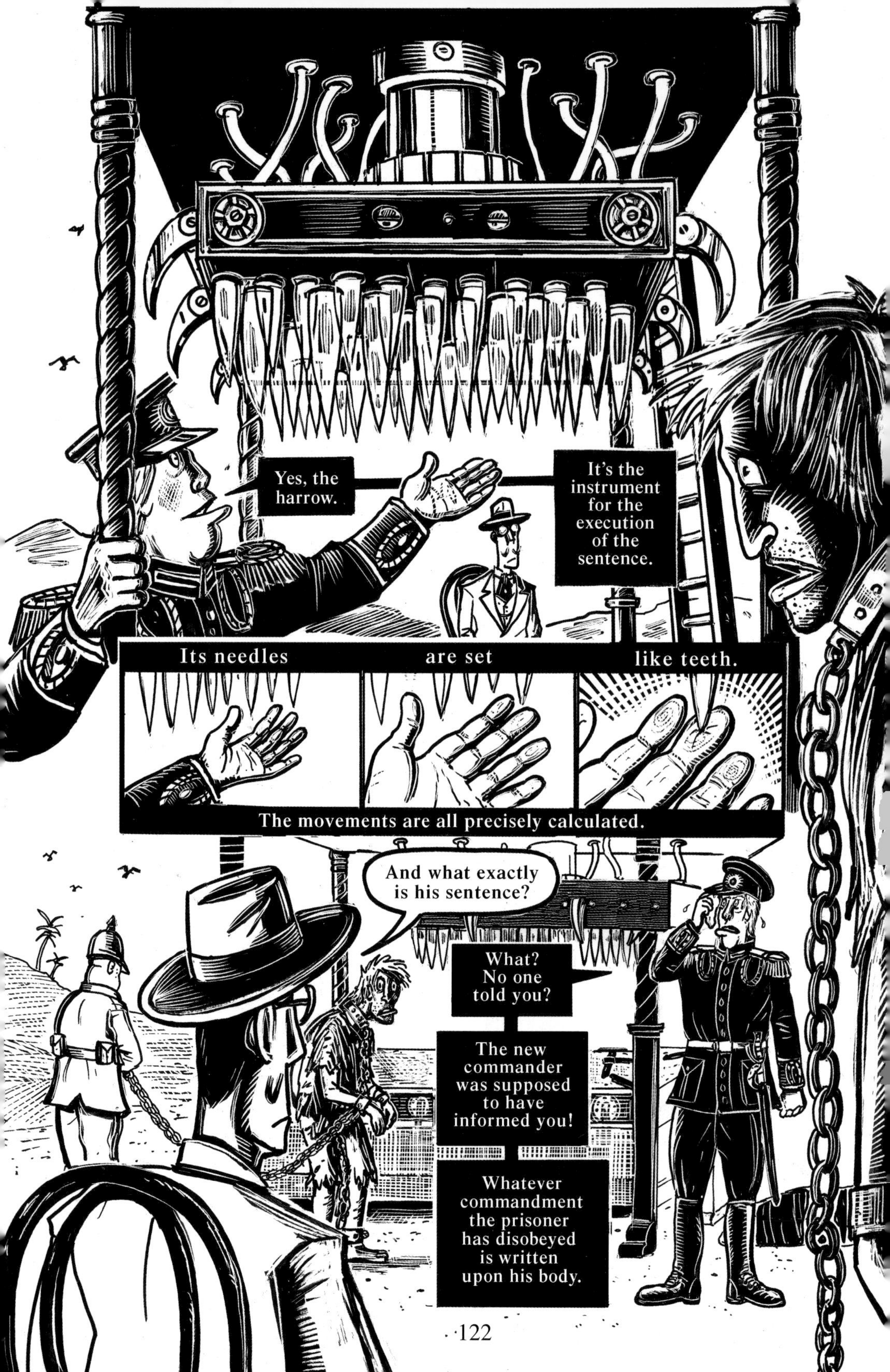

Yes, the harrow.
It's the instrument for the execution of the sentence.
Its needles
are set
like teeth.
The movements are all precisely calculated.
And what exactly is his sentence?
What? No one told you?
The new commander was supposed to have informed you!
Whatever commandment the prisoner has disobeyed is written upon his body.

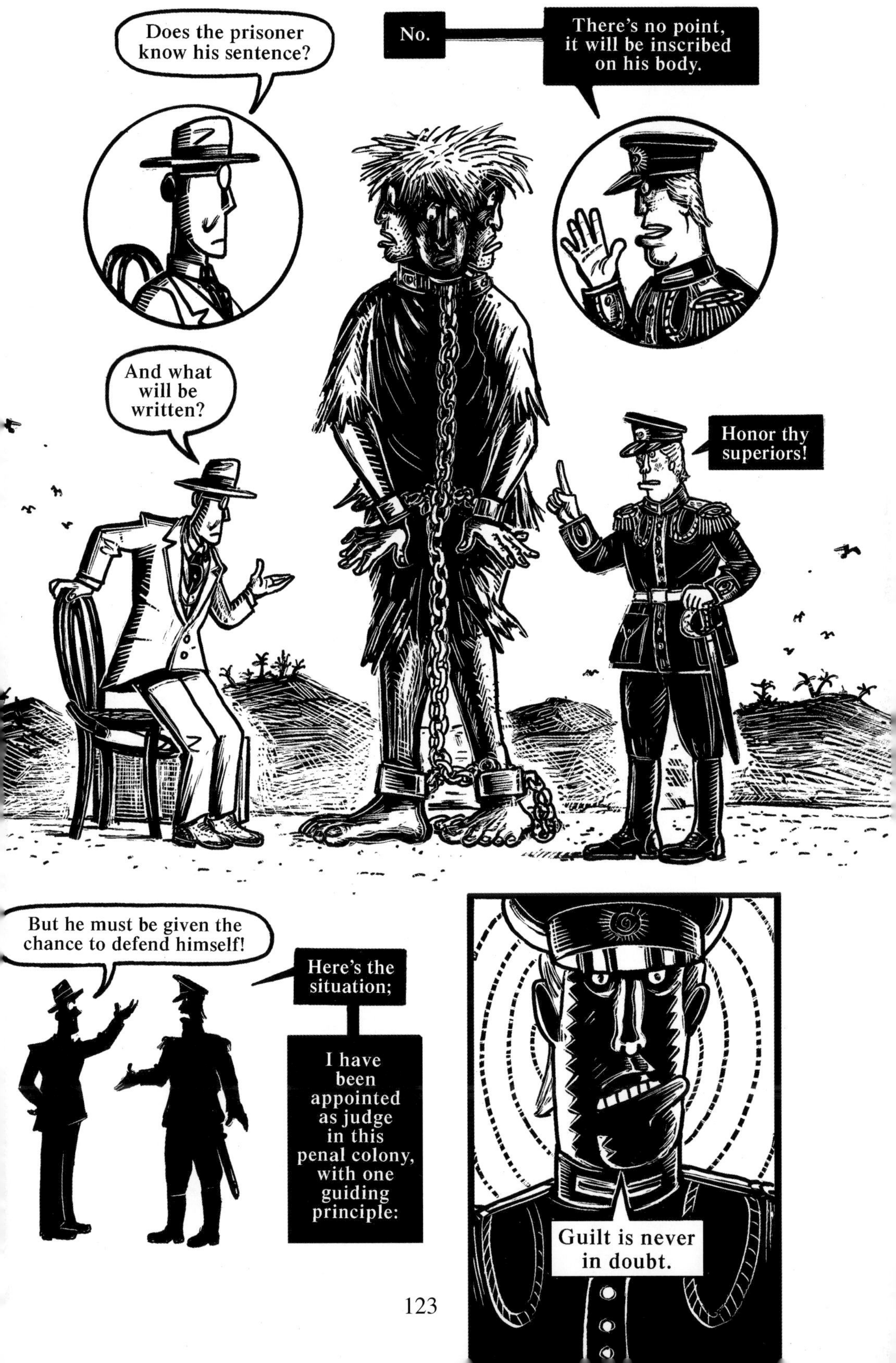
Does the prisoner know his sentence?
No.
There's no point, it will be inscribed on his body.
And what will be written?
Honor thy superiors!
But he must be given the chance to defend himself!
Here's the situation;
I have been appointed as judge in this penal colony, with one guiding principle:
Guilt is never in doubt.

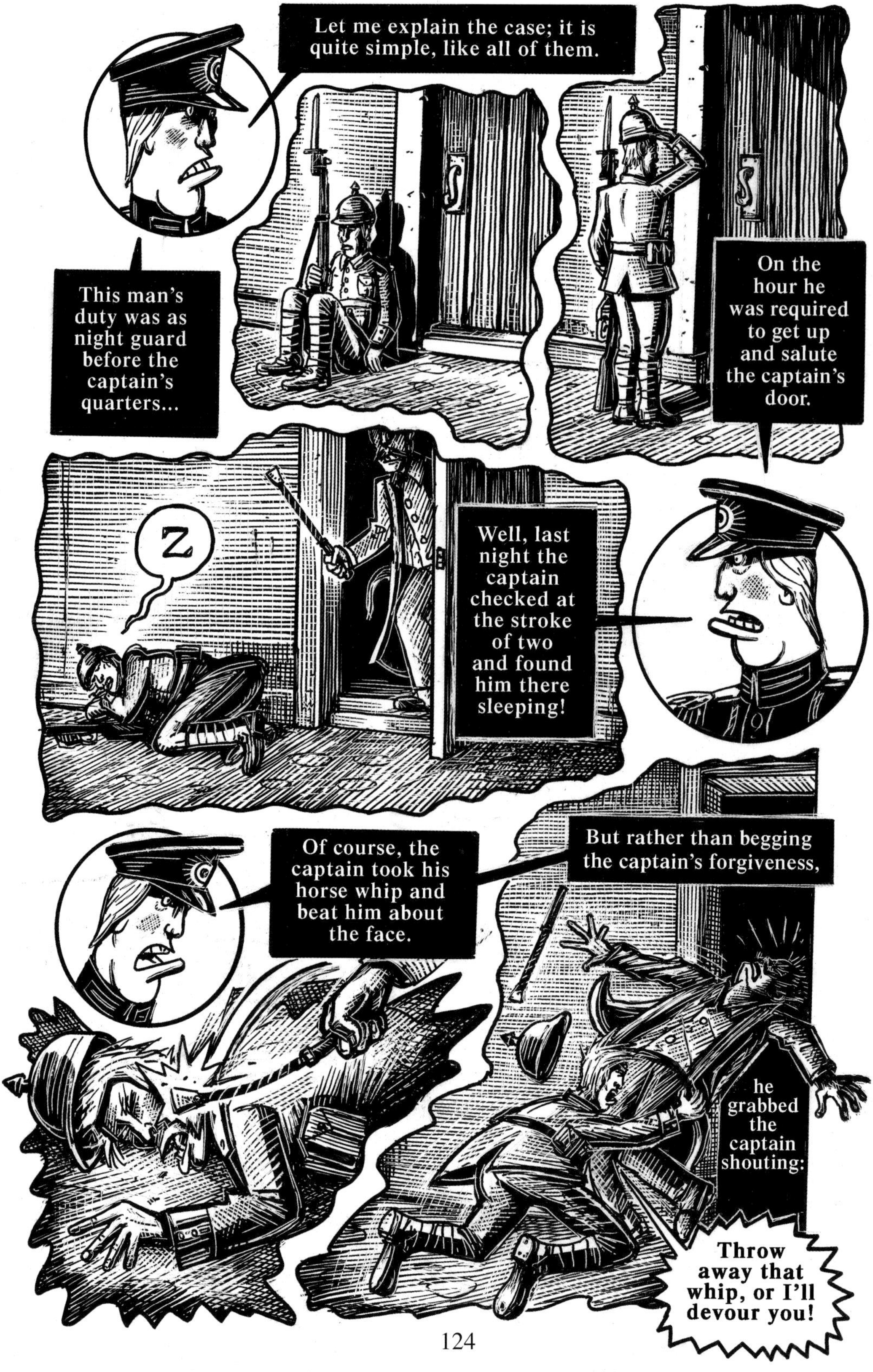
Let me explain the case; it is quite simple, like all of them.
This man's duty was as night guard before the captain's quarters...
On the hour he was required to get up and salute the captain's door.
Z
Well, last night the captain checked at the stroke of two and found him there sleeping!
Of course, the captain took his horse whip and beat him about the face.
But rather than begging the captain's forgiveness,
he grabbed the captain shouting:
Throw away that whip, or I'll devour you!

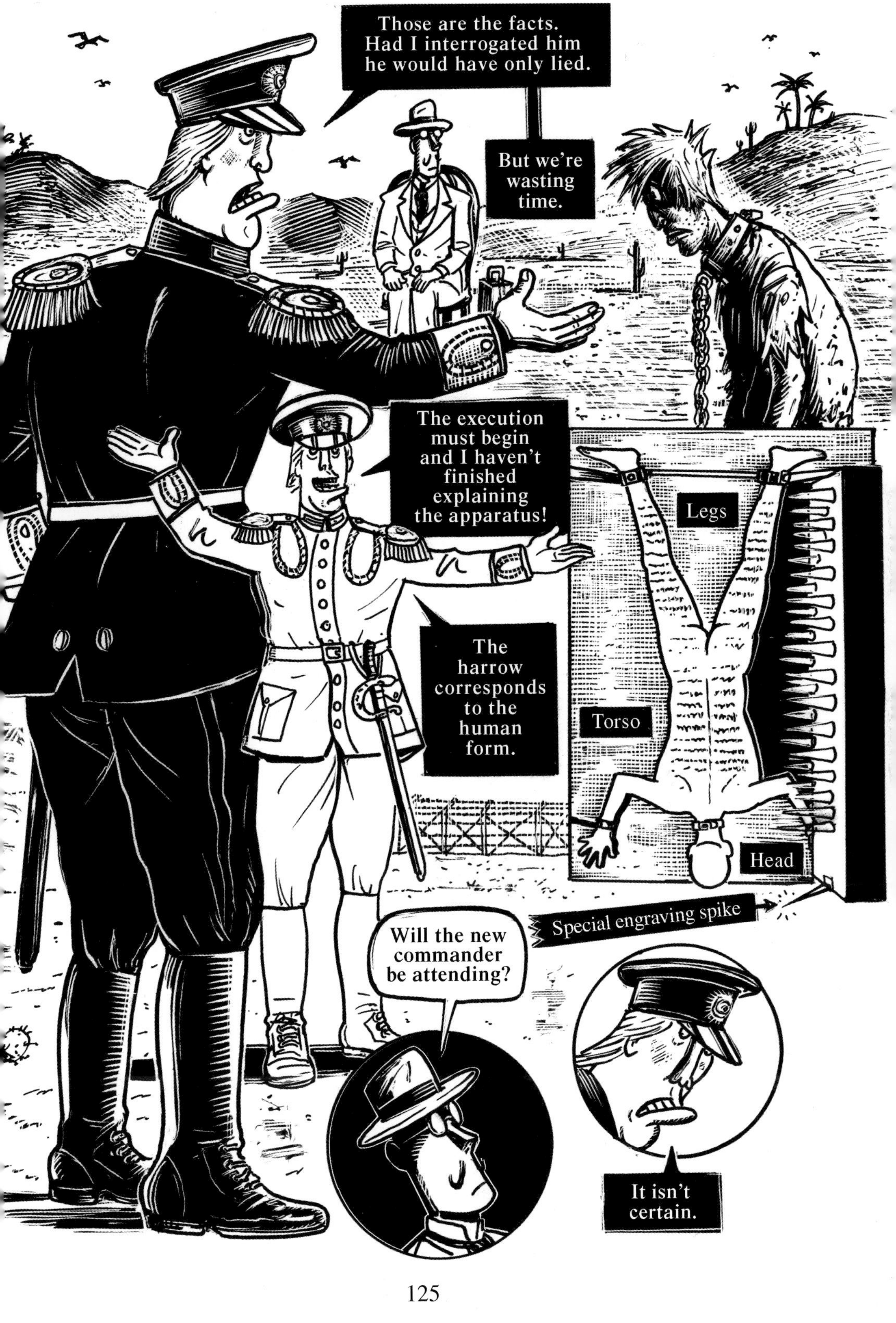
Those are the facts. Had I interrogated him he would have only lied.
But we're wasting time.
The execution must begin and I haven't finished explaining the apparatus!
The harrow corresponds to the human form.
Legs
Torso
Head
Special engraving spike
Will the new commander be attending?
It isn't certain.

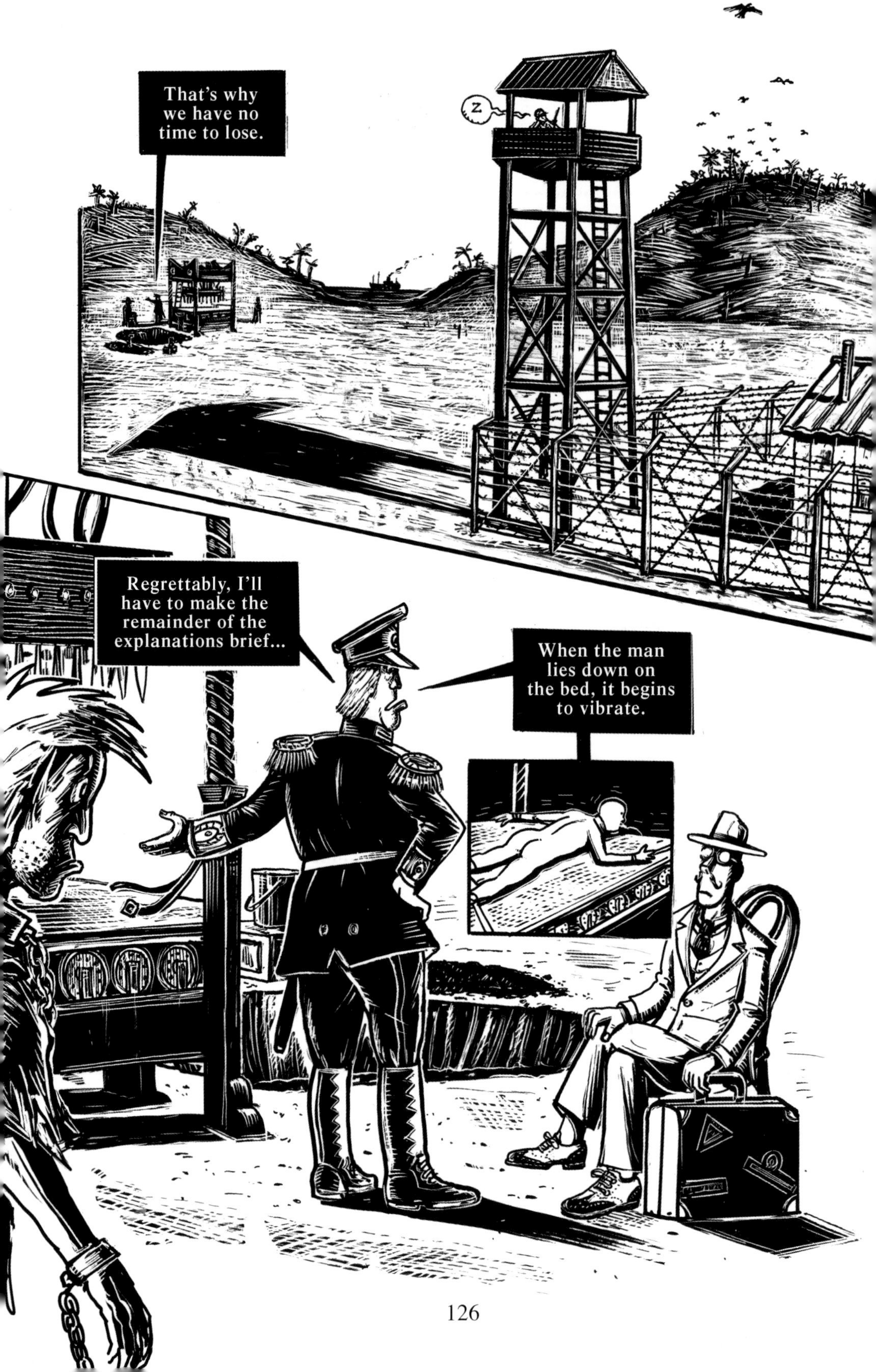
That's why we have no time to lose.
Z
Regrettably, I'll have to make the remainder of the explanations brief...
When the man lies down on the bed, it begins to vibrate.

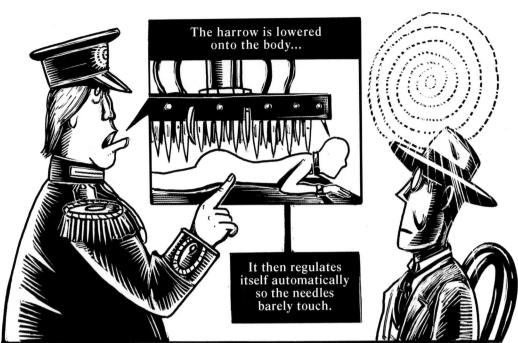

The harrow is lowered onto the body...

It then regulates itself automatically so the needles barely touch.

As the bed quivers, the needles pierce the skin.

Come take a closer look.

The harrow is made of glass so you can view the inscription as it is being written.

A shorter needle sprays water to wash away the blood to keep the script clear.

Z

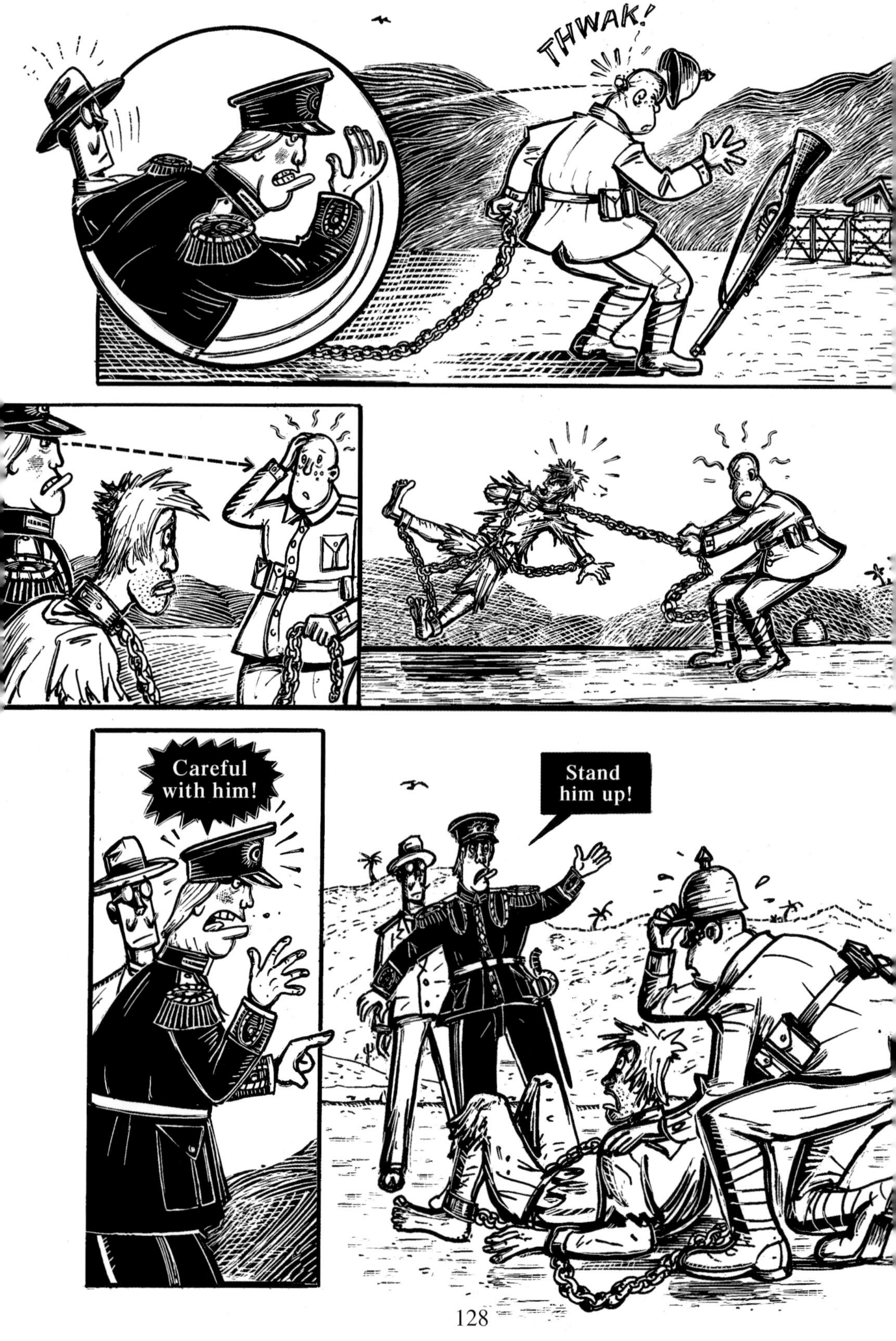
THWAK!
Careful with him!
Stand him up!

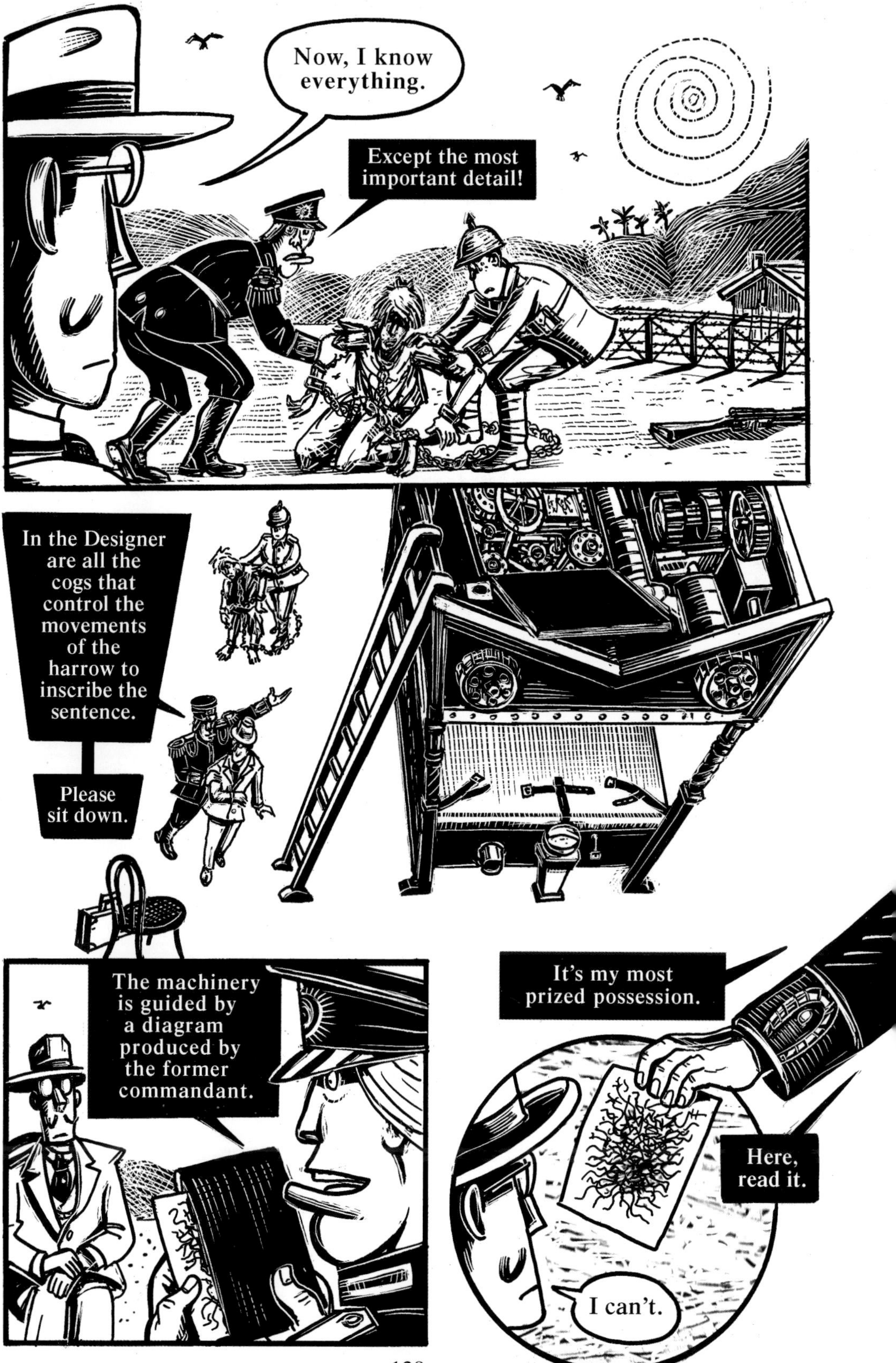
Now, I know everything.
Except the most important detail!
In the Designer are all the cogs that control the movements of the harrow to inscribe the sentence.
Please sit down.
The machinery is guided by a diagram produced by the former commandant.
It's my most prized possession.
Here, read it.
I can't.

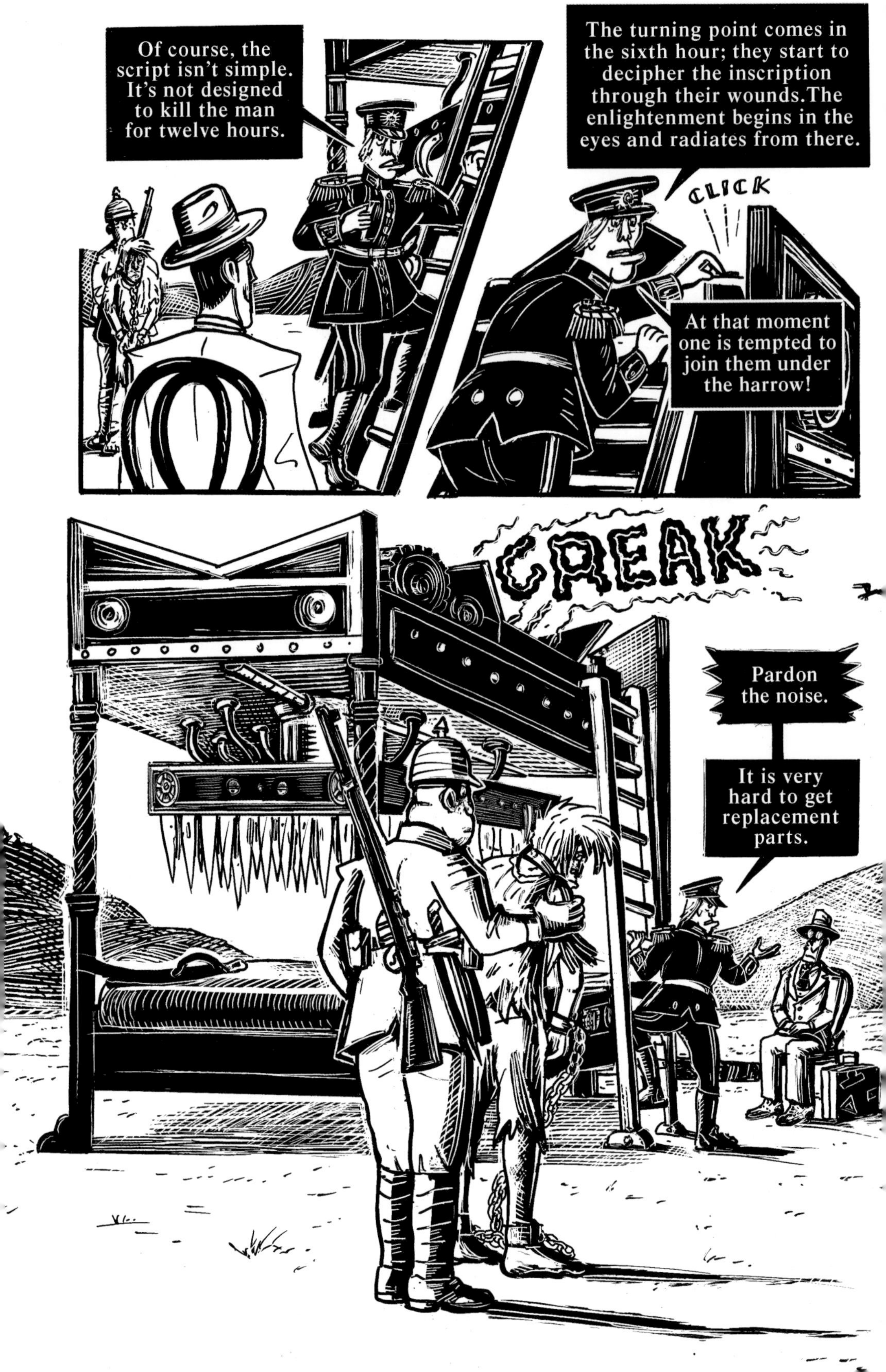

Of course, the script isn't simple. It's not designed to kill the man for twelve hours.
The turning point comes in the sixth hour; they start to decipher the inscription through their wounds. The enlightenment begins in the eyes and radiates from there.
CLICK
At that moment one is tempted to join them under the harrow!
CREAK
Pardon the noise.
It is very hard to get replacement parts.

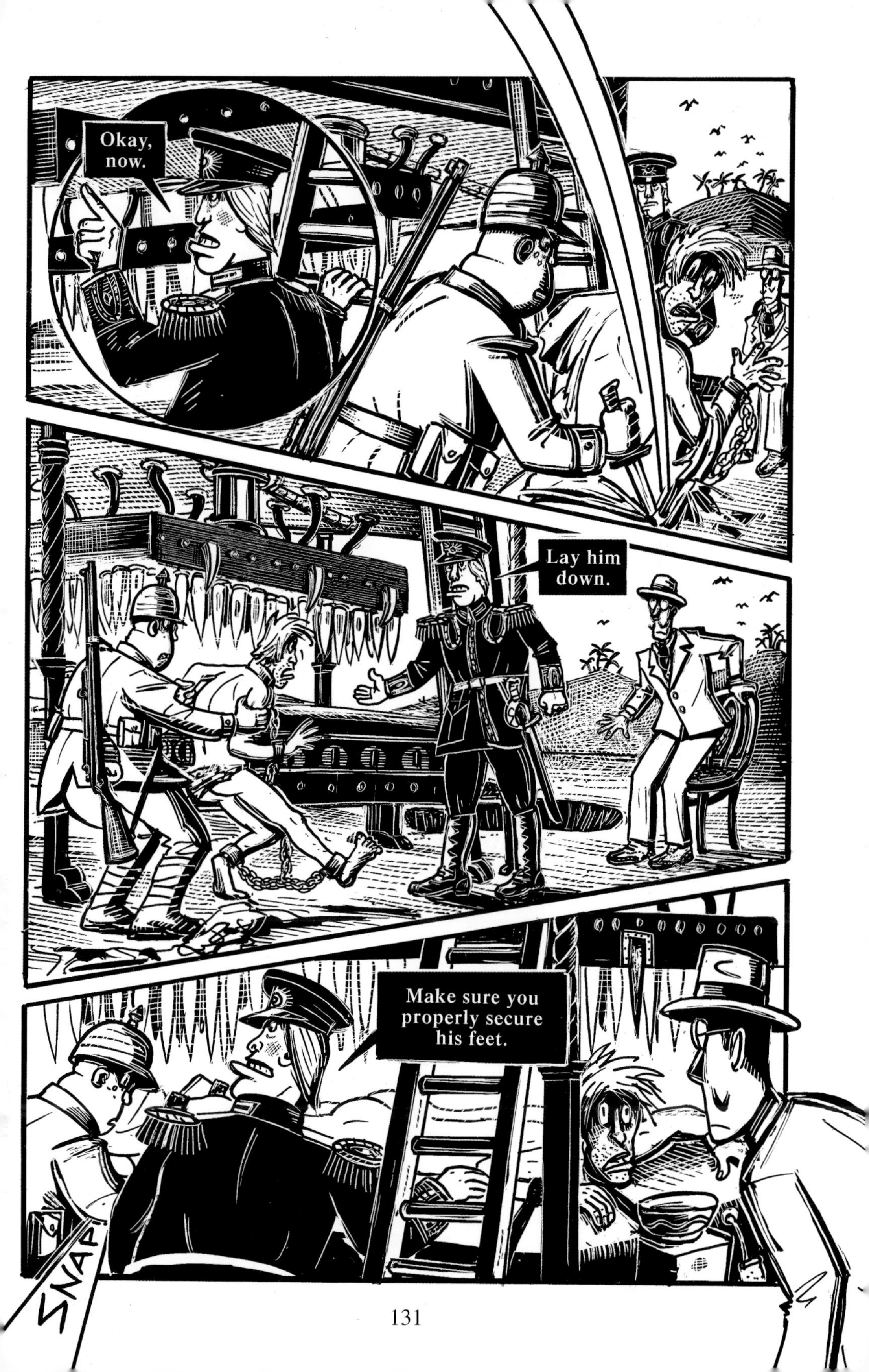
Okay, now.
Lay him down.
Make sure you properly secure his feet.
SNAP!

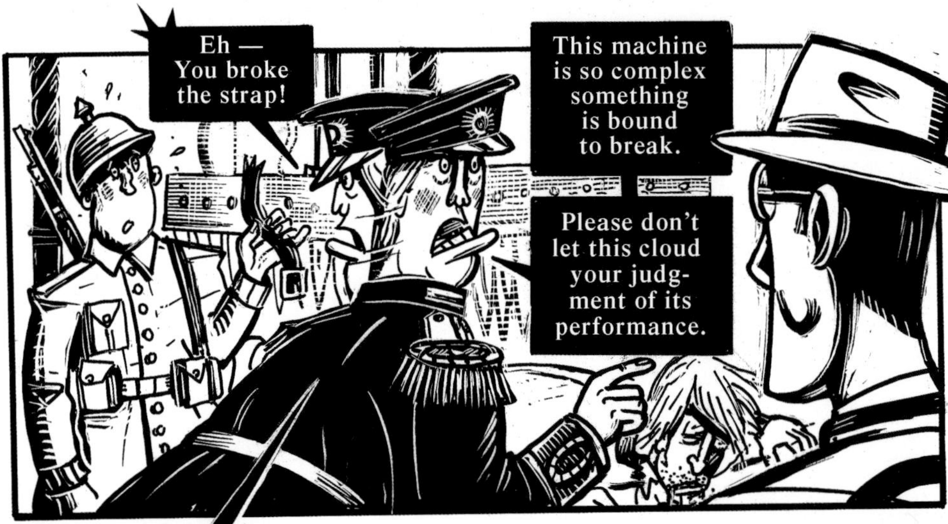
Eh — You broke the strap!
This machine is so complex something is bound to break.
Please don't let this cloud your judg-ment of its performance.

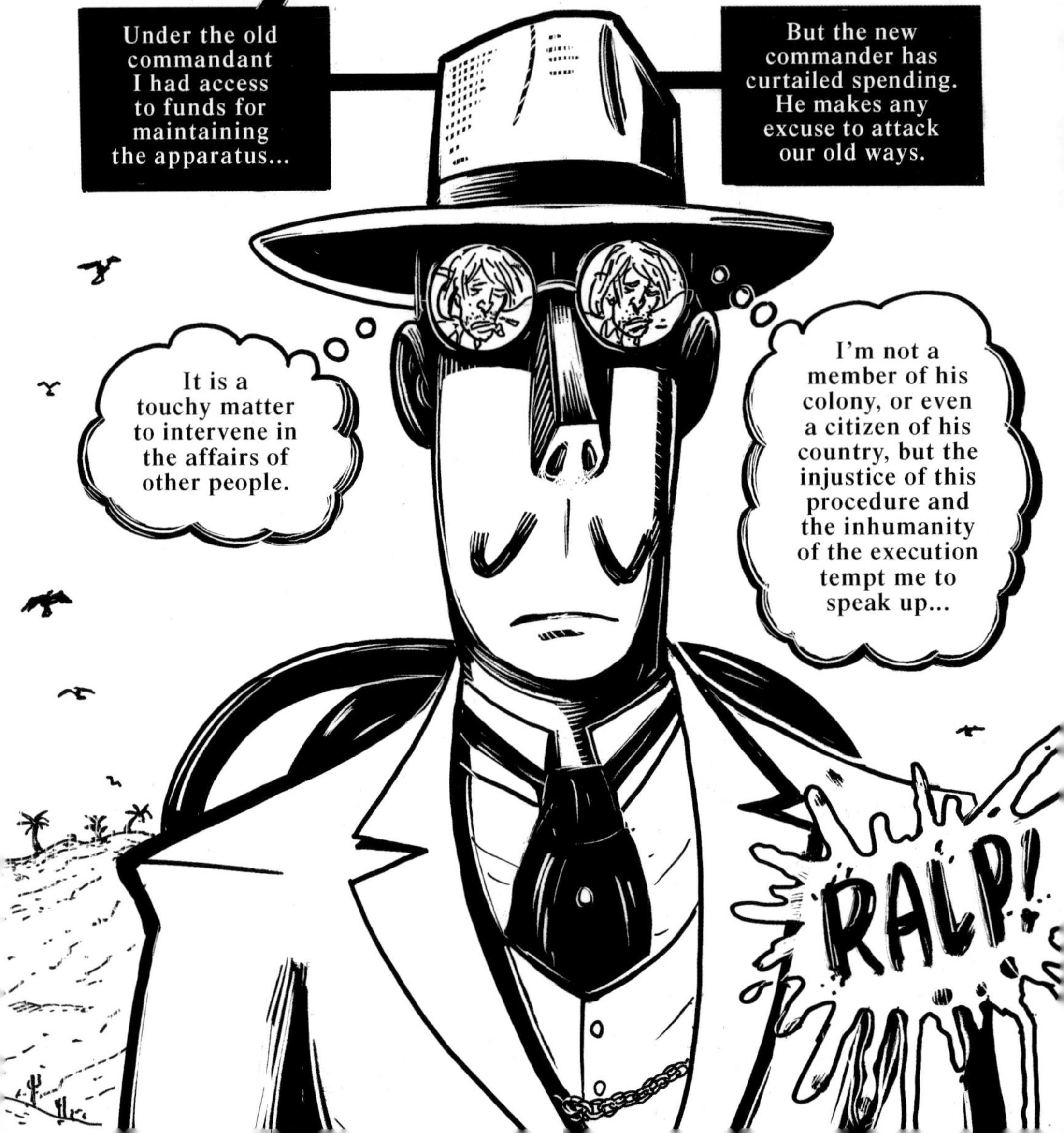
Under the old commandant I had access to funds for maintaining the apparatus...
But the new commander has curtailed spending. He makes any excuse to attack our old ways.
It is a touchy matter to intervene in the affairs of other people.
I'm not a member of his colony, or even a citizen of his country, but the injustice of this procedure and the inhumanity of the execution tempt me to speak up...
RALP!

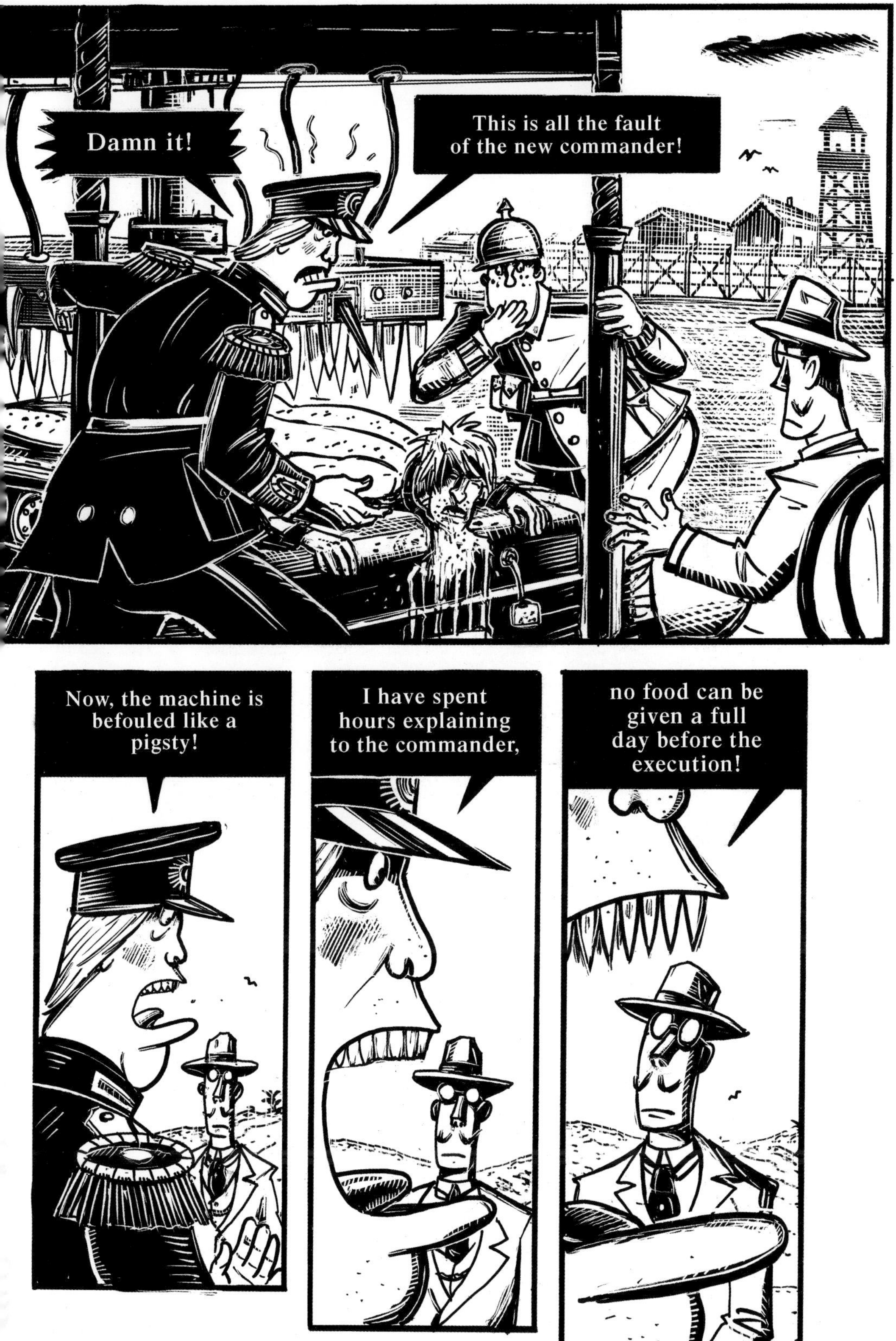
Damn it!
This is all the fault of the new commander!
Now, the machine is befouled like a pigsty!
I have spent hours explaining to the commander,
no food can be given a full day before the execution!

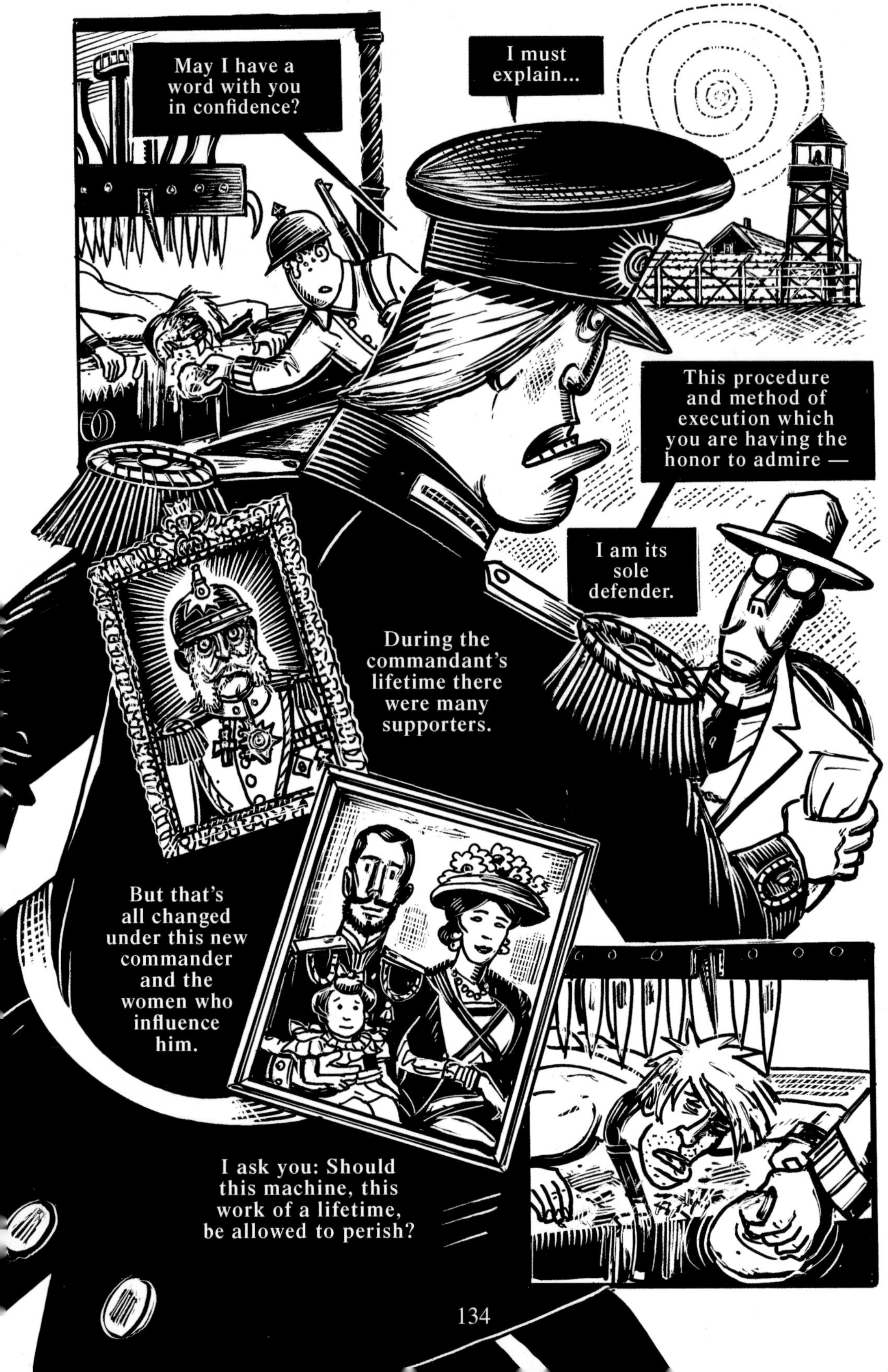
May I have a word with you in confidence?
I must explain...
This procedure and method of execution which you are having the honor to admire —
I am its sole defender.
During the commandant's lifetime there were many supporters.
But that's all changed under this new commander and the women who influence him.
I ask you: Should this machine, this work of a lifetime, be allowed to perish?

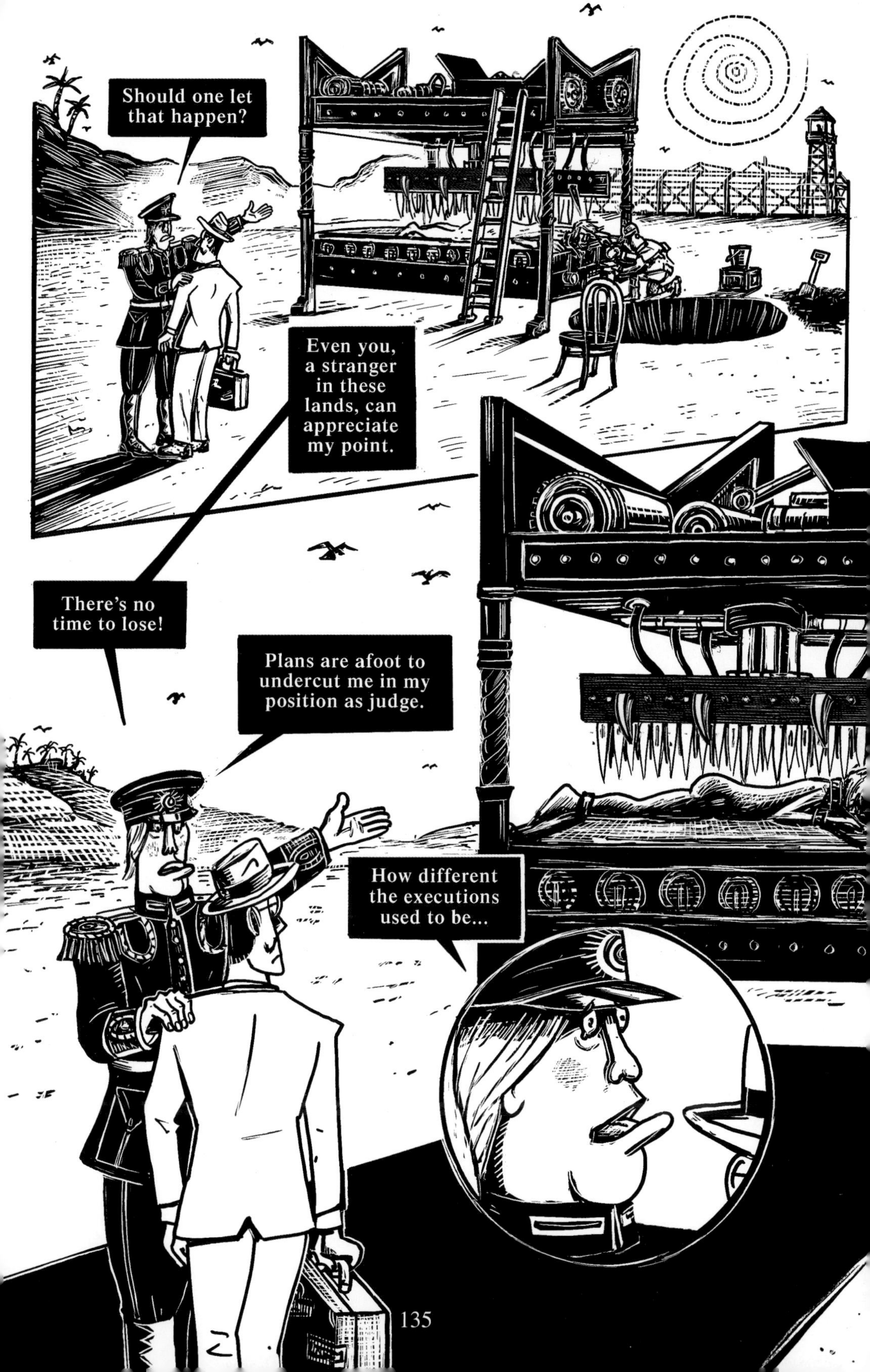
Should one let that happen?
Even you, a stranger in these lands, can appreciate my point.
There's no time to lose!
Plans are afoot to undercut me in my position as judge.
How different the executions used to be...

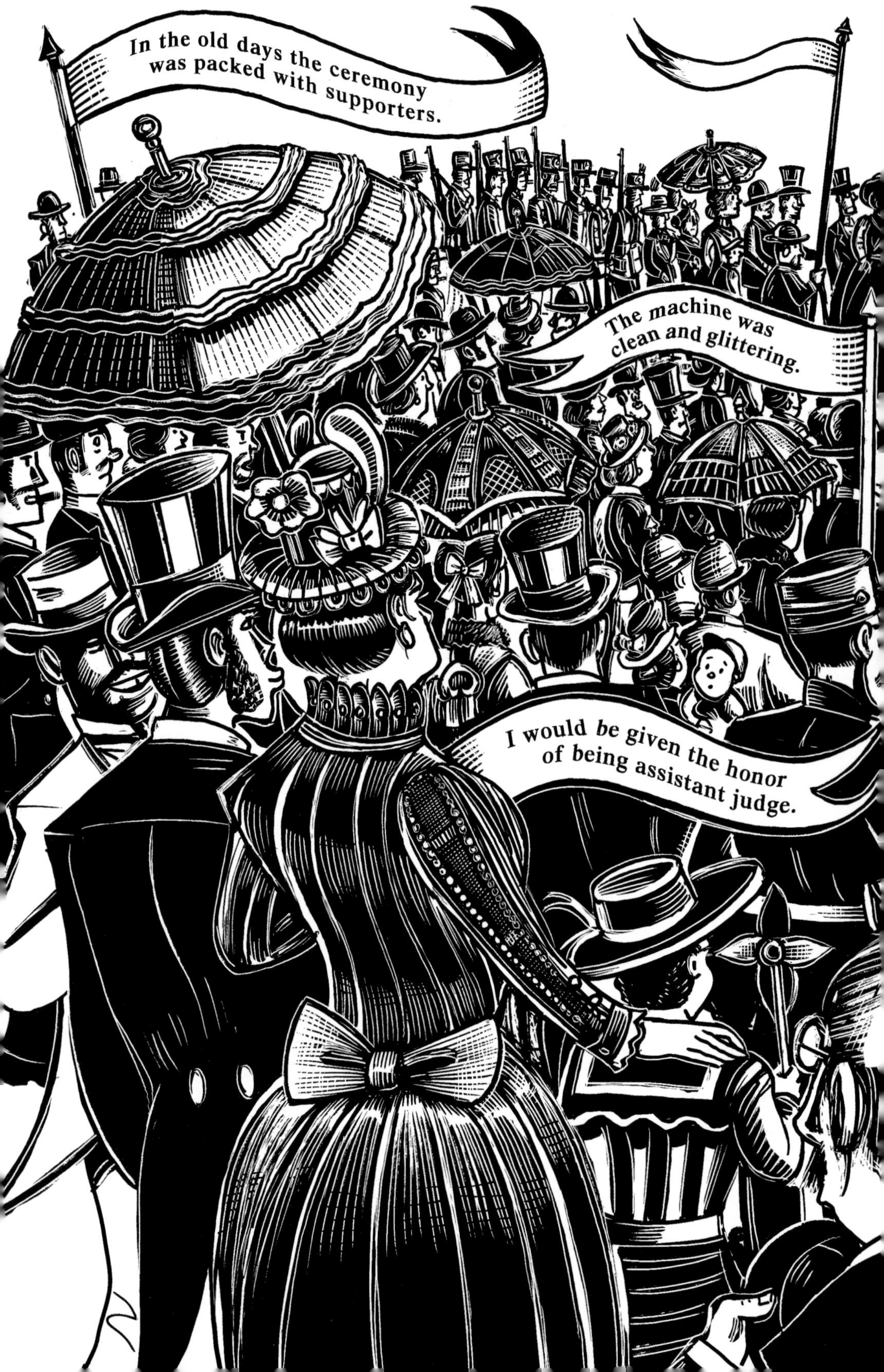
In the old days the ceremony was packed with supporters.
The machine was clean and glittering.
I would be given the honor of being assistant judge.

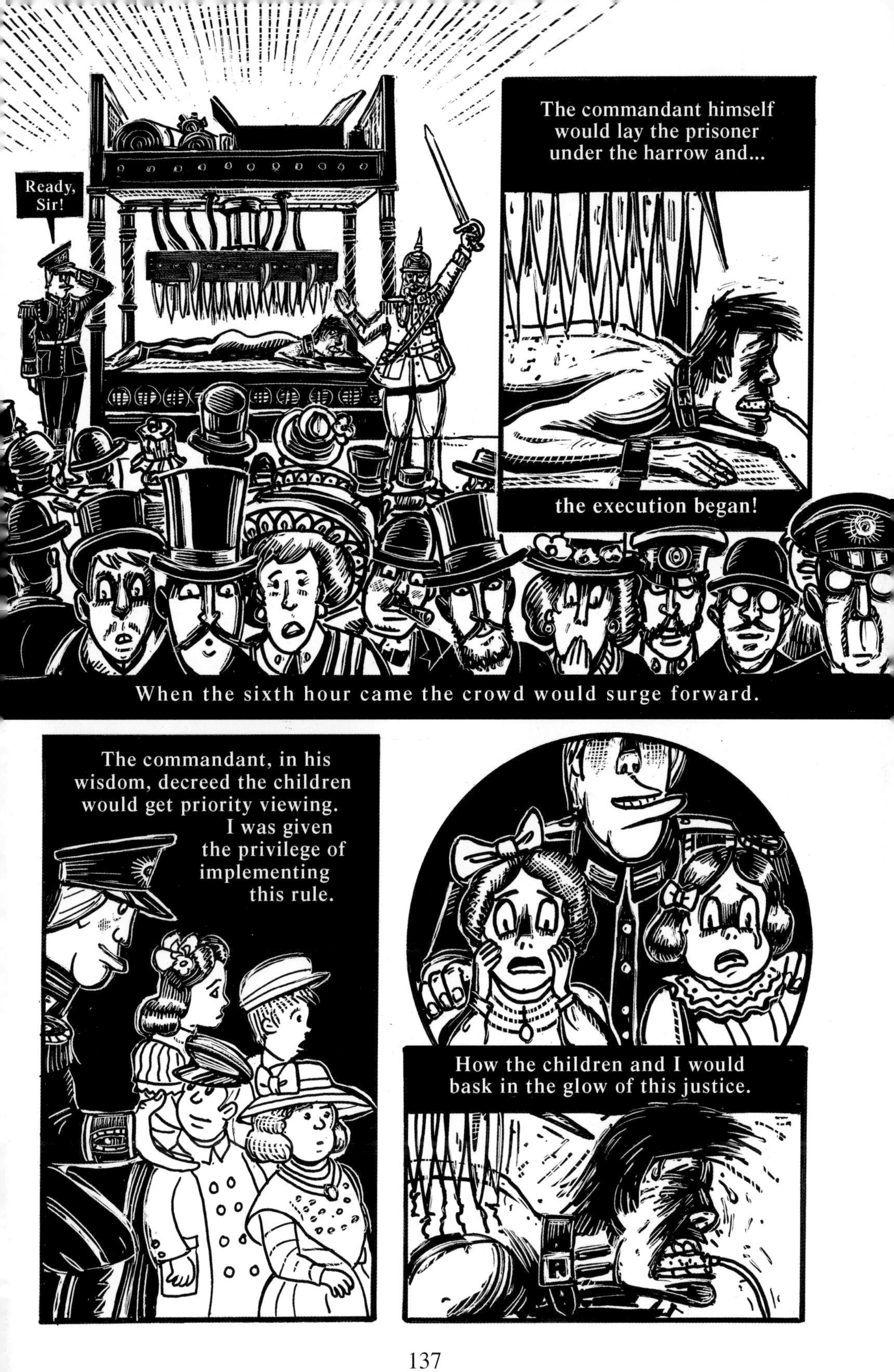
Ready, Sir!
The commandant himself would lay the prisoner under the harrow and...
the execution began!
When the sixth hour came the crowd would surge forward.
The commandant, in his wisdom, decreed the children would get priority viewing. I was given the privilege of implementing this rule.
How the children and I would bask in the glow of this justice.

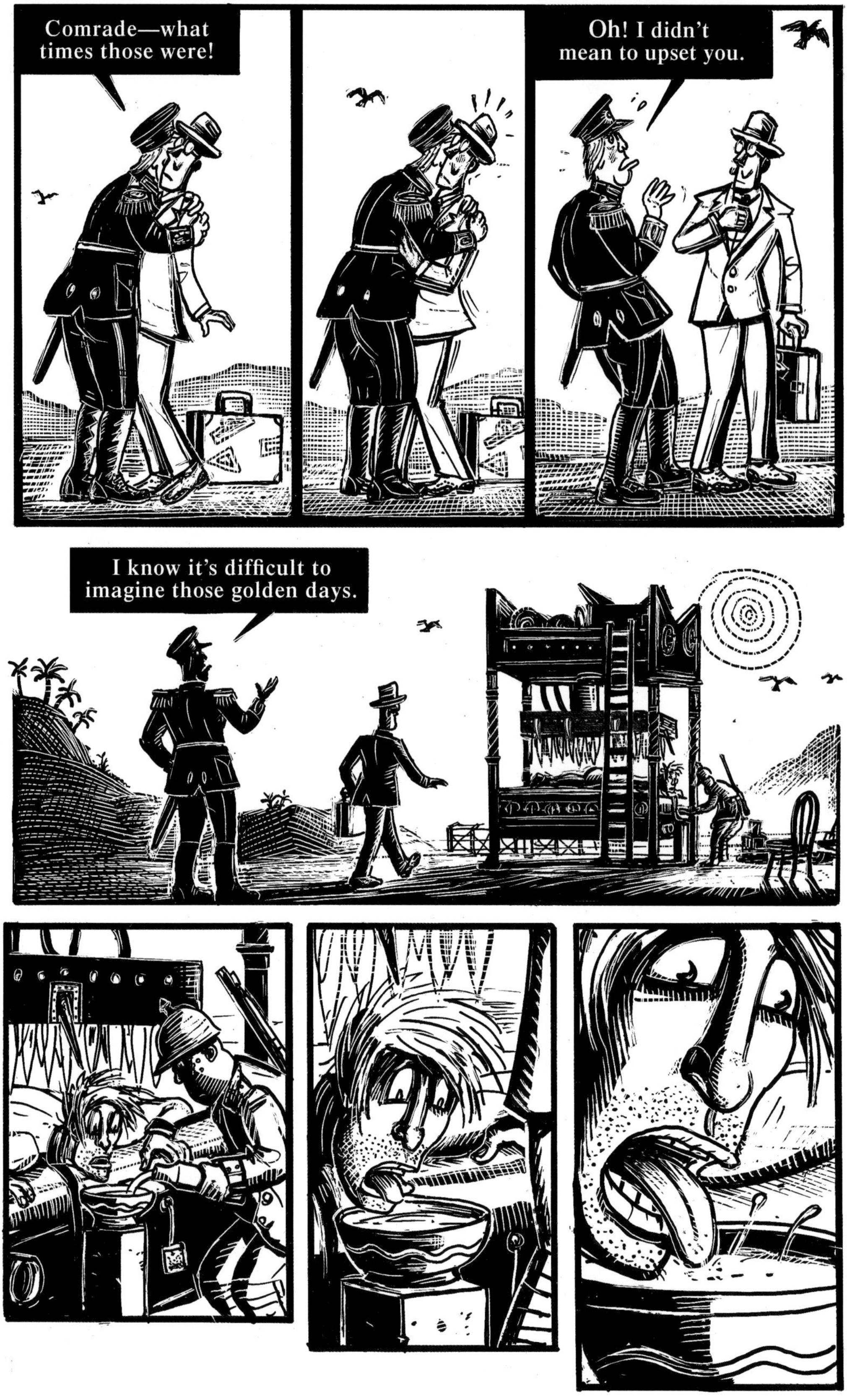
Comrade—what times those were!
Oh! I didn't mean to upset you.
I know it's difficult to imagine those golden days.

Listen–

What's important is the machine is still working, still doing its job.

Perhaps you object to capital punishment and this instrument of death.

You might say: "We haven't tortured since the Middle Ages!"

But even if that's true, you must help me preserve *tradition!*

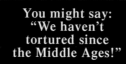

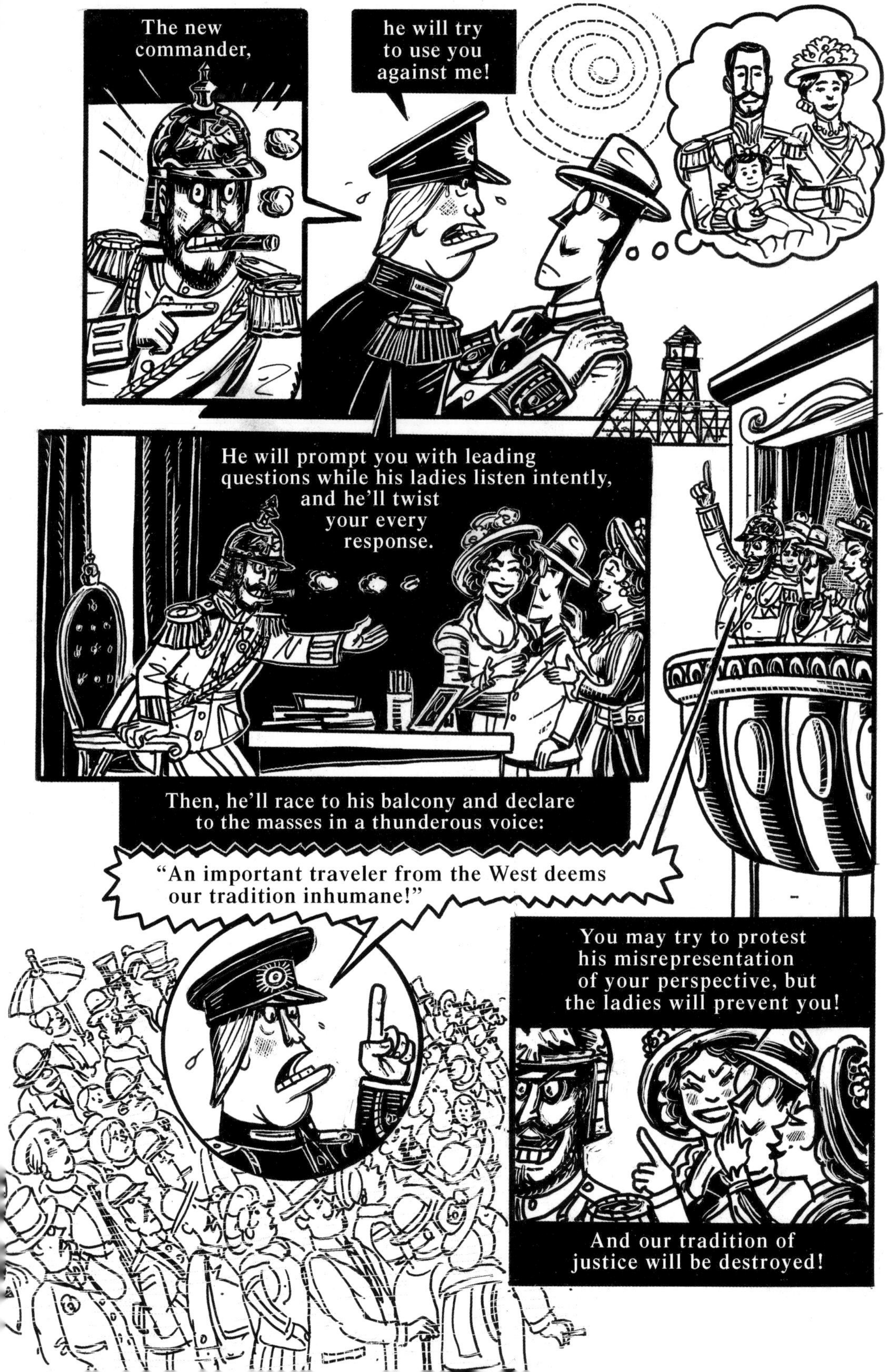
The new commander,
he will try to use you against me!
He will prompt you with leading questions while his ladies listen intently, and he'll twist your every response.
Then, he'll race to his balcony and declare to the masses in a thunderous voice:
"An important traveler from the West deems our tradition inhumane!"
You may try to protest his misrepresentation of your perspective, but the ladies will prevent you!
And our tradition of justice will be destroyed!

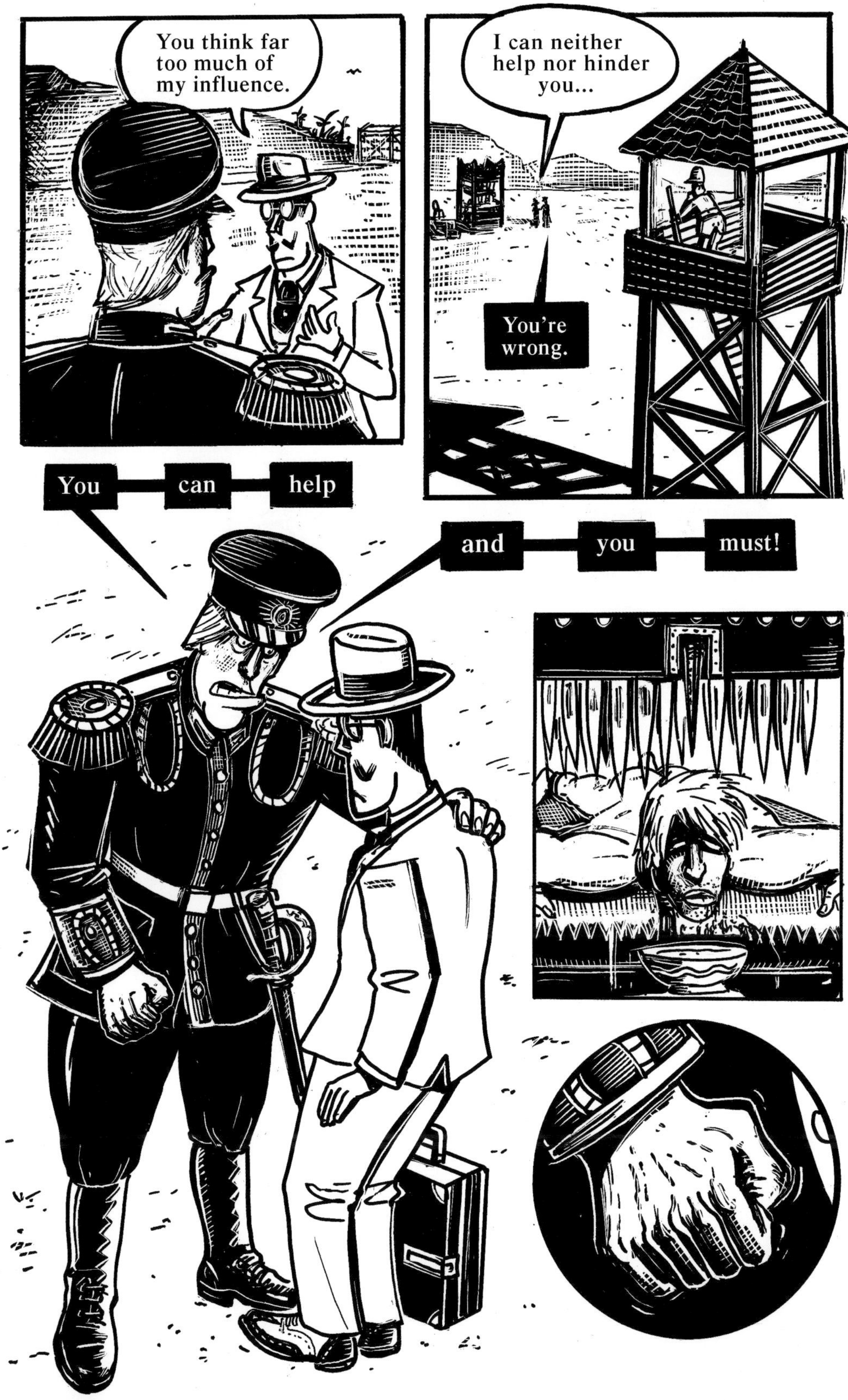
You think far too much of my influence.
I can neither help nor hinder you...
You're wrong.
You can help
and you must!

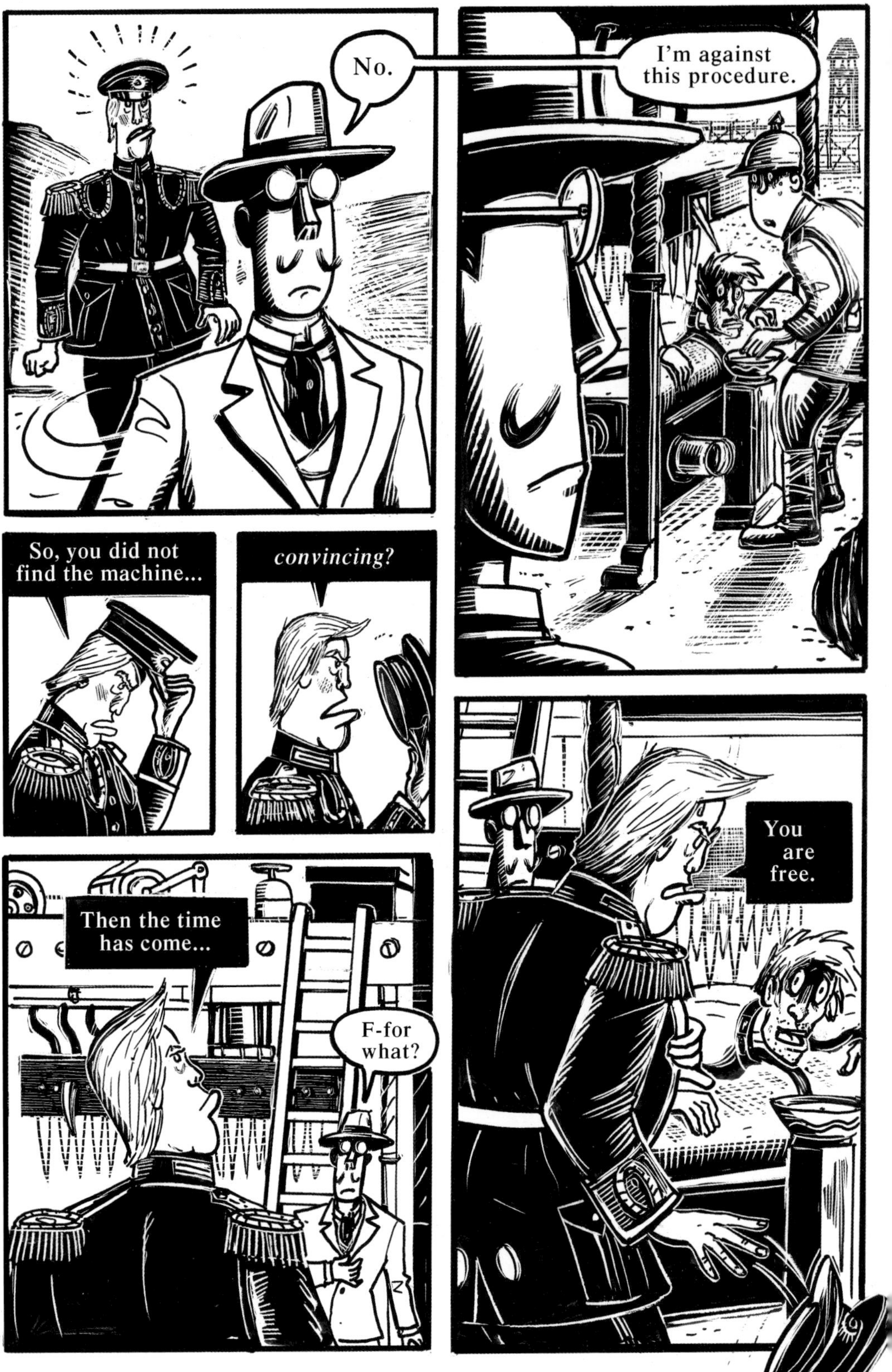
No.
I'm against this procedure.
So, you did not find the machine...
convincing?
Then the time has come...
F-for what?
You are free.

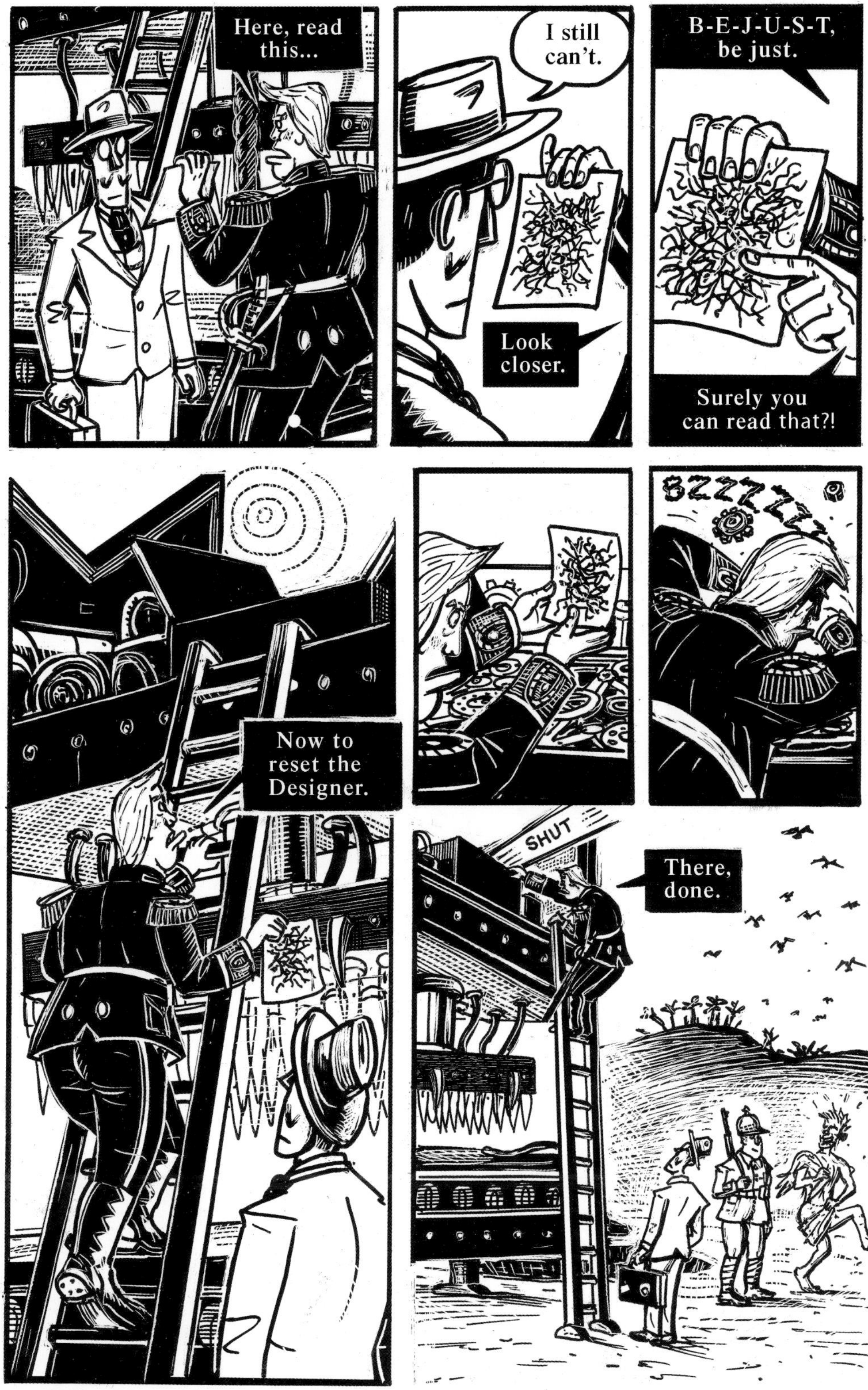
Here, read this...
I still can't.
Look closer.
B-E-J-U-S-T, be just.
Surely you can read that?!
Now to reset the Designer.
BZZZZZ
SHUT
There, done.

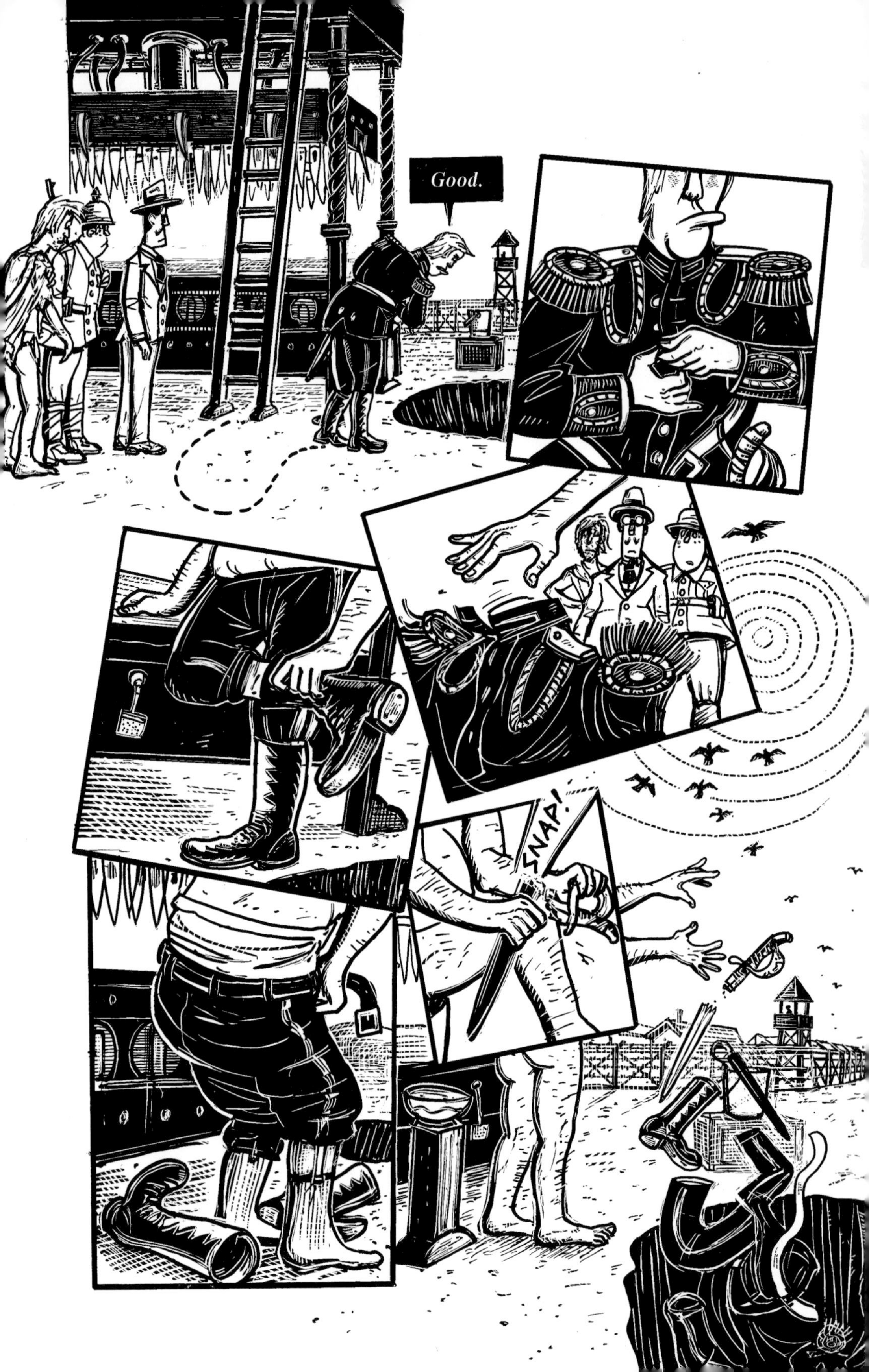
Good.
SNAP!

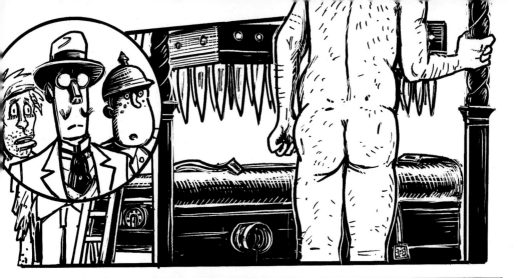

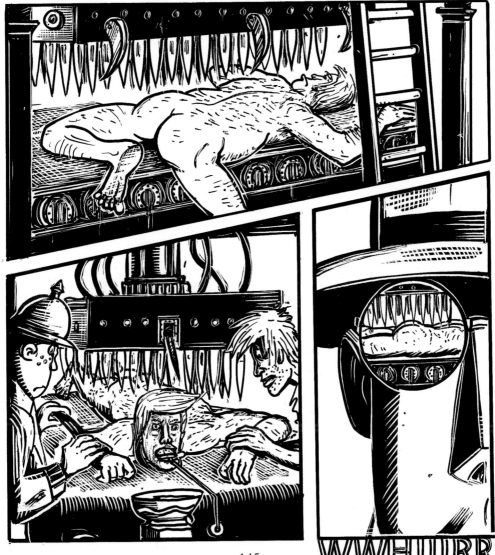

WWHIIIRRRR

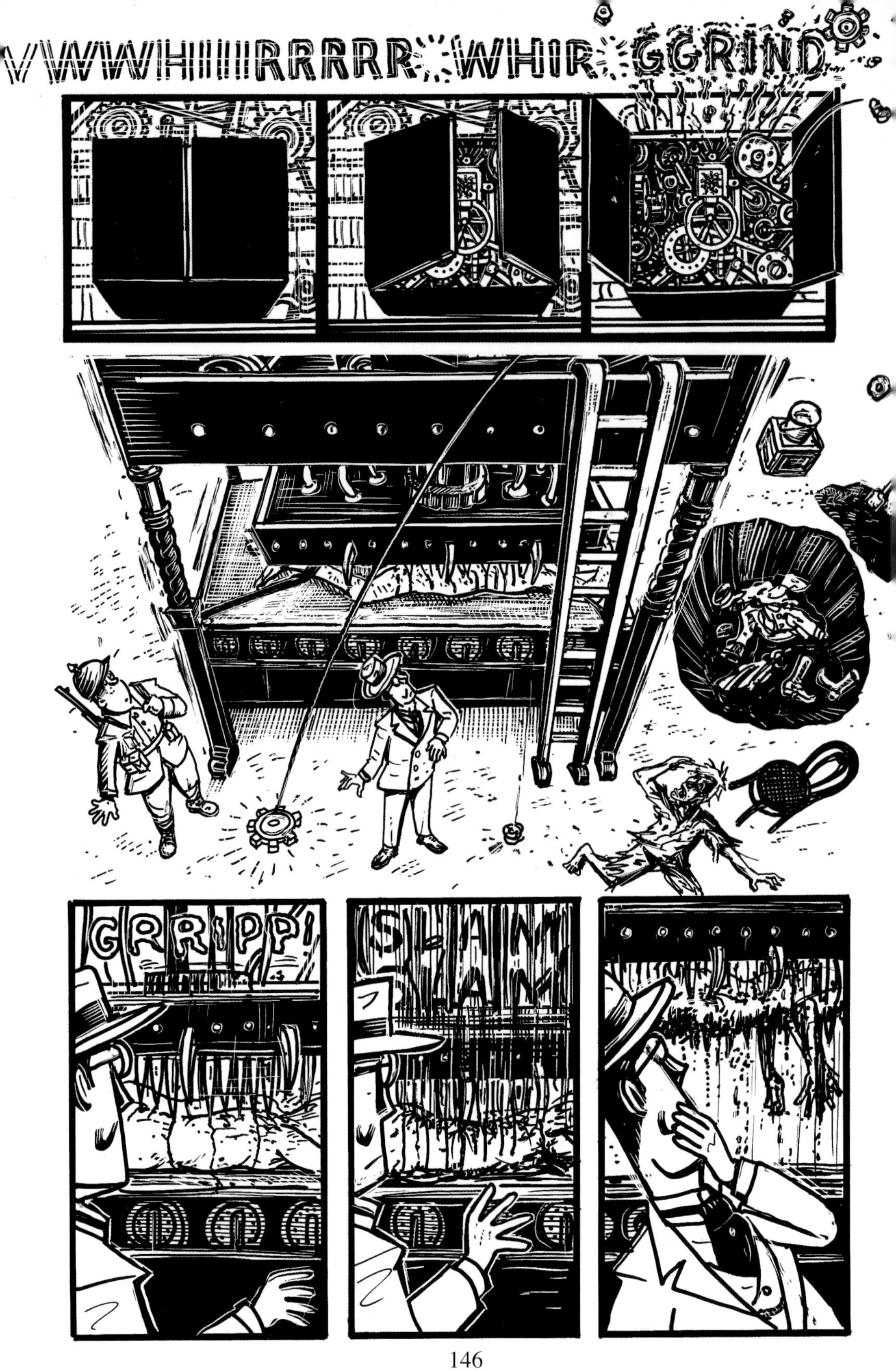
VWWWHIIIIRRRRR
WHIR
GGRIND
GRRIPP!
SLAM

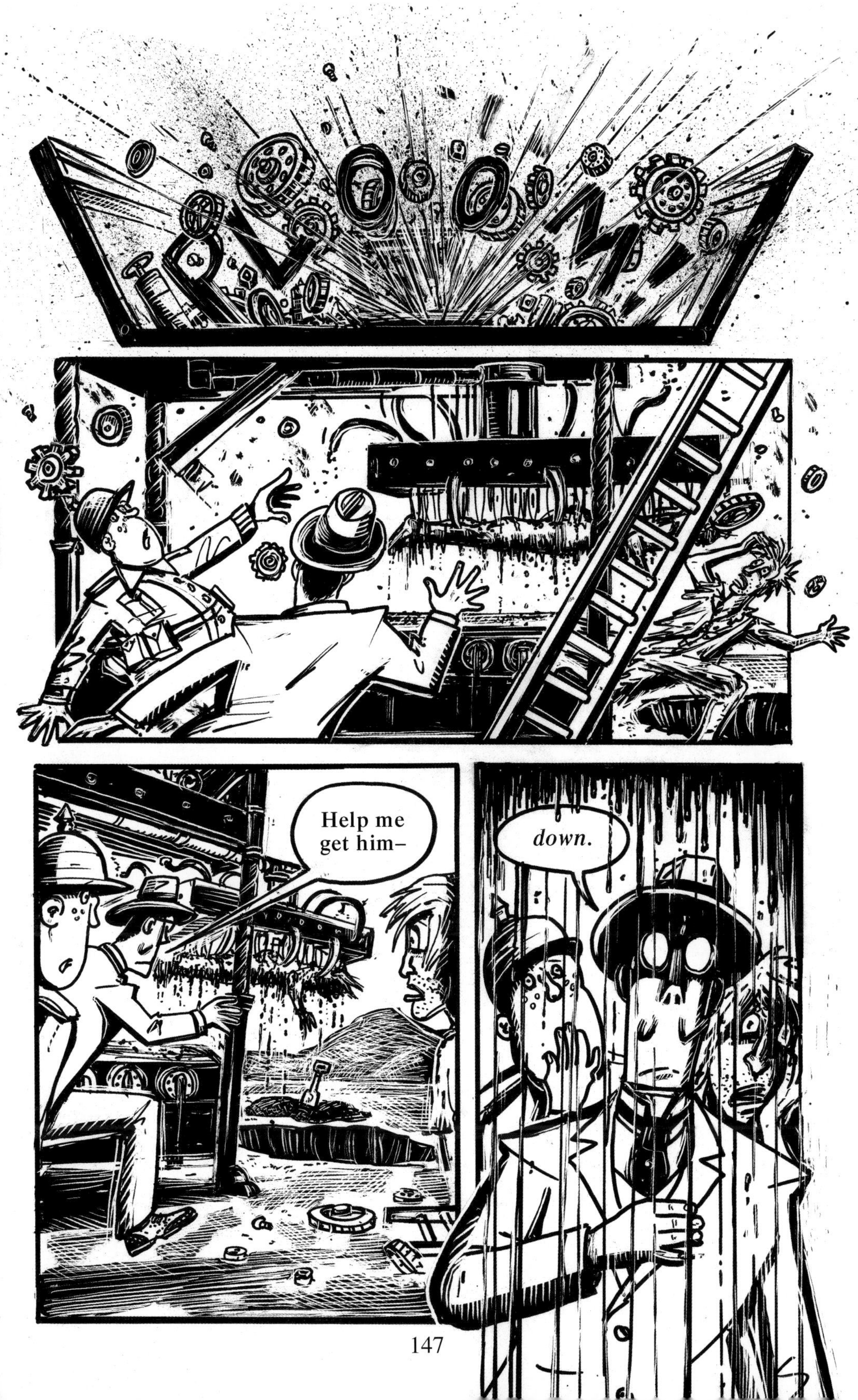
BOOOOM!
Help me get him–
down.

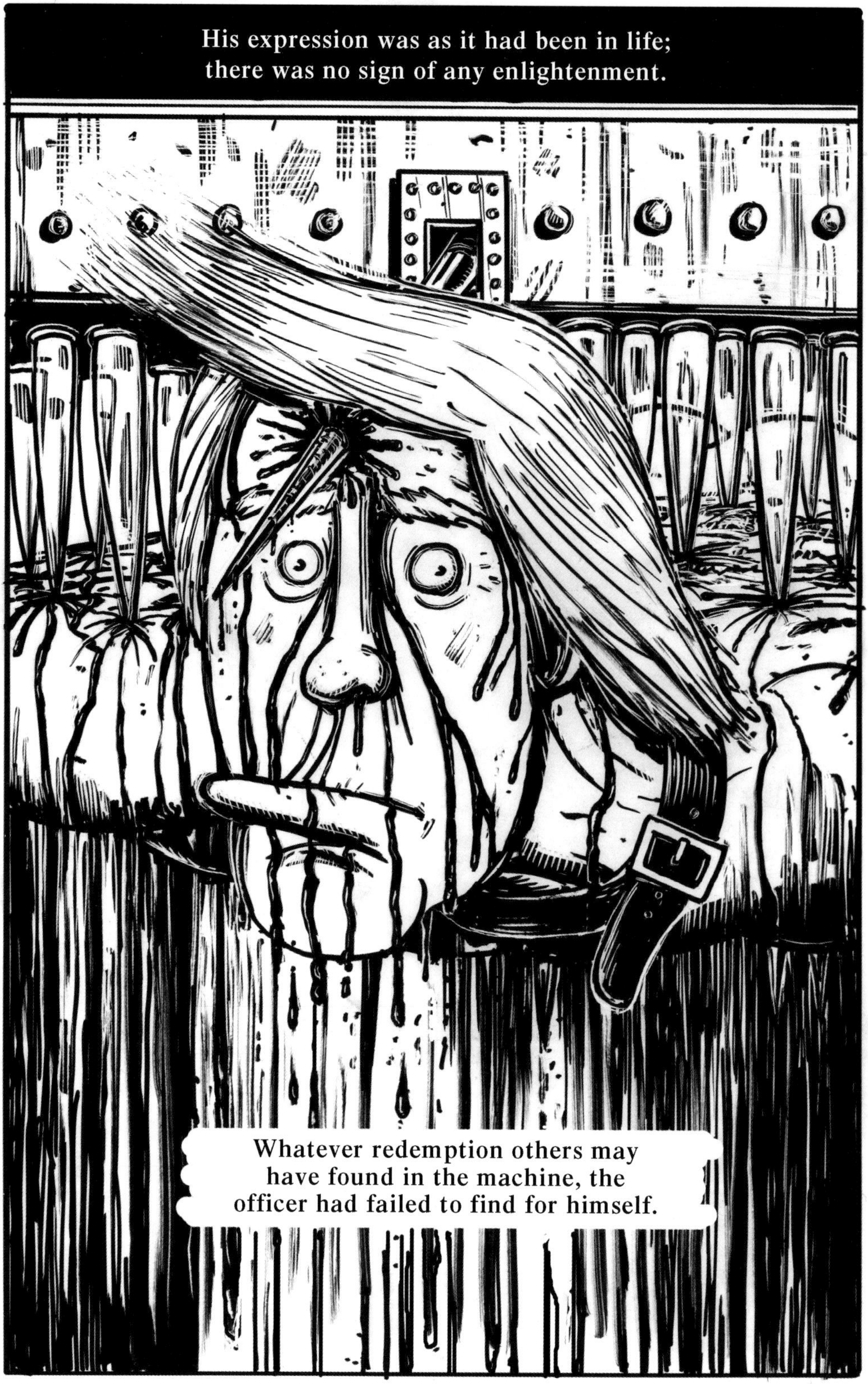
His expression was as it had been in life; there was no sign of any enlightenment.
Whatever redemption others may have found in the machine, the officer had failed to find for himself.

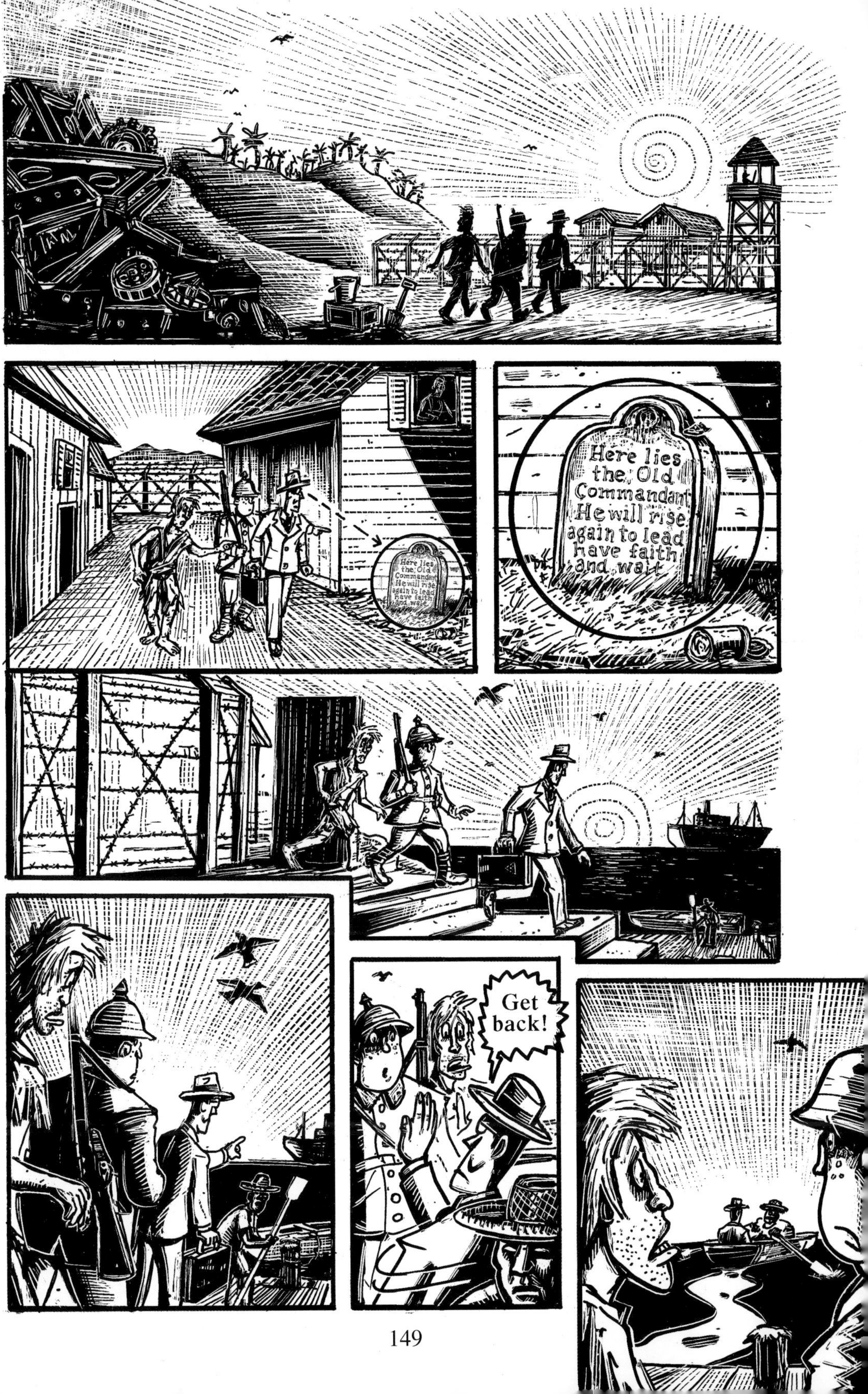
Here lies the Old Commandant He will rise again to lead have faith and wait
Here lies the Old Commandant He will rise again to lead have faith and wait
Get back!

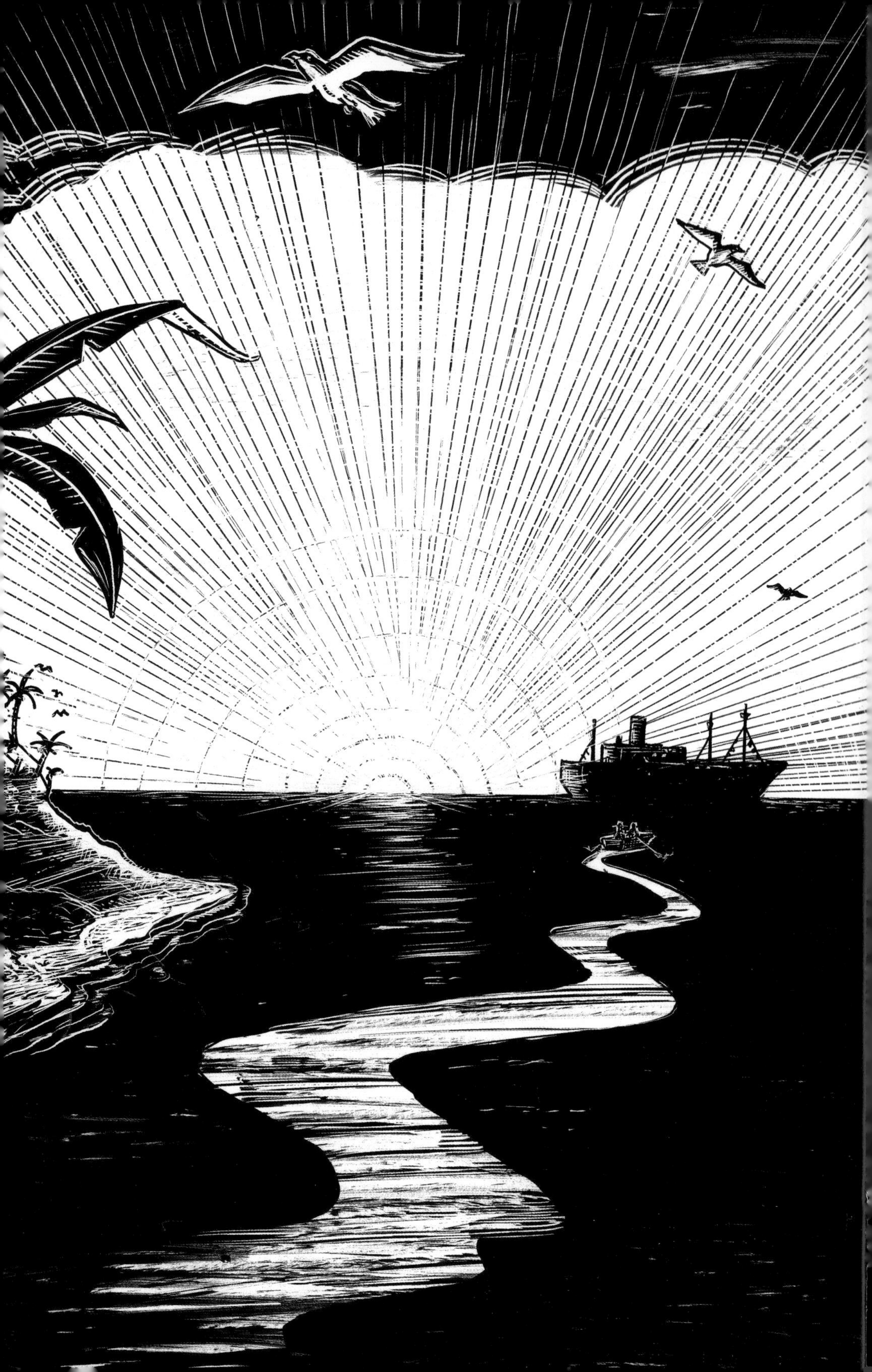

THE VULTURE

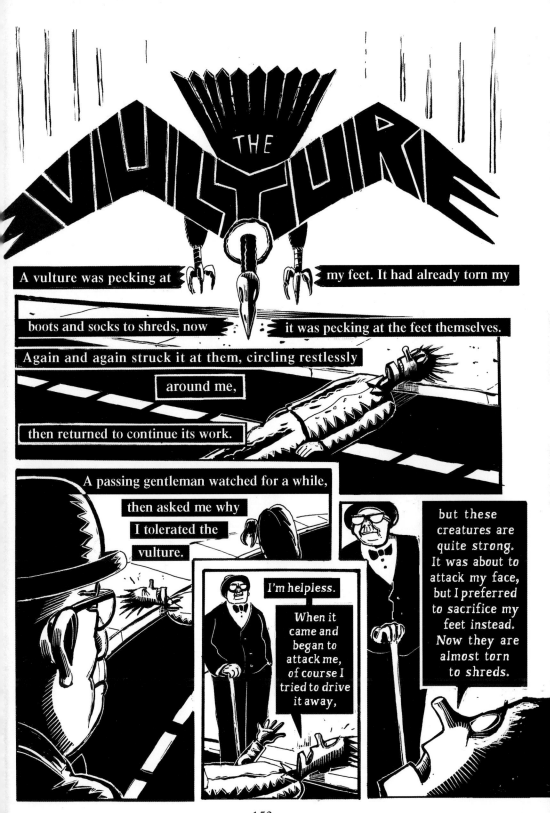

THE VULTURE

A vulture was pecking at my feet. It had already torn my boots and socks to shreds, now it was pecking at the feet themselves. Again and again struck it at them, circling restlessly around me, then returned to continue its work.

A passing gentleman watched for a while, then asked me why I tolerated the vulture.

I'm helpless. When it came and began to attack me, of course I tried to drive it away, but these creatures are quite strong. It was about to attack my face, but I preferred to sacrifice my feet instead. Now they are almost torn to shreds.

153

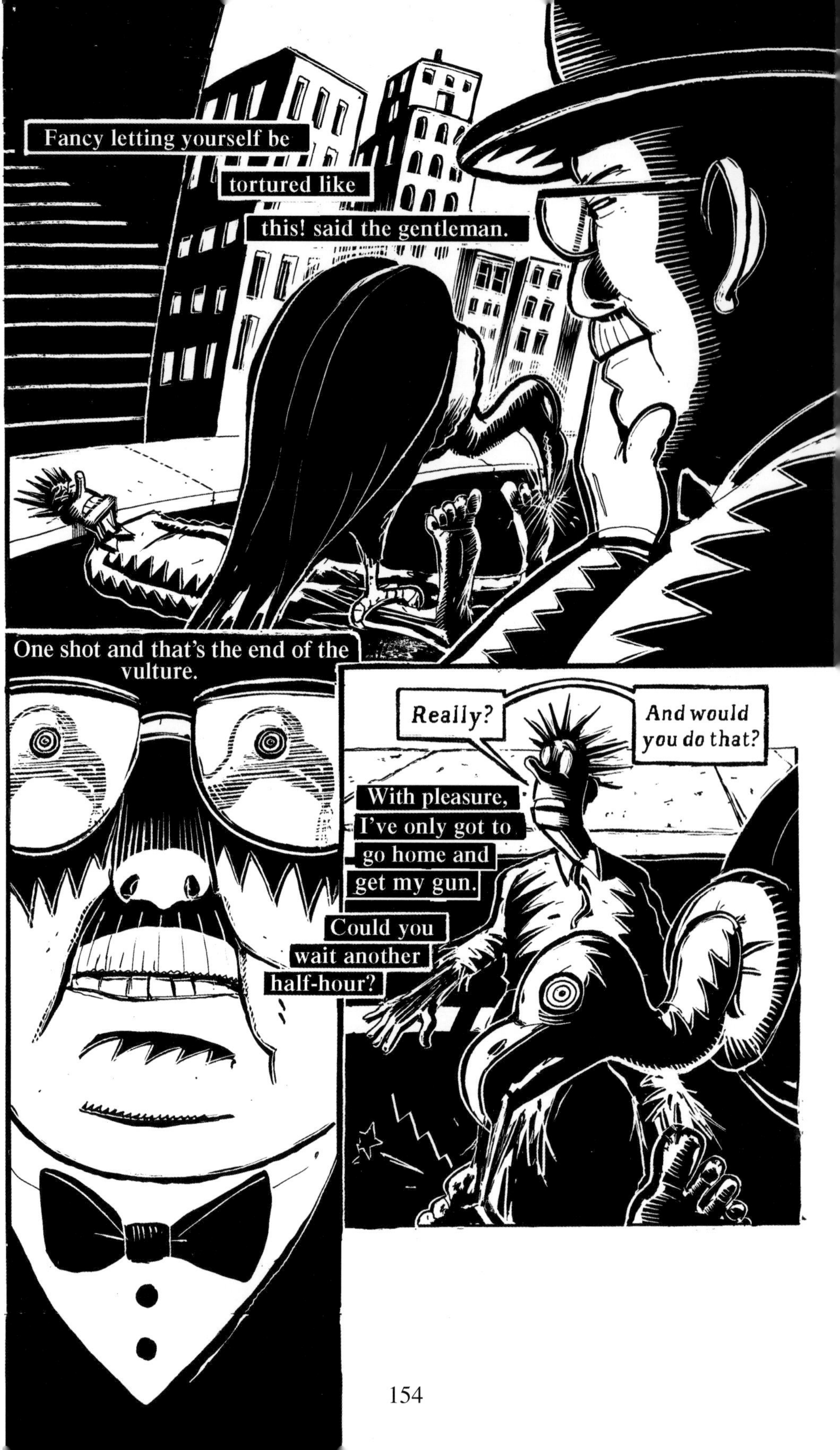
Fancy letting yourself be
tortured like
this! said the gentleman.
One shot and that's the end of the vulture.
Really?
And would you do that?
With pleasure, I've only got to go home and get my gun.
Could you wait another half-hour?

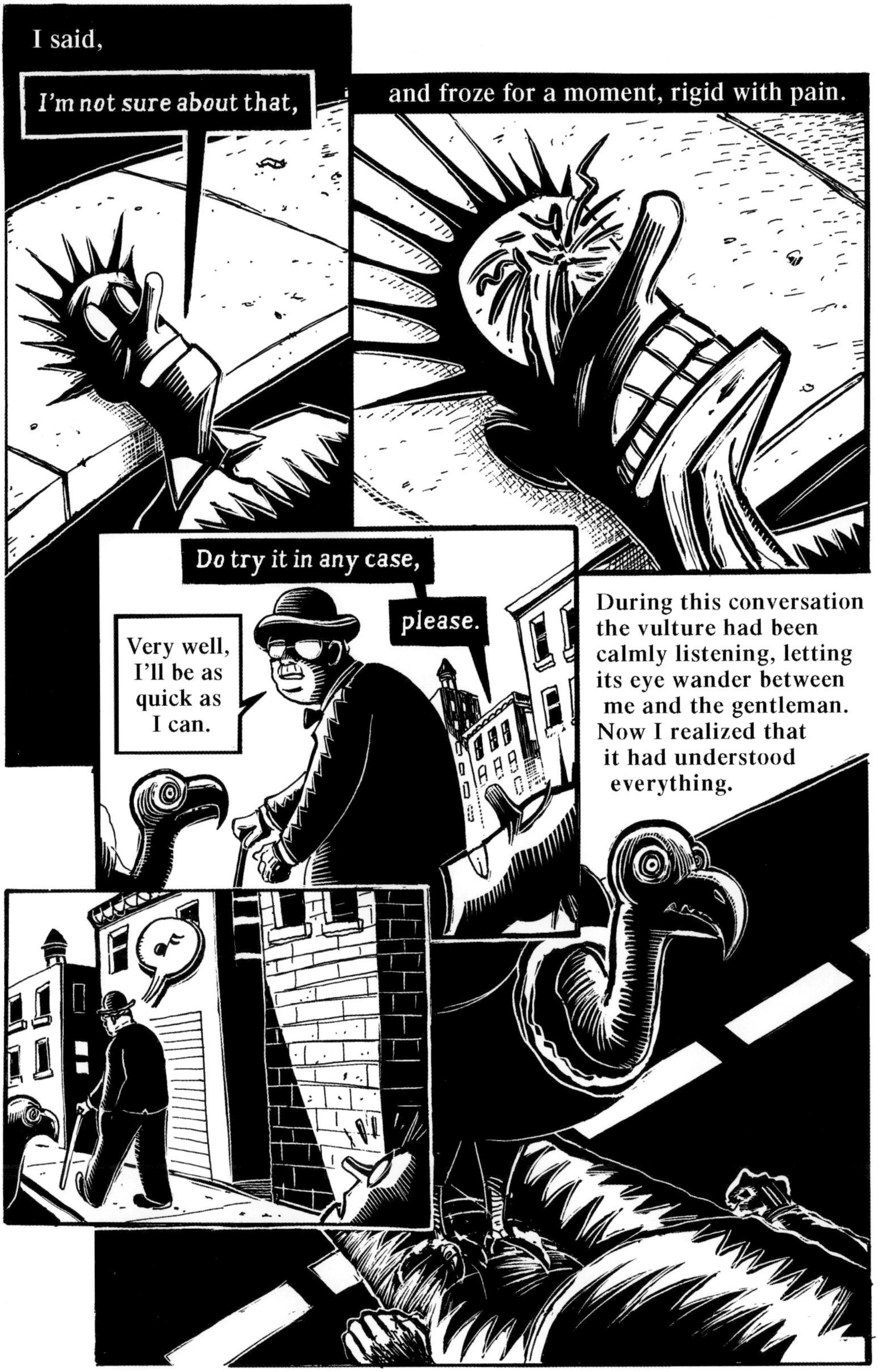
I said,
I'm not sure about that,
and froze for a moment, rigid with pain.
Do try it in any case,
please.
Very well, I'll be as quick as I can.
During this conversation the vulture had been calmly listening, letting its eye wander between me and the gentleman. Now I realized that it had understood everything.

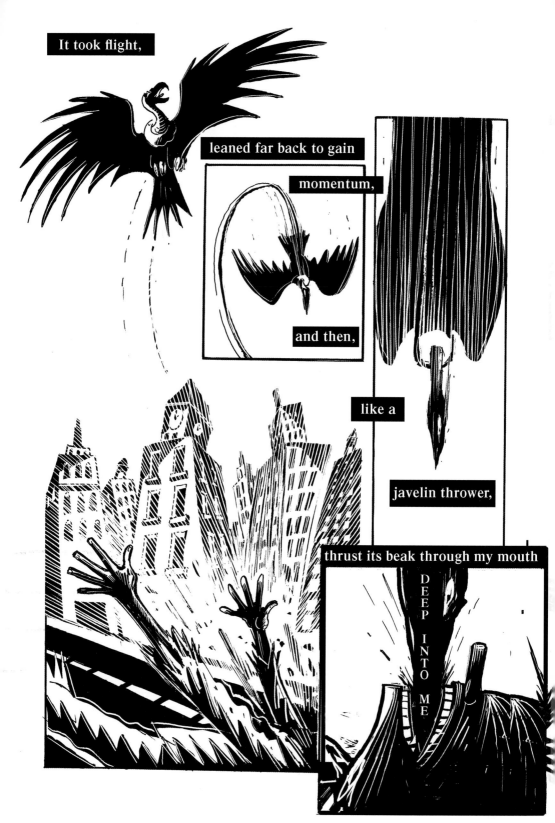

It took flight,

leaned far back to gain

momentum,

and then,

like a

javelin thrower,

thrust its beak through my mouth

DEEP INTO ME

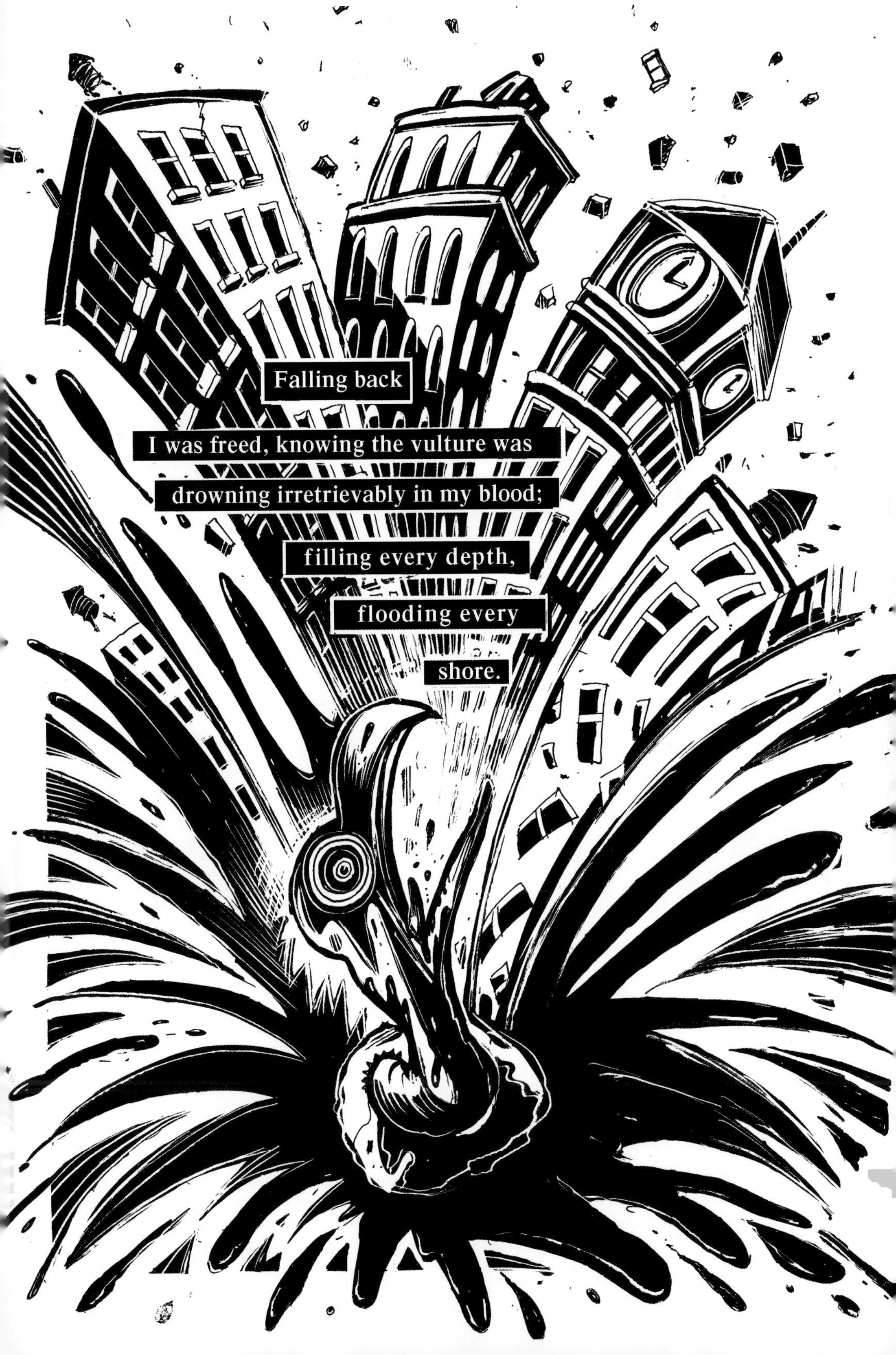
Falling back
I was freed, knowing the vulture was
drowning irretrievably in my blood;
filling every depth,
flooding every
shore.

Acknowledgments

Many thanks to all the people who helped to bring this book to light: Judy Hansen, Tom Mayer, Jeremy Dauber, Emma Hitchcock, Minah Kim, Hilary Allison, Jules Feiffer, Joe Lops, Ingsu Liu, Julia Druskin, Betty Russell, Emily Kuper, Emily Russell, Terry Nantier, Sofia Feldman, John Thomas, Seth Tobocman, Steve Ross, Max Brod and, of course, Franz Kafka.

Franz Kafka was born in 1883 in Prague, in what is now the Czech Republic, to a middle-class Jewish family. Though he completed a degree in law, he ended up as an adjuster for an accident insurance company and only found time to write after work hours. The handful of stories Kafka published during lifetime drew little notice. He died 1924 at the age of forty from tuberculosis, having instructed his friend Max Brod to burn his unpublished manuscripts. Fortunately, Brod ignored Kafka's request and edited and found publishers for Kafka's works. Originally written in German, Kafka's short stories only began to reach a wider audience in the 1940s, when they were translated and spread overseas. Today they have influenced generations of writers.

Peter Kuper's illustrations and comics have appeared in publications around the world including *The New Yorker* and *Mad*, where he has written and illustrated "Spy vs Spy" every issue since 1997. He is the cofounder of *World War 3 Illustrated*, a political comics magazine, and has remained on its editorial board since 1979. He has produced over two dozen books including *The System*, *Diario de Oaxaca* and *Drawn to New York*. Peter previously adapted Upton Sinclair's *The Jungle* and Franz Kafka's *The Metamorphosis*, which is used in high school and college curriculums in the United States and abroad. His book *Ruins* won the 2016 Eisner Award for best graphic novel. He has been teaching comics courses at The School of Visual Arts in New York City for thirty years and is a visiting professor at Harvard University.

More of his work can be found at peterkuper.com.

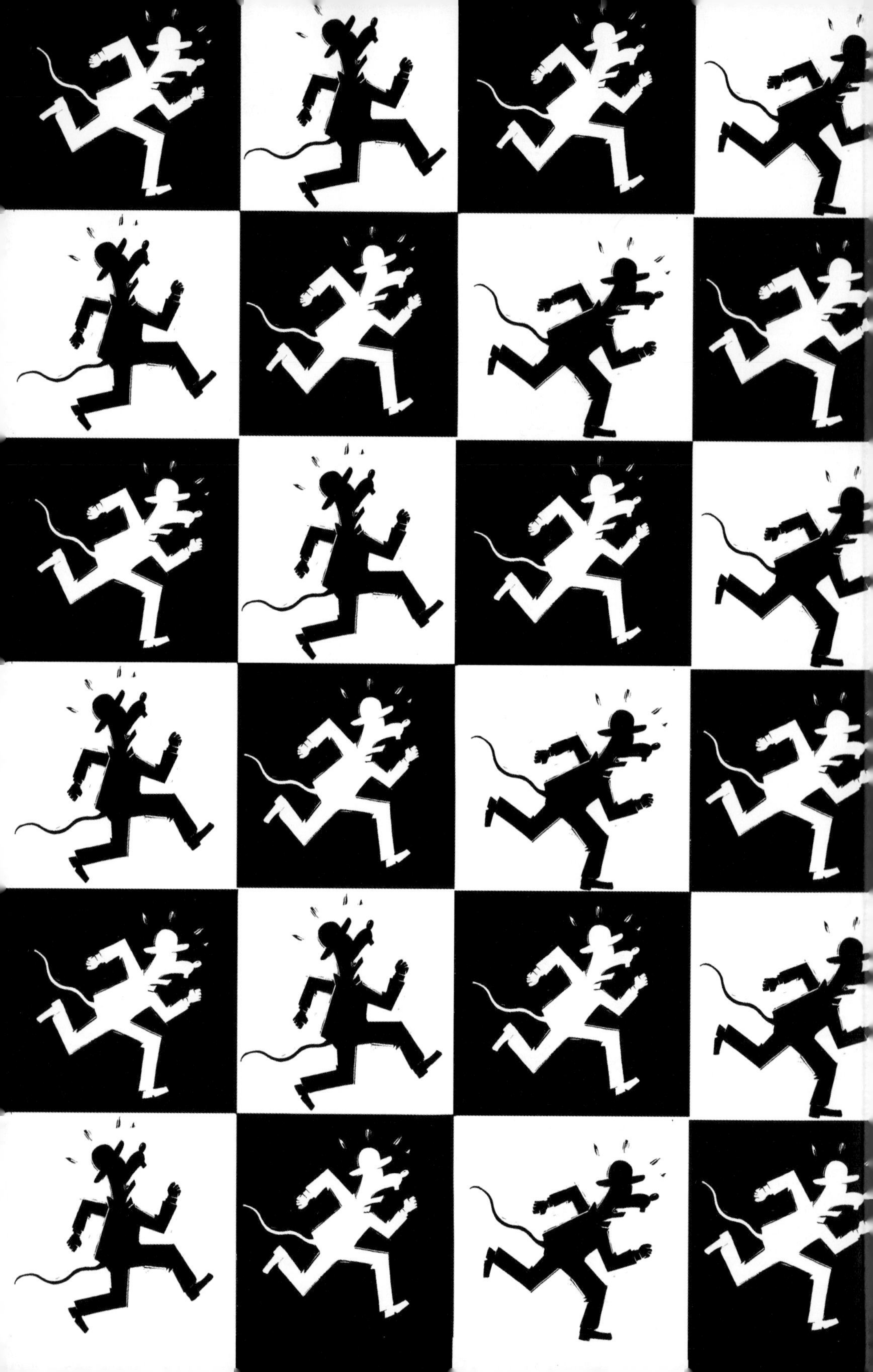

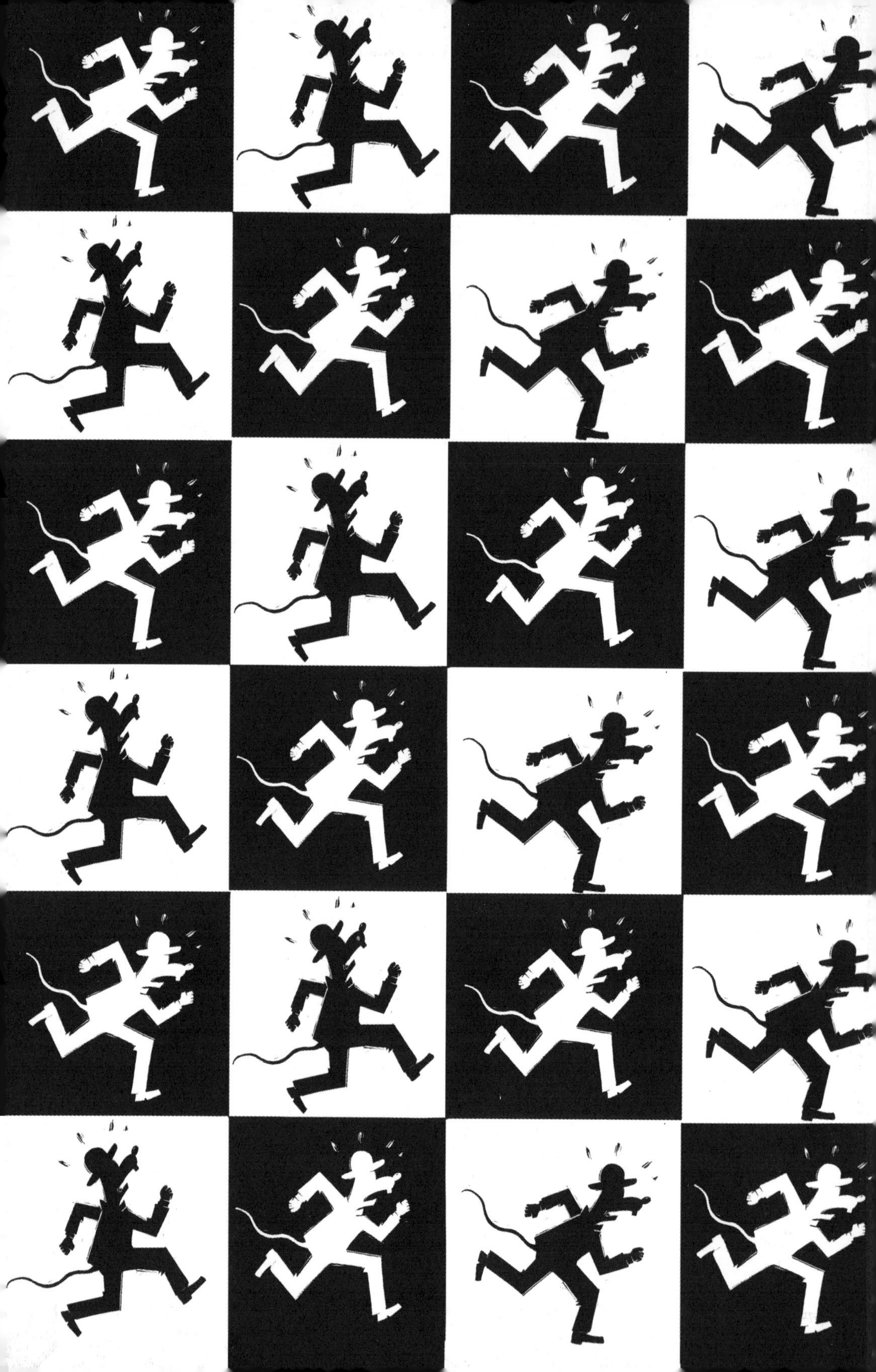